CHAOS FORGED A FABLE

THE CHAOS COVENANT ~ BOOK ONE

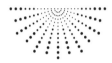

KATE CRAFT

CHAOS FORGED A FABLE

Book One of The Chaos Covenant

Copyright © Kate Craft 2022

First Edition: March 2022

ISBN: 978-1-7397349-0-9

For enquires, please visit the website below.

www.katecraft.com

Books are a gateway. A black hole of endless possibilities. A place where soulmates meet and friendships thrive. A place where villains might proposer and heroes could fall. Here, worlds begin and reality fades. Here, lies imagination.

— KATE CRAFT

To Dad.

Thank you for always grounding me…and for calming Maya down.

CONTENTS

PROLOGUE

The voices are back.

Wind rattled the windows and whipped through the trees, their branches carelessly scratching the bedroom windows. This wasn't what had woken Maya. She had yet to go to sleep like her mother had asked, too busy listening to the whispers. They were somewhat comforting against the howls of harsh winter winds, typical for England in December. As the storm grew louder, the voices dimmed, and Maya slipped from her bed with a short huff of frustration.

"Where are you going?" Jacob asked sleepily from the other side of the room.

Maya considered telling her younger brother. She had done that only once before, wanting so desperately for Jacob to hear them too, and share in the comfort they brought her. But the voices remained ever silent to the boy, the prospect of muttering ghosts or invisible people only serving to frighten him. So, like always, she lied.

"I'm just going to get some water," she whispered.

Jacob nodded sleepily and lay back down, a soft snore shortly following. Maya tip-toed from the bedroom, carefully navigating the old wooden floors of her grandparents' house. A long screech emanated from one of the uneven parquets. She froze and held her breath, waiting a moment before lifting her foot and making a note to avoid it in the future. The moment Maya's toes touched the cold tiles of the utility room, she let out a sigh of relief. A low powered lamp lit the hall, its soft glow a poor guide to the back door.

The wind continued to wail, almost in protest to the voices that whispered, beckoning Maya outside. She turned the key and opened the door, quiet so as not to wake her parents sleeping above. Barefooted, with only thin, dinosaur patterned pyjamas to protect her from the elements, she stepped outside. The voices roared, whether with delight or in trepidation, Maya wasn't sure. She moved forward, battered by the gale but barely registering the cold as it crept in to nip at her feet.

The moon hung low above the small lake, setting it beautifully alight as Maya stepped into the shallow, icy water, urged to go deeper. She distantly noted a blue glow. *Pretty*, she thought, advancing further into the murky waters.

"Maya!" Jaseen screamed as she ran from the back door towards her daughter.

Maya stopped, the water lapping against her waist as she turned towards her mother.

"Maya, stay right there," Jaseen pleaded as she reached the lake's edge and splashed into the water. "Mamma's coming, sweetheart. Just walk towards me."

Maya continued to stare at her mother, confused and oblivious to the danger behind her. There, the water dipped and swirled, a whirlpool forming. Jaseen grabbed Maya and lifted her from the water. Spinning, the pull of the current had intensified, and she battled against it, moving slowly towards the edge of the lake. Seemingly angered, the whirlpool expanded and Jaseen's movements slowed further as she began to tire. *I will make it,* she promised the entranced Maya in her arms.

The back door slammed; a sound barely audible over the veritable storm of elements colliding. Yali was running towards the lake and Jaseen gasped with relief at the sight of her mother. The current was too strong. There was no way they could both escape its pull. But perhaps one of them could. Kissing her daughter on the cheek, Jaseen stretched out her arms and threw Maya as far as her strength would allow. Yali dashed into the shallows to grab Maya's arm, dragging her quickly back to the safety of the bank. She glanced up desperately to search the water. But the whirlpool was subsiding...and her daughter, Jaseen, was gone.

1
REVELATIONS

LONDON ~ ENGLAND

15 Years Later

"Stop struggling or the cuffs will hurt you," Maya stated calmly to the wriggling man between her thighs. Taking the restraints from her belt, she snapped the first to his wrist. Her weight shifted and the wriggler saw his chance. Twisting his body, an elbow slammed into the side of Maya's head.

"Son of a–" she muttered. Springing to her feet, she took off after the criminal she had been trying to arrest. Oxford street, like the rest of London, was packed with people. Car horns blared at commuters jumping from the busy path, a desperate attempt to avoid the wanted man barrelling towards them. He veered right and into an alley, but not before pushing an old man to the ground to deter the woman pounding down the street behind him.

With a low curse, Maya dodged to the side, missing the thief's latest victim by a hair. "Jason, help that man!" she yelled to her partner; only metres behind. Maya turned down the alley. The one-cuffed man was there, trapped, with nowhere to go.

"Dead-end, buddy," she sang. The man raised his fists, taking a stance to put up a fight. Maya scoffed enthusiastically and did the same. Police training had given pointers on how to hold your own in a scrap, with the intent to subdue and cause the least amount of harm. However, Maya decided she was having a bad day and called upon her other training. As far back as she could remember, her grandmother, Yali, had been teaching the family various styles of self-defence. Fast-forward years later, and Maya felt more than confident handling guys like this one – all muscle and no skill.

Maya walked towards the thief, watching, waiting for him to make the first move. He did. With his entire bulking mass of body weight, he drove his fist towards her face. She blocked it easily and moved in close to punch him in the gut. As he doubled over, she grabbed his arm and tried to bring it behind him. Quicker than expected, the man recovered and jabbed his fist. This time Maya was ill-prepared, and her chin suffered for it. Mildly surprised and a little more than irked, she quickly swung her foot up to connect with his chest, knocking the man off his feet.

A low whistle of approval rang from behind. Ignoring her partner, Maya walked over to the criminal. He lay flopped on his stomach, making short gasping noises. Bending down, she applied the second cuff and dragged him to his feet, shoving him towards Jason.

He'd witnessed the brawl and tutted at Maya with mock disapproval. "Daniels is going to go ballistic if you've broken something...again," Jason warned.

"Never mind him. How's the old man he knocked over?" she grunted, nursing her jaw.

London dwellers continued to pass by the alley, a few

tourists stopping to take pictures before rushing from the scene.

"He's fine," Jason assured her. "How's your jaw? Not like you to let them get a hit in," he chided gently with a nudge to Maya's shoulder.

She smiled at her partner and assured him she was fine. Jason and Maya had both been a part of London's Metropolitan Police for five years now. Training and working together, they had become close. She knew at one point he had wanted something more. It was easy to convince herself, and him, that going there simply hadn't been worth the risk of ruining the friendship they already had.

BACK AT THE STATION, Jason took the tealeaf to get processed. Just as Maya sat down, Sergeant Daniels stepped out of his office.

"Constable Cross. My office. Now," he seethed.

"Bugger," Maya muttered, dragging her heels to the open door.

"For Christ's sake, Maya." He'd waited until she had closed the door; not that it mattered. The walls at the station were paper thin. "What did you *do* to the guy?"

"It was self-defence," Maya insisted with a non-committal shrug.

Daniels shook his head and sat back behind the cheap, pine desk. "You'll have to fill out another Use of Force Proforma."

"Not a problem," Maya stated happily with a mock salute.

Daniels looked at her thoughtfully. "I also want you to take some leave."

"What? Why?"

"Maya, this is the third time this *month* I've had you in my office to fill out that bloody form. If you're not careful, I'll have to consider more than just leave."

After a mild and increasingly awkward stare-off, Daniels sighed tiredly. "Something's going on with you. You've always been hard-headed, and stubborn–"

"Easy with the compliments."

Sergeant Daniels paused, his fingers tapping lightly on the desk. "It's like you've been itching for a fight all month." Despite his irritation, he was concerned. He'd known Maya for most of her life through her stepfather, David, and he considered them both as family.

Maya sighed, considering his words. He was right. No matter how much she tried to bury herself in work, one thing stayed at the forefront of her mind. In two days, it would be the anniversary of her mother's death, fifteen years ago. "Okay, I'll take some leave. Is two weeks enough?"

Daniels, pleasantly surprised, nodded his head. "That's fine, I'll submit and approve it starting now," he confirmed, waving her out of his office.

MAYA STEPPED through the door of her small apartment, dumped the keys on the side table, and kicked off her shoes. Moving into the bathroom, she undressed, released her hair from the tight ponytail, and climbed into the shower. Warm water broke the chill that had crept in throughout the day. Maya hated winter and everything that came with it. Once dressed in her hoodie and flannel bottoms, she made her way into the kitchen and poured a generous glass of Argentinian red wine. Now, suitably comfortable and appropriately armed, she picked up the phone and moved over to a small sofa by the window.

The call was picked up after only a few rings.

"Cave Residence, this is Jacob."

It had been a while since Maya had spoken to her brother; at least a year since she'd last seen him.

"*Hello?*" Jacob asked again, a hint of confusion at the silence on the other end of the line.

"Hey, long time no speak," Maya said awkwardly.

"Maya? Maya! How've you been? It's been so long. Why haven't you replied to my messages? Are you at work?"

Maya sat patiently and waited for her brother's torrent of questions to slow down. "Jesus, Jake. You plan on letting me answer anytime today?" she said with a chuckle.

"Sorry, I know you've been busy, we've just missed you."

Maya mentally swatted at the ever-familiar guilt creeping in. "No, I'm sorry, you're right. I've been busy but that's no excuse to not call before now," she admitted. "What are you doing there anyway? Why aren't you at Uni?"

Jacob was studying medicine at Oxford University, with the aim of becoming a doctor like their grandfather, Christopher Cave. Jacob was probably one of the brainiest people Maya knew personally, and he was only nineteen. She admired his patient, humble nature. He was never one to openly brag. The more Maya thought about it, the more she was convinced she was probably adopted. Jacob was just like his father, David Cross, Maya's stepfather. Though, David never treated her as anything less than his own flesh and blood. Both father and son were docile and kind-hearted, almost to a fault.

"Maya?"

Jacob's question shook Maya from her thoughts. "Sorry, what did you say?"

"I said, we're on a break, so I thought I'd visit Gran and Grandad." He chuckled. His sister was always focused when given a task, but she had a tendency to get lost in her own train of thought.

"Ah, right. Well…" Maya hesitated. "I was thinking about coming up for a visit, tomorrow."

"That's awesome!"

At Jacob's shout, a muffled voice hummed in the background. "What's awesome?"

"Gran, Maya's coming to visit," Jacob exclaimed excitedly.

"Mayara, that's wonderful," Yali cried. "We recently fixed up the sparring studio too, so you'll have to show me all the new tricks you've learnt. Oh, it's been too long."

Crazy old woman, Maya thought, cringing at the sound of her full name. First visit in five years and that's the first thing that pops into her nan's head. However, that was always one of the many reasons she loved Yali. Despite the distance, they were almost always completely in tune. "Okay, well, I was just calling to let you know. I'll drive up tomorrow."

After signing off with the promise to be there early enough for dinner, Maya ambled over to the kitchen counter to refill her wineglass. Despite the day's events, she still had plenty of energy. For the longest time Maya had been convinced she might have had ADHD, as it always took a lot to wear her out. Usually, she would go for a run before bed. Tonight, she sat on the window seat of her top floor apartment and watched the bustle of Southwest London. The waxing, gibbous moon stood proud and further lit the perpetually animated city. Maya silently swore she could feel the inhabitants' collective energy. Sipping her wine, she leant back and let the calm feelings pass through her body. She opened her eyes to the pattering of rain against the glass, before settling once again to enjoy the peaceful element.

THE DRIVE from London to the Midlands was packed with the usual commuters. As is typical for the South, it never matters when you leave, or how much planning you commit to getting anywhere on time. Be prepared with a coffee and a good audiobook, because you're more than likely in for a long, honk-heavy, finger-waving journey.

Six hours and possibly one speed camera flash later, Maya pulled up to her grandparents' driveway. With the engine still humming and one foot barely out of the car, a warm set of hands pulled Maya the rest of the way and wrapped her in a warm embrace. She settled in and hugged her stepfather back, breathing in the lingering and familiar smell of tobacco and cheap, Arabic aftershave he'd hoarded from far-eastern travels.

"Hi, Dad. I've missed you," she admitted, feeling embarrassed at having left it so long.

"We've all missed you, too," his reply came, muffled against the hood of her jumper. "Your grandpa has gone all out. I'm fairly sure we're having a three-course meal."

"All to celebrate the return of the prodigal daughter," Maya's grandfather, Christopher, interrupted from the doorway of the house. "Come on inside before we lose all the heat!" he insisted, ushering them both into the hallway.

As they stepped inside, Maya was told her grandmother was busy in the sparring studio with Jacob. Before heading out to greet them, Maya decided to drop her bag in the old room she'd once shared with her brother. She made her way down the squeaky hallway of the old house and was unsurprised to find the room exactly the way she had left it. Shelves lined two of the four walls, all filled with books that promised adventure and far-away places. Outside of England, Maya had only been to Madeira, an island off the coast of Portugal. It had been her mother's favourite place. Maya quickly banished the thought of Jaseen and left the room to find Yali and her brother.

As she walked towards the studio at the end of the

garden, she stopped briefly at the side of the lake. She had forgotten how peaceful it was here; an odd thing to think, considering the painful memories. The backyard was an acre of beautifully maintained land, surrounded by imaginatively coppiced trees. An impressive space, it consisted of open lawn, broken only by the small and elegant lake with an impressive studio behind. The garden's peaceful silence was interrupted by the sound of a yelp, followed by a distinct grunt of disapproval that could only belong to one person.

"You know, Grandma, there aren't many seventy-year-olds that can knock someone fifty years their junior on their butt," Maya declared approvingly as she stepped through the studio's open doorway. She glanced at Jacob and sighed. "Uni's making you soft."

"I'm a lover, not a fighter," Jacob claimed with a grin. "I'd like to see *you* take her on."

Yali threw a roughly carved, wooden pole to Maya, who caught it easily. This came as no surprise. Their grandmother had always insisted on training with things you may find lying around, like sticks. Maya had continued to practice when she left home because she could honestly say she had enjoyed it.

Yali lunged and Maya mirrored the same moves she'd used against the man in the alley. Blocking the hit, she thrust the staff towards her opponent's stomach. Her grandmother predicted the move and jumped back, swinging her pole by one end, causing the other to bonk the side of Maya's head. Annoyed, Maya stepped back, rubbing the sore spot and bruised ego before readjusting her posture. This time, she lunged towards Yali, a ploy to aim for her face before quickly ducking to swing the pole at Yali's exposed ankles.

They sparred like this for ten minutes, matching other hit for hit. As Maya prepared to make her next move, a slipper flew from the right and smacked her in the nose. She glared at her traitorous brother.

"I'm hungry," he said with a shrug. A smile stretched across his face. He'd distracted her.

Maya twisted – but too late. Yali spun and kicked Maya's feet from underneath her. Rolling onto her back, the end of Yali's sparring pole hung above her face. She had lost the bout...again.

LATER THAT EVENING, Maya sat in what was fondly known as the 'Garden Room'. The space itself had no plants or shrubbery to speak of, save a vase of flowers on the dining room table. It was, however, the biggest room of the house; with its two-story windows forming the wall that overlooked the land to the rear of the property. Curled up on the padded wicker-chair with a book and a glass of wine, Maya looked out to the garden and pondered the night's events.

It had been lovely seeing everyone. She had expected nothing short of a harsh telling off for spending so much time away from home. Instead, they had welcomed her back without the animosity she felt sure she deserved. *And I do deserve* it, she thought. Being here was always a constant reminder of Jaseen; the wife, daughter, and mother they had lost all those years ago.

Maya didn't remember the night itself. The family never seemed to want to talk about it, so she never pushed. The morning after, however, was hard to forget. It was the first time she had met Sergeant John Daniels, her current boss. Daniels and Maya's stepfather had been friends since their time together as boys at the local college. He had also been the one to handle Jaseen's case as a new detective. Despite the obvious, one thing still bothered her about that morning.

Maya had never seen the body; no black bag, no open casket…nothing. There had been no closure, and this was what she continued to struggle with. To Maya, it felt like an open case and, at times, itched like an open wound.

Just as she began to spiral down the mental rabbit-hole that beckoned her every time she visited her grandparents' house, a warm hand clasped her shoulder. Maya jumped, spilling the scarlet contents of the wineglass down her cream sweater and neat braid of pale-blonde hair.

"Christ, Gran! I thought everyone had gone to bed."

"Sorry, I recognised that far-off look of yours…thought I'd better jump in," she said with a wink.

Maya let out a breath and dabbed at her muddied hair with a dry part of the cheap 'Police' jumper. Choosing to ignore the stain, she began to settle back into the chair when her grandmother stopped her.

"Shall we go for a walk in the garden?" Yali asked hopefully. "It's pretty crisp out, but nice enough."

"Sure, just let me change and grab a jacket."

BEFORE MOVING OUT and joining the police, Maya and Yali would walk the garden most nights. Like the young twenty-six-year-old, she always seemed to have endless amounts of energy. They chatted, catching up on the events of the last five years, whilst inadvertently gravitating towards the edge of the lake.

"Fifteen years," Yali said softly. "I'm surprised you came."

That's fair, Maya thought. This was the first time since her mother's death that she had been able to face being at the house on the anniversary. The lake had taken someone they all treasured. Yet, strangely, it was a part of them. Maya couldn't explain why she felt drawn to the small body of water. She should want to run away from it; but somehow, it made her feel closer to Jaseen. She believed the same could be said for her grandmother.

"Why?" Maya asked. The question itself opened so many avenues of discussion. As expected, Yali averted her gaze, instead letting it fall on the swaying reeds of the sanded water banks.

Echoing her grandmother's silence, Maya left her at the edge of the lake and returned to the sleeping household. Back in the room, she unpacked and quickly climbed under the bedcovers to await the restless night she knew would come.

MAYA BOLTED UPRIGHT, something waking her, a presence whispering in her room. She flicked on the bedside lamp and squinted her eyes as they adjusted to the light.

She was alone.

With a sigh, she hit the switch, once again sinking into the black and chalked it up to being half asleep. As she began to drift, Maya heard it again. A voice. She sat up, then, and held her breath, listening. *Not just one voice*, she realised. Outside, the trees scratched as they fought against the winter wind, and something tugged at Maya's memory. With a sharp shake of her head, she rid herself the remnants of whatever dream had woken her.

Swinging her feet out of bed and stretching, she looked at her watch. 0345. Resigned to her wakefulness, she grabbed a clean jumper and a pair of leggings and headed for the kitchen.

It should have come as a surprise that Yali was already in there, but her grandmother was the night-owl sort.

With a sleepy hello, Maya noted the television's glare dimly lighting the room. "Voices," she muttered, smiling at the cause to her waking illusion.

"Coffee or tea?" Yali offered, pulling out a chair at the table for Maya to sit on.

"Coffee please, black." Maya rubbed her eyes sleepily and stifled a yawn. The ding of mugs hitting the granite kitchen top resounded over the quiet; too quiet. Maya looked at the tv and saw it was on mute. "I'm going mad," she mumbled.

Between filling the cup, Yali had been watching Maya carefully from the moment she had walked into the kitchen. She, too, hadn't slept; and didn't intend to until the following evening. "What makes you think you've gone mad?" she asked, holding out the steaming mug.

Thinking Maya had her grip, Yali released the handle. Hot liquid and porcelain fell to the floor, smashing across the stone tiles of the old kitchen.

"Shit!" Maya exclaimed. "Sorry, Gran. I'm away with the sprites – as you would say." She hurriedly ran to grab some paper towels whilst her grandmother retrieved a pan and brush.

"Mayara, why do you think you're going mad? Did you have a bad dream?" Yali asked, her wariness thinly veiled.

"I don't think I had a bad dream, but I woke up thinking people were in my room…and then I *swear* I could hear voices," Maya chuckled at the absurdity.

"Do you hear the voices now?"

Seeing her grandmother's serious expression, Maya stopped what she was doing and sat up. For dramatic effect she squeezed her eyes shut and listened. At first there was nothing, just the windy whistle beyond the windows. Then, she heard them. Soft whispers. Her eyes flew open and Yali sat back on the frigid tiles.

"You can, can't you? You can hear them again."

Maya snapped her head to look at her grandmother. "What do you mean, *again*?"

Yali's knowing look told Maya she could hear them too.

But how? The voices weren't just whispers in her ear, she could *feel* them. An embrace, pulling her, enticing her.

Yali sighed and stood up. "We're both going to need a coffee for this...though we could probably do with something stronger." She moved over to the kettle and flicked it on before grabbing two new cups and loading them with instant coffee.

"Okay, this is going to be quite hard to wrap your head around," Yali began. Abandoning the drinks, she paced across the room. She stopped and turned to face Maya. "Brace yourself, kiddo. First of all, you weren't born here. You were born in a different place, somewhere called Avalon."

Maya blinked at her grandmother's unexpected admission. "But my birth certificate–"

"I know. Like mine and your mother's, it was forged." She returned to her task, eager for something to calm her shaking hands. "Your grandfather and your boss, John Daniels, helped us with that."

"So where is this place? It sounds...familiar."

"I'm surprised you recognise it. The name has been lost in history, branded as a myth. But that's not important." Yali hesitated, preparing for the onslaught of questions. "Avalon is not in this world."

Maya looked up again from the remaining broken shards on the floor to stare at her grandmother, waiting patiently for the punch line. Waiting for her to spontaneously shout *gotcha!*

Instead, Yali gazed back, waiting for Maya's reaction.

At the prolonged silence, Yali continued slowly. "Avalon is in another realm, one parallel to ours. You're not going mad when you hear the voices, they're coming from the gateway."

Maya laughed, the sound taking Yali by surprise. "Gateway? Gran, what have you been smoking?" she continued to chuckle. "And I suppose this is a hidden closet in the house somewhere, and a lion rules over the land?"

"It's in the lake," Yali explained calmly. "That's where your mother is...and your father."

Maya stopped giggling and went quiet, dropping her head to look at the floor. "Enough, Gran. Mum and Dad are dead. A joke like that...you should know better," Maya said numbly, returning to the task at hand and collecting the larger broken pieces of her mug.

Yali dropped to her knees at Maya's side, gently willing her to look up. "I know this is hard to believe, Maya. Of course, I understand that. I was desperate to tell you, but Jaseen always wanted you to have a normal life here!" she pleaded. "Do you remember the night your mother disappeared?"

"No," Maya spat, refusing to look anywhere but the tiles as tears threatened to overspill. "I remember the morning after my mother was found *dead.* None of you would tell me anything other than that she drowned...you wouldn't even let us see the body–"

"That's because there *was* no body! This night, fifteen years ago, your mother was pulled back to the other side. She was trying to save you."

"Okay. I'll bite," Maya said, lifting her gaze to search her grandmother's face. "Tell me what happened that night." She didn't believe this otherworld nonsense for a moment, but she was desperate to close the case on her mother's death. So, she would listen.

With a sigh, Yali rose to her feet. "Like tonight, you woke up to the voices." She paused to drag out the nearest chair and took a seat at the kitchen table. "I don't understand them. I don't know what or who they are, but I believe your father is responsible. They drew you to the lake that night."

Again, Maya felt a tug on the loose string of an old

memory. Her grandmother had always been a serious woman, not one to make silly jokes at the expense of others. Abandoning the broken porcelain, Maya finally stood from the cold floor, rubbing her knees, and taking the adjacent chair.

Yali reached across the table to clasp her granddaughter's hand. "Your mother and I were awake, like always, because the pull of the gateway was so...insistent. Jaseen heard a door close and thought you kids were messing around. She went to check on you both, but you were gone. I searched the rest of the house whilst she ran outside." Yali stopped and took a deep breath. "By the time I made it out to the garden, she was trying to drag you away from the centre of the lake, where the gateway is. She knew she wasn't going to make it but wanted to save you so–"

"So, she threw me towards you...and you dragged me out," Maya finished; shaking as that string unravelled and the old, suppressed memories were finally released. Memories of the glowing lake and being held in her mother's arms. Memories she had mistaken for childish dreams. She felt sick. Felt like her world was dropping out from under her. *No,* she thought, *not my world.* She suddenly felt like a stranger.

Yali bolted from the chair and embraced her suddenly delicate granddaughter. "I'm so sorry, sweetheart."

At that moment, Jacob padded into the kitchen, his face sickly pale. The two women looked at him and quickly realised, he had heard everything.

"Mum isn't dead?" he asked quietly, clearly in as much shock as Maya. "She was dragged back to this other place? Because of Maya? Because of Maya's dad?" His shock slowly formed into anger. "Why the hell haven't you gone to get her then?" he barked at Yali.

"I couldn't. There's someone on the other side that I need

to hear word from before any of us travel back. It's not safe yet."

"To hell with that!" Jacob yelled. "She's been stuck without us for fifteen years." He regarded Maya then, emotions warring inside him. Sadness. Love. Fear. Anger.

"We could go through the gateway, but we don't know what's on the other side, Jacob. Bandaar is likely still hunting for Maya–"

"Bandaar?" Maya questioned the unfamiliar name.

"Your father, Maya. He's…misled. He was a good man but, circumstances changed him."

"I think I've heard enough," Jacob declared before running from the room.

"You can't blame him for being angry, Gran. You should have told us a long time ago."

"It's my job to protect you. There was no way I could have trusted either of you to stay put; you, especially." Yali said, crossing her arms defensively.

"You're not wrong. And now that I know, there isn't a damn–" Maya stopped as the voices, barely a whisper moments before, began to grow louder.

Yali's eyes widened and she ran from the kitchen. With Maya hot on her heels, they opened the back door to see Jacob, wading into the lake. As he got closer to its centre, the water glowed that vaguely familiar, fluorescent blue.

"No, Jacob!" Yali screamed.

Waves began to lap at his waist, pulling down in a current, a whirlpool. Yali ran to the edge. Throwing her arms out in front, she began to whisper. The water's current changed, battling whatever power lay at the bottom of the lake, pulling Jacob back towards the bank. With all his strength, he pushed forward, until he was in its centre. The water crept up to envelop him, robbing him of sight and air.

Maya stood frozen, powerless to stop the water from

swallowing her brother. With a bright flash he was dragged beneath the waves, and the water returned to its calm state. In a matter of seconds, he was gone.

Beside her, Yali collapsed onto the grass. "Gran!" She knelt and rolled her grandmother onto her back. Blood, thick and heavy, streamed from her nose and ears. Turning to scream for help, she saw her stepfather running towards them.

LATER THAT MORNING, Maya sat at the window of her grandparents' room and gazed out towards the lake, where she'd seen not just her mother but now Jacob, pulled into another realm. She shook her head in disbelief and considered googling the signs of a mental breakdown, when she heard Yali begin to stir.

"Mayara?" she croaked.

Moving from the window, Maya sat on the bed and dabbed at her grandmother's sweat dotted brow. "I'm here, try not to speak."

"No, we don't have much time. How long have I been unconscious?"

"About…five hours," Maya said, looking at her watch.

"You have to go and get your brother. He's not like you. Bandaar will try and get to him."

"I plan to go and get him, Gran. Mum too," Maya assured her.

Yali lifted her arm weakly and pointed to a jewellery box on the dresser. "In there is a necklace. Get it for me please."

Maya did as she was asked and retrieved a silver pendant. Embedded at its centre sat an opal roughly the size of a penny, milky with spectral colours. She handed it to her grandmother.

"Good. Now, look under the bed. There should be a long, black box," she directed.

Finding it, Maya opened the box and saw several smaller ones inside.

"Get the blue one, that was your mother's."

Inside were neatly folded clothes. Maya picked up a pair of white trousers which fanned out at the bottom before tapering in to fit snuggly against the ankles. There was a white top as well, with long sleeves. Her fingers slid softly over the cotton-like material. Beneath that, lay a blue, slim-fitted tunic with slits up the side and skilfully embroidered patterns along the seams. Finally, the shoes. A comparatively normal looking pair of blue pumps.

"Your mother crossed over to this realm in those clothes. You're about the same size, so they should fit you," Yali assured her. She coughed then, blood spraying into her hand.

Maya dropped the shoes and attended to her grandmother. "Why are you suddenly so sick?" she asked.

"I shouldn't have used my abilities on this side of the gateway. I was trying to draw energy through it to stop your brother." She tried to sit up. "Maya, there's no time to waste. You must go now. Take the necklace with you and bring it to Fatari."

"Fatari?" Maya asked.

"Yes, she's my…sister, and a seer. She should know you're coming now." Yali clasped Maya's hands desperately. "Do *not* go near Bandaar. Go straight to Fatari, she is better equipped to answer all your questions," she wheezed. "Now, get dressed and then help me up. I will see you off and explain everything to the others."

∾

MAYA, her grandfather, stepfather and Yali, all stood by the lake.

"Are you ready?" Yali asked.

"Ready isn't exactly the word I'd use," Maya countered as she clasped the jewelled pendant at her neck. She turned from the gateway to embrace her grandmother. Christopher, holding his wife tightly to stabilise her, leaned across and gave Maya a tender kiss on the forehead, told her he loved her, and wished her luck. David was the last in line, and quickly wrapped his stepdaughter in a tight hug.

"Please be careful, Maya. I wish I could go with you."

"You would only burden her, David," Yali insisted with an apologetic smile. "Maya, you must go now. I wish we had the time to better prepare you, but your brother won't survive Avalon if you don't get to him quickly."

"I love you all, I'll bring them home." With that, Maya stepped into lake. She had expected the initial glow of the awakened power to drown in the early rays of dawn, but the lake burst to life. The entire body of water lit in a radiant blue, disturbed only by the shadows of angry waves. Maya waded towards the centre. Like Jacob, the water crept slowly up her sides and along her shoulders, eager to encompass her. She threw one last desperate look at her grandmother, before the water closed in, and everything went dark.

2
THE FIRST ALLIANCE

AVALON ~ DANIKA

Maya woke to water softly lapping against her face. Rubbing her still adjusting eyes, she leaned up and took in the surrounding environment. Her eyesight wasn't the problem. Wherever the gateway had taken her was blanketed in a thick, violet fog. Glancing behind at the lake she was still half submersed in, it looked exactly like her grandparents. She was in some sort of forest, though its trees were like nothing Maya had ever seen before. They were enormous, twisted and eerily beautiful. The thick haze only allowed ten or so feet of visibility, the rest shrouded in mystery. She stood up and walked around the base of the tree's trunk, judging its diameter to be roughly the size of a small bungalow.

Stripped of her watch before the crossing and blanketed from the sky, the time of day was impossible to guess. *How the hell do I get out of here?* Maya thought, looking up. Remembering her grandmother's necklace, she frantically patted her chest.

It was gone.

Darting back to the water, she hunted around the spot

she'd woken up. There, half buried in the sand, its clasp had broken. Almost crying with relief, Maya cupped her hand protectively around the pendant, thinking of her grandmother's wish to return it to the mysterious Fatari. A bland glow emanated from the gem, growing brighter as a thin line of light shot from its core. More disturbingly, the forest had been stagnant of any breeze, but Maya swore she felt the wind lightly pull her in the same direction. The leaves around her whipped up in a playful dance. She released the necklace and it dropped to the floor, the faint line disappearing. After eyeing it dubiously, she bent down and repeated the movement. At her touch, the pointer appeared once again. With no other option, she followed it, calling for Jacob.

After what felt like hours of navigating her way through the uprooted floor of the forest, the haze began to dissipate. A loud shriek from above stopped her. She held her breath and leaned back against a tree, looking up for any sign of the source. The same wail ripped through the silence and leaves fell from above, disturbed, as something moved through the canopy.

"Bloody fog...can't see a damn thing," Maya muttered nervously to herself. The noise was disconcerting to say the least. It sounded big, and she had seen enough movies to fuel an imagination which now seemed relentlessly intent on conjuring grotesque creatures to match it.

The fog is starting to thin, I just need to get a bit further, she reasoned, stepping away from the tree.

SNAP.

Maya stared accusingly at the twig under her foot.

Another blood curdling screech. The creature knew she was below.

Pocketing the necklace, she picked up a large stick, and ran. Wings collided with branches. The monster was in pursuit, and it was close.

A whoosh of air rushed over Maya's head as whatever hunted her dove to make contact, its talons latching on to her thin tunic and piercing the skin beneath. She screamed and relentlessly battered at the thickly scaled legs of the beast that gripped her. Claws opened to release the wriggling prey.

Maya hit the ground hard, the impact winding her, but adrenaline coursed through her body and drove her on. Ahead, sunlight peeked gloriously through the smog. *Yes!* she screamed internally, picking up speed, praying the light would offer her protection from the dark forest's predators. Maya burst through the final line of trees and into an open glen. Like stepping through a thick curtain, the fog was gone. She stopped running and bent over, sucking fresh air into her lungs before turning to the treeline with a hysterical giggle bubbling past her lips.

"Yes! Made it."

A large, winged body, burst through the trees, landing just beyond the veil. Maya froze as the creature planted its taloned feet, readying to charge its prey. Clear of the smoky forest, she could see the beast now, in all its terrifying glory. A six-foot, long bodied lioness stood before her, with a thick hide of scales and rows of perfectly predacious teeth. Shaking its wings to tuck them back neatly, it charged forward.

"Shit!" She turned and ran, with no clue where to go. It was then, Maya noticed a man on the other side of the vale, watching.

Thelic had been walking back from his daily trip to the market looking for work, when he saw the woman. Two things happened only moments apart that amazed him. First and most incredibly, someone had emerged from the Forgotten Forest's veil, unharmed. Second, this person appeared to be taunting the fog. Not long after watching the strange woman appear, a djinca burst through the poisonous barrier. Feeling safe with his distance across the field, he watched; fascinated and amused by this new development – that is, until the woman spotted him and switched direction, leading the djinca his way. Still, he didn't panic. She wasn't going to make it. The creature would be on the woman before she got to him.

"Help!" Maya yelled to the stranger. The ground behind her vibrated with the beast's pounding mass, it was closing in. She knew she wasn't going to make it. With no other choice, Maya spun quickly to engage and swung her makeshift weapon. It connected with the jaws snapping inches from her face. More than that, a powerful burst of air accompanied her swing and propelled the snarling creature backwards across the field. Maya watched, awestruck.

Thelic perked up at yet another new development, the woman had a powerful contract. He settled himself, cross-legged on the grass, watching as the djinca righted itself and renewed the assault.

That guy is just sitting there! Maya seethed. She focussed her attention on the creature. It would be futile to attempt to outrun it. Instead, she tried to summon the gust of wind again. *Don't be an idiot Maya, you're not a bloody wizard.* She glanced around for a better weapon, a bigger stick, anything, and came up empty.

The djinca, now wary of its prey, began to circle Maya.

"Come on then!" she screamed, desperation over-riding common sense.

The beast lunged as Maya ran forward and slid under its belly. She scrambled to her feet – too slow. A hard, scaled tail, whipped to the side and battered Maya's ribs. The impact lifted her into the air before she plunged to the ground with a bone-shaking thud. She moved slowly to all fours, her fresh wound dripping onto the long grass. Black spots breached her vision at the searing pain across her body. Surprisingly, it wasn't fear or despair that came next, but sheer determination. Her brother and mother were in trouble; they needed her. The ground beneath swallowed the rich and freely flowing blood, marring the lush green. A ring of pure, iridescent yellow leapt across the ground from Maya to surround her; its suddenness momentarily stunning the creature.

Thelic saw this too and rose to his feet.

The djinca lunged.

"NO!" Maya cried wilfully, placing a hand in front of her; a feeble attempt to stop what was coming. Roots sprang from the ground to surround her. Enraged, the lioness clawed furiously at the thorns caging its prey. Beneath, the blurred ring had transformed into a wide, intricately decorated circle with symbols strewn across it.

Thelic couldn't believe it. Few were strong or stupid enough to enlist the power of a second sprite, and even fewer possessed the ability to summon a castor's circle. He watched as the djinca paced the line of roots protecting the strange woman. She sat in the circle with both hands stretched out towards the creature. Wind raged across the glen, around Maya, a frustrated sprite desperate to help its useless master.

Doesn't she know how to use it? he wondered. His thoughts were cut short as the djinca hacked at the roots, one of its large paws breaking the barrier to scrape down Maya's chest.

She screamed.

With a low curse, Thelic picked up his spear and darted towards them. The creature spotted him and hunched down possessively, defending its meal. As he ran, Thelic unwrapped the blade of its protective cloth and summoned a powerful wind of his own. Only a breath from the djinca's primed stance, he stopped abruptly, using the momentum to swing his spear in a wide arc. Acting as a conduit for the wind, the curved blade not only sliced the scale-laden face but drove the lioness back as Maya's had done.

Landing on its back, the djinca rolled over and tried to regain its footing. Thelic positioned himself firmly between beast and prey. It stopped to assess the new and considerably more dangerous opponent. With a puff and a petulant swing of its deadly tail, the creature retreated into the fog.

Thelic turned to Maya. She remained behind her wall of roots, which, like her consciousness, were beginning to wane. With a strong swing of the spear, he cut through the weakened wall. The castor circle had also faded, a freshly bloomed ring of flowers the only evidence remaining; the ground at her feet gifted with life renewed.

Rewrapping the spear head, he compacted the clever metallic shaft of the weapon to half its size, allowing him to sheath it. He bent down next to Maya and assessed her wounds.

The gash on her chest was superficial and the bleeding had stopped. Her left side, however, was concerning. The ragged wound was open and seeping freely. Removing his thick, leather-made jacket, he took off his shirt and pressed it into her side to staunch the flow. The neat white slowly turned a bright crimson. He swore. It wasn't far to the lodge, but he'd have to carry her. Tying his shirt around her waist, he re-donned his coat, lifted her into his arms and began the short run back to his home.

MAYA WOKE to a pungent and unfamiliar smell. She lay on what felt like solid concrete and everything hurt. Though, buried under several, bulky fur blankets, at least her body was warm. Flames burned brightly in a wide fireplace big enough to fit her small sofa back home, where a simmering cauldron hung in the middle. Maya suspected whatever was cooking in there was to blame for the smell. In front of the fireplace lay an expanse of fur with a long and shallow stone table resting on it; a simple, cylindrical pillow spanning the entire length for seating.

The rest of the room was modestly furnished. Maya's blanketed bed had been tucked into a corner next to the fire, the adjacent side of the room featuring what she assumed to be a kitchen. Next to the table was a crudely designed drying rack, with clothes neatly folded over it...her clothes. She peeked under the blanket.

Definitely naked.

Her entire midsection from navel to armpits had been wrapped tightly in bandages. It was then that she heard a soft snicker. Looking up, Maya noticed the balcony above her head for the first time. Leaning over, watching her, was the man from the glen.

Thelic had been observing her sleep, still wary of the woman who had managed to navigate the fog veil. As she stirred, he felt an odd sense of relief wash over him and couldn't help but chuckle as she regarded the unfamiliar surroundings. Bright, olive-green eyes stared at him now, her muscular body shifting under the blankets to better see who stood above. He had to admit, she was beautiful, and it had taken more than a strong sense of morals to stop from peeking as he'd attended her wounds.

"I'm naked," she stated bluntly.

"That's correct."

"You bandaged me?"

"I did."

"Interesting." She hiked the blanket higher, grateful but affronted by the invasion of her personal space. "What took you so long to help me back there?" she accused. "And where are we?"

Thelic made his way down the small flight of stairs. "I was watching. Also, why would I needlessly endanger myself to help someone I don't know, against a ruthless creature that hasn't been seen in these parts for well over a decade?" He ambled over to the cauldron and stirred its contents, enhancing the pungent smell that filled the small house. "Oh, and this is my home."

"You were prepared to let that thing eat me!"

"I figured if you could survive the dark spot and summon that kind of power, you would likely be ok." He walked over to the drying rack and felt her clothes. Content they were dry, he picked them up and dropped them onto the bed Maya was currently trying to burrow further into. "Get dressed. I've made some food, we have a lot to discuss, stranger."

"My *name* is Mayara, not Stranger."

An odd name, he thought. A memory of something his father had mentioned crossed Thelic's mind, but he brushed it aside and responded in kind. "Thelic."

Offering Maya privacy, he left the cabin to gather some firewood. On his return, he laid the table with crude, hand-made cutlery before filling two bowls with the grotesque contents of the cauldron.

"What is that?" Maya asked tentatively.

"Rasicus and potato stew."

"Rasicus?"

Thelic paused, bewildered at the question. "It's a small animal," he said. "Doesn't smell great, but it'll build your strength and warm you."

Her hunger triumphing over the repulsive stink, Maya sat at the table and accepted the bowl of food with thanks. To her surprise, it was good, and she happily accepted Thelic's offer of a second helping.

"You're not from around here," he accused bluntly. It wasn't a question, there were too many oddities regarding his guest.

Maya hadn't considered what to tell the locals if they asked about her background. "Not really."

"Where are you from?"

She hesitated and he smiled.

"Thought so," he said simply. "There's only one other person I know from that world. I hear the odd one slips through but, as far as I'm aware, it hasn't happened for a long time."

"I wasn't sure if I should tell you," Maya admitted.

He laughed. "It's pretty obvious. Like I said, strolling out of the dark spot is no small feat."

"I hardly strolled. That, *thing* was after me."

"That *thing* is called a djinca. They're incredibly rare in the south. When did you arrive in Avalon?"

"Today."

He whistled sympathetically. "Your first day and you're up against *that*? You did well."

"I wasn't exactly given the Avalon instruction manual before I left."

"So, you being here isn't an accident?"

Maya stared into the stew. "It's a long story. I'm looking for someone. Well, two people, but I need to meet with a woman first. Her name is Fatari, do you know her?"

He scoffed. "Fatari isn't a name, it's a title. And there's only one that I know of, but she went into hiding almost twenty years ago."

"Why is she in hiding?"

"Esterbell's Keeper is hunting the Seer, supposedly she stole something."

"Keeper?"

Thelic stared dumbfounded. "Do you know anything of our world?"

"I only found out about this place yesterday and I was in a hurry, so no, not really." Maya pushed the empty bowl away sadly. Yali was in a bad way when Maya had left, she could only pray her grandmother was okay.

Thelic stood and walked to the kitchen area. He filled two tankards with a dark brown liquid before resuming his position next to her at the table. He handed one to her.

"What is this?" she asked, sloshing the sinister looking liquid.

"It's mead, drink up, you're in for a long lesson."

Maya took a sip and savoured the rich and sweet mix of flavours.

"Bloody hell, where do I even start?" Thelic asked, raking his hand through short, mouse-brown hair; the soft waves curling back around his temple. "Okay, I'm no historian but we'll start with the basics. This realm, Avalon, supposedly parallels yours. Our civilisation, however, was born from Earth. Us humans didn't exist here until the Five Majors pooled their power to create the gateways."

"Why did humans come here?"

"Apparently, back in your world there were mortals unable to commune with the elemental sprites. They shunned or hunted the castors for their abilities."

Maya thought back to history lessons, myths, and legends; but nothing in Thelic's story resembled anything on Earth she could think of.

"Avalon itself is made up of five territories, six if you count the unclaimed outlands. These are named after the Majors; Danika, where we are; Esterbell; Cantor; Fortus; and Transum.

"Is everyone in this world a castor?"

"There are some whose mortal bloodline denies them the sight. Most Avalonians are contracted though."

"Contracted?"

"It's how you used that wind and summoned the earth. Castors in this realm are tied to different elemental beings.

From what I saw, yours are either Vasiba or Finkel sprites."
He glanced down at her arms, covered now by the thin tunic.
"You don't have the marks though, and you summoned a
castor's circle. That's unheard of."

"You've lost me. Sprites and magic circles? This all
sounds a bit farfetched," she laughed.

"You cross time and space to another world, but *this* is
hard to believe?" Thelic sighed, rubbing a hand down his
face. He wasn't an educator. Simplifying their entire system
wasn't going to be easy. "In Avalon, to use power, you make a
pact with a spiritual being. In return for using their power,
they take bits of your life essence."

"Wait, so by using those abilities in the glen, part of my
soul was sucked away?" The idea was frightening.

"Not your soul, your life. High-level castors tend to die
young for their contracts."

"Fantastic, so that little stunt possibly cost me years." It
was all hard to believe but she struggled to fight the rising
panic. Maya regarded the strange tattoos woven across his
arms. "What level are you?"

"I'm...above average." He downed the rest of his mead
and stood to refill the tankard.

She had to agree, he was certainly above average. From
behind, the tight material of his trousers clung to well-
shaped legs and a peachy backside. The muscles across his
back rippled beneath the loose cotton shirt as he lifted the
large mug of mead. As he turned to walk back to the table,
she averted her eyes and took a long sip of her own drink.
Lifting her lashes slightly, she watched the same rippling
effect across his stomach. Her gaze continued, wandering
down and past the waistline – she coughed on the heavy
liquid.

He eyed her curiously before continuing with his story.
According to Thelic, the creatures in Avalon were different,

too. No Earth-bound animals had ever been permitted to travel through the gateways. He told her about the Keepers, kings of sort, and their rule over the five territories; the elemental hierarchy up to the Gods known only as the Gouram, whose history had long been lost but had once maintained this realm; and the fog veil which now blocked those wishing to cross the gateways.

"That's quite a history," Maya said, somewhat shell-shocked. "Considering the origins of this place, I'm surprised you talk like...well, like you live down the street from me." His accent wasn't British. It was deep and drawled and difficult to place. She liked it.

"Latent born castors and their families have been guided through the gateways over the centuries, they're usually offered a place in the territories' Educator Guilds and word spreads of new terminology. We adapt."

"That makes sense, though we would call those schools or colleges. I'm fairly sure guilds are reserved for tradesmen back on Earth," she said, though admittedly it wasn't her area of expertise. She glanced around the room. No electricity, a fireplace the only heat source, and tankards as drinking vessels. "It's all so old-fashioned. Like I've journeyed years back in time. I suppose you travel by horse and carriage too?"

"I've heard of those, but we don't have horses, we have bodaari or karkili. He went on to explain that, in Avalon, the seasons never really changed. There was no summer or winter; only that some territories were cold and others warm.

"What about my abilities. Like the ones I somehow conjured in the glen to fight that..."

"Djinca," he offered.

"Right. Can I use any others?"

"I doubt it, most castors only contract to one sprite. You've contracted two. Though, without the marks, it's hard to tell the type of sprite you're channelling." He pointed to his own exposed forearms. On the left, swirls covered the length in a beautifully twisted pattern. The right featured geometric patterns, ordered in thick lines. "Like you, I channel earth and wind, but my power draws from mid-level sprites known as Vasiba."

"I saw your wind when you used that spear against the djinca." Judging from what he had told her, Thelic had sacrificed some of his own life essence to save hers. "What about the glowing ring?"

"The castor circle. I've only ever seen one in drawings. The only castors I know of that could successfully call upon it to that extent were the Five Majors. It's a power reserved by those in contract with the Gouram, the highest-level sprites, Gods among their kind."

"What does that mean?"

"That you are one of, if not *the* strongest castor I've ever met...and you have no idea what you're doing," he scoffed. "You know, Keepers would go to war for someone at your level."

"I'm flattered."

"Mayara, take my advice. You either need to go home, or tread very carefully here on in," Thelic warned darkly.

"Please, call me Maya." Only Yali and her mother had ever used her real name. "And I can't go home, but I do want to thank you...for helping me in the end. I'm not sure how to repay you."

"I can think of a few ways." He laughed as Maya leaned away with a raised brow. "Calm down, I don't bite, unless invited," he teased.

Maya shook her head and stretched. A soft howl of wind caught her attention, the weather outside turning bitter. Beyond the small, clouded windows, the pink tendrils of sunset had almost disappeared as night took its place. "Oh God," she gasped, jumping to her feet. "How long was I unconscious?" Panic gripped her and she quickly felt for the soft lump of her grandmother's necklace in her trouser pocket.

"About half a day–"

"Bugger. I really need to get going." Stumbling past the table, she began searching the room for her pumps.

"It's a bad idea to leave at this stage of day, not in the state you're in with those wounds."

Maya turned and assessed him.

Height – well over six-feet.

Build – somewhat god-like.

Talent – frightening.

She could use him. Here, in this world, Maya knew she was out of her depth. She had always taken pride in her strength and capabilities; but not in Avalon. In a single day this realm had robbed her of the usual confidence, like a security blanket had been ripped from her grasp, leaving her completely naked...again.

"You could help me," she said.

"Why the hell would I do that? You're already indebted to me, what could you possibly have to offer?"

Maya gritted her teeth. "Listen, my mother was kidnapped, and my idiot brother went after her alone. I need to find Fatari so I can rescue them."

Again, his father's face popped into his head, unwelcome. "And how exactly do you intend to find the missing Seer?"

"I think this can help guide me to her." Maya pulled the necklace from her pocket. "Look, I'll show you." She held the small, opal-stone pendant tightly in her palm like she'd done in the woods, expecting the same beam of light. Nothing happened, not even a flicker.

Thelic got up suddenly and walked to where she stood by the shoe rack. "May I see that?" he asked, his voice laced with urgency.

Maya hesitated. Whatever the necklace was, it had been important to her grandmother, and this man was a stranger with questionable integrity. Though, he *had* saved her life. She handed it to him.

Dark lashes hooded the clear grey of his eyes as he stared at the pendant before bounding over to the small bookshelf beside Maya's makeshift bed. Finding the book he wanted, he fervently flipped through the pages and stopped at the sheet which featured a drawing of a stone, one that looked just like Maya's. He turned to her then, a dark expression on his face.

"Who are you?"

"I told you–"

"What's your family name?"

"Family – oh, my last name is Cross, Mayara Cross." She realised something then. "Actually, that's my stepfather's last name. I guess I don't know my mother and father's real one."

"How did you get this?" he asked, storming over to thrust the pendant in her face.

"My grandmother gave it to me, why are you freaking out?"

Thelic paced the room, unbelieving of what he held in his hand. This necklace, according to that book, was an old relic from the time of the Five Majors, from the founding of Avalon.

"Did you think this would lead you to Fatari?" he asked.

"I don't know what it does, but a beam of light shot out of it the moment I crossed over. I guess it's broken now."

He continued to walk the length of the room; back and forth, shaking with the effort to contain his anger. "This won't help you find the Seer. This Stone is a crucial part of the first gateway. It's been missing for two generations!" he shouted; control slipping. "My great-grandfather, Winlo, was charged with guarding it for the Fortusian Keeper. It was passed down to my father and stolen under his care." Despite being so long ago, what came next still hurt. "As punishment, he was killed, and my family was banished from the territory; branded as traitors."

Maya was speechless. The odds of this, of meeting Thelic and his connection to the Stone were astronomical. Dread crept in to gnaw at her. She needed the necklace and his grip on it now told her he wasn't likely to let it go again without a fight. "I'm so sorry, but please, I need it to rescue my family."

He stared at the Stone before finally sighing. "It was a long time ago, what would I do with it now?"

An idea came to her. "If you come with me, help me navigate this place to find Fatari, you can have the necklace. You could sell it to the Fortus Keeper and get reinstated. Then everyone wins!"

Thelic scoffed. "Well, when you put it that way, it all sounds so simple."

Maya ambled over to the table to sit beside him. Truly, she had never felt so alone. Everything had happened so fast. Her mother was alive, her brother was in trouble, and now she was sitting in some stranger's house in an entirely different realm.

Thelic couldn't help but stare at the effect the fire's light had on her face. Every sharp feature highlighted and shadowed, so full of expression. He didn't need a seer's gift to know she was suffering. He pondered her offer. The market had been bare of job offers for a while now. He never wanted to return to his home territory, but the necklace would fetch a hefty sum; enough to live easy for several years.

"Fine. I'll help you...for the necklace," he said, sighing dramatically for effect. This elicited the reaction he was hoping for as she laughed lightly, the lines in her face softening again.

"Thank you," she whispered, once more grateful for his help.

"Get some sleep. I'll pack what supplies I have, and we'll head to the market tomorrow to get the rest and enquire about the Seer and your brother."

"I thought you said Fatari was missing?"

"I know someone who might be able to help."

She wanted to leave now, to search the glen and the Forgotten Forest for Jacob. What if the djinca had already gotten him? She clenched her fist, ridding the thought. Thelic was right, this was the best plan, the only plan, if she wanted to find them. Settling amongst the blankets she celebrated at least one victory; she'd made her first ally.

3
FRIENDS, FOOD...AND A BORDELLO

DANIKA MARKET

Maya woke to Thelic gently shaking her. "It's almost dawn, time to go."

Maya bolted up, momentarily forgetting where she was. Her whole body seized with pain, a harsh reminder of the djinca's unwelcoming initiation to this world the day before.

Thelic quickly returned to the bed, pulling the covers away to examine the bandages. He cursed softly, realising the wound across her ribs had seeped through the night. "We'll head to one of the market healers first thing today."

Maya was glad to be rid of the blankets as fresh beads of sweat trailed down the layer already coating her skin. She stood from the bed and a wave of dizziness accompanied the slowly surging nausea. "Bloody hell. What did you put in that drink last night?"

Thelic put a hand out to steady her. "Your wound is infected. It would be better if you stayed here; I can bring the healer to you."

"No, I'm coming. I can't afford to waste any more time."

"Why do I get the sense you're going to be a handful?" Ignoring him, Maya stubbornly wobbled to the sink. "You need to bathe but getting chemicals in your wound is probably a bad idea."

Maya whipped her head to him, mortified. "Do I smell?" she asked, looking at her clothes. They were clean. She saw a small mirror by the door and stumbled over to it. Peering at her reflection, she noted with horror that her hair - still tied in a loosened ponytail - was doing its best impression of a tumble weed; the blood and dirt didn't help matters. Self-consciously, she raked her fingers through the mess before turning back to Thelic. "Please tell you have somewhere I can bathe?"

"Of course I do," he muttered. "I'm not a savage."

IT WASN'T long before Maya emerged; clean and notably steadier. She stepped across the doorway, stretched, and shivered at the crisp morning air. Something wet nudged her shoulder and she turned to see a bulging pair of deep, purple eyes staring back at her. She jumped back with a yelp. "What the hell is that?"

Thelic had been loading the last of the supplies on to his bodaari but came around to introduce them. "This is Keero, he's a mountain beast." He scrubbed the side of the creature's enormous head as it leaned into him affectionately.

To Maya, the bodaari compared to a bear...crossed with a platypus. Size-wise, it was about six times larger than the bears she'd seen at her local zoo – with a long, flat, leathery tail. Thelic offered his hand, pulling her over to stroke Keero's thick hide of fur. Keeping hold, he then led her gently up the bodaari's tail to the blankets laid neatly across its back. His grip was warm and rough, the hard earned callouses scraping against her palm.

Jumping down to close the cabin door, Thelic put his hands together and a sharp wind whipped around him momentarily before subsiding. "Okay, Keero. Let's go," he commanded, leaping onto the creature's back to take hold of the reigns.

"What did you do?"

"Laid a trap. Now, if robbers try to break in, they'll be caught in a whirl-wind and suffocate to death."

Maya waited for the punchline she knew was unlikely to follow. Her new companion, she realised, was trouble.

THE TRIP to Danika Keep wasn't far from Thelic's cabin, and surprisingly comfortable. Maya had imagined it would be more like riding an elephant or camel, but Keero glided easily across the beaten paths; a welcome relief considering her injuries.

As they approached the Keep's major town, the road became busy with traffic in the form of carts and carriages pulled by different, smaller creatures than their own. A string of houses dotted the roadside with stalls erected on the modest front lawns, their owners selling an assortment of hand-crafted items.

Maya marvelled at just how different this realm was to her home. The dwellings here were simple but beautifully intricate, their eaves carefully carved to sweep upwards in an oriental fashion, with vibrant Moroccan-like colours of yellows, oranges, and blues blossoming the walls. She wondered if all the territories were like this, or if each one had its own architectural culture. The fashion, too, was like nothing she'd seen before. The younger women wore clothes like those she wore now but much thicker. Tightly fitted trousers with a tunic of some sort on top and a pelt to protect them from the chill.

Maya shivered and buried herself deeper into the over-sized coat Thelic had given her.

"We'll have to get you some clothes as well, you look ridiculous in that," he chuckled.

"I don't have any money."

"Figures. It's fine, I know someone...I'll just add it to your tab."

"Charming," Maya muttered, cursing her ill-preparedness.

The gates to the Keep rose before them, their high stone walls and armour-clad guards promising no unwanted entrants or escapees. As they passed easily under the wrought iron portcullis, they wound their way into the open south end of a bazaar. Blended aromas of food and perfumes filled the air, masking the stink of market stables. Past the stalls to the north, the Keep's multi-tiered structure loomed above the marketplace, elaborately designed with the same hint of oriental influence as the smaller dwellings; its red brick stark and somewhat menacing when coupled with the midnight colouring of its roof.

Thelic guided Keero into a paddock already crowded with the smaller creatures they'd seen on the road.

"Will he be okay in there by himself?" Maya worried.

"He's a bully, he'll make room."

As if prompted by Thelic's words, Keero turned and swatted two of the smaller, horse like animals with his tail and settled into their combined spot.

"See? Now, come on, we need to find that healer."

As Thelic dragged Maya through the throng of market consumers, she tugged on his grip, her senses going into hyperdrive with a need to see, smell and taste everything the vast expanse of stalls had to offer. She trundled on behind him, ferociously hungry. Thelic had promised to feed her, like you would a stray dog, but only after they had seen the healer.

A commotion to the right caught her eye, a young boy being slapped by a disturbingly large man. The child been caught summoning wind in his attempt to steal some food. The man raised a meaty hand to strike the boy again, taunting him. Instinctively, Maya broke from Thelic's grip and rushed into the crowd to intercept. She caught the man's beefy wrist and flung it back towards him, pushing the young boy behind her.

"Who the fuck do you think you are?" He looked Maya up and down appreciatively then, leering as he stepped towards her. "You can take the punishment in his stead if you prefer, sweetie?"

With a quick glance at the boy, Maya told him to scram.

Thelic had felt Maya's hand leave his and searched the crowded space. A barking laugh caught his attention and he spotted Maya, staring down the market's butcher, a man easily twice her size. "Unbelievable," he muttered, forcing his way through the gathering crowd of onlookers.

Seeing Thelic, Maya turned away from the butcher to meet him. Greasy fingers snatched at her flaxen hair to pull her backwards into the man's embrace.

"Think you can just walk away?" he said, his hot breath fanning across her cheek.

"Move!" Thelic yelled. He was close when the man's hold was forcibly released, and Maya pushed to the ground. She gasped as pain rocketed through her injured side and curled into herself defensively.

Breaking through the last of the crowd, Thelic dropped next to her. "What the hell were you thinking? Spirits, woman. This place isn't like your world–" he stopped at

Maya's short, wheezing gasps, noticing fresh blood spattering her tunic. He looked up to hunt her attacker, surprised to find him strewn across the ground with a leather boot firmly planted on his throat.

"Weren't you taught to play nice with ladies? Despite popular belief they won't want you if you're mean...unless they like that of course."

"Elkin!"

At the prompt, Maya's leather-booted rescuer turned from his prey – now thrashing about in a fit of rage – and grinned. "Thellie!" With a rib-cracking stomp on the beefy butcher's chest, Elkin took two long strides over to Thelic, still crouched protectively over Maya.

"Good timing, clear the way so I can get her to Brijid."

"Excellent, I was just heading that way," Elkin said with a humoured salute.

Thelic lifted Maya into his arms and carried her through the crowd as Elkin brusquely shoved the shoppers from their path.

The western edge of the market was laden with large tents, all offering services for sale, but Elkin knew exactly which one they needed. Finally reaching the largest, he burst through the thin cotton flap. "Brijid!" he hollered jovially.

A young and wiry woman had been sitting at a desk towards the back, eyes pouring over her medical journals when the unexpected arrival called her name. She peeked over her glasses and groaned. "No, get out, unwanted, shoo–"

"That's not very nice, not to mention completely unwarranted."

"Unwarranted?" she gaped, standing to lean over her desk. "You little terror. Last time you popped your head through my tent–"

"Brijid! That's dirty," Elkin teased with a wink.

The brunette went a very dark shade of red, not long before picking up a knife and hurtling it at him. He caught it easily and sat at one of the tables by the entrance, letting Thelic come through with Maya.

"Thelic?" Her eyes widened questioningly at the shivering woman in his arms.

"She was attacked by a djinca, yesterday."

"Then why didn't you bring her to me yesterday? You silly fool. I swear, the two of you..." Rushing from the table, Brijid directed Thelic to one of the beds. Once settled, she unclasped Maya's tunic, stopping momentarily to pull a blind to surround them. She resumed undressing her, taking note of the pale colour and high temperature. Beneath the fabric, loosened bandages were soaked through with fresh blood speckled with a yellow tinge.

"The tail must've struck her, there's poison running through her system."

Thelic pulled back the curtain stepping through as Brijid cut away the bandages covering Maya's breasts.

"Thel–"

"I cleaned her body after the attack, so I've seen it all before."

Maya had figured as much but wasn't keen to dwell on it. "Bloody pervert," she croaked.

"Ha, I like this one," Brijid laughed.

"Can you heal her?"

"Of course, idiot."

Brijid dashed from the enclosed space to a cabinet. From there, she removed a bowl and dipped it into a box brimming with soil. Next, several obscure looking potions were blended and drizzled into the same bowl. Rushing back to the patient's side, she placed the concoction on a table at Maya's head.

"Roll her onto the uninjured side, Thelic," she said,

rubbing her hands together as she regarded Maya. "This isn't going to be pleasant, but I'll work as fast as I can," she warned, telling Thelic to hold the patient down.

The healer took a handful of the mixture and pressed it deep into the ragged tear, silently calling upon the elements of earth and fire to activate the blend, draw out the poison, and cauterise the wound. The blazing sensation of the elements being thrust into her body and the poison being drawn out, had Maya thrashing against Thelic's unrelenting grip, praying she would pass out.

"Done, I don't feel the poison in there anymore," Brijid announced, stepping back from the bed.

Maya continued to shake with painful spasms as the power lingered.

"Thank you, Bri," Thelic said, easing his grip on Maya's shoulders.

"I would say thank you, but that felt terrible," Maya wheezed, smiling weakly at the healer. "Also, I figure if you're going to poke around my insides and save my life, I should at least tell you my name. I'm Maya."

Brijid chuckled as she washed her hands in the small basin at the back of the tent. "Brijid. Nice to meet you."

After grabbing a blanket for Maya, Thelic left the small space to give them room and speak with Elkin.

"How is she?" Elkin asked, concerned.

"She'll be fine. Listen, I know it's been a while, but your final job for Esterbell's Keeper–"

"This sounds interesting. That's some past your dragging up, friend," Elkin teased, leaning back in the chair to prop his boots on a small chest at the side.

"I know. I'm sorry, but I need to know where you found the Seer."

Elkin let out a long breath. "Tricky old lady that one, she'll have moved on several times by now."

Thelic scraped a hand down his face. He'd figured as much but hoped otherwise.

"Why the interest? You got a job?" Elkin asked.

"Maya needs to find her."

"Who is this woman to you? Don't get me wrong, she's very pretty, but you rarely take this sort of interest in...well, anything really. Exactly how much is she paying you?" Elkin chuckled, holding his hands up in surrender at Thelic's ill-tempered scowl. "Okay, okay, I do know someone that can point you in the right direction."

Moments later, Brijid stripped back the thin curtain to reveal Maya, her wounds re-bandaged and fully dressed. "I take it back, this one's stubborn, I hate the stubborn ones," the healer sulked. "I've given her a shot of waker, but she needs to lie down, *at least* for another day."

"Wherever we're going may take longer than that, so I can rest on Keero, right?" Maya asked Thelic.

He returned her look and crossed his arms. "Are you sure you're up for it? Bodaari don't do well with dead bodies."

"Your concern for my well-being is overwhelming, really, I might cry," she smiled back sarcastically. "Whatever Brijid did felt like having my insides ripped out and shoved back in, but it helped...actually, I feel really good," Maya realised, renewed energy coursing through her.

"That'll be the waker shot, it should last a couple of days," Brijid said, pleased with her work.

Thelic took a small pouch of money from his pocket and moved to hand it to her.

"Don't," the healer warned. "I owe you so much more after what you did for me last year, Thel."

He nodded, more to acknowledge what she meant but fully intending to leave compensation. "She needs to borrow some clothes as well, if you have any to spare?"

"I have plenty. Come to the house later and I'll put a bag together for you, Maya."

FINALLY, as they walked through the market at a more leisurely pace, Maya could better appreciate what the stalls had to offer. Vendors beckoned to the crowds, boasting clothes made of finely woven silks from the Transum Territory; Jewels sourced from the mountains south of Cantor; and soaps handmade near the Deadland lakes. Everything was new and exotic to Maya, and despite the urgency of her mission, she secretly yearned to spend the day exploring the bizarre bazaar.

"Hey, hey! Did you hear? Someone wandered out of a dark spot!"

"Yeah, at the Forgotten Forest, I heard that!"

Maya froze and Thelic tensed beside her. Two of the stall-owners were openly gossiping with one another. Maya moved closer, pretending to peruse one of the merchant's items as she listened, Thelic close beside her. Elkin had stopped to talk to an attractive young woman several stalls behind and dashed over to catch up.

"Aye, I heard the Keeper's guards picked him up."

They weren't talking about Maya. They were talking about Jacob.

"Oh, I heard about that!" Elkin chimed in. "Very exciting!"

"Where do you suppose they were taken?" Maya asked, feigning only mild interest as she continued to inspect a chunk of soap.

"Well, I heard he was brought here, to the Keep, only for Bandaar of Esterbell to buy him. Supposedly picked him up earlier today," the merchant said, clearly pleased to be the centre of attention.

Maya dropped the soap at the name. Bandaar. Her father. Yali had warned her to stay away from him, but now she knew he had Jacob.

Maya walked away from the stall, pulling Thelic with her until they reached a relatively quiet area near the western wall.

"How do I get to Esterbell?" she asked, eyes wide and desperate.

"I thought you had to go to Fatari?" Thelic wasn't sure he liked where this line of enquiry was going.

"That was before I knew my brother had been taken."

Thelic watched for her next reaction carefully. "Before, at the stall, when you froze and dropped the soap...it was like you recognised the name of Esterbell, yet you say you've never been here."

Maya considered lying to Thelic but wondered what good it would do her. She needed his help, at least to find Bandaar.

"Truly, I had never heard of the name Esterbell until you told me it was a territory. That wasn't what caught my attention." Again, she hesitated. "It's Bandaar. Apparently, he's my father."

"I'm sorry, what? Bandaar Rivers?" Elkin said, poking his head around the corner to where they stood, having clearly eavesdropped on the conversation.

"I thought you were born in the Earth Realm?" Thelic asked, confused.

"Again, what?" Elkin, apparently, was elated at this news and rushed forward to take hold of her hands.

"You must tell me everything, Maya–" Elkin began before Thelic moved forward, cutting him short.

"What are you not telling me?"

"Listen, I told you, if you help me reach Fatari I'll give you the necklace. That still stands, but first I really need to get to Esterbell."

"We're not going anywhere until you're straight with me," Thelic seethed, towering over her.

Maya rubbed the spot at her temples, warding off an incoming headache. "Okay, is there somewhere more private we can talk?"

"I know somewhere!" Elkin offered before ushering them both back into the crowded market.

AS THEY WALKED IN SILENCE, Maya studied Elkin. He seemed kind, despite his intimidating physique. The man was built like the broad side of a barn. He didn't hit the typical markers for what some might consider attractive. His hair was a shaggy mess of red, tied in a hasty bun, a stark contrast to the neatly trimmed facial hair. The most prominent feature, however, was the long scar down his cheek and another, larger scar on his neck. But the man had a charm about him that was undeniable. Like Thelic, he was tall, but much wider, most likely sporting brute strength as his forte.

Elkin led them to the northern quarter. Here, the small collection of houses posed a similar style to those outside of the Keep's walls but boasted an unequal extravagance. One in particular was painted a faded white with a red door. He walked straight in without a knock; the others trailing behind.

Inside, the air was thick with sweet-smelling plumes. People in all corners of the lower floor drank from long handled smoking instruments, each with a glass bottom. Bongs, Maya realised, fascinated. She then noticed the clientele; men, and women throughout the room, gyrating against one and other in plain view.

It was a brothel.

"Amazing. You couldn't think of anywhere else to speak privately?" Thelic snapped, batting away the touchy fingers of a man dressed in a loincloth.

"What's wrong, Thellie? Afraid you won't be able to concentrate?" Elkin teased.

The lady of the house gratefully accepted Elkin's coins and showed them to an unoccupied room on the second floor. Along the way, several women recognised and greeted Elkin like they would a lover.

Thelic groaned. Maya chuckled.

The room was quaint and looked clean enough considering the location. They thanked the lady and handed her additional coins, requesting food and wine.

"Explain," Thelic insisted the moment the door was closed.

Maya walked over to the window and looked out over the northern quarter and Market stalls just past, wondering how to begin.

"To be completely honest, I don't know all that much about my history here." She went on to explain how her mother had disappeared fifteen years ago, pulled through the gateway by her father. "I didn't know anything about Avalon until yesterday."

"So why did you suddenly cross over?" Elkin asked.

Maya told him of Yali's revelation and her brother's rash decision to cross alone; that he blamed her for what happened to their mother. She fell silent, remembering Jacob's expression the moment he had found out.

"Yali. Why does that name...Wait! Thelic mentioned he was looking for Fatari, she had a sister..." Elkin slowly put the pieces together. "You're a daughter of Fatari's bloodline? *Esterbell's bloodline?*" Elkin exclaimed standing from his perch on the bed.

A light knock on the door hushed the room, Thelic's hand instinctively reaching for the spear permanently strapped to his side.

A beautifully curvaceous woman strode in with a large tray of food and three glasses. She wore a loose belt with a bottle of wine strapped to it, and little else. Her breasts hung free of restraints as a long line of silver beads draped down their middle from a choker around her neck. Below the belt, only a thin piece of sheer material clung to what Maya thought jealously to be a very well-rounded behind.

"Ah, Lisaya!."

The woman ignored Elkin, her eyes locked on Maya as she crossed the room; setting the food, glasses, and wine down on the table. Maya thanked her, but Lisaya just smiled sweetly before leaving without a word.

"Do you think she overheard?" Thelic whispered, pacing across the room to close the door.

"Why does it matter?" Maya asked casually.

"Anyone from the other side or with a higher power is of great interest to Keepers, never mind someone of your heritage, Maya," Elkin warned. "They're always looking for some way to out-do one and other and prove they have the most power. Even now, I've heard the stirrings of a war brewing between them."

"A war for what?"

"What else? Territory and power," Elkin shrugged, uninterested. "Back to the main subject, I've heard rumours about *you*, as well."

"Me?" Maya exclaimed.

"There's actually several regarding Bandaar's missing child. According to your story, it appears some of them ring true for once."

"What do you know?" Maya asked, desperate for any information on her past.

"Well, the favourite, was that both you and your mother had been kidnapped by outlanders. However, it soon came to light that this wasn't the case. Nevertheless, Bandaar used that as an excuse to prepare for war and inquisitions, requesting aid from each of the Keeps." Elkin moved to the table and poured the wine. "It was clear to most, that he was hunting for more than just his missing wife and child, but whatever that was, seemed to elude him."

"Perhaps it was Fatari?" Maya asked. "My gran told me to stay away from him, to go straight to her."

"It's no secret that Bandaar hunts Fatari to this day, her power is immense, that's for sure, but why he is adamant to possess such a power is anyone's guess. Another rumour is that Jaseen had found a way to navigate the dark spots and crossed over to the earthly realm. She must be incredibly gifted; I don't know anyone capable of doing that." Elkin chuckled to himself then. "You don't happen to be able to conjure immense power as well, do you?"

Maya and Thelic looked at each other.

"Can you!? The old maids of Esterbell Keep tell stories of how the little girl was so powerful, she could conjure multiple castor circles. Can you really do that?"

"I've only conjured one that I know of, and I have no idea how I did it," Maya replied sheepishly.

Elkin considered this. "So, your mother really did take you to the Earth Realm, in order to protect you from Bandaar."

"Why do you say that?" Thelic questioned. He had stayed quiet until now, piecing together Elkin's information with his own.

"Well, according to the maids, Maya was *forced* to conjure the circles." Elkin looked down at his hands as he continued. "Bandaar sliced open your palms, Maya, to spill the blood necessary to conjure them. This caused you to be quite a sickly child, it almost killed you more than a few times," he finished apologetically.

Maya stared at the thin lines on each palm. Her mother had lied, she had been told she cut them on a boat propellor. Instead, she'd been systematically tortured…by her father. She stood up to pace the room. "How did he even know I *could* conjure them? And why force me to do it?" She wondered aloud.

"Ah, that I don't know. Only the folktales, sorry."

"Did the maids mention anything about what sprite Maya is contracted to?" Thelic asked.

"No." The question surprised Elkin. "Surely her marks explain that much."

"She doesn't have any."

"No marks and the ability to summon a castor's circle, my girl you grow more and more intriguing by the moment!" Elkin slapped his knees excitedly. Maya on the other hand was less pleased and felt more in the dark than ever.

"At least we have a little more information," Thelic said, pulling a chair out for Maya, pointing at her wound, and prompting her to sit. "We know you were born in Avalon, that you're pretty much Avalonian royalty, and your father is a piece of lipen-dung who's hunting you for your power."

"But we don't know why." She flumped into the chair, frustrated.

"True. You also carry one of the artefacts–"

Elkin stood up then. "You, what?" he shouted, an octave higher than intended. "Which one?"

"She has the Gouram Stone."

Elkin gawked at Maya then remembered Thelic's history with the relic. "How the hell–"

"We don't know how it got from Thelic's father to my grandmother, but Yali gave it to me, insisting I take it to Fatari."

Elkin was surprised Thelic had revealed so much to a stranger; that he'd given the Stone back to her at all. He asked to see it, to confirm this story for himself.

Maya looked to Thelic for reassurance on their new ally. He nodded his head and she removed it from her pocket, placing it in the outstretched hand.

"Bleed a rasicus," Elkin breathed. "That's the real thing."

Maya tucked the pendant back under her tunic, shivering at her own cold touch.

Thelic noticed the goosebumps along her arms. "We should head back to Brijid's soon. You'll draw attention in those clothes. Freezing to death would be a bit of nuisance as well." He pulled one of the blankets from the bed and wrapped it over her shoulders.

Again, Elkin was taken aback by the subtle change in Thelic and tried to ignore it. "I assume those were your mother's clothes?"

"Yes, apparently she crossed over in them. It was all my grandmother had for me to travel in."

"Well, you certainly look like an Avalonian, albeit a bold one wearing clothes designed for the warmer climes. Even fire masters cover up more than what these clothes have to offer," Elkin laughed.

"Is it always cold here?"

"Mostly in the southern territories, where we are, but we get the odd spell of warm weather when the sprites are feeling benevolent. Not all territories are the same though. The further north you travel, the warmer the weather. I'm particularly fond of Transum, it's a happy medium there," Elkin responded wistfully, refilling both of their glasses.

Thelic hadn't touched his wine, he was too on edge. Growing up, his father had taught him the history of Avalon, of Avalonians. What bothered him now was something he hadn't thought about for twenty years. His father's last fable, about a girl and her harshly appointed destiny, and how her fate would be entwined with his own. Ever since Maya had stepped through that forest and shown him the Stone, he had the nagging thought that his father's last tale wasn't a tale at all, but a prophecy.

"So, that's the plan."

Thelic was snapped from his thoughts by Maya's words and Elkin's burst of laughter. "Little fulsin, you're either entirely too optimistic or naïve...perhaps both?"

"Well, what then? What's your grand idea for rescuing my brother? And what's a fulsin?"

"A fulsin is a really *annoying* little bird–"

"Small and beautiful," Elkin corrected Thelic. "Maya, you can't just sneak into a Keep, you'd be killed on site; or worse, considering it's Esterbell we're talking about."

"Wait, you want to sneak into Bandaar's Keep? Definitely naïve," Thelic noted.

Maya sank in her chair. "Listen, I know I don't look like much, but I can pack a punch when it's necessary. I just need directions to Esterbell and a layout of the Keep," she said with a shrug, taking another sip of wine. "I'm not asking either of you to come along, but I *am* going to get my brother."

Elkin and Thelic looked at each other in mock despair. Thelic knew he had to go, the connection to Maya's history and his father's story had shaken him. He felt drawn to her. Plus, she was right. At the very least he could sell the Stone.

"Whatever the plan, it sounds like an adventure. Count me in, little fulsin," Elkin declared.

Maya fist pumped the air, wincing at the injury to her side.

"Well, that's a relief. While I hate to admit it, this would be entirely more difficult without your particular skill sets," Thelic sighed before downing his glass of wine.

"You're coming too?" Maya stood up excitedly. "Why? From the sounds of it, this is a suicide mission."

"Curiosity...and the Stone."

"Ahh, curiosity is a dangerous thing you know, it killed the cat," Maya joked.

Both men looked at her questioningly, the humour lost on them.

A sudden pound on the door caught their attention as a tiny woman scampered into the room and wrapped her arms around Elkin's stomach.

"You must leave!"

"Blisa? Whoa, slow down. What's wrong?" Elkin asked, calmly attempting to unfurl the escort's manicured claws from his ribs.

Thelic already had his spear extended, pointing towards the potential threat.

"Lisaya! I saw her talking with Carnass' guards and pointing to your room. Oh, Elkin, you know she still hates you."

"Damn." Thelic was by the window now, watching guards strategically take up positions outside of the brothel to block their exits. "We're surrounded."

Elkin grabbed the shoulders of the woman now sobbing into his shirt. "Blisa, where's the underground passage?"

"It's too late!" she bawled. "They already know about it."

"So, let's get captured," Maya thought out loud.

Everyone in the room turned to look at her. Blisa pushed Elkin away and walked up to Maya, slapping her hard across the face. Thelic's spear quickly found the hooker's throat and pressed.

With a squeak, the escort scampered back to hide behind Elkin's mass. "This is your fault," she screamed. "They only want you!"

"Maya, why did you say we should let them detain us?" Elkin asked.

"You said it yourself, the Keepers are looking for some way to out-do one and other. Maybe this one can help us?"

Blisa and Elkin scoffed.

"Carnass is notorious for his heavy-handed leadership, you *stupid* woman," Blisa hissed.

A stampede of heavy boots was heard coming up the stairs. Elkin quickly slammed the door shut and moved the bed in front, picking Blisa up and placing her on top.

"You three should hide in the bathroom," Maya offered. "I'll let them capture me and speak to Crampess–"

"Carnass!" they all corrected.

"–by myself. If he supports me, I'll ask him to return me to the market where I'll meet you at Brijid's."

"Brave, little fulsin, but no," Elkin said sternly.

"That could work," Thelic stated quietly. At Elkin's shocked expression he explained. "Carnass is…not what you all think, you know my history with him. We'd have to play it carefully but, he might just help if it's to spite another Keeper."

"We?"

"Yes, Maya, you're not going on your own. He'd eat you alive," he said with a roll of his eyes. "Elkin, you and Blisa hide in the bathing room as Maya suggested. We'll meet you at Brijid's house. If we're not there by sundown tomorrow, then we've failed."

Blisa squealed as the solid wooden door behind her splintered at the guard's pounding.

Maya sat on the bed in her place and passed the Stone to Elkin. With a promise to protect it with his life, he grabbed Blisa and pulled her into the small, adjacent room. Thelic took Maya's hand and asked her to stand behind him. She did, and with a flick of his wrist the bed was flung to the other side of the room. With the barrier gone, guards flooded through the small gap to surround them, swords raised and hands ready to conjure the elements.

"This suddenly feels like a very silly idea."

Thelic grinned down at Maya. "Too late now."

4

THE FIGURE IN BLACK

ESTERBELL KEEP

Jacob shivered on the stone cobbled floor; an iron shackle twisted painfully around his ankle. A small hole, bare of glass, allowed the territory's cool breeze to sweep in and around the cramped confines of the cell. He hugged his knees, desperate to retain the warmth as he listened to the sweet chirping of birds. A far-off banter from the village accompanied the birdsong, a teasing combination, considering his captivity. Out of everything he regretted, failing to put on a coat before jumping into his grandparents' lake was at the top of his list. He was scared. He wasn't angry anymore, just lost, and clueless as to what he'd gotten himself into. When he woke in the forest, surrounded by those strange trees and odd coloured mist, he knew everything he'd overheard his grandmother say to be true. At that time, he blamed Maya.

Idiot, he thought, *how is any of this her fault?*

He'd never wanted to see his sister more, to say he was sorry. Jacob knew she would come for him, though; she always did.

A bang outside the cell broke his train of thought. Scrambling weakly, he pushed himself to the far corner of the room. *Stand up you coward*, he thought harshly to himself; but the cold, hunger, and fear, had robbed him of strength.

The door to his cell opened and a man, dressed in fine black silk, stepped into the entryway. Light bathed the space around the figure, falsely casting Jacob's captor as an angel.

"What's your name?" the man demanded.

Jacob didn't respond, just clutched his knees tighter and willed the man to go away.

"You came through Danika's gateway, correct?"

Again, Jacob remained silent, unsure what reaction his answers might elicit from his captor.

The earth beneath them began to shake. Survival trumping his fear, Jacob jumped to his feet and gripped the slippery, undulating cobbles of the wall, convinced the ground was about to collapse. This man was like *them*, the strange and dangerous magic users of this world.

"Stop!" he screamed. "Please, my name is Jacob and–" his brief pause triggered a second, more powerful earthquake. A crack laced up the wall at his fingertips to the ceiling. A fist sized stone fell, just barely grazing his shoulder. "Yes! Ok, yes, I came through the lake. Now stop, please!"

The earth settled and a treacherous smile played at the corner of the figure in black's mouth. He stepped from the cell and two armoured men took his place, both moving to stand at either side of Jacob.

The guards were instructed to take the boy to the eastern quarter. As Jacob was dragged from the damp cell, the figure in black, Bandaar, studied his face, and all doubts were quashed. In those terrified, vibrant blue eyes, he saw Jaseen. Sadness crept into the dim corners of his heart, quickly swept away and replaced by triumph. With the boy, he now had double the leverage against his daughter. Mayara was here, in Avalon. He felt it the moment she crossed the gateway and his spies in Danika had confirmed as much. She would surely be tracking her brother. He had waited twenty years; but Avalon couldn't wait any longer.

JACOB WAS THROWN UNCEREMONIOUSLY onto the floor of a brightly lit room. The space boasted an obvious extravagance afforded by the territory's Keeper. Each corner was adorned with expensive looking furniture and bejewelled tapestries.

With their prisoner delivered, the guards withdrew, closing and locking the door behind them. Jacob carefully picked himself from the floor to take in his surroundings. It barely took a moment before he registered the woman standing at the far end of the room, staring at him. Almost simultaneously, recognition dawned in them both.

Though he struggled to remember her face from experience, he had cherished the pictures they had of this woman.

"Mum?" Jacob spoke first, slowly taking one step forward. In turn, Jaseen took one step back, her hand now covering her mouth.

Impossible. Her son couldn't have travelled through the gateway. Even if he did, how was he here, in Esterbell? Her own eyes stared back at her. "Jacob?" she whispered, fearful of scaring this dream away.

"Yes, Mum, it's me!" Jacob ran forward and embraced her.

The shock was overwhelming, but slowly she did the same, wrapping her arms tightly around the son she hadn't seen for fifteen years. "Let me look at you, by gods you've gotten tall!" She stroked the matted fringe from his face, wiping at his tears that mirrored her own. "Why Jacob? Why are you here!?"

He sank to the floor sobbing, dragging his mother down

with him. "I'm sorry, Mum. If I'd known you were here, I would've come to get you years ago!"

"Oh spirits, Jacob, I'm so sorry." She gripped her son fiercely. Jaseen had never wanted this, never wanted either of her children to come to this world. How he'd managed to get to her, alone… "Jacob, where's your sister? Did she come through the gateway with you?"

"No," he said, wiping away at his tears. "I came by myself; I couldn't believe it when Grandma told us."

Jaseen released a deep breath thankfully. "That's good, she can't come here."

"Mum, she *will* come. You know she will, now that she knows." He dipped his head in guilt. "I shouldn't have gotten angry, we should have come here together…but I was furious! I don't know why, but I blamed Maya."

"No, Jacob. None of this is her fault!" She sighed wearily. "There's so much about Mayara's history you don't know… that *she* doesn't know."

"I know it's not her fault. I always knew. I just didn't think. Anyway, she knows a hell of a lot more now." At his mother's worried look, he placed a hand on her shoulder. "Don't worry, she's tough and Gran's been training her. She's probably already here, in Avalon."

"She is," Bandaar announced from the now open doorway.

Jaseen moved instinctively to stand in front of her son and Bandaar sneered. "I'm not interested in the fruit of your… indiscretion, Jaseen. He is nothing to me, it's our daughter I want."

"This is…you're Maya's father?" Jacob asked, stepping out from his mother's shadow.

"Yes, and I've missed her." He looked at Jaseen then, a confusing blend of lust and loathing warring inside him. "You only have yourself to blame. Her destiny was pre-determined by your bloodline."

"There's another way, Bandaar!"

"Enough!" The ground shuddered at Bandaar's outburst, before calming along with his temper. "Save it for the family reunion." With that, he left the room, and Jaseen wept.

BANDAAR STORMED PAST THE GUARDS, instructing them to lock the door and maintain sentry. Past the courtyard, he glanced at the children training there. One of the boys, barely a teenager, cleverly manipulated the earth element and a wall shot up before him. Even those contracted with the lesser sprites were improving dramatically. Continuing down the long hallways he turned into a room in the western quarter. A large, circular table stood prominent in the centre, with charts and intelligence reports tacked to the walls. Strewn across the table, a map of Avalon showed every territory in their small slice of this world.

Mayara was somewhere in Danika. He had yet to hear from his spies exactly where, but it was only a matter of time. He couldn't afford for her to make the journey alone. The Earth Realm would have softened his daughter, with creatures docile and people comparatively unthreatening.

"Sir."

Bandaar snapped his head to the shifter standing awkwardly in the doorway. "Where is she?"

"She was taken into custody by Carnass. My man is monitoring the situation from there."

Bandaar gripped the table hard enough to splinter. "Carnass." Danika's Keeper was trouble. If he discovered the truth... "Keep me appraised of the situation and get a group together. If she's not out of there in one day, then I want them to go in and get her."

Despite his impossible task, the shifter nodded; respect and fear emboldening the empty promise. He left the Esterbellian Keeper to brood.

Alone, Bandaar regarded the map before him and the freshly painted shadows of the boundary void. Surrounding Avalon, a dark expanse of the poisonous fog had caged them from the rest of this world; and to this day it continued to grow. He looked, then, at his forearms. As was the case with all castors, beneath the brands were tattooed cuffs, once thick and bright with colour now sat pale and thin against his fair skin. With Mayara, he could stop it all. Together they could save this realm and his people. Both would suffer, both would sacrifice; but what was one life, against many?

5

THE ECCENTRIC RULER

DANIKA KEEP

"I'm so cold I'm afraid my assets might drop off…and I'm quite partial to them," Maya groaned as she paced the length of the small cell. In the guards' haste to remove them from the brothel, her coat had been left behind. The Danika dungeon had little to offer in the form of comfort or warmth, with no fires burning nearby for fear of the element being manipulated to aid escape.

Thelic gave her breasts an appreciative look before shrugging off his heavy jacket and handing it to her.

"Won't you get cold?"

"Yes, but your assets are worth it," he smiled, easily dodging Maya's retaliatory air-borne shoe.

Hours passed before several guards showed up, stating that Carnass had demanded Maya's presence.

Thelic stood from the withered and rotten bed, placing his hands on the bars separating him from their jailers. His height and build easily dwarfed the guard who had spoken.

"Well, you can tell Carnass that his favourite shifter is here, and the woman doesn't see him without me." All but one in the front line of guards stepped back and balked at Thelic's tone. The man who remained stood relaxed, picking at the under-side of his nails with a small, jagged-edged dagger.

"Terricus. Thought you were dead," Thelic goaded with a sly smile. "I was disappointed."

The man looked up at the mention of his name and returned the blade to a small sheath at his side before approaching the bars. "Thelic, what's the matter? Still sore after so many years?"

Maya looked back and forth between the two men, taking an instinctive step away at Thelic's expression.

"I suppose this means I still have a chance to kill you myself," Thelic stated, his white-knuckled grip on the bars betraying his calm tone.

The guard laughed and turned, snapping his fingers to a young man at the back, telling him to run along and inform Carnass of the new development. Turning back to face the prisoners, he jabbed his fist through the bars straight into Thelic's stomach.

Thelic gasped, collapsing to his knees, his hand grasping at Terricus' uniform.

Bending down, Terricus gripped Thelic's hair, turning his head to whisper in his ear. "How *is* Brijid these days?" he asked, glancing at Maya. "Shame I don't have more time, *she* looks like a fun ride too."

Before another word could be said, the messenger returned with instructions to bring both prisoners.

As Maya and Thelic were roughly manoeuvred through the halls of the Keep, she leaned in to his side speaking quietly. "What was all that about?"

Thelic grit his teeth, shaking his head at her in response as they were led into a cavernous chamber. Richly coloured paintings covered every wall, with deep lanterns lining the eaves of complexly carved wooden beams across the ceiling. The floor, too, was a beautiful blue marble.

"Holy crap," Maya whispered, appreciating the eclectic mix of stunning possessions.

"Impressive, isn't it?"

Maya looked from the ceiling to the man that spoke. Lounging on a lavishly decorated throne at the end of the room and dressed in jewel encrusted silk garments, was Carnass.

To Maya's surprise, Thelic bowed. Before she could react, Terricus kicked the spot behind her knees, sending her to the floor, his sword falling to her throat. "You bow in front of Danika's Keeper," he spat at her.

In a quick blur of motion, Thelic was gone from his humbled position. A strangled sound rang out from behind Maya before the body dropped to the floor at her side, a sword skidding along the marble towards Carnass.

Deep red pooled beneath the jagged slice across Terricus' throat, its hue staining the thin white divides of the blue marble.

Everyone froze as Terricus convulsed on the floor, desperately gripping his throat in a bid to hold the two sides together. It wasn't long before his eyes went wide, fixing on Maya as his final gargling gasp escaped.

With the guard's dying breath, Maya found her own, inhaling sharply as she scurried back from the quickly spreading crimson tide.

Initial shock dissipating, the other guards burst into action, hurrying to surround the man standing over their comrade's dead body.

"Enough," Carnass said, boredom lacing his tone as he raised a hand in motion for everyone to stop. "Leave us."

With a quick bow, the guards gingerly lifted Terricus from the floor and hurried from the room.

At the closed door and lack of prying eyes, the feared leader transformed; clapping like a giddy child presented with a new toy. "Thelic!" he whined. "I've missed you, my darling." Hopping down from the throne, Carnass raced over to embrace his favoured serviceman. He turned to Maya. "And who, spirits tell, is this fine creature?" Moving away from Thelic, he side-stepped the crimson stain as if it were nothing more than spilt milk.

Wiping the blade on the sleeve of his white shirt, Thelic slipped it between his belt and tailored trousers before crossing his arms impatiently as the Keeper circled Maya.

Terricus' blade. He must have gotten it when they had been imprisoned in the cell, Maya thought quietly.

"Miss?" Carnass prompted again. "What's your name?"

Still in shock over Thelic's actions, she responded numbly. "My name is Maya. I'm from the other side, or other world, or whatever you call it."

Thelic groaned and buried his face in bloodied hands. He had strictly instructed Maya not to say she was from the other realm. Carnass was known for being somewhat of a collector. Yet another reason he was glad the Gouram Stone had been left with Elkin.

"Is that right!? Carnass exclaimed excitedly, "I'd heard as much from the guards, but their information rarely rings true. And what, dare I ask, are you doing in Avalon?"

Maya didn't hear, she was staring at Thelic, at the blood now painted across his face. "You killed that man," she whispered.

Registering her meaning, Carnass gave Maya a soft pat on the head. "Not to worry, dear. That one was a bit of a scoundrel when it came to the ladies." He looked up at Thelic then, his features softening. "It was only a matter of time before little Thellie got to him."

Thelic said nothing in his own defence, just stared back at

Maya with little more than grim understanding evident in the thin line of his lips.

Turning away from both Thelic and the bloody mess, she faced Carnass. The Danika Keeper was younger than Maya had expected for someone of his position, certainly no older than late thirties. From a distance, with his long, platinum hair braided down to his waist, he'd seemed much older. "I need to get to Esterbell, my mum and brother have been taken against their will," Maya explained.

"That's terrible!" Carnass gasped, clearly missing the irony that he himself was holding Thelic and Maya captive. "Bandaar Rivers is a plague upon this realm, always has been. He's a bully, too; hateful little man," Carnass cursed. "I'm not sure how I might help you though."

"I know you have spies in Esterbell, Carnass. Which means you probably have layouts of the Keep," Thelic claimed, eyeing the Keeper.

Carnass feigned offence, his perfectly manicured hands clutching his chest before smiling wickedly back at Thelic. "I *may* have some…friends, in the territory," he teased. "The layout to the Keep though, that will be costly. Even for you, my love."

Maya blinked, looking from the Keeper to Thelic. "Are you a couple? Is that why you wanted to come with me?" Maya asked, looking at Thelic who rolled his eyes dramatically. Carnass on the other hand, broke down into fits of laughter.

"Oh dear, despite my many efforts, Thelic is a tough nut to crack," he winked at Maya.

"As fun as this is; the layout, Carnass, what's the price?"

The Keeper sighed. "Always business with you, Thelic. Okay, if you want the plans, then I want just one thing. I want you, my love, in my bed."

Maya watched, further disturbed as the colour drained from Thelic's face.

Carnass however, tipped his head back and roared with laughter. "Spirits, you are easy to tease!" The amusement dancing in his eyes changed for one of challenge as he said, "I want the Seer, Fatari."

"Fatari has been missing for over twenty years. What makes you think I can find her?"

"Oh, I know you can, Thelic. Or, at the very least, I know *she* can," Carnass said, pointing at Maya.

"How could you possibly think I can find her? I just got here!"

"Darling girl, my spies branch far. I have people in every territory, you think I don't have them in my own?"

Maya stepped back at the implication. Already, someone had betrayed their confidence. "Elkin?"

"No. Lisaya," Thelic responded. "The bodello whore."

"Indeed, one of my best! Your ties to Fatari will almost certainly see that she finds you, Maya. So, that's the deal. Interested?"

Maya considered her options and found them woefully sparse. "Fine, I'll bring you a *message*, nothing more."

"Done! That was easy. Of course, I'll need some assurance that you'll come back."

"But I have nothing!"

Thelic stepped forward, removing a necklace previously hidden by his shirt. "Here, you know I'll come back for this," he said, handing it over. On the end of the silver chain was a ring, a simple silver band with a small gem embedded. "It belonged to my mother," Thelic explained for Maya's benefit.

"How surprising, I would have expected nothing less than death for you to separate from this particular trinket." Carnass studied Maya carefully. "You must trust her immensely."

"The maps, now," Thelic said with an exasperated wave of his hand.

Carnass led them down several passages to a large room with every inch of the space lined with books, scrolls, and pages scattered across the floor. He all but skipped over to a particular section and flipped through the various parchments.

"Ah! Here it is. Keep in mind it's fairly old."

"How old?" Thelic asked warily.

"Only five or so years."

"Fuck."

"That's better than nothing," Maya insisted. "Unless Bandaar has completely rebuilt?"

"He hasn't, I assure you I would know," Carnass promised. Handing over the scroll, he summoned the guards with instructions to escort them to the Keep's entrance.

Maya walked up to Carnass and kissed him on the cheek. "Thank you, we'll be back with your message...unless we die, in which case thanks, and...sorry."

Carnass leaned in to whisper in Maya's ear. "Take care of him." Despite her feelings, the look she returned promised she would. "Now go, before I change my mind," he shouted menacingly at the pair, maintaining his image as the callous leader in the guards' presence, with a secret wink to Maya.

As commanded, the guards returned Thelic's spear and took them to the Keep's entrance, instructing the gatesmen to let them pass.

Once outside, Maya gently tucked the rolled parchment into the slip of her tunic and faced Thelic. "Told you it was a good idea."

"Like I said, he would've eaten you alive had you gone by yourself."

"Sounds more like he wanted to eat *you* alive," she laughed awkwardly. She couldn't ignore the tension, the dark shadows in his eyes a remnant of the crime he had committed. "Why did you kill him?"

Thelic peered down at her, considering for a moment whether it was his business to tell. But he needed her trust if they were going to continue together. "You remember Brijid, the woman who healed you?"

"Of course," Maya whispered, already getting a sense of where this was going.

"Terricus raped her the day before she left Carnass' service."

Maya's breath caught in her throat.

"He would have killed her had I not heard the screams. I would have ended his life there and then, but the other guards came running and…" he paused turning away to rub a hand frustratedly through his hair. "Well, I got my chance, so I'll thank you for that."

Being thanked for providing the opportunity to murder a man was not something that sat well with her. But, in a disturbing way, she could understand. "Your mother's necklace…"

"Don't worry about it, just a piece of metal and a worthless gem," he lied.

"No, I'll get it back, Thelic. I promise." Discovering the truth about Jaseen's disappearance and her brother's subsequent abduction, Maya couldn't afford the additional burden of Thelic losing his mother's ring forever.

"THAT WAS QUICK. Did you get it?" Elkin asked, embracing Maya upon their return.

"Sure did, he was a sweetheart really."

Brijid's house was easy to find as it stood adjacent to the canvas tent she worked from in the market. Like Thelic's, the charming home was open plan, with a mezzanine level that formed the bedroom. Unlike Thelic's, the place was a mess.

Every corner, nook, and cranny jam-packed with jars full of sinister looking potions.

"You!"

Maya turned towards the small, very angry healer now striding towards her.

"You're supposed to be resting, not gallivanting about with Keepers!" Brijid yelled as she clasped Maya's ear and dragged her to a seating area of blankets and cushions. "Lie down there and don't move, let me see your bandages." Brijid had already confiscated Thelic's coat and, without warning, began removing the rest of her garments.

Maya decided to keep quiet and allowed it. The small brunette awed but ultimately terrified her.

"Damn it, your side is weeping again!"

"Please don't do that fire and mud magic thing you did last time. That really wasn't fun, and I feel somewhat fine."

Brijid harrumphed in response and instructed Elkin to fetch her ointment. "That was to remove the poison and deal with the worst of the wound, but there's still the risk of infection to consider. You have to be more careful."

"I will, promise. Can I get dressed now?"

Elkin returned with the ointment and fresh bandages and Brijid went to work. "You're all staying here tonight. Rest and re-group, you can leave tomorrow. Thelic, go and get something for us to eat."

"But–" Maya was cut short by a menacing look from the so-called gentle healer.

"Don't bother, Maya. You're no match for General Brijid," Elkin warned with a chuckle. "We can use tonight like she said, to regroup and come up with a plan."

Maya sighed, thinking of Jacob. They had already wasted so much time. If Yali's warning was anything to go by, her brother was in trouble. He would be scared, alone, angry...at her.

"Okay you're done. Cloth baths *only,* for three days," Brijid announced, stepping back to admire her work.

"Great," Maya replied, still lost in thought. "I think I'll go take one now then, if that's ok?"

Brijid moved to the sink and pulled out a clean piece of fabric for Maya, with strict instructions to keep the bandages dry.

As Maya headed towards the steep wooden stairs, she watched as Thelic stopped at the front door, his hand hovering over the brass handle. Turning on his heel, he walked over to Brijid, pulling her to the side to speak privately. Fear and anger briefly flashed across the young woman's face, but slowly she softened. As her shoulders relaxed, she raised her hand to cup his cheek and uttered one word – *Thank you.* The man who had hurt her, had plagued her dreams, could never hurt her again.

In the shallow bathwater, Maya did as she had promised, using the cloth to carefully manoeuvre around the wound. She couldn't shake the look on Jacob's face when he'd come into the kitchen, when they found out about their mother, stuck here all this time. She numbly wiped the cloth over her skin.

"Need a hand?"

Maya jumped at the sound of Thelic's voice. "Jesus, what the hell are you doing here?" She looked down at her wound. A darker shade of white crept up the bottom of the bandages where the water had splashed, dampening them. "Oh, great. Brijid's going to tear me a new one now."

"A new what?"

"A new asshole! She told me to keep these damn bandages dry, and I was doing just fine until you creeped up on me."

"I've been standing here for a while now, I thought you realised."

Maya gawked at him. "Listen, I don't know how it's done in Avalon, but on the other side people don't skulk about in the shadows watching women they barely know in the bath! Well, some do, but we arrest them for it."

He raised his hands defensively. "Sorry, I'll leave."

Admittedly, Maya was struggling to reach everywhere without getting her wound wet. "Wait, since you're here and have already seen pretty much everything, do you mind?" she asked, holding out the cloth and indicating to her back.

Without a word, he walked up and took the cloth from Maya's hand. Sitting on the edge of the bath, he dipped it into the warm water and gently stroked from the base of her spine up to her neck. Maya sighed as his other hand softly kneaded away at the knots in her shoulder. Despite his rough hands, she could tell he was being careful, gentler than he was used to. She leaned forward, bringing her knees up to rest her head on them, relaxing at the sensation.

"Did you come to find me for a reason? Or just to check out the naughty goods?" she joked.

He didn't reply immediately, lost in thought. "Do you believe in destiny, Maya?"

She laughed. "I think you've got the order all wrong. *First* it's the cheesy pick-up lines, *then* you get to see me naked."

Thelic growled, leaning forward to whisper in her ear. "If you can't be serious for more than a fleeting moment, it won't be Brijid you'll have to worry about."

Thelic's threat didn't provoke the response that was likely intended. Instead, she felt a growing heat between her legs, and it wasn't from the bath water. She instinctively squeezed them closed and mentally cursed her taste in men.

"Ok then," she said, swallowing. "No, I don't believe in destiny. Or, at least, I didn't. I don't know anymore, everything's changed." She smacked the water, annoyed at the situation and feeling of powerlessness, the irony striking her once again. "I'm supposed to be this powerful wizard, yet here you are washing my back. I'm also supposed to be a regular woman. A policewoman. From Telford of all places. And yet I've travelled to this frankly insane parallel universe, hunting for my kidnapped brother and my mum who's been missing for over fifteen years!" She let out a long breath. "So, I don't know. Maybe destiny is a thing, maybe dragons and unicorns are a thing too, who knows?"

"Unicorns are a myth, and dragons went extinct a while back as well."

Maya threw her hands up in mock defeat. "Well thanks, now I know, I'll scratch those off my list."

"Also, you're a castor, not a wizard," Thelic corrected her with a chuckle. He studied her back as he brushed his hand down the softly tanned skin, admiring how the top of the waterline highlighted the dip between her cheeks and her small breasts squeezed against nicely toned thighs. She was beautiful, she also had no idea how powerful she truly was.

"Why do you ask, anyway?"

"My father told me a story a long time ago, before he was killed. When I saw you fighting off that djinca I knew you were different. But when I brought you back to my home and you showed me the Stone…" He wavered, realising this was going to sound insane. "I'm not so sure it was just a story."

"What do you mean? What did he tell you?"

"I can't remember exactly, but I do remember the general gist of it. A young hunter finds a woman – no, an heiress , I think – emerging from a forbidden forest. She had run away from her evil father, who wanted to hurt the girl for her powers." Already the story was oddly comparable to Maya's. She turned to face him as he continued. "Instead, she uses these powers to find items that help her defeat the evil king, with the young hunter to help her." Thelic sighed, explaining how he had forgotten the rest but that somewhere in the story his father mentioned something about soulmates and a seer.

"A seer? Fatari?"

He bobbed his head in response. "Your story, what you've been through, and the story my father told me, coupled with the fact that you have his missing Gouram Stone...it can't just be a coincidence, Maya."

"Wait, would that make you the young hunter? And what was that about soulmates?"

Thelic dropped the cloth into the bath and stood, raking wet hands through his hair as he paced around the room. "It sounds ridiculous now that I've said it out loud, but you have to admit, it's bizarrely close."

"Well, I didn't run away from my father."

"No, you were *taken* away from a father who did terrible things to you."

"Okay, but I'm not looking for any magical items or to *defeat* Bandaar."

"Yeah, that bit throws me too."

"Either way, the only thing I need to do now is help my family." Maya stood up to grab the towel off the stool, her body on full display.

Thelic spun, prompting her to chuckle. "Oh, now you're a gentleman?"

"I wasn't intentionally *checking out the naughty goods*, as you so eloquently put it, I'm just trying to figure you out."

"Ha! Well if you do, let me know, okay?"

Thelic turned to Maya, standing in the shallow bath water, the small towel barely enough to cover her. Seeing her there, wet, and frustrated, he wanted her in his bed. Hell, he wanted to rip the towel from her body and take her right there in the bath. Little did he know that Maya's thoughts mirrored his own. In the short amount of time, Thelic had been a rock. He had fought the djinca and faced Carnass at her side. He'd agreed to help rescue her family, and now she wanted that support in its most primal form.

A small, intentional cough from Elkin broke the moment. "Sorry, am I interrupting?" he teased, knowing full well what had likely been about to happen between the couple. "Brijid sent me to tell you dinner is being served up."

"I better get dressed," Maya said as she hurried from the room, disappointed but relieved at Elkin's interference. She needed to focus. Whatever she felt for Thelic would have to wait. It wasn't worth the risk of possibly losing someone willing to help her.

Thelic watched her leave, failing to hide his own disappointment.

"Careful, old friend. We're about to get ourselves into a sticky situation. Probably not the best idea getting...*sticky*, before we've assisted her. Not to mention, she's here for a reason, and she'll likely return to her own world. Don't you think?" Elkin asked.

Thelic was left to stand alone with his thoughts. These feelings for Maya, he couldn't explain them. The fable echoed in his mind, playing repeatedly. Guilt wracked him. He had lied to her, remembering more than he cared to admit. Revilo, his father, had spoken of the hunter's duty to protect the woman, that she was his entire world, his soulmate. But at the end of his father's story, the heiress, Maya...dies.

6

THE HOOKER AND WINKLER'S HAMLET

DANIKA

Brijid and Elkin had packed all the essentials; tents, cooking equipment, food...and a hooker named Gwinney, who seemed intent on making Maya as uncomfortable as possible.

"So, Gwinney, are you going *all* the way to Esterbell with us?" Maya asked kindly, simultaneously shooting daggered looks at Elkin. The bordello woman was unabashedly draped over Thelic's back, whispering promises of future pleasure as soon as they decided to stop and camp.

Maya, Thelic, and Elkin, along with the new and some-what unwelcome guest, had left Brijid's at the first rays of dawn. Blankets had once again been arranged between the saddlebags of the bodaari, with plenty of room upon the crea-ture for each of the travellers to ride comfortably. Thelic sat near the head, Gwinney stuck to him like an unnatural appendage.

"No, I'll be getting off at Winkler's Hamlet," she said.

"And how far is that exactly?"

"Another half a day yet." Elkin grinned, clearly enjoying himself.

"Awesome," Maya muttered, her malcontent thinly veiled. She had been lying on her back next to Elkin and rolled over to look at him. "Why did you decide to come?" she asked, curious. Brijid had warned them of the perilous journey across territories, of the creatures that dwelled in the forests between. Thelic though, had insisted they would need him.

"I owe Thelic," he said simply. "About this time last year, myself and Brijid got caught up with some nasty individuals in the mountains east of Danika. He saved our lives."

"I see. He says we need your particular set of skills. What is it you do exactly?"

Gwinney, clearly jealous she wasn't the centre of every male's attention, drifted over weightlessly to lie across Elkin's stomach. Maya had wrongly suspected the woman's elemental contract to bind her with an earth sprite, if only for her snake-like tendencies. She did her best now, to ignore the slithery hooker's scowl.

"I'm a sourcer. I acquire things for people," Elkin said.

Maya thought about this for a moment. "You're a thief?"

"If that's what's required. Sometimes I'm sent in search of materials, sometimes those materials belong to someone else."

"Is that what happened in the mountains?"

"A bracelet was stolen from a family of water-rakers, they hired me to get it back."

"Water-rakers?"

"Are you stupid? Or have you just been living in a cave your whole life?" Gwinney asked, still unaware that Maya was from a different realm altogether. "They use their contracts to hunt the channels around the territories for food."

Maya had learnt two things – first, these water-rakers sounded like Avalon's version of fishermen; and second - don't ask questions around nosey prostitutes. She had to be more careful, both men had warned Maya of the risks posed should her true heritage be revealed to unfriendly parties.

SEVERAL HOURS HAD PASSED when Maya jolted awake as Keero came to an abrupt stop.

"Are we there–"

Elkin's hand flew to cover Maya's mouth, a finger pressed to his lips signalling her to be quiet. Thelic stood on Keero's head, listening, and watching the trees to his right intently. Their journey so far had consisted of travelling through dense forest. With the fading light, their path had been cast in shadow.

The wood was eerily silent, the trees groaning despite a distinct lack of breeze. Pushing the hand from her mouth, Maya glanced from Elkin to the rest of the party.

Gwinney was gone.

At Maya's frantic look, Elkin pointed to a branch in the tree above. There she sat, with the thick branch between her thighs, waving provocatively.

A burst of fire rocketed through the trees to hit Keero on the right flank. The peaceful creature wailed, batting its side with the leather tail. Maya tackled Elkin to the floor as the fire emerged, both rolling to escape the stampeding paws of the frightened beast. Jumping to his feet, Elkin rushed to calm it. With one hand on the ground and the other pressed against Keero's burning flesh, Elkin summoned water to slowly cover and cool the wound.

At some point in the scuffle, Thelic had moved to Maya's side.

"What is it?" she whispered to him.

"Could be one of four things; a Finkel, a dragon, bandits or outlanders."

"Out…wait. I thought you said dragons went extinct!?"

"They did, so it's more likely to be one of the other three."

Maya gawked in disbelief. How could he joke at a time like this?

A creature sprang from the trees into the small open space to snap at Elkin. He dodged and swept the water from the bodaari to his attacker as it darted up and into the canopy. It was fast, faster than anything Maya had ever seen. Like a small deer, on fire, with razor sharp teeth.

"Fire Finkel!" Thelic roared, holding the spear tight to his chest.

A scream erupted from above and Gwinney fell, blood covering her shoulder. Elkin caught her and raced with the woman's limp body to Keero.

"How do I use the elements?" Maya panicked.

The sprite darted from the tree, straight for Maya. She raised her hands with nothing to protect herself. Thelic stepped in front and met the impact of the Finkel's assault, his spear extended across his body as a barrier. The drive of the attack pushed him back, knocking Maya to the side. Planting his feet, he swung the spear in an arc to disconnect himself from the fiery creature and thrust his hand hastily to the ground. A large mound of hard earth shot up, catching the Finkel under its belly and driving it back into the forest.

Maya concentrated, trying desperately to summon the air like she'd done against the djinca. A throbbing pain disturbed her efforts and she glanced at her palm; fresh blood coated the surface, having cut it when she fell. It dripped to the dry leaves below and a sharp wind rustled the canopy to whip across her feet as the earth hummed. Embers danced beyond the treeline, taunting them, the creature's movements difficult to track. Thelic raised his spear, but not quick enough.

The Finkel's head planted firmly into his chest, knocking him off his feet.

Maya screamed with frustration and closed her eyes, concentrating on the Finkel's heat, on the desire to protect her new friends. The wind responded, fuelled by anger to whip fiercely around her as a surging heat prickled her body. She opened her eyes to a tornado of fire, her fire, surrounding her, and the castor circle at her feet.

Unfazed by the conjured element, the creature retrained its focus on Thelic who had struggled to a standing position, batting at the flames across his chest. It lunged and Maya didn't hesitate. She thrust her hands out towards the Finkel, and the tornado followed to engulf it. Flames had little effect on a sprite born of the element. Oxygen, however, was vital, and denied by the furious vortex as it sucked the air from its fiery prison.

Maya shook with the effort to maintain the inferno, the hum of the earth beneath growing louder. Slowly, the Finkel began to diminish. She collapsed to one knee, the pressure crippling her. A voice called Maya's name, muffled by the earth's hum coupled with the blood pounding through her ears. With a final, gasping puff of smoke, the fiery Finkel disappeared, its remnants sucked into the wall of wind. Maya dropped her hands and the elements exploded in a bust of air.

Everything was quiet. Faint stars danced across Maya's vision as she collapsed to the ground.

Thelic, previously blocked by the elements, ran to her side. "Mayara!" he rolled her over and green eyes stared up at him.

"That was new," she chuckled weakly.

Thelic let out a whoosh of relief and slumped to the ground next to her.

"New? That was *old*. There's only a handful of people with

power like yours," Elkin announced, making his way over to the pair. The runic circle has dissipated to a soft glimmer, the dead ground replaced with small white flowers, and succulent green grass.

"I'm starving, and tired, and sore," Maya moaned before giggling at the look of bewilderment from her two male companions. "Oh god, Gwinney!"

"She'll be fine, a bit banged up but there's a healer in Winkler's Hamlet that can see to her." Suddenly realising where Maya's true concern lay, Elkin reassured her. "Don't worry, she was unconscious during your unsubtle display of immense power," he promised with a wink.

As Maya struggled to stand, Thelic carried her up the bodaari's tail, placing her gently on one of the blankets. "Damn, my legs feel like jelly," she remarked, rubbing them gently.

"Manipulating the elements puts a tremendous amount of stress on the mind and body. Castors are trained from a young age to wield their abilities carefully," Thelic explained as he handed over a satchel of water. "At least you're still conscious this time."

"Without the binding marks it's difficult to tell how much of your essence is sacrificed with each use, Maya. You should be more careful," Elkin warned. "It usually comes at an environmental cost as well. Though strangely, your use of power seems to have the opposite effect." He pointed to the freshly flowered circle. "It's like the realm feeds off your power, instead of just your essence. I've never seen anything like it." Left to ponder her oddities, they set off, and Maya was claimed once again by sleep.

IT WAS STILL DARK when they passed the final trees of the forest. Winkler's Hamlet stood on the open plain; a large collection of stone-built houses, lining the edge of the channel of water separating the territory from its neighbours.

Maya was woken soon after their arrival. Thelic had gone ahead to make camp at the riverbank on the town's outskirts, opting to save the little coin they had for supplies. Elkin pointed her in the direction of their tents, insisting he take Gwinney to the healer before joining them. Tired and unsteady, she walked through the open road of the sleeping town.

"You should have woken me earlier, I could've helped," Maya insisted, stumbling over several twigs as she navigated her way to the fire. Brijid's clothes had warded off the bitter wind, but without gloves she was appreciative of the flame's warmth.

"You did all the work against the Finkel, it was the least we could do."

Maya snorted at that. "I was fairly spectacular I must admit."

"You probably saved my life," Thelic admitted quietly. "Thank you."

"Well, I was racking up quite a debt with all the times you've saved my butt over the last couple of days," she returned, keen to lighten the mood.

"Good point. Now I know how *spectacular* you are, I guess I can just hang back in the future and let you handle all the messy business."

Maya's stomach growled comically as if in tune with the mood and they both chuckled. Thelic reached into a satchel beside him and handed her some strips of cured meat. While hard and chewy, to her surprise they were delicious, and she quickly finished them off. He handed her the whole satchel, then, with a hot mug of wine, insisting they had another and could buy more at the market when it was light. So, she accepted, and they sat in companionable silence.

"Gwinney will be fine, the bordello's mistress is with her now too, so she isn't alone when she wakes," Elkin informed them, breaking the silence. He grinned at the scene and rubbed his hands together excitedly. "Meat and wine, that's my kind of celebration!" He sat beside Thelic, helping himself and loading more wood onto the fire.

"So, where do we go next?" Maya asked between meaty mouthfuls.

"At sunrise, you and I will head to the market. Elkin will go and talk to the local water-rakers. They should be able to transport us safely across the waters here."

"Is it dangerous to cross the channel?"

"Water Finkels," Elkin mumbled.

"Oh wonderful, there's water versions of the fire fairy."

"Finkel," he corrected. "And yes, like the Vasiba and Warkoons, they're creatures made purely from the elements so there's one of each kind," he explained. "Though, Finkels are the highest-level sprites under the Gouram, and they are the only ones able to manifest physically on our plain. Would you believe they were once quite peaceful?"

"Tell that to Thelic's new bald patch," Maya lied, prompting Thelic to feel his head for the non-existent evidence, shooting her a deserved scowl upon realising he had been fooled.

"Avalonians believe it's the growing chaos that's causing them to go feral," Elkin continued.

"The dark spots?" Maya asked, popping another piece of meat into her mouth.

Elkin nodded. "The fog veils are the most concerning result of the realm's deteriorating state, they grow bigger with each passing year."

"Can it be stopped?"

"Legend has it, the Five Majors composed four scrolls, one of which details a ceremony that can breathe life back into the realm. I'm unsure of the others."

Thelic, too, had heard of them. "One is rumoured to depict dark invocations, forbidden since the beginning of our time, offering life but only in exchange for death."

Maya sighed as she placed the satchel in her lap, wiping her hands on the already grubby tunic. "That sounds cheery, and I suppose nobody knows where these legendary scrolls are?"

"Hence the name," he replied sarcastically.

"Fatari has some of them," Elkin confessed to his friend's surprise. "I told you, I found her when I was in Bandaar's service."

"You worked for Bandaar?" Maya asked, surprised by his admission.

"Another reason I wanted him to join us." Thelic stood to stretch off. "I'm going to sleep; I'll see you both at the dawn."

Maya and Elkin took their time, allowing the fire and hot drinks to ease them. He told her stories of water-rakers he'd met, able to summon incredible waves and air-masters conjuring great storms. Those people had been the rare few to contract with a Finkel, their unique abilities developed over time. With Maya it was different, she had conjured fire and air to work together at a high level, with no marks to indicate her alignment with a sprite.

Returning to their respective tents, the fire was left to burn and ward off any unwanted guests. Maya couldn't sleep as those same worries buzzed incessantly in her head, a new question among them. How was she going to control a power so different? She tossed and turned, her mind stubbornly refusing to quieten. Grabbing the blanket, she left the tent and ambled along the shore, removing her slippers, and allowing the cool waves to lap against her feet.

She looked up at the night sky. Three moons shone amongst the midnight gloom. She had never noticed; too pre-occupied with trying to stay alive, she supposed. She stared at them now, wondering where her world might be among the plethora of stars, or if her world was even up there.

A sharp crackle of noise made her jump and she spun to check the tents. Someone stood by the fire, loading it with more wood. A second, smaller shape was approaching from the shadows. Maya ran forward to shout a warning but stopped as the two figures embraced. She chuckled, assuming Elkin had invited one of the bordello women for a midnight tryst, and crept back quietly towards her tent to avoid them. As she got closer, the figures were no longer faceless, distant blurs. It was Thelic and Gwinney. He was holding her by the shoulders, until she jumped forward and kissed him. A pang of jealousy broke inside Maya's chest, and she turned to leave the intimate scene. In her haste, the blanket bunched along the ground, and she fell, snapping the dry twigs beneath her loudly.

Thelic's spear was out and extended towards the shore-line, towards Maya, who was on her feet grinning sheepishly. They'd spotted her. Gwinney smiled, pleased with her audience. Unsure what else to do, Maya waved and briskly walked back towards the shoreline.

"Why the hell did you wave?" she chastised herself.

Heavy footfalls advanced behind her.

"Oh Jesus," she muttered before turning to a frustrated Thelic. "Hey, sorry. I wasn't spying on, whatever that was."

"It was nothing, Maya."

"You can kiss whomever you want. You're a single guy, she's a professional lover, who could blame you? She's beautiful."

"I know."

A brief and uneasy silence sat between them. "I'm exhausted, I think I'll head back to–"

Without warning, Thelic grabbed her waist, his hand wrapping tightly in her hair, and kissed her. Maya pushed him away, regretting the action just as suddenly as she'd made it.

"Maya, Gwinney kissed *me*, I feel nothing for her, but you–"

Shoving what she assumed was her better judgement into the dark recesses of her mind, she grasped Thelic's coat and kissed him back.

Their desperation for each other exploded and Thelic had her on the soft sand of the riverbank within breathless seconds. His hands moved roughly over her body as she raked her fingers through his hair, holding him to her. She broke the kiss to pull the shirt from his back; her own, long since removed by Thelic's skilled hands. Naked bodies bathed in the moonlight, neither concerned of their exposure or the bitter cold; a stronger, more primal need taking over.

Thelic stopped for a few precious seconds to appreciate the woman beneath him, how the light's reflection highlighted her curves. "You're so beautiful," he whispered.

She smiled and brought his face down to hers, whispering things filthy enough to provoke a bordello hand's blush, and within moments he was inside her. She winced at the sudden penetration but relished every thrust, rocking her hips to meet his momentum. Strong sinewed arms wrapped tightly under her body, moving, and manipulating her as he quickened his drive. She was close, and he knew it, wanting them to finish together. He leaned back, maintaining his rhythm, and dipped two fingers between her legs, easily finding the spot that craved his touch. She gasped, arching her back, desperate for the release she knew was coming. Her orgasm rocketed to the surface triggering his own and they both collapsed in a heap, Maya wrapped tightly in his arms.

He rolled to the side, and they looked at each other, chuckling with heavy breaths. Neither spoke as the moment ebbed and a question lay between them.

What now?

Maya shivered despite the warmth of Thelic's radiating body heat, and he moved to grab the fallen blanket and suggested they head back to the fire.

The flames were rekindled, and they settled together once again to enjoy its gentle heat. Gwinney was nowhere to be seen, and Maya blushed at a thought – had the young bordello woman seen their tryst?

Thelic broke the silence first. "You're going back to your own world when you've found your family, aren't you?"

It wasn't meant as an accusation, but Maya felt the weight of it. "This isn't my world. After I've rescued my family, there's nothing here for me, I don't belong here," she answered softly, thoughtlessly.

"I see."

"Thelic, I didn't mean…I have family waiting at home, I could come back, visit from time to time–"

"It's fine, Maya, I'm not expecting anything. We scratched an itch, that's all," he lied.

The subtle venom behind his words stung her. They were friends, they could only ever be friends because that's all she ever wanted, with anyone. All she had ever needed or craved was human touch. Like everyone else, she had urges, and never before had she truly sought more than that. She had tried once or twice, but this was different. Maya had always been very good at pushing people away, protecting herself; but with Thelic, she didn't want to.

"You should at least try and get some sleep. We'll be up soon enough to resupply." With that, Thelic said goodnight and left the warmth of the fire, his departure inviting a cold and bitter taste in both their mouths.

Back in his tent he lay, tireless, angry, and confused. He barely knew the infuriating woman, so why did he feel like his entire life had been spent waiting for her? Was it his father's tale? The way she rushed headfirst into danger to help those around her? Or the way that golden hair framed her jade eyes? Thelic grumbled a curse. She would leave this world, so there was no point getting attached.

THE NEXT DAY, as planned, Elkin left separately to speak with the water-rakers and Thelic took Maya to the market, where an eager Gwinney awaited them.

"Thelic!" she beamed, annoyingly. "Where did you disappear to last night? Darting off like that can hurt a girl's feelings, you know?"

"Sorry, Gwinney. I was with…a friend."

Thelic's categorical choice wasn't lost on Maya. He was distancing himself from her. *Probably for the best,* she thought miserably as Gwinney looped her arm through his.

"I suppose you could show us around the market, if you're feeling up to it?" Thelic offered.

"Of course! It's the least I can do after you saved my life," she smiled sweetly.

"Well, actually it was Ma–"

"Yes!" Maya cut him off. She didn't want the fiendish Gwinney to know anything about her, especially her abilities. "Yep, that Fekel would have killed us all if not for Thelic."

"Finkel," Gwinney and Thelic said in unison. He nodded to Maya in understanding, a small smile at the corner of his mouth. She was learning the risks.

As promised, Gwinney showed them around the

market, noting specific stalls to restock from. Their journey through the forest had afforded Thelic the opportunity to hunt for rasicus, which he intended to sell at the market to buy their supplies and passage. As they walked, Maya admired the hamlet's small town square. Despite the dreary morning, its inhabitants were cheerful and greeted each customer like an old friend, their exotic stalls promising sensory adventures.

"Well, hi there!" a large potbellied man beamed at Maya and walked around the stall to stand next to her. "Haven't seen you around these parts."

The man's sheer size and Maya's previous misfortune with market men instinctively caused her to step back, right onto Thelics's foot.

"Shit!" she yelped, spinning to apologise to who or whatever she had stepped on.

Thelic groaned and the man chortled.

"You're definitely not from around here. Most ladies are a bit more mildly spoken. That there is new language, is it not?"

"She's from the west, Transum Territory," Thelic offered in Maya's place.

"Oh, I see. Not affiliated with those outlanders I hope?"

"No, they wouldn't venture down this far."

"Wouldn't be so sure, friend. Whispers have it they've been seen throughout the mountain regions bordering the territories, I've heard they're preparing for war again."

Maya's stomach growled loudly, prompting a roar of laughter from the shopkeeper. "Seems your belly is as brash as you!" he bellowed. Ducking behind the stall, he removed a leather satchel and filled it with the food he had for sale. Thelic offered some coins, but the man waved them off, insisting he ought to pay better attention to his wife's needs. With a promise to keep that in mind, they thanked the marketeer, and the red-faced Maya was steered towards the port.

As they left the square, Thelic thanked Gwinney for her help. She wrapped her arms around his neck and pleaded for him to return and visit before locking her lips onto his. Maya swallowed the bile making its way up her throat. Delicately unlinking himself, Thelic made no such promise and said goodbye, leaving to head for the harbour.

"Sorry," Maya said awkwardly as she rushed to keep pace with his stride.

"For what?"

"Your foot. And you had to lie to that man."

"My foot will heal…in time," he insisted with a grin that finally lightened the mood between them.

The port consisted of a single, large dock with two long boats moored, one on either side. Neither were particularly impressive, simple in design for the purposes of ferrying and fishing.

Elkin stood upon one now, in the midst of a heated discussion with an unhappy water-master. Seeing the duo, he shooed the man away and jumped down to meet them. The rakers were due to leave at mid-day but were happy to transport the group and Keero for a few coins each.

Maya, painfully aware of how much she had been relying on the two men, could only hope to find some way of making money upon their arrival in Esterbell.

Mid-day approached faster than expected and the group were soon loaded onto the creaking vessel along with six water-rakers, each brandishing a spear. Keero, along with their supplies were loaded into the hull.

The structure resembled a crude pirate ship bare of sails or any sort of propellant, such things proven unnecessary as the rakers manipulated the currents to push them from the wooden dock. Their drivers, one man on each side of the ship, stood with palms stretched out to the water. In unison they swayed their arms backwards and forwards, creating the momentum to drift across the open channel.

Behind them, two more rakers clawed at the air over the side of the vessel. Upon investigation Maya finally understood the namesake. Their meticulous movements formed welts on the surface of the water, that would just as quickly subside until recreated with another raking motion. Long nets stretched out along the ship's length, seemingly to relax on, when in fact they slowly filled with the slippery creatures plucked from the water's surface.

Maya watched, fascinated by the fishermen's process, interrupted as Elkin wrapped an arm around her shoulder.

"I'm not sure about your world's customs, little fulsin, but here, when you stare at people like that it tends to make them uncomfortable."

Maya realised that she'd been ogling one of the rakers, admiring his craft; and that he was becoming obviously unhappy with the seemingly unwarranted attention.

"Oops," she laughed, waving at the man, only for him to squeak and duck behind a large container in response. "Christ, I'm hardly that frightening to look at."

"It's not you, Maya," he chuckled. "These people spend most of their time out on the water where they're most comfortable, and live in hamlets such as Winkler's their whole life. I took one to a bordello once–"

"I'm sure with the purest intentions?"

"Mostly…"

"What happened?"

"He got about three paces in before a voluptuous beauty commandeered and kissed him, he screamed, passed out, and soiled himself."

Maya barked with laughter. "That's terrible!"

"Not really, he married her a week later."

This incited further giggling.

"What's funny?" Thelic asked, sauntering over to join them.

"I was regaling her with a story from Sinker's Port."

"Basik?"

"Indeed."

Thelic shook his head. "I still can't believe he married her; he's terrified of the woman!"

"Wait they really married after only one week?" Maya asked, shocked.

"Ah that's right, in your world it's customary to wait a year, correct?" Elkin returned.

"At least!" she cried. "Most people know each other for many years before they make such a commitment, unless it's an arranged marriage."

"Avalon is different, times are dangerous. When a connection between two souls is made, it's palpable, you can feel it around them. So, why wait?" Elkin challenged.

"Falling in love is hardly unmistakeable, you're implying everyone here finds their soulmate. It's a learning process, what if they have bad habits? Or snore?"

"You would deny your soul its mate because they snore?" he laughed. "In your defence, professors of the Educator's Guild theorise that the people of your world are so technologically advanced, distraction and material needs have blurred your more primal or base instincts. Here in Avalon, we live by the day and technology is basic, purely to assist with living, and less about entertainment."

Maya considered this. "So, what you're saying is, I may have already met my soulmate, but I was too busy playing on my phone or watching tv to notice?"

"I assume those are entertaining machines in your world, in which case, perhaps." He leaned in to whisper, "Or, perhaps your soulmate is here, in Avalon?"

Maya instinctively glanced at Thelic before quickly averting her eyes. He had been watching the debate between her and Elkin with interest. He didn't believe in soulmates, just that you could love someone, and they could love you in return. Though, he had to admit, his philosophies had begun to deteriorate with every new event since meeting Maya in the glen.

Maya turned from her companions to look out across the water. A hamlet similar to Winklers bustled with activity in the distance. "Esterbell," she whispered. Soon, she would finally be reunited with Jacob, and her mother.

As if reading her thoughts, Elkin once again tucked Maya under his arm. "This next part is going to be tricky. I'm excited."

7

THE OUTLANDER AND THE PESKY FINKEL

ESTERBELL

Their arrival at the port hamlet of Aqarin was met with interest from the locals. Traveling marketeers usually ventured through on their way to Esterbell's Keep, so the residents were keen to see what new trinkets were possibly being brought in. Keero's presence, too, was of great interest to the children as they approached to pet him. Bodaari were uncommon in the territory, being difficult to catch and harder to tame.

Most preferred to ride smaller animals, as was demonstrated by the two creatures trotting past the group with a cartload of freshly caught fish. These were the same beasts Maya had seen in Danika Market, in the stall where Keero had been kept.

"It's a karkili," Thelic answered Maya's unspoken question.

"They're as close to your world's horses as it gets," Elkin added. Short haired and average in size, they were similar to their earthly counterparts, the only difference an elongated snout and second tail.

Their journey across the channel on the simple vessel had

been quick, but they had landed in Aqarin with little daylight to spare and the trek to Esterbell's Keep was at least half a day on Keero. Rather than risk travelling at night, the group decided to spend their evening in the waterside town. Maya suggested heading to a local tavern to see if they could gather any intel on Bandaar and his guards. The others agreed and, after once again setting up their tents on the Hamlet's outskirts, they headed to the square.

As a policewoman, Maya had been fortunate enough to experience undercover work, gathering information inconspicuously from the street urchins and petty criminals, posing as one of their own. She hoped she could use that to her advantage here, or, if desperate, she could flirt her way to some answers. Upon entering, she was forlorn to find the tavern operated as a bordello, with beautiful men and women fawning over their customers. She was out of her league amongst the professional flirters, but determined nonetheless.

As Thelic and Elkin sat down, Maya spotted a man in the corner. Cast in shadow and a hood pulled down to his brow, he eyed her greedily. *He seems keen*, she thought. Surveying the crowded space, Maya determined this to be as good a place as any, the man unlikely to try anything untoward with so many potential witnesses. She informed the others she'd be back in a moment.

Barely two paces in, a rough hand grabbed the back of Maya's coat, dragging her back to the table.

"And what do you think you're doing?" Thelic growled, plonking her sharply onto the chair beside the wall, placing himself between her and what he was sure was an impulsive idea.

"I *was* going to talk to that man, try and get some information."

"Thought so," he nodded, confirming his theory.

"Listen, I know this isn't my world, but I've had training. I know how to be discreet."

Elkin leaned across the table, whispering in hushed tones to Maya. "That *thing* you were going towards is an outlander. See the blue marks on his face? Horrible beings. They openly target human castors. I'm surprised he's been allowed to stay, look at the room around him." The chairs near the man were empty, despite the crowded space. People were keeping their distance.

"Outlanders…" Maya wracked her brain until it clicked. "The man at Winkler's Market warned us about them." She risked a peek at the lone stranger. "What *are* they exactly?"

"They're the original inhabitants of this realm. They were here before the Five Majors opened the gateways for humans to cross over," Thelic explained, waving the attendant to bring them some drinks before continuing. "Some carry a stone dagger – his is tucked into the left side of his jacket. I've also heard that many carve their chest to mark each kill. The biggest tell, though, is their hands and facial markings."

Again, Maya glanced at the outlander. He looked completely human. She couldn't see his hands, or much of his body at all due to the long cloak. The markings on his face were a beautiful cobalt blue and shimmered, like a fish's scales. He was watching her. Unnerved, Maya dipped her gaze, just as one of the bordello women wandered over to the table and sat on her lap.

"Hello," Maya said uncomfortably to the woman staring at her.

"You are a pretty one. Don't suppose you need a job?"

Maya considered this for a second. "How much does it pay?" This woman may have just presented them with an opportunity.

Elkin and Thelic exchanged confused looks but said nothing.

"Three coin per customer, two for the house, one for you."

"One coin!? I already earn three times that at the Keep," she lied easily, leaning back in the chair.

"I should've guessed. I assume – what with Bandaar's obsession over that poor wife of his – that the guards are your best patrons?"

Maya froze at the mention of what had to be her mother. A quick mental shake and she refocused on the task at hand as the mistress continued her proposition.

"Those guards are a rough bunch though. The regulars at my establishment are far more pleasing," she insisted, casually re-adjusting to straddle Maya.

"They're darlings really," Maya insisted. "I suppose they don't travel down this way all that much, what with there being so few guards for so many beautiful entertainers at the Keep."

Not easily snubbed, the mistress caressed Maya's thighs with her own, running experienced hands over the younger woman's shoulders to dip towards her breasts. "Bandaar's recent recruitment has seen many a wanderer travel to my tavern in search of amusement."

Maya half faked an erotic moan in response to the mistress's gyrations. "The new ones are unskilled, hardly a loss to our beds," she managed to say.

The mistress cackled softly at that before abruptly kissing Maya.

A commotion at the bar broke her attention. Two men were fighting over an escort, now cowering in the corner. The mistress whistled and made a subtle gesture to a woman at the bar who, after a long groan, expertly subdued the nuisances and threw them from the tavern.

"Unskilled and unmannered it seems," the mistress said with a sigh.

Unintentionally, she had identified the two brawling men as Bandaar's guards. With a quick glance from Maya, Thelic and Elkin realised this too and stood to leave in pursuit, a hard look from Thelic warning Maya to stay put.

"It seems you've been abandoned," the woman noted, brushing a stray strand of hair behind Maya's ear. "The one in the long black jacket…"

Thelic, Maya thought as she raised the proffered glass to her lips.

"He's your lover?"

"Absolutely not," Maya coughed, choking on the wine before quickly recovering. "I mean, he wishes," she replied boldly.

"I thought I sensed something strong between you two."

"No, not us, just friends – more acquaintances in fact," she insisted taking another gulp of wine.

"Either my eyes deceive me, or your head betrays your heart," she whispered deviously in Maya's ear. "Well, as enjoyable as this has been, I have a tavern to run and patrons to please." Stepping over Maya's thighs she planted one last kiss on her cheek. "The name's Balidora by the way. Don't be a stranger," she said with a wink.

Once alone, Maya sank further into her seat and waved the attendant over for a refill. She looked up as the chair beside her was pulled out from the table, the outlander taking its place.

Maya shifted back. "I'm not in service," she said automatically, concerned the man had overheard her conversation with the mistress.

"I'm not interested in having sex with someone like you," he sneered. "Where did your attendants go?"

Attendants? Maya noticed a gloved left hand was tucked discreetly under his jacket, exactly where Thelic had told her the outlander was concealing his weapon. She leaned forward and placed a hand on his thigh, feigning a more sensual interest. "They'll be back soon, so we don't have much time," she said with a sweet smile.

He grabbed her hair and moved to swing his blade out, but Maya had prepared for that when she had leant in. She caught his fist and twisted, the blade dipping into his side. With a hiss he released her hair to punch her in the face. As she stumbled back, he swung the blade in an arc. Maya had quickly recovered from the first strike and caught his arm mid swing, curling her body to his chest and driving her elbow into his face. With a snarl he staggered back then quickly charged forward.

The outlander wasn't particularly big, or even skilled, but he was fast. Maya's body was thrown into the tavern wall. Winded, she landed on all fours and spat the blood from her mouth. Like a caged animal, the man paced in front of his prey before moving in for the obvious kill. He stopped as the tavern floor hummed, and the first glimmer of a castor's circle bled into the wood. He grinned wickedly.

"I knew you had a strong one, I could almost smell it," he spat.

Everyone in the tavern had been doing their best to ignore the brawl, until Maya's power began to manifest unintentionally. She tried to stop it, conscious of the patrons that now watched, pushed into the corners of the tavern at a safe distance.

ELKIN AND THELIC had followed and confronted the guards, knocking them out before stashing them in Thelic's tent. On their way back to the tavern they heard the commotion. More worryingly, they could see the glow of the castor circle through the crusted windows.

"Is that what I think it is?" Elkin asked.

Thelic didn't respond and ran the rest of the way, bursting through the tavern door just as Maya was picking herself up from the floor.

"Maya!" he roared, shoving her observers to the side.

She launched herself at the outlander, wielding what were once two chair legs to batter her opponent. He met her swings with his forearms, blocking the strikes from his body. Raising the makeshift weapon to his head, Maya ducked quickly to strike him in the gut. He doubled over gasping; and she used that, driving her knee into his face. With a grunt, he fell back, unconscious.

Elkin had made it just in time for the finale and clapped from the entry to the tavern. Some of the observers joined him, though most were more distracted by the fading yellow circle of light at her feet.

"What happened?" With the threat subdued, the tavern's mistress, Balidora, had run over to Maya and put a steadying hand on her shoulder.

"He was rude," Maya huffed. "He said he didn't want my services."

The mistress threw her head back and howled, "Madam, for your services in my tavern, I'll double whatever Bandaar's Keep pays you."

Maya chuckled and promised to keep that in mind. Thelic had managed to beat a path through the crowd to stand beside her, and he wasn't laughing. Whatever followed that look wasn't going to be pleasant and Maya felt certain she would rather deal with the outlander again. That wasn't an option as he led her from the centre of the room, throwing a purse to Balidora in exchange for the damage.

"Well, well, you've certainly got some fight in you, little fulsin," Elkin regarded her approvingly. "Are you ok?" he asked, wiping some blood from her lips.

"I've had worse," Maya replied with a bloody grin

"We shouldn't have left her alone," Thelic snarled. He wanted nothing more than to go back and tear the outlander apart.

"I'm sorry, I couldn't control myself, it just manifested!"

"It's not your fault, Maya. You've had no training," Elkin assured her. "We can't stay here tonight though."

"Why? That outlander is out cold and I'm pretty sure I heard the mistress tell one of her people to feed it to a...blisken?"

"Good," Thelic rumbled.

"Do I want to know?"

"No."

"Why can't we stay here then?" she asked Elkin.

"I told you before, in Danika, people contracted to high-level sprites attract attention. Desperate locals may see you as an opportunity to make some money. See—" Elkin pointed behind them. Sure enough, some of the clientele had left the tavern to follow them at a distance, intrigued by Maya's power.

BACK AT THE CAMPSITE, the two guards were no longer unconscious and tried to fight their bonds.

"You got them!" Maya exclaimed, pleased.

Elkin mocked offence before leaving the canvas tent. He walked over to the soundly sleeping Keero and procured a spoon from their cutlery pouch, along with a wooden box housing small jars of different coloured powders. He returned to place the box beside Thelic, but kept the spoon hidden in his pocket.

Temper high, Thelic was eager to release his frustration on their captives. "Why the sudden increase in the Keep's guard force?" he asked as he towered over one of the bound men.

The two guards looked at each other, silently vowing not to break the oath they had made upon their entry into their Keeper's service.

"Gentlemen, we can do this the easy way…" Elkin cooed as he removed the spoon from his pocket and waggled it in front of the wide-eyed men, "…or we can do it the *fun* way?"

Again, they eyed each other, both sweating profusely despite the cool temperature.

Elkin shrugged before directing Thelic to remove the trousers of the guard on the left.

"No, shit! Okay stop! All I know is that over the last year, Bandaar's been amassing his army and won't let any of his castors leave the territory. I don't know why, I swear," the man pleaded.

Elkin moved his attention to the man on the right.

The guards, two old friends, had recently decided to join Bandaar's service for lack of any other interesting options. Neither could fight and had never had the need to. Thelic and Elkin, however, wore their battle scars proudly and the guards knew they were entirely outmatched against the two, seasoned warriors.

At Elkin's switch in attention, the guard on the right began to cry. "Please don't kill us, I'll tell you whatever you want to know."

Maya tried to stifle her laughter at the reaction Elkin's spoon had elicited in the men.

"Today!" Thelic barked.

The guards' secrets gushed into the open and their combined knowledge turned out to be more useful than even they thought it could be. Bandaar's wife, who the group suspected was Maya's mother, was locked in the eastern quarter, along with a new prisoner. Likely Jacob. The guards worked on a quarter day rotation and mid-levelled castors patrolled the grounds.

"That's new," Elkin admitted. "Bandaar has always employed mid to high-level castors, but they never worked on patrol when I was in his service."

"There wasn't an eastern quarter on the map either," Maya remembered.

Convinced the two blubbering captives had disclosed everything of potential use, Thelic took one of the powders and blew it into their faces, careful not to breathe any in himself. Within seconds they fell back, asleep.

"What did you do to them?"

"Just a bit of memory powder," Elkin assured her. "They shouldn't remember the last day or so."

Whilst rummaging through their clothes, Thelic instructed Elkin to start dismantling the tents.

"Don't you think you've violated these poor men enough, Thelic?" Maya asked jokingly.

"I'm looking for their crests." With a satisfied grunt, he pulled a small disc from each of the guards' pockets.

Maya asked to look at them. One metallic plate fit neatly in the palm of her hand; a leather thong attached, allowing its bearer to hang the badge from their neck in plain view. She moved her finger over the insignia and tried to place where she had seen it before.

"We won't be able to fake the brands, so we'll have to dress appropriately to hide their absence." Thelic pointed to the scars on the guards' necks. Large and forever flushed, the brands formed a circle with the same insignia etched into their badges, stark against the Esterbellians' pale skin. She glanced at Elkin, he too had a circular burn in the same place, the insignia marred by newer scar tissue. She knew then, what he'd done to distance himself from the Keeper's service.

The trio had soon reloaded their equipment onto Keero,

and dragged the guards back to the tavern, leaving them unbound outside.

THEY STOPPED ONLY a short distance away in an open area surrounded by woods. Here they would have to take shifts, keeping watch for unwelcome guests, but it was safer than staying in Aqarin. Together they erected the camp and Maya offered to take first watch, still wired after her fight with the outlander. Elkin, their unofficial cook, made the group a pot of vegetable soup before retiring to his tent, while Thelic stayed by the fire to eat.

"Who taught you to fight?" he asked, blowing at the steam billowing from his food.

"My grandmother mostly, but I picked up a bit from my police training too."

"I keep forgetting you're a policewoman. That explains a lot."

"I feel an insult or a lecture coming on," Maya grumbled.

"You have a knack for getting yourself into trouble." He initially meant it more as an observation than a critique, but the low tone and incumbent irritation wasn't hard to detect, and he surprised himself at how much this bothered him.

Maya immediately fell on the defence, misjudging the source of his anger. "That brute attacked me!"

"I know, we shouldn't have left you. I didn't expect him to attack in the open."

"I told you I could handle myself," Maya shrugged helping herself to more soup.

"You can fight, that much is plain to see. But you lack elemental training. With that you'll be more powerful than me and Elkin put together, assuming we can figure out what the hell you're bound to." He raised the bowl to his lips, draining its contents before regarding Maya once again. "Until then, you have to face that you're vulnerable, Maya. You have to be more careful."

"I've never backed down from a fight, Thelic. It's how Yali brought me up." Placing her own empty bowl to the side, she stood up and stretched before moving to get more firewood. "Look at it this way, the sooner one of the baddies nabs me, the sooner you get the Stone and Elkin can return to his lovers," she laughed.

Angered by her flippancy, he rose and stalked back to his tent, leaving her to tend the fire. Stripping to his waist, he climbed under the blankets and willed himself to stay there. She had clearly been joking and storming off had been petty, but the woman infuriated him. The moment he'd seen the glow from the tavern, he'd known Maya was hurt and in trouble. Something inside him had changed after their night together. No, before that. Like his restlessness, whatever it was, remained out of his control, the thought of which only served to further darken his mood.

In the adjacent tent, Elkin shook his head despairingly at Maya's ill-conceived attempt at humour. "Soulmates," he muttered, rolling over to welcome sleep.

Beside the fire, Maya was equally as frustrated. Thelic was right. Coming to this world had made one thing plaintively clear. She was unprepared. Weak. Incensed at the thought, she moved away from the tents but close enough to keep watch. Satisfied with her spot, she sat on the ground with legs crossed, allowing her arms to rest in a meditative position.

She closed her eyes and took several deep breaths, focusing on the elements to call upon whatever sprites had been helping her. Beneath the hard earth, deeply buried channels of water sang as they flowed between the stone and roots of the forest surrounding her. The wind whipped encouragingly through her hair at the effort. Despite the distance, even the fire seemed to answer her silent appeal. She felt the lick of flames caress her face, its warmth spreading throughout her body.

Maya smiled at the elements' chorused response and refocused her demands. Nothing happened. Straining with the effort, she tried again. A whip of wind rushed across her hand, and she hissed with pain, clutching it to her chest. Small bite marks had drawn blood and it streamed down her forearm to drip onto the grass. The same wind returned to caress her cheek. Wiping her arm, she tried again.

Droplets rose from the ground to float just above the centre of her bleeding palm. Standing up, she strengthened her demand and that all too familiar hum returned. All of a sudden, a stream of water shot to the surface to circle her feet. The wind purred at this development and wrapped Maya in its embrace, resulting in a frightening whirlpool, much like the gateway. She let out a strangled cry as the water rose to engulf her.

STILL FIGHTING SLEEP, Thelic heard the noise from outside and jumped up, grabbing his spear.

Elkin drowsily poked his head out and noted the absent Maya. "Where did she go?" An angry vortex floating across the glen answered their question and the last of Elkin's drowsiness vanished as he ran after Thelic.

Maya held her breath, desperate to calm the swirling mass surrounding her.

Why can't I control it?

Through the blur of the water two figures approached. Maya exhaled, releasing the last of her oxygen to scream a warning. She covered her nose and mouth with her hand – time was running out.

Her two companions watched as Maya curled into herself, frantically trying to stop her body from taking the instinctive breath it needed to survive, the breath that would ultimately kill her.

"She's drowning!" Elkin ran forward and stuck his hands into the water towards Maya. A wave swept out to hit him in the chest, throwing him back.

Learning from Elkin's mistake, Thelic summoned a wind barrier to protect himself and sprang towards the angry mass. Maya's storm vibrated in response, pleased with the renewed challenge. Thelic's wind was no match and a wall of water separated from the vortex to enclose around him.

Anger erupted in Maya as she watched her friends being battered by the conjured elements. With little strength remaining, she shot her arms out and commanded, with every part of her being, for the hurricane to desist. Banished by its master, the water released her and retreated, back to its peaceful channel beneath the earth. Maya remained floating in the air, the wind caressing her, an apology for its bad behaviour.

Thelic was back on his feet and watched with concern from below. She smiled apologetically at him as the last of her energy dissolved and she dropped. He caught and lay her gently on the ground frantically checking her pulse.

"You'll be the death of me, woman," he mumbled feeling the soft thump at his fingertips.

"Is she okay?" Elkin wandered over, nursing a sore back and damaged pride.

"That's no ordinary wind," Thelic responded as it continued to dance playfully on the breezeless night.

"No, it seems she has a strong contract after all." Elkin regarded it warily. "More than one, actually. After conjuring fire and wind against the Finkel in the woods, that's *three* elements she's managed to summon now."

Four, Thelic thought. She had manipulated earth as well as wind against the djinca upon their first meeting, too. What was she?

AFTER RE-STOKING THE FIRE, blankets were positioned at its side for Maya to lay on. Elkin withdrew to his tent as Thelic went to work removing her soaked clothes. The summoned water had drained her body of heat and turned it a disturbing shade of blue. Once stripped, several additional blankets were laid on top to trap whatever warmth she had left.

Still dressed in his own water-sodden clothes, Thelic did the same, before burying under the blankets and tucking her into his side.

She began to stir, shivering.

"Maya?"

"It's freezing," she whispered. Upon opening her eyes, she was greeted by a small, white, fox-like creature, with striking blue eyes and tall ears, sitting on her chest.

"You need elemental training," Thelic grumbled beside her. "That thing almost killed you, and us."

"What is it?" She shivered as the fluffy creature rubbed its cold nose against hers.

"Air Finkel. You rarely see them in solid form like this. I think it's been with you since the crossing to our world."

Maya felt an older sense of familiarity towards the creature. She reached out and the Finkel stretched to nestle its head in the palm of her hand, licking the small bite marks. Dissolving to whip around her head, it finally settled on the blanket over her stomach. Maya giggled. It was cute when it wasn't trying to kill her.

"Am I contracted to it?" She checked her arms, still bare of the marks.

"I don't know. There's only a handful of people in this realm contracted to Finkels, but I've never heard of anyone having an unmarked alliance."

"How do they work, the contracts?"

"There's a ceremony to summon the sprites, usually more than one will show up and you pick whichever element best suits your needs. Water-rakers for example, are mostly contracted to Water Warkoons. Or, if they're lucky, Water Vasiba. Once the ceremony is complete the sprite's brand appears and it remains within you, feeding from your essence with every use."

"You said you're above average, does that mean both of your contracts are with Vasibas."

"Yes. Most choose to align with the weaker Warkoon sprites, but at the time I had no one to guide me and little choice."

Maya stroked the elaborate markings along his arm, admiring the complex flicks and curls across his bicep. Moving her hand down to his wrist, a leather cuff covered the skin beneath. "Do you ever take these off?" she chuckled.

"Every bonded castor has a lifeline, a band to mark the essence remaining. As you use the sprites power, that band gets thinner and paler." On the day of his ceremony, Thelic had chosen to cover the bands and live as normal a life as possible. Though, he remained cautious of the price he paid with each use of the Vasibas' elements and conjured them wisely. "Get some rest, Elkin's going to keep watch for the remainder of the night. We head to Esterbell's Keep at dawn."

Exhausted, both fell asleep in a tangled embrace to the crackle of fire and the Finkel's soft purr.

～

MAYA WOKE to the rancid smell of rasicus stew. Standing over the fire, Elkin stirred the contents of the large pot. Her initial experience of the meal at Thelic's lodge had been surprisingly pleasant and her mouth watered, despite the aroma. Beside her, Thelic still slept, one hand clasping his spear, the other a makeshift head rest. In sleep, part of the blanket had been kicked away to reveal the muscular stomach beneath.

"Hungry?" Elkin asked, his double entendre plain.

Maya blushed but nodded her head. "For that? Yes," she whispered, pointing to the pot of stew.

As she struggled to sit up, Thelic stirred beside her. "Don't push it," he said. "You're likely still drained from last night's stupidity."

"*You* said I needed training," she pointed accusingly at him.

"You do. That wasn't training, that was a reckless attempt to control something you don't yet understand," he retorted sitting up and passing Maya his shirt. "Is that rasicus stew? I'm starving."

"You're right," she said, tucking herself back under the blankets to slip the cotton shirt over her head. "I didn't think it would get so out of hand."

"Don't be so hard on yourself, Maya. You too, Thelic. We didn't know she had an Air Finkel. You know they have a mind of their own," Elkin offered in her defence.

Emerging from the blankets, she smiled gratefully at him.

"You can still control them, with *training*," Thelic countered.

"Who can train me?"

"Fatari would be your best bet, she's the most powerful

and she's a blood relative so she might know why you're so different," Elkin suggested, handing her a bowl.

Maya exhaled, frustrated, knowing he was right. She'd have to wait until they reached the Seer. The Finkel reappeared at Maya's sigh and curled up in her lap, dipping its paw into her bowl of stew playfully.

Elkin jumped at its reappearance, no longer trusting the deceptively strong creature. Sensing this, the Finkel turned to him and bared its fangs.

"You're no sprite, you're a demon." He thrust his spoon towards the small, fluffy fox, sulking at its unjust treatment towards him. The Finkel disappeared and a gust of wind rocketed under Elkin's bowl, causing the hot liquid to spill onto his lap.

"Balls!" he yelled, jumping up to scrape the stew from his crotch.

Thelic laughed. "I like it."

Pleased with Thelic's response, the sprite whirled around his head before settling down once again on Maya's lap.

"Why doesn't it look like the Fire Finkel?" Maya wondered aloud.

"They change appearance, inhabiting the shape of different creatures around Avalon, nobody knows why. All in all, little is known about the Finkel sprites. I have to admit though, whatever creature that one is mimicking, I'm not familiar with it," Thelic responded, curiously regarding the strange animal.

Maya stroked their new and mischievous friend's fur. *I am*, she thought. Though, she couldn't seem to place where exactly she'd seen the little creature before.

FESTIVAL OF THE FIVE MAJORS

ESTERBELL

After sending word with a runner from Aqarin to a friend they could trust to house them temporarily, they had journeyed in that direction all morning. Passing the last line of the forest's trees, they stepped into one of a series of large farming fields. Esterbell's Keep stood tall over the community. A fortress of black stone, its high walls were edged with spikes interrupted only by deep, flaming bowls.

Like Danika's Keep, a heavy portcullis featured as the entry's barrier, currently closed to unwanted callers, with four soldiers brandishing broadswords to guard its entrance. Around the intimidating structure, a collection of houses lined the walls. With small, cobbled streets, the community was similar in nature to that of its neighbouring territory. Homes and shops were beautifully designed, petite, and functional, their only difference a stark lack of colour where the Danikan dwellings had been painted vibrant hues. This was Esterbell's major town.

Keero's large frame paired with the bustling crowds prevented them from cutting through the settlement. So, they opted to take a longer route along the outskirts. One wide road circled the town and its Keep like a dart board, with large expanses of pastures on the opposite side. Despite their suburban route, the road was by no means empty. Maya leapt to the side as two karkili thundered towards them, pulling a large wooden cart full of cloth materials, their driver tipping his hat in apology to the victims of his high-speed wagon. Two young boys then proceeded to scurry past in front of the group, the one in the lead beckoning the other to run faster. They were probably no older than six or seven. Concerned, Maya checked behind for their parents and saw two angry mothers in pursuit, covered in mud.

"Besus Marcin, you can bet I'm going to tan your hide when I catch you!" one shouted.

The slower boy continued to run, all the while throwing back exhausted pleas of innocence and naming the true villain. The leading child stopped and turned. Glaring at the traitor, he crouched and spread his fingers across the ground. In response to the summon, a floating ball of mud formed in his hand. It dawned on the younger child what was about to happen. He screeched to a halt but too late, and the muddy projectile planted him in the face.

After what Thelic had told her, Maya was shocked to see such a young contractee use the life draining power so recklessly, with scant regard for the consequences. Unfortunately, the conjured projectile wasn't very neat, the fallout resulting in a dirty group of travellers. The older boy stuck out his tongue and fled into an alley.

"Spirits, I'm so sorry!" one of the winded mothers apologised to Maya. The other had run past to collect her son, who now sat sobbing in the dirt, a mess of snot and tears.

Maya couldn't help but laugh at the disarray, despite her own grimy appearance. "Don't worry about it," she insisted, brushing the dirt from her coat. "He's pretty skilled."

"He's been training at the Keep with the other boys at his level, but it doesn't seem to do much for his manners I'm afraid." The woman bowed in apology and dashed to help the other mother and find her soon to be very sorry son.

"This friend of yours has a place to wash, right?" Maya regarded her hands and coat sadly.

"Why is it you continue to presume Avalonians are uncivilised?" Thelic asked with a glance over his shoulder. Maya had suffered the worst of the boy's attack and mud clung to the side of her head; odd bits of hair poking out around it. That, coupled with her mournful expression caused Thelic to laugh.

Maya frowned. "Hmm, I'm not sure. It could be due to your general lack of etiquette," she said, patting her hair self-consciously.

"On another note–" Elkin interrupted, pausing to manoeuvre Keero as they passed another carriage, "Bandaar never used to train young castors. Yet another thing we'll have to keep an eye out for during our rescue."

The conversation ended there as he steered their bodaari into the yard of a farmhouse. Dwellings such as this, large and richer than those in town, dotted the outer edge of the suburban road. With two levels and a great glass conservatory to the side, the owner was clearly very wealthy. The stone was painted white with black shutters to cover the windows. In the day, these would remain open, allowing the natural light to flood throughout the house. A face appeared at one of the second story windows, switching from confused, to recognition, to anger, all in the space of five seconds.

"Are you sure he's going to be happy to see you?" Maya regarded Elkin dubiously. She watched, concerned as the man disappeared from the window, only to reappear at the door. He sprinted towards them with a high-pitched battle cry and a long, thin sword raised above his head. Elkin smirked and ran to meet him head on.

Remaining with Maya and Keero, Thelic pulled out the leather jerky satchel and leaned against the creature's side to watch as the two old comrades collided.

Seconds before reaching his sword wielding friend, Elkin slipped two curved knives from under his coat and raised them in a cross above his head, catching the opposing sword as it swung down in a movement that could have split him in two. Swinging his blades to the side, the sword was forced from its wielder's grip. Elkin quickly followed through with a round house kick, making sure to keep it low. It collided with his attacker's shoulder, sending the older man sprawling. He sat up, then, and grinned.

"I sure have missed you!"

"You're getting slow, old man," Elkin smiled in response and offered his hand.

The defeated man graciously accepted, and weary bones creaked with the effort to stand. "Pah! I didn't want to injure your pride in front of the pretty young lady."

"Sadly, this one is already spoken for."

"What?" Maya and Thelic asked in unison at Elkin's remark, both walking across the yard to join them.

"Hello, darlin'. The name's Tyler Wright, but most call me Ty." Maya's eyebrows shot up at the earth-like name, and he laughed. "Unusual I know, get that a lot, crossed over about forty years ago with my pa. No contracts for me though, skipped a generation I guess."

Ty rubbed at his lower back as he bent to retrieve the fallen sword. Standing tall, he swept at the dirt that clung to a black, fitted tunic and cursed. A green stain marred the beautiful white sash sat prominently around his thin midsection. Ty's attire along with the house, blanketed their new friend in an obvious air of wealthiness. The impeccable nature of both were matched by his hair, fashioned into a large, perfectly formed afro, peppered with grey.

"I'm Maya."

"Oh!" Ty started at the equally earthly name.

"My mother was a big fan of Earth history it seems," Maya lied.

"I see, well what can I do for you folks? Usually when Elkin comes knocking it's for one of two things. Either he's hiding from a woman, or he's trying to avoid the Keeper's guards." He turned to Elkin and placed a large hand on his shoulder. "So, which is it?"

"First of all, my last visit was purely for pleasure–"

"Ha! Two days after you'd gone, one of the bordello women accused me of harbouring you. I had to replace two windows!" Ty poked Elkin's chest to emphasise his mock irritation.

"Don't suppose she's still knocking about?" Elkin glanced around nervously.

Ignoring Elkin, Ty moved over to Thelic with outstretched arms. "I suppose it's your life he's been making a mess of then?" He wrapped Thelic welcomingly in his embrace before stepping back to hold him at arm's length. "Married yet? I know this overgrown man-child is a lost cause, but I'm still holding out hope for you."

"Man-child?" Elkin rebuffed despondently.

"Nah, who would have me? Too many scars and too little time."

"Never too busy for a family, Thelic. They are life itself," Ty chastised, steering the group to a large paddock behind the house where three karkili were grazing idly. Together, they unloaded the gear from Keero, who shook his massive body in response to the renewed freedom. A hinged glass pane in the conservatory offered them entry to the spacious dome where Maya was reminded of her grandparents' garden room. Through a set of double doors and the whole reunion began again as Ty introduced Maya to his wife Calia and two young daughters, Rifi and Torin. The girls were a beautiful mix of their mother's pearly complexion and father's hazel. Maya couldn't help but wonder though, why their hair was a startling shade of pink.

The trio were shown to the guest bedrooms on the second floor, each with a bed, a fireplace and its own bath tucked into the corner. Unlike Thelic's, the house was built with plumbing. A hand pump to the side of the tub dispensed with the need for buckets to fill the deep basin, all heated by a furnace on the first floor. Maya savoured the privacy and warmth after bathing in the cold, Finkel-infested waters they had been forced to resort to over the past few days.

After her bath, she perused the suitcase full of clothing Brijid had given her, choosing an outfit similar to her last. A stretchy band of material covered her breasts under an over-sized blouse that swamped her. An adjustable corset was added to the ensemble to sit around her mid-section, tucking the excess material neatly against her body. The trousers were a good fit, though perhaps a bit short, hidden by the knee length, flat-heeled boots that completed the outfit. Before leaving her to bathe, Calia had promised to wash the soiled coat. Maya was pleased to find it, good as new, hanging over one of the kitchen chairs as she re-joined Ty and his wife downstairs.

Thelic and Elkin, equally refreshed, were informing the couple of their reasons for visiting the town, purposely skipping information that could expose Maya.

"There's only so much we can tell you without possibly putting you in danger," Elkin explained, apologetically.

Maya pulled Thelic to the side and whispered to him. "Can we trust them?"

"There's only three people I would trust with my life, Ty is one of them."

Making up her mind, she cut off Elkin. "We need to break into the Keep," she stated calmly.

Elkin gawked at his brash companion before sighing. "So, yeah, I lied."

"I'm sorry, they're trying to protect me but, with what we're about to attempt, there's likely to be some backlash." Maya continued to inform the dumbfounded family of her journey through the gateway, and of Jacob and Jaseen's capture.

"You're from the other side too." Ty stood up and embraced Maya, hundreds of questions forming, he struggled to voice them as his throat closed and tears welled in his eyes. "Sounds like you've been through a rough time, darlin'," he said with a fatherly kiss on her forehead. "What can we do?"

Maya dipped her head; shame and fear crushing her at the possibility of putting such a kind family in danger. But she knew they needed all the help they could get if this was to be successful.

"What can you tell us about the Keep? Any updated guard schedules or new builds would be useful. Surely you still have some friends in Bandaar's service?" Elkin hoped.

Ty didn't know anything more than what they'd managed to extract from the guards in Aqarin. To everyone's surprise, it was Calia that had the most to offer. "I can get Maya in to the Keep as she is, and I can get you boys uniforms to join us as guarded escorts," she claimed.

"How?" Ty questioned.

"Pharin, the seamstress. She owes me money from a bad hand at cards, and I often help with her deliveries into the Keep."

"Thank you, but it's too risky," Maya stated.

"I agree, but at least we know where to borrow some uniforms from now," Elkin realised.

"Please let me come, it sounds so exciting!" Calia begged clapping her hands excitedly.

Maya, Thelic and Elkin shook their heads apologetically in response.

"Well, at least you'll have the festival for cover if you plan to do it tonight," Ty offered. Elkin had wondered why the town was so busy and his friend was right; the crowded streets could help them blend in.

Without warning, Rifi and Torin burst through the front door, their hair, face, and clothes now a deep shade of blue.

"STOP!" Despite her fragile frame, Calia's voice boomed with enough force to snap a troop of soldiers to attention. Crossing her arms, she regarded her two wayward children. "What have I told you girls about playing in the wood?"

Rifi began reciting the three rules their parents had set. "Home before the sun sets, don't talk to strangers…"

"*And*?"

"*And*, don't poke the nexies," Torin finished

"Bath. Now," Calia instructed, and the girls scampered off giggling, unperturbed.

"Nexies," Ty explained wearily to the confused Maya. "They're docile creatures that live in the wooded areas throughout the territories. Any kind of touch to their body though and they excrete a powder like a puff of smoke. We use it to stain clothing mostly, so you can imagine our dismay that the children have a newfound interest in them."

AT MID-DAY, the sun had chased away the last hints of morning frost. With their belongings repacked and ready for a speedy departure, the trio headed into town to scout the

Keep and flesh out their plan. Banners streamed across the streetlamps and vibrant decorations adorned the otherwise dreary walls of shops and houses alike. Folk swarmed the high walled alleyways, desperately filing through to the open central square, where the entertainments had already begun. Here, the crowds were more comfortable and added to the festive atmosphere as dancers in vibrant dresses performed to a quartet of musicians and their exotic instruments.

Maya took respite in the enchanting celebrations surrounding them. Basking in the glorious smell of street food and the infectious sounds of laughter, she allowed their combined effect to serenade her; a brief pause from dwelling on the chance that they may not survive the night.

After walking the length of the Keep's walls, they retired to one of the town's central taverns, ordering stew and mead from one of its busy attendants. They had been fortunate to find a spot outside, overlooking the entertainers. More importantly, from there they could see the guarded entrance and watch for shift changes.

A parade marched through the square, a walking production as five characters demonstrated great skill at wielding their sprites' elements. Each worked together to tell a story to the crowd of mesmerised onlookers, one conjuring small mud buildings to be wiped out by another's wind or summoned wave. Children giggled as the castor's impressively controlled water splashed at their faces.

"What are they celebrating?" Maya asked.

"It's the festival of the Five Majors," Thelic said. "They're telling the story of our beginning in this realm and celebrating each of the founders' roles." He pointed to one of the performers whose dance drew in the others around him. "That's Cantor, he was responsible for creating the bond that possessed the castors of your world to cross over." Another performer raked the air, her movement eliciting the backup dancers to shake and tumble to the ground, rolling and leaping up gracefully in a pirouette.

"Who is she?"

"That's Danika, she conjured the boundary void to prevent the dangers of the outer regions from encroaching on our territories."

"Isn't that what's threatening Avalon now?"

"Yes, little fulsin, but without it we would surely have perished all those years ago upon our arrival," Elkin said, before handing the story back to Thelic.

The third performer, a young boy, danced to the front, pretending to whistle through a wooden pipe. Other, younger children skipped forward to follow his steps. This was in representation of Transum, the only Major to remain on Earth to monitor and guide latent-born castors through the gateways.

Behind the fabled pied piper, a couple danced beautifully in unison. "Who are they?"

"The last of the Five Majors, Fortus and Esterbell." Thelic, too, watched as the actors portraying the most favoured of the founders leapt and swayed with unparalleled grace. "Together, they were the most powerful. Her abilities, bolstered by Fortus, enabled them to seal the chaos that choked this realm. They were the Gatekeepers."

Together they watched in silence as the parade wound through the square, disappearing on its route to entertain citizens with the tale of origin.

Several hours passed and the world dimmed as its sun dipped below the tree line. Maya watched curiously as a man walked along the centre of the avenue between entertainers, the streetlamps flickering to life one by one as he passed. Elkin took this as his cue and left to visit the seamstress' shop, certain she would have retired for the evening.

Soon after, the portcullis was raised, and four armoured

men stepped beneath its iron spikes. Their intel had been correct, they were changing shifts every quarter day. This meant the next guard change would happen at midnight, when the three moons were at their highest. Maya and Thelic sighed with relief. Poor timing could mean the potential of facing double the number of guards, so this news meant their plan could go ahead.

After scouting the area, they had all agreed the best course of action would be to enter the Keep from the east. Jaseen was housed in that quarter and less ground to cover meant less risk of running into additional guards or castors.

"How do you plan to get over the wall?" Maya whispered across the table.

"Jump," Thelic replied. "I'll have to take you over one at a time."

"Scared I'll project myself into space if I give it a whirl?"

"You and the rest of the town."

"Rude, but fair," Maya grumbled.

A young girl approached Maya, prompted by another to bring the couple into the centre of the square. Maya looked up and regarded the townsfolk currently dancing to the musicians' rhythm; all of them couples.

"Not happening," Thelic said, crossing his arms for added effect.

"He means, no thank you, we're ok here–" Maya stopped short as the little girl's eyes began to fill with tears.

"Fine, one dance," Thelic gruffed, grabbing Maya's hand and dragging her to the square, eager to prevent the little girl from causing a scene.

The melody that played was a soft blend of high and low strings, with a woman's voice accompanying the instrumentalists. Despite his reluctance, Thelic was an accomplished dancer and held Maya to his chest as he guided her through the steps. Mid-spin, she spotted the girl pointing to them and nudging an older man at her side conspiratorially. The man sighed and pulled a small pouch from his pocket before roughly dropping it into the little girl's palm.

"I think we've been swindled," Maya giggled, resting her head on his chest to enjoy the dance. "Thank you."

"For the dance?"

Maya stomped on his foot. She meant for everything, all he had done to help her so far, and all he was about to do.

"Keep doing that and I won't have any toes left," he grumbled.

She looked up at him and his ruggedly charming face grinned back. A rush of emotion flooded through her, flushing her cheeks, and she planted her face back into his chest to conceal it.

He chuckled knowingly, moving his hand to the dip in her lower back.

Soon, the song concluded, and the citizens retreated, allowing the professionals to resume their jive.

Only moments after the couple had gotten up to dance, Elkin had returned with the uniforms of two Esterbellian castors. He waggled his eyebrows expressively now at the couple, as they joined him back at the table.

With the costumes in hand, intel confirmed, and a plan solidified; part one of their mission was complete. Settling the bill, the three returned to the Wright house to change and prepare for their midnight infiltration.

Across the street from their table, blanketed in shadow, a woman watched. She'd been surprised to see Elkin back in Esterbell, even more surprised to see him carrying Esterbellian uniforms. So, she followed him back to his table. That's when she saw Maya, and immediately recognised her. Like their prisoner, she was medium height with blonde hair.

Even Maya's facial features, a small, uplifted nose and sharp jawline matched Jaseen. Her eyes, however, were Bandaar's; bright and olive-green. As the group drifted past, she ducked her head, pulling the coat's deep hood forward to further conceal herself. Once clear, she made her way to the Keep's front gate.

"Back already, Keela? You'll miss the end of the festival."

"Oh, believe me, the fun is just beginning," she jibed with a smile, heading towards the Keeper's quarters.

9

REUNION AND DEATH

ESTERBELL KEEP

"Right, you're first, Elkin. Maya, wait here; I'll only be a moment."

Elkin strode up to Thelic and leapt into his arms. "Be gentle with me," he whispered flirtatiously, batting his eyelashes.

"You always have to make it weird." Thelic said with a half-hearted growl. Closing his eyes, he concentrated on summoning the wind as he held tightly onto Elkin, provoking a mock seductive moan from his friend. Then, they were in the air; the element easily lifting the two men up and over the spiked eastern wall of the Keep.

A light breeze brushed the nape of Maya's neck, and the Finkel manifested, floating in front of her. "I'm going to need you to be on your best behaviour tonight."

In a muted response, the creature tilted its head to the side, and disappeared.

"Ready?" Maya jumped at Thelic's voice. She'd been distracted by her intermittent sprite and hadn't heard him cross back to her side. He didn't wait for a response and picked her up, leaping over the wall effortlessly. Within moments they were all reunited and could finally get a good look at the grounds.

Elkin pulled them into the shadow of the wall neglected by torchlight and pointed up. The Keep's central structure was formed in an impressive two-story mass of thick cobbled stone, with adjoining single-story buildings interwoven by courtyards. He had been indicating two guards, stationed at each corner of a wrap-around balcony on the top floor. Hugging the darkness, he led them towards the eastern quarter.

"Long time, Elkin," a voice droned from the gloom. Dressed in black, the camouflage had prevented them from spotting her until the last moment. Pushing from a relaxed stance against the cool stone, Keela stood in their path.

"Well, that plan went to fuggerty all too quick. How've you been, Kee?"

Like Elkin, Keela wielded two curved blades as her weapon of choice, despite her high-level contract. She flicked them, now, in circles around her fingers. "I've been waiting a long time for this," she hummed, crouching into a fighting posture.

"You two go on ahead," Elkin said, ushering the others to circle around her.

"You're not going anywhere!" She lunged for Elkin, simultaneously summoning fire to launch it at the others.

Thelic and Maya dodged the projectile easily as Elkin met Keela's blow with his own blades drawn. The redhead, seemingly unfazed by the assault, grinned and whipped his head to the side as a signal to Thelic – *get gone*.

Confident in their friend, Maya and Thelic hurried on to the eastern quarter.

"It doesn't matter, Bandaar knows she's here," Keela baited, rolling her shoulders.

Elkin bristled but focused on his opponent. "Speaking of

Bandaar, I heard a dirty little rumour that you're his love child. True?"

Keela attacked again, this time driving her knife towards his gut. He pre-empted, swinging his fist to knock it from her grasp, but failed to realise her other hand had been re-conjuring her element. A whoosh of flames consumed the back of his coat. Quick to act, he summoned water from the ground beneath him and felt the momentary relief as it made its way up his legs and across his back.

Keela wasted no time and moved in for another assault. Elkin whipped the water towards his opponent. She ducked and moved in, plunging the tip of her blade into his side.

THELIC PEEKED around the corner and held two fingers up to Maya. At first, she thought he was being rude, and held her own finger up. At his confusion, she realised he was signalling to tell her there were two guards. She tucked her finger away, smiling apologetically.

This was the only room they'd found with sentries posted, likely protecting the two prisoners. Unfortunately, it was at the end of a long corridor, and they would be spotted the moment they broke cover. Maya looked down in response to the Finkel rubbing against her shin, and pulled Thelic further back into cover.

"I have an idea. Possibly. It depends on that," she said, pointing to the Finkel.

"You can't control it."

"It's impressionable, look at the way it reacted to you and Elkin."

Thelic considered this. Returning to the corner, he knelt and beckoned the creature to his side, before pointing in the direction of the guards. "They said they don't like you."

The Finkel pranced over curiously to peek around the bend. Spotting the guards, it wandered down the corridor.

"I'll admit, I did *not* expect that to work," Maya said.

Being small and quiet, the guards only spotted the sprite as it reached halfway.

"What the shitting hell is that?" The female guard pointed at the white fox heading towards them.

The second guard bent down to inspect the creature as it neared. "Whoa...I think it's a Finkel!" Hesitantly, he reached out, allowing the tips of his fingers to brush the top of Loki's head. "It's...cute."

"Little traitor," Maya sulked from their hiding spot.

"Get rid of it," the female guard instructed. "I hate Finkels."

At the woman's unfriendly words, the sprite went from friendly to feral in two seconds flat, launching itself at her face.

Maya fist pumped the air triumphantly. Thelic, taking immediate advantage of the distraction, burst from cover, summoning the wind to accelerate his speed.

The female guard screeched as she batted at the angry fox attached to her face. The man turned at the sound of approach, just as Thelic's fist collided with his nose. He fell back, blood spurting from his nostrils. The woman's nose was having an equally bad time as the Finkel bit down, using the appendage to maintain its grip. Thelic moved behind the flailing woman and placed his arm around her neck, squeezing until she passed out. Maya called the Finkel back to her side to reward it with a scratch between its tall ears.

She turned to the large, wooden, double-doored entrance; the only remaining barrier between her and her family. With both hands she pushed. It didn't budge. Before Thelic could help, anger surged through her, and she called upon the Finkel. In understanding, the sprite reappeared on her shoulder and bolted across the outstretched arm towards the doors. They burst open, one breaking from its hinge to bang deafeningly on the marble floor.

Two figures stood defiantly at the end of the room, ready to fight whatever was coming, and saw Maya.

Jacob ran forward and embraced his sister. "Maya! Thank god, I'm so sorry. I didn't mean to go off by myself, I mean, I did, but–"

Maya was staring at Jaseen. Her mother. A hand flew to her mouth as the dam broke from fifteen years of grieving her loss. Jaseen, too, had been gazing at the daughter who'd grown so strong and beautiful in her absence. Unable to bear another second apart, Maya rushed forward into her mother's arms.

"Mum," she sobbed, clutching onto the thin white tunic, terrified she would once again disappear.

"Spirits, Maya! I'm so sorry," Jaseen's heart broke, ecstatic but frightened by her daughter's presence, here at the Keep.

Maya stepped back. "Don't you dare apologise. I'm the reason you're being held prisoner!"

"No. None of this was your fault. Your father–"

"Mayara."

Spinning towards the unfamiliar voice, Maya saw Thelic with a blade to his throat, and a man standing behind him. "You must be Bandaar," she bristled. "Release him, it's me you want, right?"

Jaseen moved to stand protectively in front of her children. "I'll die before you touch them, Bandaar."

Thelic attempted to reach his spear, but Bandaar had the arm closest to it locked tightly behind his back. In response, his arm was pushed up, joints and muscles burning with the tension. He winced as the blade at his throat dug deeper.

"Stop! Please don't hurt him," Maya begged, pushing past Jaseen to take several steps forward.

"I've been looking for you for *twenty* years," Bandaar growled.

"And I'm here now, so please let the others go."

"Mayara, no. He...he plans to kill you." Jaseen felt the weight of the words as they left her. Her husband, Maya's father, wanted to end the precious life he once cherished.

"Why?" Maya asked him.

"Because your power can stop the chaos."

"And that requires my death?" Maya remembered the Five Majors' fabled scrolls, and the dark ceremony that required death in exchange for life. "You have one of the scrolls, don't you?"

"Clever girl. Part of your contract was inherited, marked only in your blood, a major ingredient required to summon the castor circles. I need your essence to save this realm. With my ceremony your power would pass to me." He regarded Maya coldly. Years of obsessing over recreating her contracted bond had hardened him with each failed attempt. "If your mother hadn't taken you, I may have been able to develop your skills to a level that would have saved your life. But we no longer have that time."

"That's a lie, Bandaar," Jaseen spoke icily. "You never intended to safeguard her life. Why won't you listen to me? What you're trying to do is impossible, but there is another way!"

Maya turned to her mother. "Another way?"

"Your grandmother knows of a second ceremony, one that will save the realm with far less risk to the castor."

"I like that option, so why don't we head back to Yali, and she can walk us through it?" Maya suggested.

Bandaar's deep chuckle reverberated through the room. "It seems your mother has been keeping a great deal from you. Yali is not your grandmother, and that incantation is a fallacy."

"The gateways must be closed, Bandaar, and Maya is the only one that can do it."

"What the hell are you both talking about?" Maya yelled, looking between her mother and father.

"Maya, the chaos that leaks from the gateways is a remnant of spirits and sprites from the other world, ones that crossed over to Avalon. They aren't like the sprites here. On Earth they are referred to as demons." Jaseen focused once again on Bandaar. He had changed so much, his own contract warping him into something she no longer recognised. "These demons were trapped in another realm, with only a thin barrier separating them from this one. Your father wishes to release them, to use their power for his own gain. Isn't that right?"

Bandaar sneered in response. She never understood, her bloodline blinding her from the truth, that they could never live peacefully in this realm until the outlanders were destroyed. "You're wrong, but without Maya's power, this realm will cease to exist in the years to come. Either way, Maya, you must relinquish your power to me, to save the people of this world."

"Bloody hell," Maya muttered.

"Why the fuck are you listening to him?" Thelic grit his teeth at the pressure in his shoulder.

Bandaar had temporarily forgotten about the man in his grasp. With a quick movement, he twisted the arm until it popped. Thelic fell to the ground with a yell and Maya ran to his side.

"Come willingly, Mayara, or I *will* kill everyone in this room."

Her throat closed as panic set in. The debilitating emotion refusing to let her think, to come up with a plan, to choose. Thelic gripped her arm, and that panic was replaced by fury. This man, her father, had imprisoned her mother, kidnapped

Jacob, and injured someone she cared for. Spotting the spear still strapped to Thelic's side, she grabbed it.

"Don't be foolish. You may have that power, but you have no idea how to use it," Bandaar said with a dark chuckle.

She helped Thelic to his feet and placed him in her mother's care, before turning and facing Bandaar. "I can try." She unsheathed the spear and ran its head across her palm.

"Maya, don't!" Thelic and Jaseen shouted.

In response to Maya's blood, the Finkel danced into action and a stormy wind exploded across the room, flinging Bandaar back into the only remaining door. With one arm temporarily incapacitated, Thelic used his body to push Jacob and Jaseen onto the floor behind the protection of the room's king-sized bed.

Maya's blood pooled beneath her as it continued to run freely from her hand, and the glow from the castor circle came to life. Praying that her episode in the forest wouldn't repeat itself, she begged the fire element to help as she pulled it from the open fireplace. Flames wrapped around her body, enraged that someone so unskilled dare call upon it. But Maya's desperation won out and she thrust the fiery mass at her father as he recovered. Momentarily stunned by her control, he howled as the blaze covered his body.

At the commotion, several guards and castors had rushed to the scene to find their Keeper writhing in agony. One castor sprang into action, dousing her leader in water while others crowded the door and summoned their own sprites to battle Maya.

She cried as their wind ripped through her own, shredding her. Jacob ran forward in a feeble attempt to reach his sister, only to be thrown back, his head slamming against the wall with a sickening crack.

"No!" Jaseen's scream broke Maya's concentration and the Keep's castors' winds enveloped her, reaving her of oxygen despite the element's nature. Thelic slammed his good hand to the floor and called to the earth and stone. The ground beneath the castors rumbled with menace and hunger as it cracked apart.

Finally, Maya sucked in a breath, just as the window to her mother's room burst apart. A familiar glint of red hair appeared on the other side of the broken glass, catching Maya's attention. Elkin.

"What did I miss?" Elkin yelled over Maya's wind, still raging chaotically around the room.

Maya looked to her mother crouched over Jacob, a pool of blood crowning his head. "Get them out of here!"

Elkin climbed through the window, crouching just metres from Maya as a painting, caught in the storm, flew overhead.

Maya once again called upon fire, this time though, it wasn't so compliant. Like her wind, it raged around the room. Straining to keep it from the others, her body protested in the effort to direct its rage towards their enemies. The wall of fire rushed forward and greedily latched onto the wooden frame above their heads. Maya risked a look back. Elkin had managed to get Jacob through the window.

"Father!"

At the cry, Maya snapped her head back to the scene in front of her. Still battling the castors' wind, she squinted through the blur as Keela ran to Bandaar to attend to him. He had recovered, partial burns to his face and hands the only visible damage. He grabbed Keela by the throat and lifted her off the ground.

"You failed!" he roared. Dropping her roughly, he whipped around to face Maya and summoned the earth. A large marble tile flew towards her, its intent to maim, not kill. A wall of stone appeared, taking the hit. Thelic's summoning had saved her. A second, larger cobble, quickly followed Bandaar's initial attack and crashed through Thelic's protective wall. Maya was knocked to the ground, her leg ripped open, and concentration broken. With its chains unbound, the Finkel went into overdrive.

Thelic manipulated the broken floor upwards, blocking them momentarily from view as he pressed against the wind to reach Maya. She screamed in agony, the castor circle absorbing the blood from her wounds. Reaching her side, he pressed his hand to her leg to staunch the bleeding.

The barrier was blasted out of the way and Bandaar faced them all once again. "I told you, Mayara. I told you I'd kill them all." He raised his hands and sharp, broken tiles mirrored his movement to rise from the ground. With a flick of his fingers, they cut through the air towards them.

Jumping in front of her daughter, Jaseen summoned a wave of water that pushed their assailants out of the room before freezing and blocking the door.

With the threat removed, the Finkel evaporated, the room suddenly quiet. Jaseen turned and smiled at Maya, blood spreading across her chest around the shards protruding from it. She collapsed.

"Mum!" Maya dragged herself to Jaseen and held her head. "No, please, Elkin!" she screamed.

He reappeared at the window and climbed through. "Jacob is in a pretty bad way–" he stopped at the sight of Jaseen.

"Maya, sweetheart, you have to go. That won't hold for long." With bloodied hands she stroked the tears from her daughter's face, streaking it with red.

"Elkin, help me get her out of here!"

As Maya instructed, he moved forward but knew they had little chance of saving her. She was bleeding out too quickly.

"Take your brother home–" Jaseen coughed, her blood, peppering Maya's hands. "Go to my mother, go to Fatari," she gasped desperately.

"No! Stop it, you're coming with us, I just got you back!" She fought futilely to stop the blood that pooled around her fingers.

"Mayara, I love you." Jaseen wheezed a final breath, and her piercing blue eyes froze, glazed forever more as her head lulled to the side.

Maya wailed, gripping her mother's dead body.

Guards and castors pounded on the ice wall as a muffled order was barked by Bandaar.

"Maya," Thelic whispered.

"No!"

"Maya, we have to go, Jacob needs help," Elkin pleaded.

Jacob. She had to help him. But leaving her mother…they had only just gotten her back. Maya leaned down and kissed Jaseen's cheek, wet with the tears of her final goodbye. Thelic laced his uninjured arm through hers, helping her stand. At the window, she turned and looked at Jaseen for the last time. As a child, Maya had thought a part of her had died when she'd first lost her mother. Seeing her now, murdered at the hands of her father, a darkness welled up within.

OUTSIDE, Jacob was lying on the floor, motionless, a crude piece of material wrapped around his head now saturated in blood.

"Jacob!" Maya crouched next to her brother and checked him. Still breathing.

Thelic and Elkin ran to the Keep's eastern wall and, using their combined strength, manipulated the stones until a large section broke apart, crashing to the ground and providing an exit. Returning to the siblings, Elkin lifted Jacob as Thelic supported Maya's weight, her leg still weeping blood.

Despite the thunder of rocks dismantling, the noise garnered little attention from the festivities in the town centre. Grateful for the celebration's cover, they ran to a tavern stable and hijacked two karkili for the ride back to the Wright house.

~

"TY? CALIA?" Elkin called as he lay Jacob gently on the family table. Footsteps pounded down the stairs followed by two sleepy faces. By now, Maya was all but being dragged through the Wright's front door. Pale and shivering, she'd lost a lot of blood. That, coupled with the power she'd used fighting at the Keep, she could barely keep her eyes open, let alone walk.

"Spirits, what happened!?" Calia ran to Maya's side but was waved away.

"My brother," she croaked.

With a nod, Calia moved to the table to assess Jacob, instructing her husband to fetch some hot water and bandages.

Elkin rushed to his belongings, placed neatly with the others by the door, and retrieved Brijid's powders. "Will these help?"

Calia regarded them, unsure. "I'm not a healer, but they might." Flicking through the bottles she read the labels to herself: *Sleep; Awaken; Memory; Pain; Diarrhoea; Cleanser; Blood Staunch*– "Yes!" She removed the larger jar containing a thick, muddy paste. Carefully removing the crude bandages, she first applied the cleanser, then carefully smeared the topical paste to Jacob's head wound. "Here, go and use these on Maya," she told Elkin. Grabbing the bottle labelled *Awaken*, she tipped some of the yellowed powder onto a cloth and held it to Jacob's face. Several seconds passed and he sprang up quicker than a jack-in-the-box, his hand flying to his head at the pain rocketing through it.

"Jacob!" Pushing Elkin and Thelic to the side, Maya hobbled over and hugged him.

"Maya? Where are we? What happened?"

Maya cried with relief at her brother's familiar prattle. "You're safe, these are friends," she assured him, waving to the four strangers. One face, however, was missing.

"Maya, where's Mum?"

More concerned with keeping him alive, she hadn't considered what she'd tell Jacob when he finally woke up. She dropped her gaze, panicked at provoking the look he'd given her in Yali's kitchen. "She died, Jacob. I'm sorry."

"But we just got her back." Tears rushed down pale cheeks streaked with the blood from his head wound, hands curling into the Oxford University hoodie he'd manage to keep hold of. Their mother had been so proud when he'd told her how he was studying to be a doctor. "How?" he sobbed.

"Bandaar tried to kill us. She took the hit and made sure we could escape," she choked.

"Again?" Jacob whispered.

Maya winced. This was the second time their mother had been taken from them to protect her. Only this time, it was forever, Jaseen was never coming back. Maya waited for her brother's outburst, be it physical or verbal, she would take it. Instead, Jacob leaned forward and pulled her across the table in an embrace.

"I'm sorry, I know it's not your fault, I shouldn't have said that."

He was right, it wasn't her fault, and deep down she knew that. Maya had been thrust into this chaotic world as quickly as he had. Nevertheless, the relief at his words mended the first of many open wounds in her heart.

"Sweetie, you're bleeding all over my carpet," Calia said, hesitant to break up the sibling reunion but desperate to treat Maya.

In the meantime, Calia had tended to Thelic's shoulder and given him some of Brijid's pain medication. Elkin's own wound had been superficial and easily treated with a few stitches. So, once patched up, he cleverly manipulated his ability to summon water and covered Thelic's shoulder in a rapid form of hydrotherapy.

With her brother awake and the burden of guilt lifted, Maya's remaining adrenaline dissolved, and she crumpled to the floor.

"For spirits' sake," Calia muttered. "Elkin, grab her. You, off the table please so I can treat your sister."

Jacob acquiesced and gingerly slid himself from the wooden slab to sit on one of the chairs. "Is she going to be okay?"

"She's tougher than she seems, and more stubborn," Thelic assured him with a nudge, despite his own concern.

"Oh, I know that much. But she's also a jinx," he said, just about managing a sad smile.

"I can still hear you," Maya groaned, gripping the table as Calia crudely stitched and applied the topical paste to her leg and hand.

"I could give you some of the powder for the fatigue, but I'm not sure what it would do to someone who's already awake."

"I'll be ok for now. Thanks, Calia, Ty, for everything." Maya pulled them both into a hug, grateful for the risks they'd taken to help them.

A harsh knock at the door broke the mood as everyone in the room span towards the sound.

Ty put a finger to his lips, signalling the others to be quiet and waited a beat. Mussing up his hair and rubbing his face to mimic the signs of a man recently woken from sleep, he walked to the door; bellowing in mock anger to hide his fear. "What time of the night do you call–" he opened the door and stopped at the pretty, Asian-descended woman that faced him. "Hey! You still owe me for those broken windows, young lady!" Ty shook a finger in Keela's face.

"I know they're here, tell them I come in good will."

Ty considered for a moment before turning and shouting back to the kitchen. "That hooker is here."

"What did you just call me?"

Ignoring her, Ty held his arm across the doorframe, barring entry.

Elkin stood up to poke his head around the kitchen corner. "This is who you were talking about before?" He laughed, composing himself at Keela's glare. "Here to do Bandaar's dirty work?"

"I'm here to warn you, some of the town's people pointed this way during the guards' questioning. It's only a matter of time before they find you."

"Why warn us? Surely the reward for our capture wouldn't be worth passing up? Perhaps you would get that fatherly attention you've always craved," Elkin suggested unkindly.

Curious at the commotion, Maya had hobbled over to the lobby entrance. "I *did* hear that correctly then, back at the Keep. You're Bandaar's..." She paused momentarily, looking to Elkin. "You knew she was my sister?"

"I heard rumours suggesting Keela and Bandaar's relationship was familial, but nothing confirmed."

"We have to leave. Now." Keela was in no mood to talk about her father, or her older sister.

"*We*? Surely you don't expect to travel with us?" Elkin remarked.

"Damn right I'm coming with you. *She* can stop the chaos," Keela said, pointing to Maya. "If there's another way to accomplish that then I'm all ears. But, if Fatari's way *doesn't* work, then she's coming back with me."

"We could just kill her," Thelic suggested darkly, his narrowed eyes and grim expression assuring Keela he was more than serious.

"You could, but you're going to need all the help you can get trying to avoid Bandaar's shifters."

She was right. At the very least, Keela could identify any spies that attempted to befriend them. "Fine," Maya said on behalf of the group. "But the moment I even suspect you're going to betray us; I'll kill you myself."

Jacob flinched at his sister's easily uttered threat. The new darkness in Maya creeping to the surface. Unperturbed, Keela offered her hand in agreement.

After inviting in their new and unexpected ally, Calia took Maya to change, her clothes shredded from the castors' wind summons. Elkin and Thelic too, left to remove their Esterbellian uniforms. Once dressed, Ty and Keela helped lash together everyone's belongings and prepared Keero and the stolen karkili for their journey.

"What the hell is that?" Jacob asked, pointing towards the bodaari. Thelic chuckled at the similarity to Maya's first encounter with Keero, before offering the introductions.

After securing their belongings, Maya, turned to Ty and Calia and embraced them. "Thank you both so much for everything."

"You are welcome here anytime, I hope you know that," Ty replied, placing a hand under Maya's chin and lifting it. "You saved your brother. You did well, darlin'."

"What will you say to the guards? What if they hurt you, or the children?" Maya shook with the thought.

Calia reached into her pocket and removed a small, balled-up handkerchief. At Maya's puzzled look she pulled back the folds, revealing at its centre a fine, white powder.

"What is it?"

"It wipes our memories of the last day or so," Ty

explained. "Should do the trick when the guards come knocking and find us all asleep. They'll test for it too, so it's handy you brought some."

She dipped her head again, a humble apology for the lengths they were having to go to in order to protect the group.

After helping Maya onto the bodaari, Jacob and Thelic took their seats alongside her. Elkin and Keela, being the least injured, opted to ride the karkili.

"Where's the nearest portal?" Maya asked.

"Towards the north, but it's too risky. We should head south, get out of the territory and head to Cantor's portal instead," Elkin insisted.

"Cantor it is."

10
DECLARATIONS

ESTERBELL ~ THE BLOODYWOOD

Although dawn had already broken, thick foliage kept the eerie forest in deep shadow. An endless chill permeated the air and a thin layer of frost remained encapsulated, a result of the sun's broken reach through the dense canopy above, forcing the group to ride with blankets wrapped around their shoulders.

Through the wooded labyrinth, Keero's plods crackled along the frozen leaves of the iced undergrowth. Small birds dipped from the canopy, flying through the tangled branches to spread their song and bring an element of light to an otherwise dark place.

"Why can't I go to Fatari with all of you?"

"Because you're weak and provide no tactical advantage," Keela stated simply in answer to Jacob's question.

Maya shot her a scowl. The woman was going to take some getting used to. "*Because*, Jacob, I promised Mum I would take you home."

Jacob couldn't argue with that. He couldn't deny their mother's dying wish; Maya knew that.

"How exactly do you intend for us to get to Cantor?

Bandaar will have guards at every port in Esterbell far sooner than we can hope to get to them at this pace," Keela noted.

"We'll cross the ice in the south."

She scoffed at Thelic's plan. "Brilliant. Facing Bandaar is probably a safer bet. If this forest doesn't kill us first, the ice certainly will."

Maya shifted uncomfortably, Brijid's medication was wearing off.

"You should get some sleep, little fulsin. It's going to take us a day and a half, at least, getting through the Bloodywood to the south."

"Bloodywood?" Maya asked.

"As in, *never go into that bloody wood*, as my mother used to say," Elkin chuckled. "The name, simple in nature, is used by Esterbellians as an adopted warning to children."

True enough, this wood was known to be a haven for all sorts of Avalonian creatures. Esterbell was ripe for stories of children playing near its edge and disappearing, never to be seen again. The lack of humans meant the beasts could live freely, without the threat of being hunted. This resultant isolation was no doubt jealously guarded and would be swiftly and ferociously defended. They would have to remain alert, should they hope to survive the journey south.

Jacob searched the canopy above, uneasy.

Hoping to distract her brother, Maya asked him what had happened when he passed through the gateway.

"Well, I woke up in a massive forest, with trees like nothing I've ever seen before, and I could barely see because it was so foggy. Somehow, I made it out and a little girl took me to her home to see her parents. They told me I had to go to the Keep, to register. I tried to insist I was just visiting, to find Mum," he paused, holding back his tears, the news of her death still raw. "They sent word to the Keeper's guards who came to pick me up and took me to see

Carnass." Jacob blushed and covered his face with the blanket.

"He didn't hurt you, did he?" Maya asked, concerned by his reaction.

"He was a weird one," Jacob said, hesitating slightly before adding, "I mean, I'd never been propositioned by a man before, and..." Sweat trickled down his brow despite the cold. "Well, this one seemed pretty important, and I didn't want to insult him, so…"

"So?" Maya scooched forward along the bodaari.

"So, I let him kiss me," Jacob admitted shyly.

Thelic laughed. "Well, at least the man finally got some attention. Maybe he'll stop harassing *me* now."

"We heard he sold you to Bandaar," Maya remembered what the man at the market stall in Danika had said.

"No, he wanted me to stay but I told him what had happened to Mum and that I needed to find Bandaar. He sent word and the next day I was picked up. Travelling was pretty awful, they barely stopped, and we moved through the night."

"And Bandaar? Did he…"

"Mostly he ignored me. I was thrown in a jail cell when we arrived and stayed there that night. The next day I was taken to see Mum."

Maya bobbed her head, happy that he hadn't suffered too much during his time in Avalon without her. "How was it, seeing her?"

"We didn't recognise each other at first, but after that we cried a lot," Jacob smiled at the memory despite the pain it caused him. "She wasn't mistreated by your dad–"

"Don't. Please don't call him that," Maya said softly. "He'll never be that to me. David Cross is our father and always will be." She lifted a hand to ruffle his hair but stopped at the bandages wrapped around it. "I'm sorry about that, too," she pointed to his wound.

"Ha, don't worry about it. That will *definitely* be the last time I run towards a tornado though. Did you know you could do magic?"

"Nope. First time I realised, I was being chased by a big, lion-dragon thing called a djinca, and I somehow managed to summon wind and earth." Maya swayed her hands in the air, mimicking a witch casting spells.

"You're a wizard!" Jacob gasped and they both chuckled.

"No, no, I'm a Castoor," she drawled an imitation of Thelic's accent and yawned, provoking a ripple effect throughout the group.

"We should get to Brushkin's Break by nightfall. It's been a long day though and you lot are injured, you should sleep," Elkin suggested. "Kee and I will keep an eye out."

Keela scoffed outwardly at the implied trust but turned her gaze to the privacy of the forest, a small rush of pleasure prompted by his words.

"COME ON. WE SHOULD KEEP MOVING."

"We can't just leave them, Keela. Those outlanders will kill them!"

"That's not our problem, Thelic. Plus, you can't fight with that shoulder," Keela said coldly as she pointed to Thelic's injury.

"What's going on?" Roused from sleep by the argument, Jacob and Maya sat up. They were still in the Bloodywood but had reached a treeline which formed the edge of a clearing. Screams resonated from the small group of houses at its centre.

"Outlanders most likely," Thelic answered.

"How does it look?" Maya swung her legs over the side of Keero and slid down his fur. As she landed, pain rocketed up her right thigh. She hissed and immediately threw her weight to the opposite leg.

"You, as well – both of you would be useless in a fight."

Maya hated to admit it, but Keela was right. Still, she felt she had to do something. "Maybe I could still summon..."

"Ha! You'll likely destroy the whole community," Keela said scathingly.

"Well? What then?" Maya watched helplessly as a small child stood by a well, wailing, his mother running to him just as an outlander caught and tackled her to the ground. "Fuck this," she spat at Keela. "Either you do something, or I will."

"Hang on, Maya." Elkin emerged from their right, returning from a quick recce of the wood surrounding the commune. "Keela and I will go. You, Thelic and Jacob stay here and assist if you see us struggling."

"What makes you think I want any part of this?" Keela asked, crossing her arms.

"There's no need to be frightened, if you don't think you can handle it–"

"I know what you're doing, Elkin Slator, and it's not going to work."

"How about a bit of friendly competition then?" he offered with a grin.

Keela considered that for a moment. "Loser cooks?" she asked. While she hated to admit it, she had missed his signature lipen-broth soup.

MAYA, Thelic and Jacob watched from the treeline as Keela and Elkin made their way to the eastern edge of the clearing. From here, the houses were closer to the wooded line. With less open ground to cover, they had the element of surprise.

Keela appeared first, racing from her tree to the back of a house within moments. Close by, one of the outlanders was tearing the clothes from a woman's chest. The villager tried to summon water, to deter her attacker, but suffered a sharp slap in the face for her efforts. Keela snuck up and drove a dagger between the outlander's shoulder blades, her hand covering his mouth to muffle the scream.

Elkin swiftly passed Keela and headed into one of the houses. His reconnaissance had revealed at least five outlanders, three of whom were in that house. Inside, two women and a man were ploughing through the owner's belongings and packing them into large sacks.

"I'm not sure that belongs to you," Elkin declared. "If you drop those bags and leave, I won't have to kill you," he smiled sweetly, unbefitting of the situation.

"Look here, little castor human thinks he can take all three of us." The two women cackled at their leader's jest. Dropping the bag, the man dashed forward, assuming the stranger was distracted by his women.

He wasn't. Elkin threw one of his daggers and planted it straight through the man's throat.

"That was my mate!" One woman squawked, her eyes darting from the man – choking on the blood flooding his oesophagus – to Elkin.

"My sincerest apologies, but he did start it." Elkin shrugged.

Enraged, she lunged towards him. To Elkin's left was the family's dining table. He quickly grabbed one of the chairs and launched it at the woman. She fell to the ground howling, clutching her shoulder, just as the second woman hurled her spear. The surprising speed and accuracy caught Elkin off-guard, but he dodged to the right, its tip cutting through the arm of his coat. The injured outlander's shrieks filled the small house, masking the second woman's rapid footfalls as she pounded across the open space. Elkin looked up just as she reached him, her fist pummelling into his chin, simultaneously knocking him through the door of the house.

Outside, Keela was tangled in a brawl with a man twice her size but with half her skill. She easily dodged the attacks, his bulky weight slowing him down. Manoeuvring herself to duck behind, she threw a series of swift punches to his back and sides. He dropped to his knees and a round house kick sent him to the floor, Keela's hard soled boot delivering the final blow to the outlander's already broken face.

Elkin wasn't faring quite so well. One of the women had ferally latched her teeth into his arm while the other clung to his back, battering his head with a small rock. Keela chuckled at the sight but prepared to step in, unaware that a sixth outlander was sneaking up. A strong arm wrapped around her throat from behind, the other knocking the dagger from her grasp.

Elkin caught the sound of Keela's strangled cry, just as he managed to grab the woman on his back by the hair. Swinging the outlander like a Scotsman's hammer, he timed the release, her body smashing into the corner of a shack leaving her slumped and bleeding copiously. In quick succession he shook off the biter, grabbed her face and twisted, her neck snapping with an audible pop.

Elkin rounded on Keela's attacker just as the outlander unsheathed a blade. Without warning, the burning barn beside them exploded, startling everyone in the clearing. A split second later, a large rock embedded itself into the outlanders skull, killing him instantly.

Keela and Elkin looked up to the treeline.

"That's why you're not allowed to summon, Maya!" Thelic scolded, indicating the poor family's barn, now reduced to splintered ashes. He helped her back onto the bodaari and led the creatures into the clearing to meet the others.

Maya hopped over as Elkin checked the broken bodies of the outlanders, all confirmed dead. Upon closer inspection, their hands were remarkably different to a human. While they maintained four fingers and a thumb, each digit stretched another carpal length with sharp, elongated nails curved at the tip. Additionally, from the wrist down, every inch was the same blue as the runes they bore on their face.

A young woman approached Keela to thank her. She had been mere moments from rape before the rescue. Keela waved her off, insisting it was no trouble, but smiled at the woman's sincerity.

"Was that...did you just...*smile*?" Elkin grimaced. She ignored him, refusing to allow the moment to be ruined.

Nine people lived in the clearing's tiny hamlet. Their humble living sustained by growing vegetables and hunting small animals to trade at the market in Brushkin's Break. In return for their help, the families offered the travellers several satchels of vegetables and dry-cured rasicus meat, along with a rare bodaari pelt. With thanks, they accepted the food but thought best, for obvious reasons, to decline the pelt.

Discreetly, Maya pulled Thelic to the side. "Maybe we should give them some of that powder you use to wipe memories, just in case Bandaar's men come through here."

Thelic pointed to Elkin, already removing the small bottle from a satchel on Keero's back.

The family's generosity meant the group would only have to stop at Brushkin's Break for a tent and vital medical supplies. With no idea how far the Esterbellian soldiers would have reached, stopping in an open market would be risky, but necessary before the crossing.

~

THE SUN WAS SETTING across the territory when they spotted the village, their half-way point. Being the least recognisable, Thelic was elected to check the area for guards and signalled to the others that the coast was clear. With few houses and no tavern, the villagers had retired for the night, packing away their stalls ready for the next day. Passing through the town, the group led their mounts back into the southern edge of the Bloodywood, where they could rest unseen, and wait for the market to reopen in the morning.

With only three tents to share between five, they had hoped to reach the town before nightfall to purchase another.

"I'd be happy to share with you." Elkin threw a casual arm over Keela's shoulder and pulled her in. With a smile, she lifted her knee until it collided, satisfyingly, with his genitals.

"Why?!" he groaned, cupping his tender spot and sinking to the ground.

Maya shook her head in dismay at their lecherous friend. "I can share with Jacob, so why don't you and Thelic take the other tent and Keela can have the third?" she offered.

"Suits me," Keela decided, slipping into the tent to deter any further suggestions.

"Great, I'll take first watch tonight, I slept pretty well on Keero for a while back there."

"Everyone's exhausted, Maya. It would be better having double-guarded shifts," Thelic insisted. "So, I'll take the first watch with you. Elkin and Keela can do the second."

"What about me?" Jacob asked.

"We'll camp again once we've crossed the Ice Passage. You can take up one of the shifts then and let someone else get a full night," Elkin reassured him. "For now, get as much sleep as possible, whenever you can."

The smell of vegetable stew drew Keela from her tent. After grabbing and filling a bowl with food she quickly retreated, followed shortly by Elkin and Jacob, who bid their two watchkeepers goodnight.

"Are you cold?" Thelic asked. The fire had been banked the moment their food was warm. With only the embers left to burn, it removed the risk of smoke drawing attention to the campsite. Maya had gathered several blankets and snuggled into them, shaking her head in response to his question.

"Do you really think Keero would have recognised the bodaari pelt that family offered us?"

"The last bodaari pelt I was gifted, Keero refused to let me ride him until I got rid of it. They're smarter than you might think."

Maya chuckled at the thought.

"I'm sorry about your mother." Thelic had been hesitant to bring it up, but after the loss of his own, he knew the quicker you came to terms with loss, the easier it became.

"Me too," Maya sighed. "We lost her once when we were little. This was different though. It was painfully real. Saying that, I feel an odd sense of closure. I'll never have to wonder what happened, which makes it harder *now*, I suppose, but it'll help in time." Maya had been studying the dying embers and looked to Thelic. "Your mother–"

"She's dead."

The blunt finality of his statement struck her, and she immediately regretted her words. "I'm sorry, I shouldn't–"

"It's okay, she got sick, after my dad."

"How old were you?" Maya couldn't help herself, she wanted to know more about him, the good and the bad.

"I was ten when the Fortus Keeper, Jaxum, executed my father. My mother died two years later."

"You've been on your own since you were twelve? How did you survive?"

"I contracted with the Vasibas and lived in the woods for about two years, in an area between the house I have now, and Danika Market. One day, a guard caught me trying to steal some food and I was taken to the orphanage."

At the mention of Thelic's contract, Maya eyed the leather cuffs at his wrists, frightened to think what the hidden mark below would reveal about his remaining lifespan. "Is that how you met Carnass?"

"Not quite, well I suppose. I was taken to see Carnass after releasing his prized karkili and burying the Keep's stable in a minor earthquake."

"And here I thought *I* was a difficult teenager," she laughed. "Any particular reason?"

"In my defence, it was an accident. I was trying to steal one of the creatures to get back to the woods. When the guards found me, I was frightened and lost control, hence the earthquake. Carnass took a shine to me though, he was quite young then. He offered me a deal – stay and train to be a shifter, and he would give me the land to build a house on the outskirts of town."

"What *is* a shifter? In my world, anyone who said that would be expected to transform into an animal."

"I can't transform into an animal, but we do transform into different roles. Shifters are trained to be hunters, labourers, couriers; but mostly we're utilised as spies or protectors."

"When we were with Carnass, you introduced yourself as his favourite shifter. Were you his bodyguard?"

"At a time, yes. But I spent the three years before this one, spying on the Fortus Keeper."

"The one who killed your father!?"

He nodded his head, a muscle ticking in the hard line of his jaw. "I think Carnass expected me to kill him, and I came close. I was quickly employed as his daughter's protector. It's because of her that I couldn't do it in the end."

Maya's gut tensed, and a sullen curiosity drove her next question. "Were you in love with her?" She prayed he would say no.

"I thought I was, at the beginning. But it wasn't love." He watched Maya subtly exhale the breath she'd been holding. He knew he wasn't in love with Alaara. He hadn't known the meaning of the word, until recently.

The embers sparked to life, a result of the southern breeze or whatever passed between as the couple gazed at one another. Neither moved to stomp it out or drown it. Despite their mutual desire, they hadn't kissed since that night by the water. Maya needed space, and he knew that. They both knew, if they went down this road, she wouldn't just be choosing him, she would be choosing his world.

To Thelic's surprise, she stood up and hobbled over to sit beside him. With the blankets still wrapped around her, she leaned in, laying her head on his shoulder. She had been with Thelic for such a short amount of time, and yet with everything they had been through she felt like she'd known him for years. She felt comfortable, safe, but ultimately on edge. Should she go there? Go that extra step and let these feelings she'd always preferred to tuck away crawl to the surface? At the thought she released a frustrated sigh.

"What's wrong?"

"You're what's wrong!" She threw her arms in the air dramatically, letting the blanket fall from her shoulders. She didn't replace it, figuring the cold air might clear her head.

"What the hell did I do?"

"You...well, you're messing with my head."

"I'm messing with *you*!?"

"Yes. Back home, I had a boyfriend for a while and it was slow, and nice, and sure there was no spark, but it was normal. This, these feelings I have for you, they don't make any sense, Thelic!"

"You're telling me. You turn up out of nowhere, ruin my quiet little life, drag me across the territories, almost get me *killed,* and then you plan to just disappear. What we have isn't anything special, Maya, I realise that now. But it's strong, I've seen it throughout Avalon. Some souls just speak to each other."

Maya rolled her eyes. "Soulmates, right. I struggle to believe there's one person in all the realms that you're destined to be with."

"That's not what Avalonians believe either. There are many potential matches but when you find one, you stick by them, because there's no need to find another. I never believed in this shit, but it makes sense." With a flick of his wrist, earth rose around the fire to fall on the re-kindled flames, once again inviting the dim shade of night. "It's like the sprites, most castors fit with particular ones, it matches them; the same can be said for people."

"That sounds a bit more reasonable, I guess." Calming, she pulled the blankets around them both and returned her head to his shoulder. "What am I supposed to do with that, Thelic? Am I expected to give up my world? My life?"

"No. I know how I feel for you, but you *always* have a choice, Maya."

"I have feelings for you, too," she whispered.

"I know, we just need to figure out what those feelings are." He leant down and kissed her hair. Neither spoke for the rest of their watch, instead listening to Elkin's soft snore, a small noise in the dense confines of the Bloodywood. A creature squawked high in the trees, fleeing from a larger predator, kept at bay from the campsite by the human guardians.

∼

SEVERAL HOURS PASSED and the guard switch was made. Keela was not overly impressed at being woken up but understood the need for two bodies on watch. Crawling from her tent, she took a seat on the blanketed floor, accepting a cold mug of broth from Elkin.

"Did you sleep okay?"

"Well, between yours and the bodaari's snores, it was an intermittent sleep at best, but I got what I needed," she replied honestly.

Elkin and Keela had been close during his service to Bandaar and shared a bed on more than one occasion. But he'd never truly understood what they were; if they *were* more than friends.

"What happened between us?"

"You betrayed your territory and left," she said with a casual shrug. Lifting the last of the broth to her lips, she drained the contents before moving to a small stream running adjacent to the tents. Kneeling amongst the broken twigs and vines that littered the forest floor, Keela took her time, rinsing and re-rinsing the bowl, each dip in the cold water a sobering reminder of what this man had done to her.

Elkin watched the meticulous rhythm at which she worked. She was upset, that much he could recognise easily enough. "I had to, Keela," he stated quietly, rising from the blankets to stand behind her. "If I had stayed, my death was certain."

With her hands still submerged in the icy water, she turned her head slightly up and to the side to glance at him. While he showed no signs of it, he had to be lying. Elkin had always been whimsical, always thinking with anything other than his head. That's what she had always believed; that he had gotten bored and left the territory, left her.

"Go on," she prompted, shaking off the bowl before taking a seat on the blankets.

"My last task, before I left, was to find the Seer," Elkin said, settling in beside her.

"And you failed and thought Bandaar would kill you? He's not inherently evil you know?"

"Let me finish. I found her. I was going to bring her back to Esterbell with me, but she changed my mind. Fatari prophesised my death, told me if I remained under Bandaar's command that I would surely die before my time."

"Did you ever stop to think she was lying to you to save herself?"

"Of course I did, but she convinced me. She told me things about you."

Her head perked up, once again searching his amber eyes for signs of deception. "What things?"

"That you would die with me."

She chortled at that. "You're saying you left to save me? Come on, Elkin, admit it. Things were heating up between us and you got itchy feet." Keela shook her head. "I'll give you this though, that's one of the more inventive excuses I've heard."

"It's not a lie, I valued our friendship–"

"Why didn't you take me with you then? You knew how Bandaar was with me, how he pushed me."

"You wouldn't have left."

"Why do you think I was at the Wright house searching for you?" she seethed, anger resurfacing.

"To bring me back!"

"You fool!" She rose from the ground to stand over him. "I came looking for you because I wanted to go *with* you. I would have left everything behind!" Grabbing her blanket, she strode angrily from the firepit. "You like being alone so much, you can stay out here by yourself," she spat, and disappeared through the canvas flap of her tent. With no intention to go back to sleep, she took to cleaning her weapons, cursing the man who had broken her heart.

Elkin wallowed in the discovery of what he'd done. If only he'd known, everything would have been so different, *he* would have been different; but it was too late now. Fate's path was set and there was nothing he could do to change that.

DAWN BROKE and with it the Bloodywood returned to life. The smaller creatures remerged noisily from their hidey-holes, a refuge from the larger night-time predators. Despite this, the wood still held its dusk-enshrouded persona, the only light being that which managed to break through intermittent cracks in the canopy.

Breaking camp, Thelic was sent into Brushkin to resupply. The small town's position on the woodland outskirts meant it was bare of travellers and most of its trade remained within the town. This benefitted the group as they were less likely to come across any guards. Still, hesitant to take risks, the remainder waited in the shadowed confines of the forest for Thelic to return with the purchased goods.

The voyage from Brushkin's Break to the southern point of Esterbell would take them another half day through the wood. So, they settled onto the fed and rested creatures with hopes of an uninterrupted journey.

The night's events hung heavily on each of the travellers' minds at what had been revealed. Even Jacob rode in silence, his own thoughts crowded with what was to come. Where would this gateway lead him? How would he get home? Was he a coward to leave Maya and this chaotic world behind?

The dim light of the canopy brightened slowly as they

approached the southern edge of the Bloodywood. Past the treeline, a large expanse of ice stood between them and the snow-covered mountains over the channel to the south. From here they would move west, across the ice to Cantor's flat lands. The great freeze groaned in welcome. Daring its desperate contestants to try their luck.

11
THE ICE PASSAGE AND THE
TRIBAL ELDER

ESTERBELL ~ CANTOR

"This is a bad idea," Keela muttered.

"You have a better one?"

"Yes, Maya. We drag your ass back to Bandaar and you two can hash it out."

"That's nice. Why are you here again?"

"You two, cut it out and help us," Thelic said. He and Elkin were unloading their gear from Keero to pack smaller and more manageable backpacks. The karkili had already been released of their harnesses, now grazing on some lower trees nearby.

"We're just going to leave Keero here? By himself? Will he be ok?" Maya asked. She'd grown fond of the bodaari and hated the idea of leaving him alone to fend for himself.

"In this area, Keero is one of the biggest creatures around. He's saved my neck against meaner things than what he might find here. He'll be fine," Thelic assured her. Though Keero could find his way home, Thelic would miss his friend. The only remaining concern wasn't the other beasts in the wood, but the bodaari himself. Thelic knew that Keero would likely stay in the area to wait for their return, and he was increasingly unsure if they would make it back.

On foot, their trek over the ice would take longer than the water crossing between Danika and Esterbell. Elkin's previous excursion had taken him a quarter day, but with a group this size, he expected it would likely take them longer.

"Right, let's go over some safety tips and tricks, shall we?" Elkin addressed the others. "Just a couple of things to look out for. First, stick to blue ice, it'll be thicker there; Second, if you see logs or anything protruding, stay away from it; Finally, if the ice starts to crack, get low, spread out your body weight and try to roll away from the area."

With bags packed, Elkin took the lead several paces in front of the others and stepped onto the glacier. It groaned and creaked under his weight but held. Keela on the other hand, chose to take up the rear, her theory being that – if it could take the four people in front, then she would be fine.

A ferocious wind from the mountains ripped across the icy plains and whipped up the loose snow to batter the travellers. As they reached an old quarter waypoint marker, the storm had thundered over the peaks to unleash its torrent. But they couldn't afford to stop. Being caught on the ice at dark would mean walking blind.

To their left, toward the mountains, Thelic spotted movement from the shoreline. Outlanders. The storm was likely keeping them at bay, but he kept a wary eye nonetheless, in case they decided to risk it. Further ahead, Elkin had seen something that worried him more. Enormous shards of ice had frozen, standing on their ends to tower up vertically. Something had broken through from beneath. Only two creatures could survive the severe conditions of the southern frost, and he wasn't keen on their group facing either.

Thanks to Brijid's powders and the pain medication from Brushkin's Break, Maya's leg was doing much better than the day before. Nevertheless, powering through the storm was proving to be a challenge. Thelic, wary of this, walked at her side with Jacob just ahead. Despite their blood ties, he didn't trust Keela to step in and help if it became necessary.

They passed the halfway marker. The sun was low, and it wouldn't be long before it dipped out of sight. They were running out of time. Elkin increased his pace, confident that Thelic and Keela would bring up the rear.

They passed the final quarter-point marker. The outlanders had been tracking them but remained on the shore.

What are they waiting for? Elkin wondered. He'd spotted their stalkers at the halfway point and had been on high alert ever since. It was unlikely the outlanders had managed to set a trap for them on the ice, but he wasn't taking any chances.

The ground rumbled.

Elkin raised a hand, but everyone had already stopped at the shudder. A huge shadow passed under the ice, beneath their feet. If Maya didn't know better, she'd have thought it was a whale, but she was slowly coming to grips with the Avalonian philosophy that, if it's not human, it's probably going to try and kill you.

CRACK.

The ice beneath Elkin fractured but didn't break. He was sure the creature below was a shropsin and prayed it wasn't a Finkel in shropsin form. The sun caressed the horizon, its final rays painting the world above the shoreline an amber red.

They were close.

The beast was circling the water beneath them, its body large enough to swallow a raker's ship. They waited, barely breathing, for Elkin's command. In the water it was fast, faster than any human, but on the ice they could outrun it. The beast disappeared into the depths.

"Now! Spread Out!" Elkin bellowed to the others behind him.

Watching Elkin run forward and to the left, Thelic grabbed Jacob and Maya, dragging them to the right. Unsure what to do, Keela bolted forward. The shadow shot from the ice, large shards splintering upwards as the shropsin broke through. Keela had been above as the ice sheet broke, its momentum throwing her clear into the air. With nothing to break her fall, she landed several feet away, with a bone-jarring thud.

The shropsin's rubbery, fluorescent skin rippled in tune with its roar. Using the claws at the tips of the two front winged fins, the beast dragged its impressive form onto the surface of the glacier. The tail whipped menacingly, its length – down to a webbed fin – decorated with curved barbs. It had been too long since the creature had eaten, and these five travellers would do well to fill a hungry winter belly. The shropsin swayed its long neck from side to side, evaluating the closest target.

Keela.

"Run to the shoreline!"

Spurred into action by Elkin's command, the group bolted.

The shropsin's dorsal fin fluttered with excitement, and it gave chase. Adequately equipped for the glassy surface, the creature was closing the gap on Keela, its talons cutting into the icy surface blasting her with frozen shards as it gained.

"Hey!" Just behind Elkin, Jacob stopped and raised his arms to flag down the beast.

As they caught up, Thelic tried to grab him, to drag him along with them. Maya intervened, instead spurring on her brother.

"You've got this," she called, dragging Thelic towards the shore.

Jacob continued to wave his arms as Keela and the shropsin drew closer. Just as she passed, he scurried between her and the creature, switching its attention. The blue giant shuddered to a halt, preparing to snap up its prey, but Jacob danced to the right and ran, staying parallel to the shoreline.

This new, more playful game excited the creature, and it resumed the hunt. Jacob stayed ahead with ease before once again veering right to circle back around and meet the group on land. The shropsin, too large to make chase through the densely packed treeline, wailed in anguish at being cheated of its meal, and crashed back through the ice to its murky depths.

"Guess all those track medals actually stood for something then," Maya laughed breathlessly, hugging her brother. Jacob smiled back, adrenaline and relief coursing through him.

Keela stepped forward, awkwardly reappraising their tag-along. "I owe you my life. That was reckless and idiotic… thank you." She wasn't accustomed to relying on others. Nevertheless, Keela had felt her last moments under the breath of the shropsin, and was grateful to be alive.

"It's going to cost you I'm afraid," Jacob said, accepting a water satchel from Maya.

"Oh?" Keela said, her eyebrow raised as she crossed her arms defensively. "And what, exactly, is my life worth to you?"

"Two things. First, stop looking so damned miserable all the time. And second, you owe Maya."

"Ridiculous," she replied, miserably; but nodded in understanding. He was scared she was going to betray them, and with good reason.

Away from the shore and out the other side of the small wood, there was little protection from the elements. Cantor was known as the 'Flat Lands', a simple farming nation, most of whom had contracted with lower-level earth sprites. This meant that, despite its frigid climes, the territory was ripe with pastures and very little forestry.

The group soon set up camp, huddling beneath blankets in their tents, the harsh elements and need for stealth denying them the comfort of a fire. Jacob took the first watch, as promised, and used the time to contemplate his return to normalcy.

THE FOLLOWING MORNING, the storm had died down, and the air was clear and crisp. Conscious of their wounds from the previous few days, the group remained in camp to address them.

Maya groaned, unwinding the bandages to reveal snapped sutures in her leg, a result of their marathon across the ice.

Keela watched as Maya removed a small sewing kit from the medical pouch. "You can't stitch that again," she said. Moving to her side, she noted the hardened edge of the healing wound. "You would risk trapping what's already healed under the new stitching. Do that, and you'll almost certainly incur a sinus, then a cyst, and then probably die of infection."

Despite her reservations, Maya was impressed. "How do you suggest I treat it?"

"It needs to be wrapped securely and kept clean and covered." Keela reached into the pouch and removed the cleansing tonics. Kneeling, she dabbed the ointment onto a clean piece of cloth and moved to place it on Maya's leg, before catching herself. Maya's deep green eyes bore into hers, assessing but grateful. "I had a similar injury several years ago, and I know people who have died from these infections," Keela offered sheepishly in explanation.

Maya continued to stare as Keela worked on her leg, cleaning the edges with each tonic in a precise order. "Thank you," she said, earnestly, with a responding grunt from Keela that it was no trouble. The growing relationship between sisters would be slow, but this was progress.

Elkin attended to Thelic's shoulder, providing the same hydrotherapy treatment he'd applied at the Wrights' home. Thelic rolled the joint satisfyingly, the pain barely an echo of what it had been only days before. Jacob's head, too, was faring well, and the bandages were removed with only a large scab remaining.

Digging into his backpack, Thelic revealed a map of the region indicating the journey to Cantor's gateway would take them less than half a day.

"You've had that this whole time?" Maya asked, grabbing the thick parchment from him. "I thought you were leading us by memory." With worn ends from over-handling, the world's features were beautifully drawn. Creatures and words melded along its edges in handwritten notes and drawings. Each of the five territories were marked as being their own island, all encircling one unmarked landmass in the centre. Surrounding the territories were mountainous areas and then nothing, only a roughly scribbled shadow encompassing the region, disconnected from the rest of their world.

"I knew where I was going then, but I'm unfamiliar with Cantor. Hence, the map," he said, snatching it back from her.

"I'm relatively well acquainted with Northern Cantor, however I found the women of the South to be as cold as their environment, so I tend to avoid it." Elkin shivered at a memory.

"Are we to expect any dark and mystical forests, Claw-bearing ice beasts, or disturbingly clingy hookers on this leg of the journey?" Maya asked her two guides, hands on her hips, the corner of her mouth pulled up in a light tease.

"Outlanders have been said to frequent this territory, if that helps?" Keela offered.

"Typical," Maya scoffed with a dramatic eye-roll.

"I can't wait for you to see Transum, it's glorious!" Elkin said.

"Bordello central I presume?" Maya couldn't think of anything else that would put a grin like that on his face.

"Only the best! It's an Avalonian Metropolis, I would live there if I didn't have a bounty on my head."

"Dare I ask?"

"Nothing major, I accidentally set fire to a bordello when we were…experimenting with candles," he said with a wink and nudge to Maya.

Jacob was quiet. As they set off, he'd remained at the back of the group, lost in thought. Maya was teasing Thelic about his crude drawings on the map when she noticed her brother several steps behind. She motioned to the others to carry on and fell back to speak to him.

"I smell smoke, so clearly you're overthinking something."

He looked up from his feet to Maya, her eyes bright.

She was excited for Jacob to return to their world and determined to get him there in one piece. "What's going on in that head of yours?"

"I'm scared," he admitted, dropping his head once again.

"To travel through the gateway? You know Dad's number. Find a phone and call him as soon as you get there. Or, if you wake up somewhere dangerous, come back through and we'll take you back to the portal in Danika."

"I'm scared for *you*, Maya."

That caught her off-guard, but she could understand why. This world hadn't been particularly welcoming over the short amount of time since they had arrived.

"You're strong, I know that but, we already lost Mum. I can't lose my sister too."

Maya stopped to wrap him in a hug. "You're not going to lose me. Gran would kill me if I died," she chuckled, trying to ease the tension.

They walked, arms linked for the rest of the journey. Together they reminisced about the times Jacob's father had scolded them for venturing too far from home, or Yali had sulked after a poor training session. Jaseen's disappearance had been the only thing to truly darken their childhood, an event that left a scar so deep, Maya had pulled back slightly. She regretted that now.

Across the open fields, they could see the fog-enshrouded wood from several miles away as it grew with their approach. The sight was just as it was in Danika, the shifting purple miasma an impenetrable force to Avalonians. Upon reaching its edge, Jacob's rucksack was re-packed to include a satchel of meat and some water along with his tent, just in case. Elkin dragged Thelic over to wrap their departing friend in a sandwich hug, offering hopes that he would return one day when it was safe to visit. Keela grunted a goodbye before laying on the grass, using her bag as a makeshift pillow. With assurances to the others to return once her brother had safely crossed, Maya and Jacob passed through the veil.

Frustrated by his inability to follow, Thelic stood silently and watched, waiting.

∾

MAYA COULD FEEL the gateway the moment they stepped through the mist, its energy guiding her gently through the forest trees. It wasn't long before they came across a small lake, its essence a pulsating beacon. Protected by the layers of

saplings and shrubbery, the water was peaceful, uninterrupted by the howling winds beyond its barrier.

"Where do you think it will spit me out?" Jacob asked,
each foot like a lead weight as it plodded through the dense
undergrowth.

"I don't know, but if you're in danger, just come back
through. I'll wait beyond the veil with the others tonight, so
you have plenty of time to get back to us."

He felt better at that. He wasn't scared the first time. It
was only when the water completely devoured him that he
felt true fear, like he was dying. He grabbed Maya, desperately pulling her to his chest. "I love you so much. *Please* be
careful."

She leaned into him, the reality that she may never see
Jacob again nipping at her conscience. "I will, pinkie-
promise."

Leaving her side, Jacob stepped into the icy water and the
lake began its powerful glow. As before, ripples turned to
waves that dipped in a whirlpool to surround him, rising to
envelop the traveller in its embrace. Maya stepped forward,
her instincts screaming to save him, to protect him from the
element. With a flash of light, he was sucked down into its
depths; gone.

Slumping to the floor, the tears she had kept at bay for so
long erupted into sobs that racked her body. The masked
smile and light humour replaced with despair in the privacy
of the empty wood. He was safe now, away from this roguish
and treacherous world. She had considered, for a moment,
following him through to their family. But Maya had made a
promise, to send him home and go to Fatari. There was too
much she didn't know, too much to do; and there was Thelic.
At least Jacob could go back to university and study to be the
doctor he always wanted to be. To Maya, his presence here
had been home, she hadn't felt so far away. With his depar-

ture and Jaseen's death, an overwhelming loneliness ached inside her.

After several moments, she picked herself up off the forest floor and wiped her tears as she began the short walk back to the others.

A branch cracked underfoot somewhere behind. She spun and took the blade Thelic had purchased at Brushkin on her behalf from the thin belt at her waist. Despite its small size, she appreciated the feel of the weapon now.

A woman stepped from behind one of the trees, smiling. Branches cracked to Maya's right; her left; she was surrounded. The woman held up a hand, instructing those in the shadows to remain where they were and walked towards Maya. She was an outlander, an old one. Tattooed, cobalt runes marred the sunken cheeks of the old being, her long and simple blue dress dragging along the floor as she moved.

"Bugger this," Maya muttered. The woman was too close now, and Maya held out the dagger with a warning shout. "Do *not* come any closer."

Long, white hair fanned the woman's face to flow behind as she continued her approach.

BEYOND THE VEIL, Thelic continued to pace along the spot where Maya and Jacob had entered the wood. He stopped at the muffled shout.

"Fuck!" No longer concerned by the miasma, he darted into the woodline. Within two steps he crashed to the floor, choking, every breath a shard of glass.

In the same instant, two sets of hands lifted him to his feet and dragged him back. Keela and Elkin had held their breath, but the fog's toxicity provoked a similar effect to the eyes. Breaking through the mist, they all collapsed, crippled by the poison.

. . .

MAYA STEPPED BACK; she'd watched these people, or ones like them, rip into that poor village in the Bloodywood like a hurricane. "I said, stay there!" She had to maintain some distance between them. Fighting a single outlander was one thing, but there were possibly a number of them. If they attacked, her best chance would be to get to the others outside the fog. "What do you want?"

"Please, Mayara, I just want to talk."

Her name. Only those closest knew its true form. "How do you know me? Did Bandaar send you?"

"That cretin has nothing to do with my being here," the old woman harrumphed, slighted by the implied association. "I've been waiting for your return. I'm sorry we couldn't get to your mother in time to save her."

At the mention of Jaseen, Maya stopped. "Who the hell *are* you? And how are you here, in the fog?"

"I'm a Tribal Elder, one of many," she admitted humbly. "But I had to get you alone. We've been following you since your arrival in Danika."

"Why me? And how do you know all of this?" The idea that these things had tracked the group, unnoticed since Danika, sent shivers up her back.

"There is too much to explain and too little time," the woman insisted desperately. "Fatari will explain all when you see her, but for now, please know that my people mean you no harm."

"I was already heading that way–"

"You must hurry, Mayara. She is fading, and it won't be long before she transcends this realm, all realms, for good."

"I don't understand."

"Just trust that we are your allies, my kin will accompany you from the shadows for the rest of your journey. The human are too untrusting of our kind for them to travel with you in plain sight."

"I'm not sure if you heard, but the last outlander I met tried to kill me." Maya gestured to the still healing crack across her lower lip.

"I know. My tribe is currently hunting his group. He will pay for his offence. You and all the Avalonians – the humans – have been misled. Go to Fatari. We will see each other again, soon." With a departing smile, the old outlander turned and walked away, fading into the mist.

12

OUTLANDISH WARNINGS

CANTOR

Maya ran through the forest and broke past the fog barrier, straight into a hard chest. Rubbing her nose, she looked up to find the chest belonged to Thelic. He was angry, his eyes red and swollen.

"Why are you crying?" she asked. Beyond the looming mass of muscle, Keela and Elkin lay on the grass, a wet cloth covering each of their faces. "What the hell happened to you guys?"

"We heard you shout and went in to find you!" Thelic yelled, anger outweighing his initial concern. He knew it was misplaced, but at the time, he'd never felt so helpless.

"Correction," Keela said, removing the cloth from her eyes, equally as teary and blood-shot. "This senseless meat stick ran into the fog. *We–*" she waved dramatically between herself and Elkin, "–pulled his sorry ass out before he choked to death!"

"So, little fulsin?" Elkin asked. "We were quite alarmed. What was it that startled you?"

"Outlanders."

"What!?" the three warriors jumped to attention,

weapons drawn, Thelic stepping protectively between Maya and the fog.

"Behave, you lot. They're gone. Well, sort of." At the chorus of raised brows demanding an explanation, Maya told them of Jacob's departure, her promise to wait one night, and the impromptu meeting with the old tribal leader.

"They're planning to shadow us?" Keela asked, checking her surroundings.

"How did they walk through the miasma when only a moment of it damn near killed us?" Thelic wondered aloud.

"I don't know, but then, I don't really understand why I can walk through it either."

"What else did they say?" Elkin asked.

"Just that we have to get to Fatari as soon as possible. Apparently, she's dying."

"It might be a trick; they could be using us to locate her hiding place. You can't trust outlanders, Maya," Keela insisted.

"Yes, but according to whom?" Thelic had always found the origins of outlanders to be a bit hazy. They were brought up as children to fear and despise the inhuman mutations.

"According to our history," Keela began, confused by the question. "They've always hated our kind. They started this war in the first place and wonder why we fight back!" She went on to explain how, according to Avalonian history, passed down from the generation of the Five Majors, outlanders have been the epitome of malevolent casting. Their powers employed to try and drive the humans away, unwilling to share their world any longer. "Since the first war, their aim has always been to destroy the gateways and anyone that manages to make it through."

Elkin nodded along in agreement with Keela's retelling. "It's rumoured that some of the outlanders, those that shed blood by elemental means, anger the Gouram, the most powerful of the sprites. In retaliation, the essence of all outlanders has since been corrupted."

Maya thought of her mother's warning, about the sprites or demons from her world. From the sounds of it, Jaseen had sided with the outlanders. But why was that left out of Avalonian history? Was her mother wrong? Possibly sensing Maya's growing distress, the windy Finkel popped out of thin air and wisped across her shoulders, burying its face in her neck.

Keela's blade was out and soaring towards the sprite before Maya could blink. It brushed just below her ear, where the creature had been nuzzling. Keela missed and the Finkel reappeared in her face, baring its fangs at the insult.

"Keela, no!" Maya screamed. "It's a friend, I swear it won't hurt you."

Elkin scoffed at that. His memory of their previous altercation with the sprite begged to differ.

"Hey, come over here, ignore the mean lady," Maya beckoned it back to her side, stroking the thick fur upon its return.

"That thing was there, in Esterbell, at the Keep!" Keela remembered the violent maelstrom that the Finkel's energy had conjured at Maya's command. "I don't understand. Why is it *not* trying to kill you?"

"It's just a little mischievous, we're working on that. I was thinking of calling him Loki, after the God of Mischief."

"I've never heard of that god, is it a sprite too?" Elkin asked, intrigued.

Maya laughed and offered the cliff-notes version of the mythological Norse God.

"It suits him," Thelic decided. He moved forward to stroke the newly named Finkel, who'd reclaimed his spot across Maya's shoulders. Thelic lingered there, stroking Maya's neck before leaning in to whisper in her ear. "I won't be letting you out of my sight again." Especially now, knowing the outlanders were immune to the fog, and shadowing them.

Maya flushed, heated by his touch and the distress that remained in the crinkle of his eyes.

~

THE NEXT MORNING, Maya was hesitant to leave, concerned her brother would return to find them gone. With one final glance at the wood, she gave the nod for their journey to continue, north to Cantor's Keep.

"Why north? The outlanders told me to go to Fatari, but I forgot to ask them where exactly she is," Maya said as she readjusted the heavy backpack.

"I know a man in Transum, he can point us in the right direction," Elkin assured her.

Unlike Esterbell, which boasted several ports around the island, Cantor claimed only one. Produce would be brought from all reaches of the territory to the Keep's major town, where the harbour would buzz with the daily commotion of exporting their goods to the remainder of the islands.

As they journeyed, Elkin mostly regaled them of his sexcapades within the small capital, insisting that, despite its small size, its overall quality was unquestionable. To the untrained eye, the six-foot, scruffy sourcer was nothing more than the average womaniser; but Maya had come to learn that Elkin loved in his own way. All of his companions they'd come to meet had loved him back, but to a degree that suggested they weren't led to believe more than was possible. Except Keela. Maya was sure a deeper history lay between the two Esterbellians.

A long winding road branching off in different directions every few miles was their route to the Keep. It was sign-posted, and carts hauling vegetables of foreign shapes, colours, and smells, continued to pass them on a regular basis.

As one of the first towns rose from the distance, tall posts bordered the roadside. Upon closer inspection, severed hands had been nailed to their wooden sides. Colours sprung from the crisp red of blood that spattered the post, some a cobalt blue, all with long fingers and talons at their tips. Maya, having stepped closer to investigate, jumped back in recognition of the outlanders' hands.

"That's new...and mildly disturbing," Elkin remarked, not as bothered by the sight. To him, to all Avalonians, the outlanders had always been the enemy.

"This territory, along with Esterbell and Fortus have been preparing for war with the outlanders all year. This is a warning," Keela said, regarding the body parts with disinterest.

"Why now?" Thelic asked. He'd heard rumbles around Fortus before he'd left their service last year, but nothing to suggest an all-out war.

"Bandaar believes they've renewed their efforts to destroy the gateways."

"To trap the demons, like my mother said?" Jaseen had been adamant in Esterbell, that the gateways had to be closed to stop the foreign sprites from breaching this realm.

"Ha! That's an old folk's tale, Maya. Conjured up by the outlanders to justify trying to rid this world of humans. Bandaar believes they want rid of the gateways to weaken the Avalonians before a strike. He simply wants to protect his people," Keela said, shrugging. She had no reason to believe otherwise.

This confirmed Maya's theory. Two competing histories seemed to have been written regarding this realm, with both sides willing to go to war over them. "That's why there were so many guards in Esterbell, and the young castors..."

"Yes, they too are part of the war preparations." That was the only part of her father's rhetoric Keela had felt conflicted over; they were just children, too young and ill- prepared for combat.

The markers continued all the way to a minor settlement, some featuring different body parts of their alleged enemies.

Maya felt sick. The cold, Cantorian air seemed to slow the rate of decomposition, but the smell of rotting flesh renewed with every passing.

Hands.

Feet.

A severed head.

Maya was no stranger to death or body parts. Being a policewoman, she'd seen more dead bodies than she would have liked. But the sheer brutality of these messages and their actors' indifference disturbed her.

It had begun to snow now; the beautifully thick, crystallised flakes painting the green world a majestic, clean white, temporarily blanketing the mottled red of the dismembered body parts.

Elkin whispered a welcome to the small town of Stiks, warning everyone to stay alert. Passing beyond the wooden gates, they were met with hard, assessing looks.

The area was bustling with its townsfolk going about their daily lives. Farmers hurried from shop front to shopfront, seeking the best price for their goods. Children played in the streets, weaving in and out between the carts and karkili. The houses themselves were nothing like that of Danika and Esterbell. Made of stone, they stood bare of the colour seen in Danika; these dwellings simple and fit for purpose. The snow had grown thick by the time they passed the final pillar to coat the already dull town; the barren features and cold stares an unnerving combination.

"Hello there." A woman stepped from behind a cart to

address the newcomers. She was younger than her appearance suggested – a result of the hard, Cantorian lifestyle – but approached the strangers with a confidence beyond her years. "You folk aren't from around here." It wasn't a question. Her eyes, hard and calculating, belied the smile she wore.

Thelic and Keela, too busy assessing the threat of the woman and four additional men, didn't answer. It was Elkin that stepped forward to meet their host. "You're right, we've travelled from Esterbell."

The woman's expression said she didn't buy it.

With a tight smile, Elkin continued. "We came from the ice passage in the south, we're a bit short on coin and couldn't afford the extortionate prices of Esterbellian waterrakers," he offered in explanation for their risky choice of route.

She considered that a moment. "I see. The weather down that way was good last night I hear, perfect for the passage."

She was trying to catch them out.

"I'm not sure who told you that, it was terrible. Luckily, I've travelled that way many a time, and the quarter waypoint markers are still in good enough condition to guide." The test had been double edged, only a handful of travellers knew about the waypoints; those who didn't and thought to cross the ice either changed their mind or perished.

"Right," she mumbled, checking each of their hands and faces for tell-tale signs. "Don't suppose you came across any outlanders on the way?" At the question, the four men inched forward, ready to grab any potential information or imprison any sympathisers.

"No," Maya replied, something in her tone catching the woman's attention. Thelic shifted closer, his hand hovering over the spear, the blade's cloth removed the moment they had been waylaid.

"Well, we didn't *meet* any, is what she means; but we think we might have seen some, in the mountain regions south of the ice."

The woman looked to the two men on the right and nodded her head. Without a word they left to hunt. "Thank you, and sorry. Can't be too careful these days," she laughed, the smile finally touching her eyes.

"I've been to this town in the past, and it was never this…"

"Scared? Paranoid? Unwelcoming?" she offered, finishing Elkin's thought and chuckling for his attempt at courtesy. "We've had a number of outlander attacks recently. Many of the townsfolk have had to abandon their homes and livelihood for fear of being targeted."

"Would they be so brash, or stupid, to wander into a town though?" Keela asked.

"We caught one, wearing gloves to hide her hands and paint to conceal the runes. I'm sure you've already met her, in fact, on your way into town."

The severed head.

Maya looked away, lost in thought. The Elder had seemed genuine. Why spin the tale that Avalonians were misled, that she meant them no harm, when her people continued to seek war with Avalon? Either way, she was beginning to learn that, for a farming people, the citizens of Cantor were brutally intent on their mission; indoctrinated from a young age to dispel or dismember their decided enemies.

With assurances that they simply intended to pass through on their way to Cantor's Keep, the woman and her militia granted them access. Thelic had originally intended to buy a couple of karkili at the town with the last of their coin. Elkin's lie to the woman, however, was built on the foundation that they were poor. With their observers still in sight, the idea was abandoned, and they quickly departed the hostile village.

WITHOUT THE KARKILI, the journey to Cantor's major town had taken them two days longer than they'd hoped. Upon their arrival, the travellers were cold, hungry, and desperately tired. After sleeping in tents on the open plains, exposure to the bleakness of Cantor's weather system had left them raw. So, as traffic began to develop on the road into the Keep's bordering town, they were relieved and eager to find a guesthouse within which to rest.

The Cantorian city was similar to its smaller counterpart, with houses lacking flair, and market abuzz. Unlike the other Keeps, there was no wall to separate the leader from his or her people, but it remained an impressive fortress none-theless. A long staircase ascended its front facing wall, reaching two stories up. At the top, a large, wooden double-door with wrought iron hinges framed the entrance – wide enough to fit two bodaari side by side. Above that, on the highest level, a pagoda featured at its pinnacle, a guard station. Standing against the boring and monotonous town, it was easily the most striking structure in Cantor.

Amongst the throng of citizens crowding the wide streets, more guards were interlaced patrolling the town. Maya and the others pulled their hoods forward to conceal themselves, unsure if Bandaar's men might be hiding amongst the masses.

Elkin guided the weary group to a small tavern just outside of the town centre. Inside was dark and musty, but the rooms were clean and featured a bed and bath. Low on money and intent on saving some for their karkili, Thelic and

Elkin shared a room, allowing Maya and Keela one each to themselves.

Without a moment to waste, Maya ran a bath and stripped, stepping into the bubbles of hot soapy water, finally relaxing. As the steam billowed around her, she sank further into the deep tub, sleep overcoming her.

Strong, calloused hands lifted her arms as someone shouted her name, waking her roughly.

"Hey! Can you hear me?"

"The whole goddamn town can hear you, Thelic!" Wet hair clung to her face, and she realised where she was. He had knocked on the door but with no answer he'd been concerned and entered to find Maya half asleep.

"Well what kind of idiotic…you are just so…" He groaned and pushed back from the tub, swiping at the long, stubborn wisps of auburn hair hanging down to brush the side of his face. With neither the time nor the inclination to stop at a barber during their travels, his hair had grown slightly, a short stubble handsomely peppering his face.

"I don't know how the contraptions on your side work, but here it's simple; you sleep in the bath, you drown in the bath."

"No, it works pretty much the same way in my realm too," she said wistfully. "Except our water system is automatic and takes a lot less work."

Thelic moved to sit on the bed. Maya, increasingly aware of her nakedness, grabbed the towel from the chair at the side of the tub.

"Why didn't you leave?"

Maya knew what he meant. Admittedly she had been tempted to follow Jacob through the portal. Her world was safer, more familiar; whereas this world couldn't seem to decide on how best to make a meal of her.

"I couldn't. Not while knowing you…and everyone else were there waiting for me."

"So, you stayed for me?" He looked up from his clasped hands with a grin.

"You *might* have had a small – a *very* small – part to play in my decision to stay," she admitted, grinning back.

Thelic rose from the bed. Within two long strides he was in front of her, and their mouths collided. They had barely eaten for the last two days, but it wasn't the need for food that drove their hunger, it was each other.

Gripping the backs of her thighs, he lifted her from the deep tub to wrap her legs around his waist. Fingers raked through his hair as her kisses trailed a line across his neck. Moving to the bed, he lay her still wet body on the rough sheets, the shirt pulled from his back and flung carelessly across the room. She fumbled with the button at his waist, jilted by the fact that she was the only one bare of clothes. He stepped away to remove the bottoms and knelt to place his head between her legs.

The world dropped away, the only thing left – Maya and this man, whom she was coming to love so unquestionably it frightened her. She gripped the sheets, starved of the attention she desired from him night after night, coming hard and fast at the command of his skilled tongue. Before the wave could subside, he was inside her.

He, too, had craved and wanted to hold Maya, to ravish and possess her. She flipped him onto his back, taking control of the pace; wanting more, telling him she needed more. He growled in tune with his own rising climax, flipping their positions to take the lead once again, and she was happy to relinquish as he brought them both to a shattering finale.

Exhausted from their travels and their tryst, they collapsed next to each other on the bed, weary but content.

Breath back, Thelic rolled on to his side to face Maya. During her fight with Bandaar, or possibly before then, he'd only suspected. But since that day at Cantor's gateway, when she returned to him, he knew then, that it was Maya who utterly possessed *him*.

13
OLD FLAMES AND MASQUERADES

CANTOR

The following morning, Maya woke to an empty bed. After dinner at the inn, Thelic had stayed with her that night, and they'd made love again and again, stopping only when exhaustion demanded it of them.

Love, she thought, shaking her head at the absurdity of falling so quickly. But if the light, knotted butterflies in her stomach were anything to go by, there was no denying it. Back at the gateway, when she had considered following her brother, Thelic's face had hung in her mind. That, and the promise to her mother. She sighed and dispelled the heavy thoughts, burying beneath the coarse blankets of the bed.

The door to Maya's room opened.

"I could join you?"

Under the covers, her stomach flipped again to the sound of Thelic's voice, more so to his offer. She pulled the sheet down just enough to see his tall frame filling the entrance. Elkin, ambled up to stand beside him, an arm lacing across his friend's shoulders.

"Well, I don't know about you two, but I slept fabulously last night." He winked at Maya, who flipped the sheet back over her head, mortified he may have heard their midnight activities.

"Actually, as much as I'd love to crawl back under there with you, we have a lot to get through today," Thelic said, his eyes grazing the thin sheet that left little of Maya's figure to the imagination.

A long, drawn out sigh emanated from the bed. "Fine. Go away, I need to bathe and change," she moaned.

THE GROUP MET downstairs and shared some breakfast before heading out. With funds dwindling, Elkin and Keela would look for two days work and they'd stay at the inn a second night. Maya offered to try and find work in one of their places and Keela laughed so loud and hard, the man behind her jumped, choking on his bread. Maya's hand twitched with the temptation to summon Loki, stopped only by Elkin who explained the technical training required for the services they intended to offer. Instead, Maya and Thelic would re-supply and find some karkili to continue their journey.

Cantor's streets and eastern houses were bathed in dawn's soft, orange glow by the time they left the inn, with the capital's many inhabitants spilling onto the streets. By Avalonian standards, the major town was modestly built, but teemed with humans and their creatures going about their daily routine. Children raced their friends to the scholarly hall; men and women to their jobs; and the rare elderly – cared for by the Keeper's pension – took to having a leisurely stroll.

With their shopping notes in hand, the first stop on their route was the bladesmith. Keela had listed this as her only request, for the couple to have her weapons serviced before they left the territory. Thelic was also keen to have his spear sharpened and replace Maya's small weapon for one of better quality.

Cantor's market was divided into sections, separating the stalls that sold fine, Transumian silks from the marketeers offering a myriad of delectable treats. Seeing the food on offer, their breakfast porridge at the inn was a woeful comparison. Thelic marched through the square, stopping only at the stalls which offered what they needed. Maya, as usual, dragged her heels behind him; savouring the rich mix of sweetened scents, potent enough to rouse the five senses.

Elkin's list was not quite so plain. They would need enduring ingredients for their meals on the road: cured meats, dried vegetables, herbs, spices, and stock powders. Additionally, bold letters at the bottom of the list read: *WINE*. Maya followed, watching closely as Thelic carefully chose those fruits and vegetables suited for travel.

Their final stop was the village stables. Three rows of long, wooden barns lined the paddocks on the town's outskirts. Here, the trees and lawns alike faced a perpetual battle for vitality, a fight often lost against the harsh Cantorian temperature. Nevertheless, several karkili roamed lazily, grazing on what remained of the withered grass.

In search of the owner, Thelic left Maya to admire the odd creatures. He walked from structure to structure, peering inside and calling out. As he reached the last, a petite redhead exited through the door and ran straight into him, bouncing backwards onto the floor at his feet. Mumbling an apology, he reached down to help her stand. Their eyes met and recognition flashed in both.

"Alaara?" Thelic said, surprised at seeing the young woman in such a place.

Stunned, she remained seated for a moment longer before taking his hand. "How are you, Thelic?" She brushed her long skirts, avoiding his eyes to hide her shock.

Without answering her question, Thelic looked around before asking, "Where's your guard? Your father wouldn't allow you outside in your *own* territory without one, never mind travelling here."

"He's by the paddock." She studied Thelic longingly. His hair had grown slightly, and his hands held new scars. But he was still her Thelic. "He's a bit of a brute though, I much preferred having *you* as my shadow."

Thelic nodded his head, unsure what to say. They'd parted ways not long before he'd returned to Danika. Spying on Jaxum had taken its toll. Despite Thelic's efforts, being so close to his father's executioner had opened those old wounds and he was forced to leave his post, before acting on the dark thoughts that swelled at the Fortus Keeper's presence. By that point, Alaara had been falling in love with him, with the idea of him. Thelic had grown to realise what they had wasn't a match, wasn't love, so he'd let her down as gently as he could.

She continued. "So, who are you shadowing now?"

"One of Carnass' investments." It wasn't a lie, Carnass had a vested interest in Maya. But under Alaara's kind and sweet exterior, lay a spoilt and often jealous persona.

"Danika's Keeper? I suppose that means you'll be coming to Sika's gathering tonight?"

Sika, Cantor's Keeper, supposedly one of the strongest earth wielders in Avalon. One of the few bound to a Finkel sprite. So far, two of the five Keepers knew of Maya and her abilities, he wanted to keep that number as low as possible.

"Not likely, she isn't fond of festivities and has no relation with Sika."

"Ah, so you shadow another *woman* now." Alaara slipped behind Thelic and wrapped her hands around his waist, whispering into the space between his shoulder blades. "Does she please you like I once did?"

Thelic removed her hands to pull her in front of him. "You need to move on, Alaara. I was under your father's service and a toy for your amusement, nothing more."

"Sure, you might have started out that way, but we both felt something towards the end," she purred. "Don't deny that."

Despite the shake of his head, he *had* felt something at the time, whispers of affections for the fiery woman. With Maya, those whispers had drowned, replaced with a roar that echoed his desire and devotion.

Alaara was stung by the rebuttal and wanted to convince herself the love she felt was long gone. Nevertheless, she felt a need to possess the warrior like a child would a toy.

A laugh at the paddocks turned his head. Alaara's recently appointed guard had approached Maya out of boredom, waiting for his master. He now entertained her with a story, regarding a time he'd been in the unfortunate position to assist in the birth of a karkili's pup. Being unskilled, a misplaced finger had caused the pup's mother to boot him in the face. Maya was in hysterics at the theatrical display performed to the story.

"It seems Dixol has found his company for the evening," Alaara goaded, her eyes flicking to gage Thelic's reaction.

Thelic strode towards them and watched as the guard brushed a strand of hair from Maya's face, and her casual attempt to step back, unnerved by the sudden gesture. Thelic clenched his fists. Alaara was on his heel, giddy with anticipation at seeing her warrior once again in action, even at the defence of another woman.

"Hello!" an old man shouted, appearing from a house towards the end of the paddock's road. "You folks here to see me?"

At the shout, Maya had looked up to see Thelic, with another woman close at his side. Her hair, like amber, billowed around slim shoulders, while perfect, hourglass hips swayed with every step.

Alaara casually placed a hand on his arm, all the while raking her ochre-tinted eyes over Maya's body, judging the competition.

Upon seeing his approaching mistress and her companion, Dixol raised his hands, taking two steps back from Maya as a cold, grey glare was thrown towards him.

Drawing close, the stable owner waved again to get their attention, and Thelic finally turned to greet him. "We'd like two of your karkili."

"Oh. Sorry, but you're too late. This young lady has just purchased the lot!"

Alaara smiled wickedly at Maya; her eyes unwavering as she spoke. "I can, perhaps, part ways with two of the beasts." She broke her gaze to look up at Thelic. "But I want something in return."

Ignoring her, Thelic resumed talking to the old man, who had stopped several steps away, clearly sensing the thick atmosphere. "I don't suppose there are any other sellers in the area?"

"Hmm, 'fraid not. Only other seller is south of here, little town called Stiks."

The town with the trophy spikes, Maya thought with a shiver. She was in no hurry to return there and knew the others would feel the same way.

Thelic released an annoyed sigh and thanked the man before turning slowly back to Alaara. She beamed, knowing she was going to get her way, delighted to command his attention once again.

"What do you want in return for the creatures?" he asked, convinced he wasn't going to like the answer. Alaara had always been fond of playing games and manipulating those around her, a trait inherited from her father and position as the bored Princess of Fortus.

She clicked her nails together, thinking carefully. She wanted Thelic to return to his former role as her guardian, but knew he would decline. There had to be another way to persuade him.

Maya held her breath.

"I want you to accompany me tonight, to Sika's gathering," she decided.

"That's it?" Thelic asked warily.

"That's it. You know how much these things bore me, but my father insisted on my attending in his stead," she whined, stroking Thelic's arm.

His eyes were focused on Maya, who failed to hide the mix of jealousy and anger the silver-tongued woman provoked in her. "Maya?" he finally asked. They needed the karkili, but she needed to know that he was considering her over everything else.

Maya shrugged, feigning disinterest. "We need the creatures...and apparently this young woman needs a babysitter."

Thelic smirked and Alaara turned viciously on her. "Who are *you* to speak to the Fortus Keeper's daughter in such a way? Filthy little peasant." She snapped her fingers and pointed at Maya.

Dixol, no longer the playful flirt, moved behind Maya and pulled her hands back in a vice-like grip.

Thelic extended his spear to land at the nape of the guard's throat. "I wouldn't," he snarled, eyes daring.

Maya lifted her foot and slammed it down onto Dixol's leather boot. He loosened his grip with a yelp, and she spun, thrusting her knee into his softer parts.

"You really shouldn't be forceful with a lady," Maya insisted, stepping towards Thelic and Alaara. "Right, you–" she pointed at the red-haired and now equally red-faced woman, "you're being pushy, stop it. And you–" she pointed at Thelic, "you said it yourself. If we're to get to...you know where in time, then we need those creatures." She dropped her hand and placed both on either side of her hips, taking charge. "Go to this party, drink some wine and indulge the Princess. Then you can return to me, and I'll take all the painful memories away." She winked at Thelic in a bid to wind up Alaara.

He chuckled.

Furious but determined to ignore the snipe, Alaara said, "Good, that's settled then. You will accompany me, *all night* at the gathering, and then you can have your karkili." She flipped her hair back and readjusted her dress, before stalking away.

The guard quickly approached to offer an apology and request the address of their inn, before rushing after his temperamental mistress.

～

UPON THEIR RETURN to the guesthouse, raised voices drifted from inside. Thelic entered first to find Keela sitting at one of the far tables, and Elkin pacing across the room.

"We should leave, tonight. You shouldn't go to the gathering."

"How did you know about that?" Maya asked the obviously distressed redhead.

At some point in the day, Elkin had found the time to go to a barber. The hair that had hung in a loose, shaggy bun was now much shorter; his beard trimmed to a thick, sharply designed stubble. Without the mess of hair, his scars stood with a renewed definition, but he had transformed into the charming gentleman that suited his exploits.

"You look great!" Maya exclaimed with more surprise than she'd intended.

Elkin snapped his head up at her voice and tried not to sigh at the meaning. He stopped pacing and took a seat across from Keela, pushing an accusatory finger in her face. "She's been invited to the Cantorian Keeper's gathering, tonight."

Keela groaned and flicked his hand away.

"Thelic has too. At least they'll have each other," Maya offered, trying to calm the bear.

"What? Who invited you?" Elkin screeched.

"Alaara," was all Thelic said, but it was enough, and Elkin cringed for his friend.

"This is unwise. Bandaar might be there, and he'll want to know why Keela disappeared."

"I didn't just *disappear*, Elkin. He thinks I'm carrying out my own search for Maya," she said with an over-dramatic roll of her eyes.

Elkin scoffed. "And why should we trust that you're not just going to walk right up to the fearless leader and give us all up?"

"Because she hasn't given us any reason to distrust her yet," Maya answered on Keela's behalf. Everyone turned to look at her. "At the end of the day, she wants the same thing everyone wants; to stop the chaos."

Keela gave a solemn nod in agreement, insisting that Bandaar was unlikely to come anywhere near the Sika's gathering. "He never comes to these things. I'm usually sent in his place, and it will seem suspicious if I fail to show up."

Elkin had been about to protest when the front door of the inn crashed open violently. A large, dark skinned man in an elegant fur coat filled the doorway.

"Sika." Keela grinned in welcome at the Keeper.

He smirked back. "Seems I couldn't wait until tonight to

see you; I brought your clothes." He tore his gaze from her long enough to acknowledge the others in the room. The inn was empty of additional customers, its usual inhabitants prowling the town for an evening's entertainment.

"These are my companions. Thelic will also be attending your gathering this evening," Keela waved in Thelic's direction, who nodded respectfully to the Keeper.

Sika was studying Maya, who had stood to attention when the door burst open. "And who is this fine young woman?" He walked up to her, his long, muscular legs closing the distance in three paces. Once there, he lifted her hand to his lips and placed a warm, gentle kiss to her palm.

"Maya. *She* is Thelic's."

"Excuse me?" Maya gawked at Keela but blushed at Sika's lingering touch. Thelic tensed but said nothing, knowing better than to idly pick a fight with the leader of a territory on his own turf.

Sika gave a side-ways glance to Thelic before gently releasing Maya's hand and straightening. "Apologies," he said, a hand raised to lay across his heart as he bowed. "You don't intend to join the gathering tonight, Maya?"

"I'm not feeling very well," Maya lied. Despite Keela's assurances, she didn't want to risk Sika somehow finding out about her gifts.

"You look well enough to me. I insist you come. I'll have my man drop off some medicine and your clothes." He dismissed Maya's rising protest with a flick of his hand. "Elkin can accompany you. Right, old friend?"

Elkin had been sulking at the Keeper's presence and Sika lapped it up. "I see, so I'm invited now?"

Sika released a roar of laughter that shook the small confines of the inn. "Of course! You'll attend the gathering, but not as Keela's escort," he said, enjoying the moment.

"The warrioress will be attending at *my* side tonight. I've missed her dearly."

"And I you," Keela declared, her feet propped lazily on the table as she picked at the evening gown.

Elkin said nothing, for fear of saying something he might not live to regret.

"Excellent, I will meet you at the gate when the bells toll." With a wink at Maya, he turned and left the now all too quiet room.

MAYA CARESSED the jade green material of the dress she was expected to wear to the gathering; like chiffon it glided through her fingers, delicately thin. It was slightly too tight. Whether this was a misjudgement of her size or a result of Sika's lechery, Maya wasn't sure. She was, however, inclined to go with the latter as Keela, too, had been given a dress similarly dyed and fitted. Both items had been delivered, each with a thick fur coat to guard them from the brisk air on their walk to the Keep.

The innkeeper's wife pampered and fussed over the two women upon hearing of their invitation to the gathering. Keela had growled in annoyance initially, but the hulking woman was not to be trifled with and soon had her way with the irritable warrioress.

Not long before the town's bells were due to toll at the last ray of light, the two sisters made their way down to their male companions.

Elkin whistled. "Who had to die to get *you* into a dress?" he asked Keela, eyeing her appreciatively and silently thanking whoever it was for their sacrifice.

"Here," Thelic walked up to the two women and handed them each a mask.

"It's a masquerade ball?" Maya asked, surprised but pleased.

"Thankfully. We should go or we'll be late." Thelic placed his hand at the small of Maya's back, leaning in to whisper privately. "If we didn't need those damn creatures, I would haul you back up those stairs and keep you all to myself tonight."

"You have a date tonight, or have you already forgotten your former lover?" Maya teased, urging the heat between her legs to subside before she dragged him back up the stairs herself.

Thelic growled in annoyance at the reminder, wrapping his arm around her waist in a subtle and welcome indication of his loyalty.

Alaara had sent him clothes she deemed fit for the gathering; black shirt and trousers with a carefully tailored silk coat, dyed a beautiful, violent red. Maya stroked at the trimmed stubble and appreciated the innkeeper's efforts to tame his hair. Thelic wasn't beautiful. A scarred body and rough nature denied him that title. But he was handsome, with a rugged charm that oozed unsubtle danger.

THE BASE of the Keep was crowded with a queue of guests, all waiting to make their way up the impressive stone staircase into the grand hall at its head. The evening bells tolled. Perfectly on cue, Sika appeared at the top step and beckoned the guards to grant them access.

"You look exquisite," he said to Keela as she mounted the final step. With a kiss on the cheek, he gazed at her lustfully, turning to Maya with an equal show of appreciation. "I will be envied by all tonight, as you both parade in my colours." He spied the arm wrapped tightly around Maya's waist and smiled.

"What does that mean? *In my colours?*" Maya whispered to Thelic. She had suspected a trend in the different territories. The people of Danika, while multi-toned, seemed to favour the colour blue along with their Keeper. In Esterbell, the colour black seemed a common theme, with clothes and houses splashed with the dark hue.

"Each of the territories' armies don a colour, one that matches their lifestyle or particular affinity with the elements. Cantor is a farming community, so their army identifies by its sigil, and its colour, green."

"How bizarre," she muttered, glancing at Sika's plush, jade-coloured tunic.

Sika had managed to catch the end of Thelic's hushed explanation. "Could it be?" He lifted long fingers to his lips, pausing in contemplation.

Maya gave an awkward smile in response, praying they hadn't spilled the beans already.

Before Sika could commence his interrogation, a hand snaked around Thelic's waist and tugged him away from Maya's side.

"You're late," Alaara sang, stopping to give him an appreciative once over. "But worth the wait."

"Lady Alaara, glad you could make it," Sika boomed. With arms held wide, he stepped forward to embrace the Fortusian, his enormous build swamping her. "Well, now that we're all present, perhaps we should go and greet my guests?" he said, once again linking his arm through Keela's.

The hall was enormous and teemed with brightly dressed revellers, their masks a complimentary addition to the air of mystery. Glass eyes of dead creatures looked down upon the partygoers, the heads a well-maintained declaration of the Cantorian leader's considerable hunting skills.

Above, an open mezzanine level buzzed with activity as entertainers danced and juggled and surrendered their throats to fire and long knives. On the bottom floor, they passed rows of freshly prepared food, enough to feed the guests three times over. Waiters danced across the room, skilfully wielding bottles of wine as instruments of their performance, stopping only to fill the guests' goblets. Front and centre of the soiree, a woman sang to a beautifully eclectic mix of baroque and what Maya could only describe as celtic reels, infecting the crowd with its upbeat rhythm.

Sika stroked the bottom of Maya's chin, which she was certain was hanging open. "You can blame Carnass, the fiend. He said my parties were boring." He waved a hand gesturing to the grand hall. "So, I had to step it up."

Maya and Elkin were left to wander the hall, the others dragged away by their evening partners. Since the crossing to Avalon, Maya had been neglected the opportunity to indulge herself and have fun. Considering the serious nature of her being here, this was understandable. Nonetheless, she now realised how much she yearned for some semblance of escapism as she looked longingly at the dancers swaying along the centre aisle, gracefully riding the musician's melodic wave. She remembered the dance with Thelic in Esterbell and cast her eyes across the room in search of him.

There.

Alaara had her perfectly manicured fingers wrapped across his forearm, laughing about something unintelligible above the din.

"Shall we?" Elkin extended his hand to her, the mask doing nothing to hide the glint of amusement in his eyes. She returned the smile and accepted his proposal with a mock curtsy.

The mood was infectious, easy, and relaxed. Maya couldn't help but laugh as they flitted across the floor. With the mask as her cloak, she was invisible. She could be bold and unrestrained. She could dance. The musicians beckoned the new couple as they upped the tempo. Some left the floor, annoyed at being upstaged, others entranced by the entertaining duo. A breeze rushed through her hair as Elkin lifted her into a spin; upon touching the ground she flitted away, teasing her partner. Again, a sharp breeze seemed to dance along with them.

Loki, the Air Finkel, had deemed it fun enough to join in, his wind lifting the petals from a series of decorative bowls to explode around the room. For a moment, the space became a blossomed snow globe, and those around them stared at the fascinating couple. The song gave its final notes and they spun to a stop, both giggling.

Nearby couples clapped in appreciation, though wondered at the peculiarity of their show. Panicking, Maya quickly bowed, nudging Elkin who followed suit. The room burst to life with applause and Sika weaved his way to the surprising duo. Maya glanced again and spotted Thelic. Alaara remained firmly attached to his arm, but all attention was on her, his eyes burning; with desire or fury at their risky fun? She was sure she'd find out soon enough.

"I know leaders who couldn't dream to command their soldier's attention the way you just captured my hall," Sika bellowed, his hand flying to pat Elkin on the back. "And, I see you have been gifted the devotion of a Finkel," he indicated to Loki, now nestled into the crook of Maya's neck. His eyes dipped to regard her exposed arms, bare of the contract's mark.

"He saved my life and he's been with me ever since," Maya admitted, crossing her arms behind her back nervously. Keen to switch the topic, she took the chance to gather some information. "Speaking of soldiers, yours are truly impressive," she gestured to the men and women lining the walls, each wearing the Cantorian emerald-green armour and equipped with a long spear.

"Our numbers are building nicely." Sika rubbed his freshly shaven face. "It's a shame though, if not for..." he shook his head and released a frustrated breath.

"I've heard the outlanders are terrorising your land, why do you think that is?"

"Because they're heathens, nothing but thieving, robbing, murdering sons of whores."

"That can't be the only reason," she insisted. *There must be more.*

"The outlander elders have requested a meet, insisting they have nothing to do with the attacks. But we have proof, and that proof lies upon bloodied spikes across my lands," he seethed.

Stiks. Apparently only one of many small settlements across the territory to dress their gates with the dark signs of impending war.

"I'm sorry, this is too dark a topic for such a wonderful evening. I should let you get back to your guests." Maya bowed her head lightly and turned to leave with Elkin.

Sika's hand grabbed the back of her arm, spinning her to face him once again, his anger gone. "You're an otherworlder." He'd seen and heard just enough now to be sure.

"I–" she didn't know what to say. This man was in league with Esterbell to fight the outlander threat. Who knew how deep that collaboration went, or what he would do should he discover who Maya truly was. Before she could attempt to formulate a lie, a small pastry soared across the room to slap against Sika's cheek.

Keela leaned lazily against a table, checking her fingernails; plates of the same tartlet stacked behind her. Further back, only a few tables away, Thelic was storming towards them. Maya shook her head, silently pleading for him to stop. The last thing they needed was to cause a scene. With a scowl, he did as she asked, perching nearby to monitor the situation.

"Sika, you seem intent on playing with every female here but me," Keela accused, her voice softly serenading the Keeper. From the table, she glided over and slipped between him and Maya to rub her hands over his chest. "I may not seem it, but I'm a jealous woman." She edged her hands down to his hips, grabbing and crushing them to hers as she leaned up to kiss him. He returned it, distracted momentarily from his former interest. He wrapped a hand roughly in Keela's hair, mussing the elaborate bun the innkeeper's wife had painstakingly fashioned.

Elkin's jaw clenched.

During the awkwardly long moment, Maya admired the two. Keela's sharp features, inherited from her mother's Asian lineage, were all the more beautiful when coordinated against Sika's dark skin and hardened body.

Keela broke the kiss with a rough push to Sika's chest, wagging her finger at him. "Only this much, my Lord," she teased.

He rumbled longingly in response, but her distraction had worked. "Did you come here simply to drive me crazy, little warrior?" he crooned, readjusting the bejewelled mask.

"As amusing as that is, I'm here on an errand for my father."

"I see, and I suppose there's something you need from me?"

Keela played with a loose strand of hair, relaxed, the lies as easy to her as breathing. "My father requires me to head north, we could use safe passage to Transum."

He scoffed. "Consider it done." Pausing momentarily, he added, "But you will return to me, at some point, so I can convince you to be my wife, my mate…my queen." His final title of affection was spoken so immodestly, a young woman passing by fanned her face dramatically, her blush climbing as Keela was crushed into the Keeper's embrace.

"Perhaps, when my father's errand is taken care of."

A hush came over the room like a ripple in a pond, followed by a smaller swell of whispers.

"And what errand might that be, Daughter?" The crowds had parted and Bandaar, along with several of his guards, strolled towards them. Dressed purely in black, his green eyes were a burst of colour against the midnight ensemble. Towering before them, he looked delightedly from Keela, to Maya.

14

UNEXPECTED GUESTS

CANTOR KEEP

"Bandaar! You made it, old man," Sika bellowed.

Keela shrank under the weight of her father's accusatory glare. It lasted only a moment, but the look was warning enough of a grim future upon their return to Esterbell.

"Sorry I'm late. I was hunting." Bandaar's eyes danced. He'd finally caught up to the prey, the hunt coming to its conclusion. "Might I steal my daughter's friend? Just for a moment."

Maya wanted to run...or fight. Going anywhere alone with Bandaar was only going to end one way; locked away in preparation for a ceremony that would claim her life. The opportunity to do either, vanished as he gripped her arm and led her from the party.

Stepping forward, Elkin was met by Bandaar's guards who subtly blocked him from their master. He couldn't afford to start a fight, not here. All he could do was watch as Maya was led from the hall to a side door.

The festivities had resumed, and couples swayed around the centre aisles in blissful ignorance of the troubles afoot.

Scrambling through the drunken crowds, Thelic was at the door moments after they passed through. It was locked.

"Fuck," he roared. Turning, he spotted Elkin, surreptitiously surrounded by Bandaar's guards.

Elkin gestured with a tilt of his head to another door at the end of the great hall.

Thelic ran for it. Once through, he spotted Maya immediately. They had stopped in the centre of a large room, bare of furniture or decor. Her arm was held at an awkward angle, a heated argument passing between them. Thelic sprinted forward and grabbed Maya, pulling her roughly away from her father.

Stunned at the interruption, a smile played at the corner of his mouth as recognition dawned. "I remember you." He regarded the man in front of him as one might an insect. "How's the shoulder?"

Having been forced to leave his weapon at the inn, Thelic kept his arms loose and palm facing the ground, ready for whatever the Esterbellian Keeper threw their way. He rotated his shoulder. "Good as new," he snarled. "Nice of you to stop by, now fuck off."

Bandaar's eyes widened, though his fury at the young man's insolence was quickly replaced by amusement. Thelic had moved his body to block Maya, one hand securing her behind his back as she attempted to step forward. "You're lovers," he chuckled.

"What would you know of love?" Pushing Thelic's arm down, Maya stepped forward, the shock of seeing her father again subsiding. "How can you even contemplate love when you killed your own wife, *murdered* the mother of your child?"

Bandaar flinched, the motion almost imperceptible. "I didn't..." he struggled to finish the sentence. "I lost control," was all he could manage.

"That's all you have to say? You never loved her, or me," Maya spat.

Again, a brief look of sadness crossed his face before the cool, detached look of disdain once again held her. "You're coming back to Esterbell so we can finish this once and for all," he snarled, every sharp word a threat.

"She's not going anywhere with you." The ground rumbled lightly under Thelic in his own warning.

"Why won't you at least let me try Fatari's way? Or are you so intent on my death? A punishment for abandoning you all those years ago with my mother?"

"Fatari is a meddlesome, traitorous woman. She isn't one of us and her methods and prophecies suit only herself!"

Maya was taken aback. "What do you mean? Her ritual saves Avalon, isn't that what you want?"

He growled, pacing a short line in front of them. "Her ceremony doesn't simply stop the chaos, it closes the gateways for good." He laughed darkly. "She wishes nothing more than the destruction of human-kind and would have one of those creatures rule these lands."

Jaseen had said the demons' power was leaking from the gateways, causing the chaos. His reasoning made no sense if he truly wanted to save the realm. "Why do you want the portals to stay open?"

"Without the crossings, castors on the earthly plain would be doomed, hunted to extinction for their abilities. They are already so rare as it is. With the gateways open, Maya, we can bring them all here. We can save them all."

"Why release the demons? What purpose could that possibly serve when their power chokes this realm?"

"She was wrong about that. The sprites of our world have nothing to do with the chaos. *That* is born from the third realm in which they're trapped. It's leaking into Avalon. By releasing them, our kind can fully inhabit this world." He clasped his hands tightly together, willing her to understand. "But that can only happen with you, with my ceremony, where your powerful contract to the elements will pass to me."

"Power. That's all you really want. You've deluded yourself into thinking it's the only way, because then you get whatever power lies in me," Maya whispered, shaking her head in disbelief at the man whose blood ran through her veins.

"To protect Avalon! You don't understand, the outlanders and their gods will destroy us!" He roared, grasping her shoulders with a violent shake.

Thelic pushed forward, wrapping his hand around the Keeper's throat.

Bandaar chuckled at the empty threat. "I knew you would never understand, Maya. You're barely human," he rasped through Thelic's grip.

Maya recoiled at the sound of her father's voice. Something was wrong. Though she didn't claim to know him, his tone was unnatural; another, somewhat whispering sound seemed to join it. "What the hell do you mean—"

Maya was cut off as guards crashed through the locked door and ran towards them. Just as the first reached Maya, the window at the far side of the room shattered. A thin, wooden arrow with an iron head ripped through the empty space, its sharp tip easily piercing through the skin and bone of the guard's neck. Maya fell back to land on the floor, a thin cut lining her cheek from where the projectile's edge had grazed her.

The guard beside Maya dropped to his knees before falling flat on his back to convulse at her feet, gripping the fatal wound.

Behind the fragmented window, a shadow dangled from a rope, the second arrow already nocked and primed.

At the crash, Thelic had released Bandaar to stand over Maya. He bent and retrieved the dead guard's sword, his attention divided between the figure at the window and the Esterbellian Keeper's guards.

Spurred by the uproar, Sika stormed into the crowded room, his own soldiers and Elkin close behind.

Keela was nowhere in sight and Maya wondered if she'd fled rather than face their father's wrath.

Striding to stand at Bandaar's side, Sika stopped. Even with the domed ceiling, his height dominated the room to tower over the others. "You know you're all ruining a perfectly good party?" The Cantorian leader's voice, although calm, held a menacing edge. He flicked his gaze to the dark figure at the window. "I don't believe you were invited, outlander."

Everyone now stared at the threatening shadow, his arrow, still primed, glinted in the light of the three moons. He didn't waver, the string to his bow taut with no signs of tiring. He silently waited for his opponent to make the first move.

"You're *with* them?" Bandaar seethed at his daughter. "Restrain her!"

Thelic raised the sword, ready for the first challenger as an Esterbellian soldier warily stepped forward.

The shadow released.

Blood sprayed as the arrow found its mark. The guard dropped, dead, still several feet from Maya and Thelic.

Sika raised a weary hand. "Enough of this." With his body still firmly facing the window, he glanced over his shoulder to Maya. "Leave. But know this, Maya, you've made a powerful enemy here tonight."

"Sika–" Bandaar was cut short as Sika's guards raised and

dropped the heel of their spears, the echo clanging throughout the halls, a gavel finalising the Cantorian's decision.

Addressing the outlander, Sika flashed a smile. "I'll be seeing you again, I'm sure, when our armies finally collide."

The archer flexed long fingers around the bow, a subtle acceptance to Sika's challenge. Maya and Thelic turned to leave.

"You can't let her go," Bandaar raged, desperate now as Maya reached the door, "Sika! If she leaves here today, then Avalon, *Cantor*, dies!" he begged.

"Maya, one of my guards will see to it that you aren't stopped. Bandaar and his men will remain here," Sika insisted, with a pointed look at the Esterbellian.

As Elkin, Maya and Thelic were escorted through the great hall, all was silent. At the commotion, the music had stopped, and everyone stood as they were, watching as the miscreants were removed from their festivities. Alaara stood to one side, her eyes daggers. Maya silently prayed they wouldn't be venturing near the Fortus territory anytime soon. Thelic dreaded the day they would. As they made their way down the stone steps outside, a booming voice commanded the party to continue, and it did, like nothing had happened.

Down the long steps of the keep, their escorts kept a hurried pace as they wove through the streets. "Where are you taking us?" Thelic asked the guard. The inn and their belongings were in the opposite direction.

"The harbour, as instructed."

"But our things!" Maya insisted.

"They are being collected. Sika asked me to give you this when we were out of sight." The guard handed Maya a note and continued herding them towards the docks.

She opened the crumpled paper to find some hastily written scribbles.

Maya,

My vessel is at your disposal and will drop you and your party anywhere you wish. Keela has informed me of your quest to reach the Seer, Fatari. I trust her and so I am placing that trust in you. Should you fail to calm the chaos, I will hunt you down myself and offer your body to the spirits. I know of Bandaar's plans for you. If you should succeed, please consider a matrimonial partnership.

"What does it say?" Elkin asked, peering over Maya's shoulder.

"In short, if I fail, he'll kill me. If we succeed, he wants to marry me."

Elkin chuckled. "I've always liked that about him, straight to the point."

Thelic mumbled something about a spear and Sika's throat.

As promised, Sika's ship stood tall and rakers rushed to ready it for the sudden voyage. Its entire length had been stained the Cantorian green with swirls of gold, and decorated with brilliantly carved, bright white panels. Its shape was much like the water-rakers at Winkler's Hamlet, but boasted wealth and military prowess. Racing past, two of Sika's guards had collected their belongings from the inn as promised and carried them to the ships bow, where a stable held four karkili.

"These are from Sika too?" Maya asked, indicating the creatures as she stepped aboard.

"He insisted – an early wedding present, or so he says," Keela replied. The others turned to find her leaning casually against one of the six pillars that supported the ship's shelter.

"You're here!" Maya exclaimed, later admitting she'd thought that Keela had fled.

Unimpressed, Keela explained. "Someone had to secure our escape. Plus, I told you, I'm not going anywhere until we've seen Fatari."

Eager to make way, the captain – a high-level water-raker – requested their intended destination. Elkin was confident his contact would have remained in Northern Transum. Mikosh had been the same man to direct him previously, a predictable man, and their only hope of finding the Seer. He relayed their heading to the captain.

EXPECTING to arrive at the northern port of Transum by the following afternoon, the group unpacked their blankets and prepared to settle in for the night. The three moons hung above, their reflection setting the ship and water alight. Just below the surface, small, vibrant creatures surfed the ship's waves, their scales bringing the colours to life against the midnight gloom of the water.

As the others settled, Maya walked from the bow to the

stern, admiring the fish-like creatures. Along the centre of the ship, the shelter's blinds had been closed to allow the water-rakers some privacy to sleep before their shift. Maya crept past the captain's cabin; her steps soundless along the well-preserved floorboards. From the stern, Cantor's flickering firelight could be seen fading into the distance, her father with it.

ON THE ROOF of the cabin, the shadow now sat, watching Maya. Seeing she was alone, he dropped to land just behind her, the sound faint. Grabbing her waist, his free hand wrapped around her mouth, forbidding the startled scream.

"Don't make a sound," the shadow instructed.

Maya held her breath, hand reaching for the dagger she'd immediately re-strapped to her side upon being reunited with their belongings.

"I swear I won't hurt you. We need to talk." His voice was deep and soft. Maya felt his jaw brush along the top of her head as he spoke, the taut muscles in his arm tensing as she squirmed. "Please," he whispered.

Maya went still and nodded her head in a muted promise to do as he asked. As he relaxed his grip, she sprang forward and turned to face the man who had fired the arrows at Cantor Keep. "Who are you?"

"My name is Kadhim, I'm one of the tribesmen sent by Prisia, the Elder you met at Cantor's Gateway."

Maya remembered. "You're an outlander."

A muscle in Kadhim's jaw tightened and his eyes turned hard. "We don't refer to ourselves in such a way. That label was designed by the humans in their ignorance."

Maya leaned her back against the barrier along the ship's rear and sighed. There was so much she still didn't know.

She was risking her life as a promise to her mother, but beyond that, she knew nothing.

"You're being too careless. Attending the gathering was beyond foolish."

Maya bristled at the stranger's reprimand. "Who do you think you are?" she asked. "I wasn't given much of a choice, and I managed to gather some information."

"I've never seen dancing used as an interrogation technique," he mocked. Maya blushed. "And what did you manage to uncover?"

She told him of Bandaar's plan to use her power to release the trapped demons and stop the chaos. "We also found out that Cantor and Esterbell have joined forces in preparation to destroy the outland–" she paused to correct herself, "your people."

"That much we already know, and Bandaar is deluded. He knows too little of his own history to be playing with gateways."

"Why is your tribe attacking the human settlements?"

"Like Prisia said, those attacks are being carried out by a minority, extremists. They believe the humans are still contracted with the sprites of your realm, the demons. They've grown impatient with our mistreatment as well." He crossed his arms, drawing Maya's attention to his hands.

"Your hands, they're…different, not like the others."

He glanced down and realised what she meant. While his were longer than the average human, his claws were cut down and shaped, not gnarled like the outlanders she'd seen. The colour of his hands was also unusual. While the others had been an azure blue, his were tattooed a shade that blurred the line between red and amber.

"I'm from a higher tribe, one of the only ones left, that we know of."

"Maya?" Thelic had come to check on her, concerned after

their encounter with Bandaar. Seeing the darkly clad figure looming over her, he reached for the spear that usually hung at his side, only to remember he'd left it by the blankets. "I leave you for two moments! Get the fuck away from her," he stormed forward, closing the distance between them.

Maya stepped in front of Kadhim, standing between the two men. "It's ok, this is the man who saved us from Bandaar's guards."

Thelic eyed him warily. Any other time, an outlander was considered an enemy, but now, he wasn't sure who their enemies were. Another figure dropped beside Kadhim, a woman dressed identically in tight black cloth, her blade pointed at the new arrival.

"Enough, Zarina," Kadhim warned. The woman remained silent but lowered her weapon.

"Everyone needs to calm down." Maya sighed and turned back to Kadhim. "Why does your elder want me to see Fatari?"

"A long time ago, the Seer foretold two prophecies; a fated decision that would lead to our salvation...or to our destruction," Zarina answered.

"What are these prophecies?"

Zarina looked to Kadhim. With a nod of approval, she continued. "Either our people will unite under one leader and the chaos contained...or the obliteration of both sides and the realm in ruins."

"And Maya's inherited power is what saves it? What is she contracted to?" Thelic asked.

"We don't know exactly, that is why she must go to Fatari. Only the Seer knows Maya's role to play in these prophecies," Kadhim finished.

Again, Maya was left with more questions. "How do we get to her?"

"Your friend is on the right path. Mikosh will know of her current whereabouts," Zarina insisted.

Kadhim stepped closer to Maya. Ignoring Thelic's cautionary look, he brushed a loose strand of hair from the side of her face. Leaning down, he whispered, "We'll be close by, should you need us." Then they jumped, higher than Maya had seen any human, and disappeared over the lip of the captain's cabin.

15

AVALONIAN METROPOLIS

TRANSUM

Maya had been transported to an entirely different realm. At least that's how she felt, staring up at the towering buildings she was no longer used to. It wasn't like London, there were no skyscrapers here; but the colourfully painted buildings stood tightly compacted into what was said to be the second largest city of the five territories. Maya supposed it *could* be like London, possibly Chinatown, if it were the early 1900s. The architectural theme rang true and featured the same oriental style as some of the other territories, only more squished, the clear intent to fit as many houses into one area as possible.

After leaving their karkili with a harbour stableman, Elkin led the others down a series of winding alleyways. Congested and stuffy, the streets reeked with the strange and contrasting smells of baked goods and body odour. The sun's rays and subsequent high temperature of being farther north seemed to accentuate the different smells, making them somewhat pungent and sour. Men and women ornamented the doorways of various inns and taverns. Dressed in fine, powdered makeup and elegant silks, most relayed offers of a good time or work available. Some lay in the street, vacant expressions lining their faces.

Maya stopped beside a young man sat motionless below one of the shop windows, pale and gaunt with glazed eyes. She checked his pulse. It was there, the light breath caressing her arm. A cloud of sweet-smelling smoke swamped her; the cause, a remarkably intoxicated woman opening a nearby door. A brief glimpse revealed the interior. A room, laden with smoke and naked humans draped over long chaises. Each held a long silver pipe in one hand, with instruments of various shapes and sizes clasped in the other; instruments for what? Maya wasn't sure she wanted to know.

The man at her feet stirred, moaning, craving the quiet of sleep. Keela put a hand on Maya's shoulder, hurrying her along.

A tailor was the first item on Elkin's agenda. Their old clothes had been well suited to the colder climes of the southern territories. Here, and further north, the excess material was unnecessary and only stood to draw attention to the tourists amid crowds of immodestly swathed Transumians. The fashion clearly revolved around their silk trade as all who mingled or meandered through the streets wore finely crafted silk in their sleeveless coats, trousers, and dresses. Many of the men walked the streets with chests exposed, while the women adopted short dresses sewn with ornate beading and embroidery.

Elkin turned left, past several dens, if the columns of smoke were any indication. Then right, over a small bridge. Then right again, into an alley only wide enough to walk single file. If Maya hadn't already known that Elkin grew up in Esterbell, she would've guessed he was born and bred walking these dilapidated streets. She looked up and glanced around, wondering whether the outlanders were able to follow them here. They finally stopped outside a glass fronted shop. The sign read: *Wilix Wishes*.

Inside, large rolls of dazzling, silk material hung from the walls and mannequins displaying the tailor's work. Frustrated shouts rose from a room behind the counter, and a red-faced, blue haired man dashed out at the sound of his door's bell.

"I'm closed, g-go away!" he stuttered, patting his thin cloak, and feeling around his desk.

"Even for me?" Elkin asked, his arms outstretched to the frantic man.

Locating his glasses, Wilix donned them and squinted, readjusting his sight. His face brightened at the sight of Elkin. Navigating his way through the piles of material at his desk, he came forward, his own arms outstretched before stopping abruptly. The warm smile quickly morphed as he scrunched his face in a mix of horror and disgust. "Wh-what is that?" Wilix pointed to Elkin's winter-suited travel attire.

"Don't judge me, lover. You know the Danikan tailors are all...blah."

"Lover?" Maya asked, louder than intended.

"Ha, he wi-wishes," Wilix tutted, winking at Elkin. "The man adores f-femininity, but can appreciate a handsome man." He flicked his blue locks to emphasise the point.

"As you can see," Elkin waved a hand to his companions, "we need your help."

"Indeed, you all do." Wilix sighed and appraised the group of travellers in front of him. "Wh-when do you need the items by?"

"We'll take whatever you have that's ready to go, now."

"Nothing is ready, it must be f-fitted," he said with a dramatic eyeroll. "You two," he pointed to Maya and Keela. "In the back, I have a few th-things that might do," he said, herding them into the large backroom before shouting back to the men. "E-Elkin, you find something for you and hand-some there in the meantime."

Standing in front of an extravagant mirror, Maya regarded the new clothes prescribed for her by Wilix. She cringed, the ensemble screaming – *take me, I'm easy.*

Elkin walked in as she tugged at the lace bottom refusing to cover the areas she was determined to keep private. "Per-fect," he sighed lecherously.

"Not on your life, Elkin," Maya muttered, before looking to Wilix desperately. "Sorry, but do you have anything that's a bit...more?"

Wilix sighed but obliged, handing her a bundle of clothes. Within the pile, she found a pair of cream, elasticated silk trousers that tapered at the ends. The teal top was cropped but ribbed to provide ample stability for her breasts, leaving her midriff bare. A long and white, open silk coat completed the ensemble, sleeveless and beautifully stitched with designs of golden flowers.

Keela, too, had refused Wilix's first suggestion and opted for a simple pair of silk trousers with a netted top that exposed all but her nipples, a thin line of material stretching across the front. Outside, Elkin and Thelic wore similar outfits, sleeveless coats hanging open to reveal hardened chests and thin silk trousers. Not much was left to the imagi-nation, and Maya could appreciate that.

"These will help us blend in a bit more, they'll do well in Fortus too, should we have to travel that way," Elkin figured.

"You p-plan to cross east?" Wilix asked.

"We're hoping to avoid it, but we have little control over our options."

Wilix held his chin and considered the travellers once again. With a click of his fingers, he disappeared into the back room, appearing moments later with four bags. Inside were white garments, several alternative outfits for each of them.

"There's shirts and trousers for all with a dress or two for both you l-ladies." He bobbed his head, content with his choices. "The fashion there is a bit more...plain, I suppose." His eyes went to slits as he glanced sideways at Elkin. "And I suppose you want this on your t-tab?"

Elkin's cheeky smile was answer enough and Wilix shook his head with mock despair before shooing them out and wishing them luck on their travels.

The relief felt from the fresh, light-weight clothing was immediate when met with the wave of Transum's late-afternoon heat as Elkin led the group to a nearby tavern. Like all the others, inside was small and dim, but delightfully featured a fenced outdoor area in the rear for guests to sit in the sun. Passing by the few customers, they settled towards the back to order food whilst Elkin disappeared to find his contact.

"I've missed these parts," Keela remarked, relaxing into the deep wicker chairs at their table as she lifted her face to enjoy the sun's bounty.

In the rare moment of peace, Maya seized the opportunity to learn a bit more of her half-sister. "Do you travel the territories a lot?" she asked.

"I travel when it's necessary, usually as an emissary for Bandaar, so I have little time to myself."

Maya hesitated before asking, "Does your mother travel with you?"

Keela continued to bask in the sun and several moments passed before she finally responded. "My mother died a long time ago."

"I'm sorry, I shouldn't have pried." Maya rubbed her face, convinced her nosiness had deepened the rift between them.

"It's fine. Like I said, it was a long time ago. She was from here though."

"From Transum? Do you still have family here?"

"My grandfather, but we don't talk."

Baby steps. Maya was pleased with the progress they were making as new-found siblings but thought better than to push the topic any further. Elkin returned along with a waiter carrying their drinks. The message had been sent, and now it was merely a case of waiting.

"Don't you have a bounty on your head in this territory?" Thelic asked, causing Elkin to shift uncomfortably in his seat at the reminder.

"I do. Luckily it's in one of the towns further south, so we should be ok."

By coming to Transum, Elkin had risked the most in comparison to the others, and with little to gain.

"Why did you come with us after Esterbell? Surely your debt with Thelic has been paid?" Maya asked.

Elkin laughed. "I should hope so!"

"Then why?"

He let out a long breath and mirrored Keela, sinking into his chair. "I would like to say it's purely something as honourable as assisting the hunt for the cure to this world's chaos." Elkin paused, his forehead creasing as he battled with the thoughts that crossed his mind. "I suppose that *is* the larger of my reasons for accompanying you. But I also have my own motives for finding the Seer now."

Keela lifted her head, interest peaked, and Maya willed him to continue.

"She gave me a prophecy, of my own fate, three years ago. It didn't go exactly as she'd said and now, I'm wondering if there was something more to it." Keela watched him fiddle with the cutlery and understood his reasoning. Fatari had insisted that if he stayed with Bandaar, both her and Elkin would have died. The question remained, why did the Seer fail to mention that Keela would have gone with him?

MIKOSH HAD SENT word for the group to meet him at a bordello by the harbour. Even without the sun overhead, the mild breeze was refreshing as they weaved their way through the narrow boulevards to the marina. Unsurprisingly, sweet smoke clouded the air as they stepped into the sizeable den of vice. Immediately upon entry, beautiful men and women descended upon them, offering drinks and silver pipes. A man, completely bare of cloth, took Maya's hand to rub it down his muscular chest, a low growl from Thelic stopping him, barely inches from the course hair at his pubis.

Elkin informed them of their business with Mikosh and all but two of the harlots skulked away in a huff at the loss of potential customers. The two remaining women proceeded to drag Elkin and Keela through a set of wide double-doors. Inside, an old man lay upon a bed of luxurious pillows, several women among them.

"It's a marvel Fatari stayed with you as long as she did, Mikosh," Elkin said with a chuckle at the man's appearance.

"Damn woman had it good," Mikosh grumbled from his cushioned throne. Refusing the proffered hands of help from his companions, he slowly and awkwardly clambered up to formally welcome his guests. "You keep wonderful company as always, my dear boy." He hobbled over to Maya and Keela, leaning up to kiss them both on the forehead in way of greeting.

"We've heard the Seer is ill, Mikosh. Is this true?" Elkin asked, conscious of their time constraints and eager to hurry the old man.

"How did you hear of this?"

Elkin lifted a hand to Maya by way of explanation and she retold her story of meeting the Elder by the gateway in Cantor.

"Pah, bloody woman. Lifaya needs peace!" He dipped his head sadly. "She doesn't need more bloody chaos, she's already fighting so much as it is."

"Lifaya, that's Fatari's true name?" Maya asked.

"It is. Well, it was. She rarely goes by anything other than her title now." He lifted his head, cold determination in his eyes. "Who are you to ask for her whereabouts? Eh?"

"You know you can trust me, Miko. You gave me her location in the past, and I kept my word that no harm would come to her."

"My Lifaya was strong then. She could fight a petty thief!"

Elkin didn't flinch at the intended insult, instead rolling his eyes at the old man.

"Please," Maya said. "I promised my mother I would find Fatari."

"Why? Who was your mother to bear such a ridiculous request?"

"My mother was Jaseen Rivers, former wife of Bandaar, and Lifaya's granddaughter."

"Ridiculous. You really expect me to believe that? You're not the first to boast such a claim," Mikosh spat. "Jaseen crossed to the other side many years ago."

"You're not wrong, but she was brought back here against her will fifteen years ago and has been here ever since...until Bandaar killed her." Maya said, her voice rough with desperation for the old man to believe her, and the devastation of reliving something still so raw.

Mikosh stayed quiet, searching her face for the lie he felt sure was hidden amongst her pleas. "Then, you are Mayara?"

She nodded her head and released a long breath, relief washing over her.

"If you *are* Mayara, kin to Fatari, descendent of Ester-bell…" Mikosh reached under his cloak to reveal a jewel encrusted dagger, "then you must prove it."

"What?" Thelic stepped forward, anger bubbling to the surface.

"That's fair," Maya said, taking the dagger. "What do you want me to do?"

"Lifaya told me of your birth, of four castor circles that formed around you and Jaseen upon your entry to this world, the earth beneath you renewed." He smiled in anticipation. "Summon them for me." He knew she would either fail and humiliate herself, or succeed; both prospects equally exciting.

"All four!? I've only ever managed one and that damn near knocked me out. Summoning four will likely kill me!"

Mikosh simply shrugged and everyone became painfully aware of the small confines of the room. Maya suggested they move somewhere else. Mikosh, however, didn't believe this small woman was the true blood relative to the great Major. He shook his head and settled into a chair at the edge of the chamber with a wave of his hand, demanding she proceed.

"Fine, I'll try, but you better know where Fatari is." She jabbed her finger in the old man's face before stalking into the centre of the long room.

"This is a bad idea. She has no control over her contracted power, Mikosh!" Thelic warned, concerned not just for Maya but her spectators and everyone else in the general area. He was beside her now, his hands on both of her shoulders. "You don't have to do this. We can scour the Outlands for the Seer."

"Don't worry, I'll keep it as low key as I can," she tried to reassure him, and herself. "Plus, Loki is better behaved now." She called its name, picturing the furry creature in her mind, and a bushy white tail whipped playfully against face. To those in the room, Mikosh appeared impassive. But the

Finkel's conjuring had surprised him, and with the lack of contractor's marks on her body, he began to wonder.

Thelic and the others moved to the far side of the room, Keela with one hand on the door handle. She had seen the extent of Maya's power, her capacity for destruction, and wasn't happy with their current proximity to the inevitable disaster.

Maya uttered a small prayer to Loki and dragged the dagger across her open palm. Blood sprang to the surface and Maya allowed its escape to pool at her feet. She concentrated on the Finkel, on its energy, as a yellow circle began to glow beneath her. Loki, excited by the surge in power, danced about the room. Maya wanted to join in, the energy from the circle elated and filled her with warmth.

"Concentrate, Maya!" Thelic hollered over the wind's roar. "Think of the elements combined, not just Loki."

But she loved the feel of Loki, his bushy tailed form fit with his nature so perfectly as his wind brushed across her face to tangle her hair. Thelic was right, though. Mikosh wanted to see *all* the circles. Next, she thought of earth and the ground shuddered at her summons.

Keela twisted the handle to the door, ready to bolt, convinced the building would collapse around them.

Outside, frightened squeals filled the bordello and people rushed for the exit. Yet still Mikosh sat, unperturbed in his chair, willing her to continue.

Maya realised she would have to allow her blood to flow more feely if she hoped to succeed. She dragged the blade across her other palm, the sting of the cut like fire, blood met with earth and the room flooded with light.

~

THE WINDOWS at Mikosh's back exploded. Two figures were through the wall and sprinting for Maya. Spear met sword as Kadhim and Thelic clashed.

Flames rose from the ground at Maya's feet, summoned from the flickering and dull red ring that now encompassed the air element's circular seal. She had summoned the second. As before, Maya struggled with the temperamental element. The high-pitched clang of metal broke her concentration and she looked to see Thelic and Kadhim, their weapons were drawn but their eyes were on her, on the fiery waves that grew.

"Water, Maya, think of water!" Elkin roared over the chaos. On approach, Zarina had been hit by a fiery tendril and stood nursing her wound by Elkin's side, not daring another step.

Water. Cool, calm, a peaceful element, Maya thought.

Nothing happened.

Maya felt the lick of flames caress her legs, her arms, her face. Again, she tried to summon the fire's alter-element. Sweat ran down her neck, both from the heat and her exhaustion. A startled yelp snapped her attention to the others, her friends. Elkin was on the floor, his trouser leg scorched. Fear gripped her; she had no control.

"Get out!" she shouted, begging the others, but they remained. Even Mikosh, now on his feet, held an arm across his face in a feeble shield to the blazing waves of heat; but he remained, mesmerised by the sheer force of her power.

Maya screamed in pain and desperation, thinking only of water.

The water in Yali's lake.

The rain outside of her apartment window.

WATER!

The element sprang to life and embraced her. The room flooded, pooling out of the window and calming the other elements. The red castor circle disappeared, replaced with an equally dull and broken blue ring. Black spots appeared at the edge of Maya's vision and the water began to dissipate. Within moments, the circles had vanished completely, and the water retreated beneath the floorboards of the bordello.

As the last of the elements were dispelled and the floorboards revealed, Mikosh gasped in delight. His hard, oaken floor was gone, replaced by a myriad of flowers, moss, and grass. Maya smiled sadly at the old man, before succumbing to the exhaustion, her blood a steady stream that dampened the moss beneath.

Kadhim and Thelic rushed forward, Thelic catching her head before it could collide with the ground.

"Maya?" No response. He checked her pulse. It was fast, but beginning to slow. Slower. Slower still. He checked her breathing. "Fuck!"

"Move, boys," Mikosh hobbled to stand over her, lifted his cane, and slammed it into her chest. Water exploded from Maya's mouth, and she rolled to the side, emptying her saturated stomach.

"I swear, that element is bi-polar," she laughed weakly. "First it saves us and then it tries to kill me," she coughed and wiped a bloody hand over her mouth, still it bled.

"Elkin, get some bandages. We need to stop the blood," Thelic yelled. Maya's head rolled in his hand; she had passed out. "Hurry!"

Mikosh told them of an infirmary he had in one of the back rooms. Thelic lifted Maya carefully, Kadhim supporting her head, and together they carried her to the small room.

WITH THE BLOOD flow staunched and bandages applied, Maya was left to sleep-off the exhaustion her summons had caused. The others gathered in the now empty bordello and looked to Mikosh. He shivered at the memory of what he'd seen. While it had appeared to them broken, incomplete, the woman had shown tremendous power. But she was frighteningly unskilled and dangerous.

"Surely you believe her now?" Thelic snapped. He was pacing, incensed, his warning had gone unheard and now Maya lay in a crude infirmary.

"Her contracts are powerful, I'll admit."

"Powerful? The people in this room are powerful!" he warned. "Hers is supreme – no, it's blessed!"

Mikosh regarded his once hardwood floor, now buried beneath Maya's summoned flower garden, and he had to agree. While Maya had failed to fully summon the four rings, all of the elements had indeed answered her call.

"What the hell does she have to…" Thelic remembered the Stone. He stormed off to retrieve it, returning moments later to thrust it into the old man's face. "Is this proof enough?"

"Spirits, is that?" The Gouram Stone confirmed what he had already come to realise. As Maya had summoned the castor circle, he'd seen Lifaya as a youngling, when her hair had held the colour of sunlight and life's hardships hadn't begun to show in the lines of her face. She had been a force not to be taken lightly. Many had feared and respected the power of Fatari, she could have ruled territories and commanded great armies, but instead her visions spoke of another, lonelier path.

"Well?" Thelic demanded.

"Yes, yes, I know she is who she claims," Mikosh said, waving him away.

"Then you'll tell us where Fatari is?" Elkin stepped forward, hopeful.

Mikosh disappeared into a small, adjacent study, reappearing with a map. Laying it out on the table, he pointed to a mountainous area in the Outlands, east of Fortus. The island territory of Transum, where they currently dwelled, sat eternally *west* of Fortus. Journeying through the dividing channels would take them twice as long, as no raker or ferryman would pass near the centre island. They would have to cross the Fortus territory to make it to the Outlands in good time.

The old man regarded the five warriors at his table. "There are too many of you, you'll stick out like harlots in a temple if you traipse into Fortus as a group."

"Zarina and I will stick to the shadows," Kadhim said.

"I'm surprised you managed to keep up and stay hidden," Thelic admitted. The outlanders' stealth and skill had impressed him.

"We would have remained concealed, but I saw Maya's light. I was worried," Kadhim admitted, his brows pulled tightly down as he glanced at the infirmary door.

Thelic nodded but struggled to understand. The outlanders' role in this was still as veiled as the shadows they kept to. Kadhim's concern appeared genuine, and if he was as invested in Maya's safety as he seemed, then they could use that.

"You were right, Elkin. Lifaya is fading. Last I heard she had little time left," Mikosh said. He dropped his gaze to look at his feet, shame and sadness a lead weight on his heart. "I would go to her, but the journey would almost certainly kill me."

One of the remaining bordello women emerged from the infirmary to inform them that Maya was finally awake.

Thelic walked in and sat on the bed beside her, closing the door to the others. The bandages were well strapped, and the blood hadn't yet seeped through. He looked then to her eyes.

Their bright flair had diminished and now sat dull and weary against a pale face.

"I told you that was a bad idea," he said.

"Did Mikosh tell you the location?"

Thelic nodded. He felt deeply for Maya, for what she was going through, what she'd been through, and what was likely to be expected of her in the future.

"Hey." She lifted his chin so he was once again looking into her eyes. "Stop sulking. I'm ok, just a bit tired."

"You stopped *breathing*, Maya."

She hadn't realised. "Oh, well I didn't die." She grinned, the only comfort she could offer.

Thelic shook his head, "If something happened…"

"Stop. There's no use thinking like that."

"Maya, my father's fable, I didn't tell you the ending," he whispered, scared to utter the words in case they became prophecy.

"Whatever it is, it's just a story." The look on his face told her she didn't want to know, not now, not when she felt so broken. She mustered what remained of her strength to ask the only question that mattered. "So, where are we going?"

"First to Fortus, then to the mountain region of the Outlands."

Maya sighed wearily. "Delightful."

16

THE MARBLE CITY

FORTUS

Dawn began to break over the mountains as Mikosh's hired oarsmen pushed from one of Transum's eastern docks. The barge provided for the group's crossing was small and a poor comparison to that of Sika's, but it was big enough for the six travellers and their creatures, and it was free.

Across the still waters, the firelight from the western shores of Fortus danced like fireflies in the distance, each one snuffing out with the sun's yawn. Maya sat at the bow and watched their approach, a mix of awe and dread warring inside her. In the short amount of time it had taken to gather their belongings and the karkili to the barge, her strength had barely returned. Again, she was left paying the physical toll a summoning demanded. Nevertheless, she felt slightly stronger than she had, like training a muscle. Bandaar's words rang in her ear like an echo.

You're barely human.

Was it her power that dictated her humanity? Or something more? Maya added it to the mental list of questions she'd been compiling for her grandmother, Fatari.

As the boat docked at the Fortusian port, a woman harbouring a scroll of paper and a sour demeanour was there to greet the early morning arrivals. With a grim face, she demanded a reason for their visit and the length of their stay. Thankfully, Kadhim and Zarina had felt it wise to slip into the ripples of the boat's wake before they docked to avoid any trouble. The woman eyed the four remaining travellers dubiously, her stare lingering on Maya who had struggled to stand in greeting.

Elkin assured the woman that they were merely passing through to the territory's eastern docks to solicit passage home to Danika. She determined this trip by karkili to take them no longer than five days, and so they were issued a travel document stating as such. A warning was given that, should they be caught in Fortus beyond this period, they would likely be executed as spies or illegals.

Beyond the gates of the dock stood a beautiful city. Marble, crystal, and white stone lay before them in pristine splendour. Here there were no ramshackle houses or decrepit barns; only dwellings, shop fronts and taverns spaciously laid-out and divided by spotless stone roads. This was a city fit for the high-society inhabitants that Fortus bragged.

Again, Maya was taken aback at how this territory, separated only by a small body of water from its neighbours, could be so vastly unique. Danika's major town had been a vibrant place, its Moroccan-like colours exploding to life. Esterbell in comparison had been muted in its decorative style and Cantor even more so. Transum had been the biggest cultural shock to Maya, until now.

While Transumian fashion was similar to that of Fortus – falsely claiming innocence in its ivory-white colours – Fortus was a heavenly comparison, right down to its pearly gates. The only indication that they still in fact remained in the world of Avalon, were the karkili that carried the few early morning risers from their homes to their places of work.

They rode the widened carriageways of Transum's city streets, under a line of trees that offered a splash of green in a somewhat colourless place. Even the structures bore no resemblance to their neighbouring islands. Here there was no sign of the oriental fashioned eaves. Instead, the dwellings featured domed roofs and shutterless windows.

"This place is…" Maya couldn't find the words.

"Boring?" Elkin offered.

"I was thinking more along the lines of beautiful, impressive, stunning and possibly intimidating," Maya chuckled, her head butting against the underside of Thelic's chin. He shifted back on the karkili and readjusted his grip on the reigns. Until she regained her strength enough to risk riding the creature on her own, Thelic's hard chest at her back was a welcome reassurance.

"Sure, it's all of those things. But it's too sterile for me, not enough grit or action," the scruffy bear winked mischievously.

"I suppose when you're a professional thief, a sourcer, that makes sense in a place as rich as this. I imagine the citizens here aren't found wanting," Maya said.

"Oh, don't be fooled. Some of my best clients have been Fortusian. Their need to possess that which others do not is part of the society lifestyle," he explained.

"I see." Maya recognised the similarity in her own world, where some of the wealthiest would buy items unnecessary for anything other than to boast that they could. "So, I assume these travel tickets are to keep the riffraff from staying longer than might be considered desirable?" She held hers up, a simple card with a stamp, a date of arrival and a date of expected departure.

"Of course, terrible to have such dregs plaguing the

Fortusian streets for longer than necessary." Elkin imitated the air of a regal – straight backed and pompous.

A woman brushing her already immaculate front steps frowned at the scruffy group as they passed. She stopped sweeping, only to place a chubby hand on her hip; clearly displeased by Elkin's impression. Atop his karkili, he bowed dramatically to the woman, who tutted before storming back into her marble palace.

Maya wheezed with the attempt to contain her giggles; an arm wrapped around her stomach. Thelic, too, rumbled with concealed laughter and the group once again found themselves in good spirits at the territory's expense.

Before their departure, Kadhim had requested the group meet with them at an inn positioned in the northern sector of the city. Thelic's familiarity with the territory made it easy to navigate the near-desolate streets. The quiet walkways, bereft of children or rumbling carts, emphasised the echo of the karkili hooves and denied the travellers stealth or privacy.

Thelic felt Maya's body tense against his own, and assured her that, here, the people had no reason to rise with the dawn and soon enough the streets would be bustling. She relaxed. Thelic, however, remained aware. His service with Jaxum had ended swiftly and left a suspicious taste in the Fortus Keeper's mouth.

It wasn't long before Thelic stopped them outside a large inn; The sign above its door simply painted with the words: *The Origin*. Thelic reached up to help Maya from the karkili and lightly clasped her elbow as she found her feet. Inside, marble stairs took centre stage of the room, with a bar to the left and tables to the right. A man with a notably scarred face, dressed in a simple white robe, rushed over to greet his early morning customers.

"Hello, valued patrons," he said as he curled his body into

a low bow. Elkin's eyes flashed to Maya in humour at the dramatic reception.

"We're meeting some acquaintances here," Thelic said.

"And who might that be?"

Thelic wavered at the man's question, unsure what name the outlanders may have given, if they'd concealed their identities.

Maya instead stepped forward to offer an explanation. "We have no name unfortunately, but they would have arrived early this morning, or…" she realised, "they may not have arrived yet. We could be slightly ahead of them."

The owner regarded the three strangers and twiddled the oversized cuffs of his robe nervously, unwilling to betray his customers anonymity should they require it.

"Takarum, they're with us," Zarina's voice drifted from the top of the marble stairs.

The owner whipped his head back to Maya and clasped her hands in his. The fingers, previously hidden by his long robes were cold and hard, not human. Maya realised then that they appeared to be made of hard, animated clay. She jerked her own back instinctively, regretful as the owner's face dropped.

With the will of a professional who was used to the cold reaction, he quickly adopted a wide grin and bowed again, this time in apology. "Please forgive me. These hands of mine are quite unusual, and I didn't mean to alarm you."

"You're an outlander," Keela realised, a cruel grin stretching across her face. "And you're in hiding."

The scars that marred a once pleasing face rippled with annoyance. Before his arrival, Takarum had taken a blade to the runes that marked him as an outsider to the Avalonian territories. His hands too, were removed and replaced with the enchanted earth element, an extreme but effective method of concealment. Choosing to ignore the demeaning label, he clasped his stiff hands together and said, "I've heard you are sympathisers to the cause; I welcome you."

"We are no such thing," Keela hissed, her eyes dancing around the inn for any possible eavesdroppers.

The owner stumbled back at her verbal assault, his eyes whipping to Zarina who was making her way down the marble stairs. Kadhim had joined her and made his way over to Maya, assessing her state. She remained standing, barely, Thelic's arm wrapped lightly around her waist by way of support.

Kadhim's eyes narrowed, frustrated. "You need rest." He stood directly in front of her, the violation of her personal space of no consequence to him. She noticed the subtle change in Thelic's grip, tightening possessively. Kadhim noticed too and stood to the side; he'd voiced his concern and would push no further.

"Will you be staying, Master Kadhim?" the owner asked, the slight tilt in his tone subtly betraying his wish for them all to leave. The young outlander looked to Maya for a response. She shook her head weakly, determined to continue with their journey.

"We will stay for some food and then be on our way, Takarum. Please have some additional supplies ready for departure by then." At Kadhim's request, the owner bowed before rushing gratefully from the room.

～

"WHERE DO YOU THINK THEY ARE?" Maya asked, searching the surrounding buildings and trees of the city's outskirts. Upon their departure from the inn, the two outlanders had retreated with the promise of remaining close by should they require help.

Thelic, too, looked to the sky but had no answer to give. It was one of the many things about the odd beings that unnerved him – the lack of presence until they were right on top of you with a blade at your throat.

"Apparently they can turn themselves into animals," Elkin said.

Keela chortled. The rumour was well-known but unproven – a tactic to frighten children from wandering too close to strange animals. To her, this likely explained Elkin's belief, what with him being an overgrown child in her eyes. She looked at him now, disdainfully.

"What?" he asked, sensing her contempt. "You've heard the stories."

"Exactly. They're stories. Nothing to say they're true. Plus, I wouldn't presume an outlander to be so talented," she sneered.

A black bird with red-tipped wings dove towards her, twisting sideways to skim the karkili's ear with a light brush. The surprise caused the larger creature to buck, mildly throwing its rider who grasped for the reigns with a low curse.

"I think you've offended them," Elkin chuckled.

As they rode past the eastern sector of the city, the rows of houses began to dwindle, and tall trees took their place. Even the woods of this territory denounced any room for criticism. Fully bloomed and healthy, they stood tall but far apart, allowing the sun to grace its visitors. Past the final house on the city's outskirts, guards stood on either side at the end of the stone road. Beside them was a tall bird cage, its inhabitants chirping in a joyful chorus.

Thelic pulled his hood further forward to conceal his face and instructed everyone to have their cards ready. As expected, the guards demanded their travel documents and peered at each, examining the stamp and dates with a careful eye.

A second guard had been staring at Thelic, eyebrows scrunched together and head tilting from side to side. With a nod from their inspector, the guard broke his gaze and reached into the cage to remove one of the colourful birds. A quick note was written and attached to its spindly leg before being thrown into the air, soaring away to its predetermined destination. With a grunt, the guard allowed them to pass with a warning to remain on the east-western path.

"Why do I get the feeling this place doesn't get many tourists?" Maya said quietly with a quick glance back at the path's guardians. They continued to stare after them, one of the guards leaning in to speak with the other.

"It used to. People would travel from across the territories to visit the Marble City and its citadel. All of this is new," Thelic said, gesturing back to the makeshift guard-station.

"It's probably down to the brewing war with the outlanders. Do you think that guard recognised you, Thel-lie?" Elkin asked.

"I hope not, but it's possible. I trained a number of Jaxum's soldiers during my service here."

"Would it be bad if he recognised you?" Maya twisted to face Thelic, concern lining her face.

"Depends. Jaxum has always been a paranoid bastard, but hopefully he's distracted enough to ignore the return of a former hand."

With nothing to do on the road, Maya quizzed the others on the territory. Keela had visited the area only twice and seemed disinclined to contribute to the discussion, instead leaning further into the high-backed saddle to get some sleep. Elkin had only travelled as far as a village by the eastern docks, where his requested quarry was often stored to be picked up. That left Thelic to educate Maya with what he'd learnt during his service.

He began with the citadel; a gargantuan temple that

honoured the Five Majors. At the heart of the city, it stood in all its crystalline glory and claimed the title of the oldest and biggest of all the buildings in Avalon. Several smaller temples around the outskirts had been erected to honour the Gouram, though they had long been forgotten and rarely saw visitors.

Next, he spoke of his service with Jaxum. The Fortus Keeper had been difficult and paranoid, giving Thelic menial tasks until he could prove his worth. A stroke of orchestrated luck had seen Thelic quickly promoted to train Fortusian fighters. That day, a fighting event was being held at the arena. Thelic's intelligence told him that Jaxum and his family attended these fights religiously. So, he anonymously paid a group of tourist ruffians to start a brawl on the viewing platform above the Keeper's personal podium. As the fight spilled onto the neighbouring platforms, Thelic had stepped in and quickly overpowered the louts in full view of Jaxum and his daughter. Upon seeing this, Alaara had requested Thelic as her personal guard. After several months proving himself as a trainer, he spent the next two and a half years shadowing her.

Maya remembered the entitled woman from the stable; possessive, spoilt and temperamental with copper-red hair becoming of her personality. She glanced at Elkin – his own scruffy red hair rustling in the breeze – and retracted her last thought.

Along the east-western road they reached the first of a series of small towns and their simple, typically Avalonian dwellings made of white stone and cedar shingled roofs; a far-cry from the Marble City's opulent perfection. At their approach, children clutching items for sale rushed to the visitors.

To spare the young ones the disappointment of failing to sell, Elkin and Thelic purchased a small item from each.

Keela remained stone-faced, immune to the well-crafted looks of despair the children used to manipulate their clientele. Refusing to buy anymore, the children were shooed away.

"Wow, those kids saw you two coming a mile off," Maya declared, one eyebrow cocked as the two males recounted their remaining coins.

As they set off, Thelic released the reigns of the karkili and slipped a small metallic object into Maya's palm. A pendant, beautifully crafted and surprisingly weighty considering its source.

"The children of the villages here mine for metals. This particular type is only found in the Northern Opal Mountains of Fortus." He fingered the object in her hand. "It's stainless and impervious to any singular element."

"How do they manipulate it then?" she asked, admiring the twisted shape of the precious metal.

"They freeze and burn it, warping its molecules. At a particular stage they're able to shape the material." At the questioning gazes of the group, Thelic mumbled something about Alaara forcing him to accompany her visits to the local towns.

Maya appreciated the talisman. "The symbols, do they mean anything?" The metal had been beautifully warped to form an odd combination of shapes, thin and no larger than a human eye.

"They represent the four elements, and spirit."

"I figured it was something to do with the Five Majors," Maya admitted.

Thelic held her softly from behind. "Considering your power, your link to the elements, I thought this would be more personal." Leaning back, she stretched up and kissed his cheek. It *was* more personal, though she wasn't sure why. Maya's experience with summoning the elements had been anything but pleasant so far, but she had always felt them. Looking back, even at her low-rent apartment in London, she remembered all the times she felt the wind in her hair, watched the rain pound against her window or felt the earth's vibrations as she ran through the Richmond Common. The thought struck her, that the elements, or her link to them, may have been there all along.

THE SUN SET on the third day of travelling through the Fortus territory. So far, they'd passed several villages, all offering hand crafted items, food, and drink like the first. Opting to maintain a stealthy presence, they refused the proposals of a place to stay and instead slept off the path in the open woods.

By the end of their *second* day, they had reached halfway – a day ahead of their appointed schedule – and aimed to maintain this rate of progression. Despite their intentions, the hard-backed mount of the karkili and long distances caused their muscles to ache and eyes to fall heavy, forcing them to retire each night at sundown. Maya suspected this was more for her sake. Unlike the seasoned warriors, she wasn't used to the rough travel.

As they rode atop the hard saddles on the creatures' backs, each member became more and more grateful for the light and soft material Wilix the tailor had given them. Abandoning the silk coats and flared trousers, they had opened their given goody-bags from the Transumian on the first day of travel through Fortus. Inside were clothes comfortable enough for the journey, though with adequate hardiness to save their thighs from chaffing.

Over the past few days, Maya had found her strength had returned enough to ride her own karkili. She missed Thelic's bodaari, Keero; his wide back and fluffy, blanketed fur had made travelling long distances a comparative luxury.

BY MORNING on the fourth day, the blankets were rolled and the creatures mounted. It wasn't until mid-afternoon that they reached the third guard station and repeated the process of showing their travel documents. As the guard carried out his inspection, a bird above squawked, announcing its arrival before landing gingerly on a nearby branch. Moving to intercept, a second guard strolled to the branch to retrieve the bird and its message.

"These are fine, you're making good progress," their inspector said, handing back the passes. "Continue along the east-western path and don't deviate," he reminded the group for a third time. Pocketing their documents and giving their rides a light tap to the rear, they trotted towards the second guard. He stepped in their path, the bird's delivered message hanging in one hand, his other held out to the travellers.

"Stop," he demanded, signalling for the first guard to join him. "Are you Thelic Anthon?"

Thelic went still, his hand gripping the central shaft of the spear.

"You *are* Master Anthon, correct?" The first guard read the message as it was handed to him, and his jaw dropped.

"I remember you! You trained my brother in the 2nd division," the first guard beamed, before remembering the contents of the letter and curbing his excitement. "You're to meet with the Fortus Keeper at Yatiken Point, immediately," he instructed.

"I am no longer under Jaxum's service, and am therefore under no obligation to follow their commands," Thelic reminded them, his eyes hard and tone low, dangerous, daring them to object.

The second guard spluttered, outraged at the insult. "You are a *guest* in Fortus territory and will obey the Fortus Keeper's demands!"

"Gentlemen, Yatiken Point is out of our way, and we are on a deadline for Danika's Keeper," Elkin pleaded on Thelic's behalf.

"You will proceed, *accompanied*, to Yatiken Point," the guard insisted.

They could fight, three warriors against two measly guards. They would win with ease, Thelic mused. But if they ran, word would reach Jaxum and they would be stopped at the harbour, possibly executed on sight.

"Fine," he decided. "I'll go with you and my companions will continue on their travels."

Maya snapped her head to Thelic, an objection mounting with her next breath.

"Good idea. Your Keeper requires only Thelic's attendance, does he not?" Elkin asked, his eyes conveying to Maya what his lips could not – *trust me.*

The guards looked at each other, unsure but ultimately deciding he was correct. The letter requested only Thelic Anthon's presence. "That's fine, stick to the east-western road."

With a nod, Elkin took control of both his and Maya's reigns, and led them away, down the path and out of sight.

"What are you thinking? We can't leave him, you know his history with Jaxum!" she hissed between gritted teeth in quiet rage, unsure of the guard's proximity.

"Don't worry, we'll follow them at a distance," Elkin said with a grin.

"I thought you were unfamiliar with the territory?" Keela questioned, perturbed by their new plan and far more inclined to do as they'd promised the guards and continue to the eastern docks.

"I am, somewhat. But this territory is well paved, and Yatiken Point is known to stand upon the cliffs overlooking the Outlands. It shouldn't be difficult to follow them," he assured Maya, resting a hand on her shoulder.

"Why do you think Jaxum wants to see him?"

"It could be a number of reasons, little fulsin," he offered unhelpfully. "Maybe suspicion over Thelic's unexpected departure, or he may want to re-enlist him, or…"

"Or?" Maya and Keela asked in unison.

"Or, the letter was written in Jaxum's name *only*, and it's a certain redheaded enchantress that requires his attention." Elkin shivered at the thought.

Maya felt a burning, possessive fury and uttered one name. "Alaara."

17
A WOMAN SCORNED

FORTUS ~ YATIKEN POINT

They would come for him. Elkin was always like that, always a trustworthy companion, not that Thelic would need rescuing. But the thought was reassuring. Despite their history, Keela and Elkin made a formidable team, and he was lucky to have them at hand. Even Maya in her untrained state could probably take out the entire Fortus observation deck. *Maya.* Thelic sighed at the thought of the brash woman and could only hope she wouldn't do anything reckless in the meantime. He didn't want Jaxum anywhere near her. His personal history was holding up their journey and leading Maya to danger; his jaw clenched at the thought.

The steep incline to the clifftop fortress was not easily navigated by the karkili. A rough path cut through the rock was their only route, offering views of the dividing channel between territories and Outlands beyond. As they mounted the final, rocky lip, Yatiken Point stood proud against the barren cliffs. Strategically placed, the fort fulfilled its purpose as the Fortusian eastern observatory. A tall, stone turret climbed to heights unchallenged, its sights set on the surrounding neighbours.

With the visitors' appearance, four additional guards made their way from the tower entrance. Thelic dismounted from the karkili as instructed, his eyes combing the surrounding rocks for his companions. Nothing. Since Maya had irrevocably upended his life that day in the glen, they hadn't been apart. Being away from her now stirred a strange feeling, clawing at his chest and willing him to return to the calamitous woman. A flash of red caught his eye; hidden by the rocks but unmistakeable. *Elkin.*

"Oih," a guard bellowed at the stationary Thelic. "What were you looking for?" he asked, his own eyes now assessing the surrounding area.

"Grokus. I heard they've been spotted in this area recently," Thelic replied, his eyes darting from left to right dramatically.

The guard stilled, grip tightening on the hilt of his sword. "That's a bunch of snubcokey," he said, a nervous laugh escaping him.

Thelic shrugged before turning to head for the open gate, hissing under his breath.

The guard spun at the grokus-like noise; blade unsheathed. A sobering clang to his helmeted head grounded the young man when coupled with the angry commander yelling, "They don't dwell in this region, you fucking idiot."

Inside, the cavernous stone structure was bare of decoration. Weapons racks and cots were scattered across the inner confines of the lower level, harsh conditions for the lengthy year-long post.

After reluctantly handing over his spear, Thelic was shoved to the right and up a winding circular staircase that climbed the turret walls to the observation deck. From here the guards were afforded a 360-degree view of the surrounding area and beyond. The cruel Shadow Mountains of the barren Outlands stood in terrifying glory to the east, their summit hidden beneath a perpetual dark cloud. Thelic walked over to the edge and gazed out, his eyes searching hopelessly for any sign of life. The Seer had settled somewhere in that impossible region.

Light footsteps from behind broke his reverie. He didn't turn, instead he said, "I figured you'd be too busy preparing for this war to chase old shadows across the territory."

"You're not just any shadow though, are you, Thelic?"

He tipped his head to the sky and breathed a mixture of relief and frustration at the silky, feline voice of his ex-lover. "Ah, I see Baba has finally put you to work," Thelic said, his emphasis on Alaara's term of endearment for her father lined with a condescending tone.

Hardened to the frequent taunts of high society prims, Alaara rolled the insult off her shoulders. "My guards tell me you're traveling to the eastern docks."

"*Your* guards?" Thelic laughed.

"What happened between you and the Esterbellian Keeper, Thelic? Are you in trouble? Is that why you're going through the other territories to get back to Danika?"

Her concern took him by surprise, and he turned to look at her. This was the Alaara he'd known, the Alaara that cared. She had entered society at the age of twenty-two, like all men and women of higher class. They'd been together for a year by that point, and he believed he was in love. But as her circles changed, so did her personality.

"We were taking the scenic route," he offered in answer to all her questions.

"Don't lie to me! That peasant woman has dragged you into something, I know it," she yelled, her hair, a dramatic fan of red, only emphasising her temper. "I could have sent word to my father, I'm sure he'd be equally as interested in your business here."

"What do you want from me, Alaara?"

She baulked at the look he gave her. It was a look she had cherished when brandished at her defence, but frightened her now. "I...I just want to help you."

Thelic raked a hand through his hair and turned his back to her once again. There was a time when she'd had the power with one word, one look, to stop him mid-swing from separating a man's head from its perch. Arms curled around his stomach as her face pressed into his back. He sighed and leaned over the stone barrier separating him from a drop to the sharp rocks below. Green eyes in a whirl of golden hair stared back from mid-way up the turret wall. His heart stopped.

"WE COULD TAKE THEM," Maya insisted. Pacing between the rocks, she risked a peek every now and again at the fort's entrance.

"No, *we* could take them, you're more likely to kill all of us," Keela said scathingly. Maya gave her a look, simply implying that now wasn't the time.

"We have no idea how many guards are in there, little fulsin; and Jaxum is no small mission."

"He's powerful?" she asked, biting her nails. Elkin wasn't helping either.

"Like you, he is bound to a Finkel sprite making him quite strong to begin with. But he's also well versed with an assortment of weapons." Elkin sat on one of the rocks and removed his blades along with a small stone.

"You're sharpening your knives, now?" Maya crossed her arms to stop the nervous habit.

"Mm-hmm."

She paced. A flick of movement at the top of the observation deck caught her eye, strong arms hanging over the banister. Thelic. It had to be. All of Jaxum's soldiers were forced to wear long-sleeved tunics, despite the unforgiving heat.

"I'm just going for a wee," Maya whispered, slinking off. Keeping low, she switched direction and slipped between the dusty rocks. No guards were present outside of the gates and Maya navigated her way easily to the base of the eastern wall.

The crumbling stone was marred with cracks and divots. *I can climb this,* she thought, slowly numbering each fissure as she picked out her route. The turret was easily over a hundred feet tall, higher than she'd ever scaled before. With no safety lines or crash mats to save her, Maya experienced one of those life-saving moments – when survival instincts kick in and tell you this is a particularly bad idea, and natural selection takes a back seat. Ignoring it, she gathered dust from the rocks and coated her hands, sending a mental note of thanks to Wilix for his choice of rubber soles in her flat plimsoles.

Halfway up the turret, her arms shook with fatigue and her right thigh burned. She stopped momentarily, wiping the perspiration from her hands onto the dusty walls. A black bird with red-tipped wings swooped nervously beside her before diving to the rocks below. She looked up to check her progress, and silvery blue eyes met hers. Eyes that went from mild disbelief to sparkling rage. She smiled and continued climbing, suddenly nervous to reach the top.

～

"THELIC, PLEASE," Alaara whispered.

He'd momentarily forgotten about Alaara, her voice reminding him of the danger to Maya should she reach the top. He turned back and held her by the shoulders at arms-length. "Tell your guards to give us some privacy," he said coolly.

Her eyes shone with hope, and she instructed the guards to leave. Nervous glances were passed between them, but the guards did as commanded, closing the thick, wooden door behind them.

She embraced him again, her face looking up longingly at his. "Come back to me, Thelic. Tell me what you need."

"Maya–" A hard shove to Thelic's chest cut him off as Alaara pushed away.

"Why? What is that stupid, low-born woman to you?" she screeched. "You were mine; we were good together and could have ruled over Fortus, *together!*"

"Now, there's needy–" Maya leaned heavily on the frame of the stone balcony, heaving one of her legs up breathlessly, "– and then there's crazy stalker," she wheezed, dragging the rest of her body up and over onto the observation deck floor to land with a graceless thud.

Alaara took a step back and turned to run for the door, ready to order her guards' return. Thelic's hand wrapped around her mouth, the other gripping her waist.

With shaky knees and little breath, Maya managed to rise to her feet. She glanced at Thelic who returned a look of unmasked fury and disbelief.

"You–" he stuttered.

Maya walked up and kissed him on the cheek, winking as she said, "You would have done the same."

She was wrong. Thelic wouldn't have thought or had the skill to climb that wall. If it were Maya that had been taken, he would have barged through the front door.

Walking unsteadily back to the edge of the balcony, Maya looked down to where Elkin and Keela had been sitting. The two were standing now, in the midst of what seemed to be a heated argument. She gave a low whistle and waved from her perch, they ducked and looked up. Maya waved and gave a thumbs up. Elkin seemed to laugh as he waved back. Keela, apparently less impressed, dropped her head into her hands.

With their friends warned, Maya faced the entitled Fortusian woman with a menacing look. "Nasty business, abducting former lovers."

Alaara mumbled a response barred by Thelic's fingers still gripping her mouth. With Maya's nod, Thelic loosened his clasp and a torrent of verbal abuse erupted from the captive woman.

"You'll be skewered for this. My father will have you *both* hanging from the citadel walls you pathetic–"

Maya unsheathed the small, unimpressive sword from her side and swung it up. The skin at Alaara's throat dipped as the tip of the blade pushed into the nape.

"Maya…" Thelic warned, sensing a darkness he was all too familiar with.

Maya echoed Alaara's words from their initial meeting at the stables. "*Who are you* to threaten the daughter of Bandaar?" She nudged the sword, a trickle of blood lacing down Alaara's throat. "What business is it of yours what we do?"

"You…you're the missing daughter, Bandaar's–"

"I am, though I want nothing to do with him *or* that title," Maya said as she lowered the blade to her side.

"Where have you been this whole time?" Alaara whispered in awe, no longer concerning herself with summoning the guards.

"Like I said, I don't believe that's any of your business, Alaara."

"I heard rumours of what he did to you, of his obsession with the outlanders and the chaos."

Despite his stoic expression, Thelic was surprised. Alaara was more informed than he'd expected.

"So I've heard," Maya replied with equal indifference.

"Is that why you're here, why you're travelling through the territories? To fulfil his wishes?"

Maya laughed at that, at the prospect of working alongside her twisted father. "We're working *against* him. His goals are misguided."

A low growl rumbled from Thelic, another warning. Maya was giving away too much. Alaara twisted in his grip. He released her and stepped to the side, an imposing wall of muscle between their captive and the exit.

"I can help you. I can secure your passage through Fortus," she assured them, confidence returning.

"Why would you do that?" Maya asked, increasingly dubious of the woman's intentions.

"Because you were my fable," she admitted shyly, rubbing her fingers together in a nervous gesture. "I always imagined that you escaped with your mother to somewhere that people weren't cruel, and you were no longer bound by expectations."

Thelic realised, then, what had changed in the future leader of the Fortus territory. She had stepped up misguidedly into a role she didn't want but was expected to uphold.

Shouts emerged from behind the door, and everyone turned as Dixol slammed through, furious his mistress had been left alone with the prisoner. The scene before him did nothing to temper his rage. Maya raised her sword and Thelic stepped back, one hand gripping Alaara's wrist.

"I remember you," Maya said. "How's the old honey-sacks?" she referred to his genitals after their encounter at the stables in Cantor, where she'd slightly lessened his chances of reproducing.

"Surround them!" he ordered the guards who filed through the door behind him. Maya and Thelic had their backs to the stone balcony and six guards blocking their exit. "Release her, now," Dixol barked.

The sound of small wings fluttered around them. Maya looked up and saw what appeared to be the same black bird. Another had joined it – white with the identical red tips.

The birds dove, aiming for one of the guards. The man raised his arms to protect his face, both hands clutching Thelic's confiscated spear. But they didn't attack. Instead, the spear was plucked from his hands, and they leapt back into the sun's glare overhead.

Just as suddenly, two bodies clad in white armour fell from the sky, landing gracefully on the stone wall behind Maya and Thelic, the spear clasped between them.

The outlanders.

The guards gasped and stepped back. One outright screamed and dropped his weapon, before catching himself and scrambling to retrieve it. The outlanders remained crouched; their long, taloned fingers draped over their bent knees, and faces covered with a material that flapped open with the wind . Without a word, they lunged, one grasping Maya and the other Thelic. Then they dropped, over the side of the balcony to the stony rocks below.

The guards rushed forward and Dixol grabbed the screaming Alaara, sure the two had been dragged to their death.

"They're...floating...they're alive!" One guard squealed, unsure whether to be impressed or horrified by what he'd just witnessed.

"Go and get them!" Dixol ordered.

"No! Leave them." Alaara bent over the balcony and

watched as Thelic, Maya and the outlanders were met by two others before disappearing into the surrounding forest. "We know they're heading to the eastern docks, send word to the path patrols that they are *not* to be stopped."

"But, Mistress–"

"Send another message to dock patrol with their description. I want them followed, discreetly. Find out which direction the water-rakers take them." The guard commander nodded in understanding and left to relay the order.

"What about your father?" Dixol asked.

"He forgets that we face more than one enemy. Those outlanders were helping them. There's something we're missing," she explained, her eyes assessing the thundering plains of the Outlands.

MAYA and the others raced through the woods to their three remaining karkili. Unwilling to risk the guards catching up, they set off immediately.

After several hours of hard riding, they slowed their steeds to a steady trot. The sun had set on Avalon, the three moons taking its place to light the way. Ahead, large beams of light pierced the canopy, reflecting the white armour of their rescuers.

Zarina sat patiently on the thick branch of a tree. At its base, Kadhim had been pacing a small trench into the earth. Spotting them, he strode forward with one taloned finger extended at Maya.

"You! Spirits curse you!"

Maya put a hand to her chest and dropped her jaw, the picture of innocence. "What did I do? He's the one that went and got himself kidnapped by a psycho ex-girlfriend!"

"I don't care about him! I'm talking about *you*, climbing

that wall, and almost getting yourself killed!" He scrubbed both taloned hands through his short raven hair and resumed pacing.

"I thought it was impressive," Zarina offered with a grin, stark white hair neatly plaited across her shoulder swung free as she leapt stylishly from the branch to greet them.

"As did I." Elkin pushed his karkili forward and offered a high-five to Maya, a gesture she'd taught him on their travels.

"I agree with Kadhim, it was pretty fucking reckless," Thelic said, the image of Maya hanging above the rocks burned into his memory.

"And *you!*" Kadhim's finger was redirected. "Your personal problems could have cost us this entire quest!"

Thelic's mouth twitched at the crumbling outlander, hand flexing on the hilt of his spear. "You want to remove that mutilated finger from my face?"

"Boys, boys." Zarina pranced over, one hand on Kadhim's shoulder and the other resting on Thelic's thigh atop the karkili. "As fun as it would be to watch your battle of prides, we're wasting time," she purred, her voice and logic calming the storm of colliding egos.

Kadhim dropped his hand and Thelic relaxed his grip, a wary eye on Zarina's claws so close to a vital member of his body.

In exasperation, Kadhim transformed into the red-winged bird and vanished into the canopy above. With a quick wink, Zarina disappeared in pursuit.

Elkin stared after them, suspicions confirmed of the outlanders' shapeshifting abilities. "I *told* you they could transform!" he gloated, shooting a smirk at Keela.

With no time to spare, the group continued through the night. Travel by firelight was deemed too risky, their aim to sneak undetected past the final guard station. The moons' glow, however, proved to be an ample light source as they traversed a path parallel to the east-western road.

Hours passed and the moons ran their course to swap shifts once again with the unrelenting sun. Maya wiped away at the sweat blanketing her skin. They all needed a shower, or a bath or any form of clean water to wash away the stink of five days travel. She leaned forward, suddenly conscious of Thelic at her back.

By mid-afternoon the trees thinned and houses once again appeared, bustling with activity. Forced from the wooded veil, they raised their hoods and dismounted to walk beside the exhausted creatures that had carried them so far. Carriages flurried by, full of goods for trade, and dockhands barked orders to their workers. The buzzing waterside town was loud and the air ripe with the stink of dead creatures, their blood lining the roadside drains from gutting stations.

Thelic led them to a small inlet that sat apart from the larger merchant ships. Water-rakers sat along the banks with long, broken nets, and replacement string to repair them. Young rakers played in the shore of the inlet, the watchful eyes of their parents monitoring the water for any tell-tale ripples of unfriendly critters. Maya was tempted to join them, to wash away the stench that seemed to grow worse when mingled with the unpleasant aromas of the dock.

Thelic broke from the group and approached a young man. Maya watched the raker raise his hands and shake his head, clearly unhappy with Thelic's request for passage. On receipt of a heavy pouch of coin, the man seemed to reconsider and motioned for them to follow.

Around the bend sat a vessel, much like the one Mikosh had provided for their voyage to Fortus. This one was marginally bigger with enough room for several additional passengers which, in this case, would be the owner's two sons to help launch the boat across the water. Even from the shores of Fortus, the Outland's ominous mountain range stood tall against the thundering back drop. The hairs on Maya's arms stood on-end, a sixth sense of what was to come. Elkin slid his arm casually around her shoulders and leaned his head atop hers, calming her. She wasn't alone.

Keela was scanning the crowds, her own sixth sense picking something up. They were being followed. She searched for familiar faces, anyone from Esterbell that she may recognise. No, Bandaar would be smarter than that. He would no longer trust her after the scene at Sika's gathering. Nonetheless, she searched for any suspicious behaviour, any lone bodies that stood idly by.

"What is it?" Elkin asked.

"Someone's following us," Keela mumbled, not bothering to look at him. "I'm sure of it."

"You're not wrong," he agreed. "One of them has been following our trail since the Marble City."

"One of them?"

Elkin gave a nod, his own eyes assessing the crowds. "The other is new, only spotted him earlier today."

"How did you know? And why didn't you tell us?" Maya chimed in.

"Kadhim told me while you were busy on your one-woman quest to rescue your beloved."

"Where was I?" Keela asked.

"You were sleeping, I think," he muttered, unimpressed by the Esterbellian's lack of interest in the lives of her travel companions.

The three of them stood now, eyes scanning the crowds, wary of their uninvited shadows. Even if they happened to spot them, nothing could be done. Jaxum's guards swarmed the docks like a colony of ants, checking crates and taking the names of travelling passengers. If they created a scene here, they would almost certainly be hauled back through the territory to the citadel.

It didn't take long for the small family of water-rakers to load their vessel with the group's belongings and the agreeable karkili. The water rippled as it answered their call and they pushed away from the shores of the Fortus territory; towards the Outlands, and Fatari.

18
A WATER GOD'S OASIS

THE OUTLANDS

The wooden hull of the water-raker's vessel scraped across the black sands of Outland's shores. Midnight loomed and the moons' light reflected off the surrounding lifeless trees. The water was still, only the soft waves of the boat disturbing its glassy surface. Nobody breathed a word as the karkili and passengers disembarked. The water-rakers held their breaths, frightened, recoiling at the sound of the soft sand underfoot and what the disturbance might conjure from the night. With their cargo unloaded, the raker-family pushed off silently into the bank of mist, not daring to look back.

Thelic reached into Elkin's satchel for the map. According to Mikosh, Fatari was camped temporarily by the water's edge of Slitter Ridge. At least a five-day hike through the mountains, north of where they stood. Maya stepped around to see and he pointed to their destination, explaining the timelines.

"Five days," she whispered, crestfallen, the small sound lost in the vast landscape.

"Fatari will be dead by then, we're wasting our time,"

Keela said, pacing back and forth and failing to conceal that she was frightened of this place. Maya wanted to batter her, but understood the hesitation.

Thelic folded the map and placed it back in the satchel, taking his place on the karkili and lowering a hand to Maya. He had no hesitation, if there was a way for Maya to stop the chaos without the expense of her life, he'd cross the fabled fiery gates of Hell.

"If you're there, best make yourselves known," Thelic said, his head tipped to the sky above.

Kadhim and Zarina emerged from the shaded line of silver, barkless trees.

"It would be unwise to travel at this hour, the creatures here covet the cooler nights and hide during the day," Kadhim advised. "We've searched the surrounding area and nothing too concerning seems to prowl this close to the shore. Though, I would suggest moving slightly further inland."

Maya watched as a small swell broke the surface of the reflective waterline. Stepping aside so Thelic could dismount, they grabbed the oblivious karkili by the reigns, and moved them further up the bank.

"We can take your watch tonight so you can sleep," Zarina offered cheerfully, unfazed by the territory's eery atmosphere.

"We work in two-person shifts and, as far as I'm aware, you both need sleep as much as we do," Thelic reminded them. It wasn't that he didn't trust the outlanders. They had saved their lives twice now and had certainly proved their value, and the group would need that extra strength if they hoped to make it through the mountains alive.

Kadhim bobbed his head in understanding.

The schedules were divided evenly so each member of their party could sleep. Thelic offered his tent to the outlanders with the intention to sleep in Maya's. Both gave their thanks but declined, accepting only the proffered blankets, preferring to sleep under the sky. Maya and Thelic took the first watch and decided to risk bathing in the still shoreline only metres from the makeshift camp.

With the outlanders out of view, Maya stripped and waded into the tepid water, instantly soothed as the layers of sweat, dust and grime peeled away from her body. Thelic watched as the reflected light bounced off the tranquil waters onto her skin, the result a sleek, ethereal figure. Maya lapped the water over her arms, stroking its stream down to her flat, muscular stomach to dip below the waterline. Not daring to go any deeper, instead, she bent her knees and leaned back, allowing herself to fully submerge.

Unable to wait a moment longer, Thelic relinquished his own clothes to join her. As the water reached his waist, he sighed in bliss as the weariness suffered from their days of travel shed itself from his body. Maya chuckled, wading behind to wash his back. The muscles rippled at her touch as she stroked the long contours down to the base of his spine. Moving closer, her smaller body slid against his bulking mass as she reached around to wash his chest. A low groan escaped his lips at the feel of her breasts pressed against the centre of his back. Whipping around, he grabbed her thighs and lifted her to straddle him. In the same breath he claimed her mouth, his need overwhelming. Maya laced her fingers into the short lengths of thick hair, savouring the rare moment of private intimacy she'd been starved of.

Thelic broke the kiss, breathless, his silver eyes holding hers. "Spirits, what have you done to me?" He reached down to the depths below, to Maya's intimate depths, and stroked her, relished her cravings that mirrored his own as she gyrated against his skilful pulse. He pulled away just as she reached the mounting precipice, "I want to punish you for being so reckless at Yatiken," he rumbled, his fingers returning to drive her once again. "If I had a choice," his rhythm intensified, "you wouldn't walk for a week after I was done with you," he growled into her ear. A shiver of blissful anticipation rushed through her core as she once again reached the breaking point. His fingers disappeared. It was all she could do not to whimper at the aching absence, only for the shock of something bigger, stronger, harder to plunge into her.

She gasped, her body straining to accommodate the sudden mass, a blissful harmony of pain and pleasure pushing her over the edge as he pumped his full length deep inside her. She clutched his shoulders, her half-bitten nails digging into the muscles that heaved with tension as he devoured her. And that's what they did. They weren't making love. The pressure and need between them was too great for the slow undulations of love making. She matched his rhythm whole heartedly; permitting, encouraging, enjoying his callousness as she rode the second wave. His head dropped into the nape of her neck as he, too, shuddered with release. They held each other, tightly, too afraid to let go and miss what might be their last chance for a moment alone. As they caught their breaths, knowing smiles were exchanged, and the tempo began again; warring need abated, they made love.

BY MORNING a deep fog bank had rolled through the camp; the sun, reticent in the early hours, failing to shift it. Kadhim and Zarina had departed at first light to monitor the area, returning in time for Elkin's stew-like breakfast.

"So, is it just those birds that you two can transform into?" The party chef had been dying to ask since their suspicions were confirmed and sat down with his bowl, cross-legged, eagerly awaiting their reply.

"In our tribe, yes. We worship Svingora, the Gouram of air," Zarina said.

"I've heard of that. It's old though, the names of the four Gouram." Elkin tapped the spoon to his forehead, willing himself to remember the others.

"They are the original Gods of this realm, before your Five Majors."

"Thelic mentioned the old temples around Fortus, is that what they were worshipping?" Maya asked.

Zarina nodded sadly. There had been a time when the outlanders were welcome at those temples, several generations ago before the first war, before her time. She longed to see them in their prime.

"Are there other, Gouram-worshipping tribes?" Maya continued as she picked at Elkin's latest concoction, too distracted to notice Zarina's melancholy.

"Yes...at least there used to be. There are four Gouram – Svingora, of air; Batshari, of water; Ragashi, of earth; and Pavinic, of fire. Each of the tribes worships a particular one. Since the Five Majors first brought humans through the gateways...since the elemental chaos, we've been cut off from the other tribes. It's hard to know how many are left."

"I don't understand, I thought the tribes were banding together for war with the territories?" Thelic pressed. He didn't believe for a second anything that suggested or claimed otherwise.

Sensing the Avalonian's suspicion, Kadhim answered in Zarina's stead. "Of course we prepare for war, how could we not? What she means is, our tribes didn't just extend to the six territories."

"I know that much," Thelic said, exasperated. "Apparently they span this entire globe."

"That's right. But what you may not realise, is that the boundary veil cut many of the tribes in half, the rest living on the other side, removed from their loved ones."

"I thought the veil only surrounded the portals?" Again, Maya was thrown by the new information, a reminder of how little she truly knew of her birthplace.

"*That* chaos is an elemental leak, a result of too much power concentrated in one area. The fog that surrounds the territories, this little slice of *Avalon*, is man-made."

Maya didn't fail to notice Kadhim's sarcastic intonation placed on one word in particular. *Avalon*. Did the outlander's have their own name for this world? Before she could question further, Keela spoke.

"The Major Danika saved the humans with that barrier; your kind would have destroyed us. When humans traversed the realm in search of somewhere they could be free from persecution, they arrived here only to be hunted once again. I doubt she intended for the veil to get so out of control."

"She was a foolish woman," Kadhim spat. "Conjuring that boundary may have been to save the human castors, but it's likely going to kill us all with the rate it's encroaching on the territories." He rose to his feet and suggested the group move on. With no room for further discussion, he transformed and soared into the sky beyond the mist.

SURPRISINGLY, no boats had turned up by their campsite through the night or even that morning. Whoever had been following them at Fortus docks had either abandoned the cause or docked elsewhere along the shoreline, out of sight in a bid to remain stealthy.

The bare, ashen trees groaned as their wood expanded with the mounting heat; the sound neither a welcome nor a warning to the those who wandered the abandoned territory, merely a reminder of their presence. The dry, cracked limbs scattered the ground like bones, snapping under the heavy footfalls of the karkilis' hooves. Like the trees, everything at the base of the mountains was dead, with no signs of life in the sound of birds or the smell of grass and flowers.

By the end of the first day, the trees had begun to thin as the land inclined, and they reached the base of the Shadow Mountains, aptly named for the permanent gloomy cloud that rumbled at its peak. The karkili, bred in a pampered environment, were deemed to be unfit to cross the desolate mountain pass. With no other choice, the creatures' harnesses were cut and their ownership revoked, abandoned on the barren lands to feast on the deadened bark of the ash trees.

The following days of trekking the uncompromising mountain terrain were slow and repetitive. Scrambling along the rocks had rubbed their fingers raw, with ankles aching and swollen from one too many missteps along the uneven channels. At the outlanders' suggestion, they had chosen to weave along the lower echelons. The journey would take them twice as long this way, but promised to be half as perilous as going over the mountain peaks.

Maya tripped for the umpteenth time on the scraggy rocks, her once pristine white clothes now muddied with dusty grey and crusted blood. Thelic took the opportunity to stop the group for the second time that day, to rest and take on some water. The heat didn't help matters; every breath was thick with the humidity.

Kadhim appeared at her side and assessed the open and gnarled wounds across Maya knees. "There's an old temple not far from here, we should move there and rest for the night."

"It's barely mid-day," Maya said, desperate for the

extended rest but all too conscious of how much time the trek was taking.

"We can use the time to treat our wounds, rest and have a proper meal," Elkin assured her.

Maya glanced at each member of the group, belatedly realising that they were all looking to her and waiting for a decision. Kadhim continued to nod encouragingly at his own suggestion and Maya sighed. "Fine, I suppose we could stop for a few hours."

As promised, it wasn't long before they turned a bend and were gifted with the sight of something so beautiful and out of place, Maya was sure she was hallucinating.

An underwater river had carved a path through the mountain's belly, spilling out of the rocky gullet into a crystal-clear pool at its feet. The body of water was edged with flowers and vines that crept along the decrepit remains of a temple, its domed roof collapsed, and pillars crumbled. After the days of lifeless surroundings, the greens and blues and pinks of the oasis were revitalising, and everyone sagged with relief.

Without bothering to ask if it was safe, Elkin dropped his gear and jumped into the cool waters of the pool. Maya, more wary, looked to Zarina who nodded with a smile of encouragement. Without further hesitation, everyone leapt in to join him. For the first time in days, smiles were shared as body temperatures plummeted and wounds were cleaned by the lagoon's natural salt content. Even the air was significantly cooler, leaving their lungs feeling wonderfully refreshed. Only Kadhim remained on the bank, his face devoid of the same infectious joy. He was waiting, the only member of the group with knowledge of what was to come.

Expecting to reach Fatari's camp the following day, Elkin used what remained of their meat supply, and cooked a grand meal for the weary travellers. By the temple, fireflies danced through the long grass, lighting the oasis in the absence of moonlight. Stories of old wars and mythical creatures rumoured to dwell in the area were shared, both outlanders and humans coming together for the first time with ease.

Maya's vision began to blur, her exhaustion overwhelming. Refusing to leave the soothing company, instead, she curled up on the blanketed ground and closed her eyes to the soft lullaby of her friends' voices.

The sounds drifted further as Maya floated into an empty void, reminding her of Yali's, when she'd heard those whispers as a child. Something tugged at her conscience. Something was wrong. She was too aware, too present of mind to be dreaming. She opened her eyes, but it wasn't the crackle of firelight she saw, she was home, at her grandparents'.

"MAYA?" Thelic was hesitant to wake her. Like everyone, she was exhausted, but the sun had risen on the fifth day, and they hoped to reach the camp by nightfall. Even as they had each packed their belongings she hadn't stirred. Even now, she lay undisturbed, the soft rise and fall of her chest the only sign she was still alive. Concern crept in as he shook her again, this time less gentle.

"Don't move her!" Zarina hissed, pulling Thelic back. "If her body moves, even slightly, her soul will struggle to reunite with it."

"What the fuck is that supposed to mean? She's soulless?"

"What's going on?" Elkin came to investigate. "Is the sleepy fulsin refusing to rise?" he chuckled, empathetic to the weariness they all still felt.

Thelic was crouched over Maya's empty shell, willing her to wake up and damning himself for trusting the outlanders. "You set this up, didn't you? You knew this was going to happen!" he growled at Zarina, fingers itching to grab his spear and bury it into the white-haired deceiver.

"Not me." Zarina turned and pointed to Kadhim. He, too, lay motionless…soulless. "He's acting as her anchor, he'll make sure she makes it back, Thelic."

"Why? What have you done to her?" Keela demanded, temper flaring.

"This temple was once a sacred place of worship, before the first wars of our two sides," Zarina explained.

"Worshipping who? Or what?" Elkin bent down to Maya's side and placed an ear to her chest, relieved to hear the soft thump of life.

"The oldest and most powerful of the water-sprites, a Gouram."

"Get her back, right now, or you can say goodbye to your feathered prince over there." Thelic's eyes were steel now, and hostile.

"I can't do that. And to kill Kadhim would almost certainly seal Maya's fate," Zarina warned. "Without him, she would face an eternity wandering the space between, like so many before her."

MAYA RACED through the old manor, searching for Yali, Jacob, anyone. Nobody came to greet her. It was abandoned, forgotten. Whispers echoed through the empty space, calling her name, beckoning her to step outside towards the lake. She followed them.

There.

At the water's core, lay the magnificent, fluorescent form of a shropsin.

Maya's breath caught in her throat at the sight; the long, barbed tail, winged fins and sheer size of the water creature so out of place in the Earth Realm. But then, she knew this wasn't her home, not truly. This world was cold and mono-chromatic; not the heart-warming place she was used to.

"Who are you?" Maya whispered.

The beast, whose purple eyes featured long, lizard like pupils, scrutinised the human before him. His even breaths rumbling around her.

Maya walked forward. "What am I doing here?" She stopped at the taloned wings resting on the bank of the water.

"You are Mayara. The halfling. Breaker of promises," the creature rumbled, flashing teeth that would easily make a meal of the young woman, should she fail his test like the others.

"*I am* Maya, but I'm not a halfling and I have no recollection of breaking any promises." She took in the full size of the terrifying creature and said, "I think I'd remember that."

The shropsin chuckled and with it the earth trembled. "Your mother made the promise on your behalf. Perhaps I should just eat you, punishment for her deception."

"Don't talk about her like that," Maya growled. "She was a good woman."

"Oh? Did she not deceive you? Did you not spend your youth basking in blissful ignorance?"

He was right. Her mother had lied, about everything. "Who are you?" she asked again.

"I am Batshari, the Gouram of water." His neck extended proudly as his title was revealed for the first time to the igno-rant human. "Every drop of rain, every current in the vast oceans, even the moisture in the air; all water is an extension of my essence."

Maya considered this, considered her former attempts to manipulate the water element and risked saying, "In that case, I need your help."

Batshari rumbled, humoured by the woman's audacity. "A God's help should not be beseeched with too light a heart, just as your mother found. Though that burden was destined to lie on your shoulders."

"What did she promise you?"

"A life, for a life," he grinned.

"I don't know if you heard, but my mother is dead, so whatever bargain she struck has been paid," she said, glaring at the tricky God.

"Her promise was a life of servitude, your servitude, to the Four Gouram."

"Bollocks! You're lying!"

Maya was swept off her feet with a swing of the shropsin's front fin, its claws ripping through the clothes and skin of her stomach. She screamed in pain, clutching the open wound. Long, yellowed teeth snapped, globules of drool falling to either side of her face.

"You dare challenge me? Stupid, ungrateful child," Batshari hissed. "What reason do I have to lie? You are a speck, a mere ripple in the ocean of time."

"My mother would never do that!" A scream burst from Maya as the God dug one talon deeper into her stomach.

"She would, and she did. To save your life." The shropsin slithered from Maya back into the shallow gloom of the otherworldly lake. "You were born with a failing heart, youngling. Your mother cried out to the Gods, and we answered."

"Was she contracted to one of you?"

"No. At the time she possessed a bond with one of the Finkel sprites, along with remnants of power passed down from your ancestor, Esterbell."

The slashes and puncture to Maya's stomach had calmed, the trickles of blood slowing to a stop. "What happened?"

"We were watching and deemed your life worthy of our

intervention. We offered Jaseen a choice. She could let you die, left alone to surf the afterlife as intended by fate's fickle scheme; Or, in exchange for your servitude, we would bestow a small dose of our combined essence."

"Why would you want me? What could a God possibly have to gain from a human's subservience?" she asked, desperate to know the consequences of her mother's poorly chosen benefactor.

"You are a child of two worlds, a mixed breed with powerful, lingering ties from both parents."

"But my parents are both human."

Again, he chuckled in a low, teasing rumble. "No, Maya," he said slithering forward, his face once again a breath from hers. "You are of the Earth Realm, *and* this one. Your mother was one of the...I believe you call them, outlanders."

Maya!

～

"FUCK, she's still bleeding, why is she always fucking bleeding? Get some more material and heat some water," Thelic instructed, trying desperately to staunch the sudden wound at Maya's abdomen. One minute she had been sound asleep, the next, a large slash and pools of blood. "Maya, wake up, please!"

Zarina did as he asked and ran to fetch what was needed. Kadhim hadn't moved. It had been half a day since Thelic had tried to wake Maya. Half a day of watching her rhythmic breathing for any changes. Elkin and Keela had gone to hunt, realising that their meat supply was gone and only vegetables remained. They took the distraction gladly.

Just as suddenly as it had started, the blood began to slow, trickling to a stop. Thelic swore, concerned, and frustrated. This was the second time she'd gone somewhere he couldn't follow. First it was into the fog, where he had tried and failed to reach her. Now, even her soul was wandering off by itself. What the hell was he supposed to do with that?

~

MAYA COULD HEAR Thelic calling for her. He was worried.

"Summon my element," Batshari demanded, stretching his winged fins taught in anticipation.

"Hang on a moment, you haven't explained *anything* yet! What is this promise? What am I expected to do for the Gouram? And if my mother was an outlander, does that mean one of the Five Majors–"

"Do not speak of them!" The shropsin growled. "You will do as I ask and go to your seer, she will enlighten you. We have wasted too much time already. I must ready you... should you live." He grinned, a toothy wicked thing, and Maya shivered. "Now, summon my element."

Batshari's claws had seen to Maya's spilt blood, the castor circle's offering. She concentrated on the lake, watched its ripples before closing her eyes and allowing the other senses to take over. Moisture hung in the air, droplets clinging to the tiny hairs on her body. She swallowed, the heat robbing her tongue and throat of that smooth mucus lining. She lifted her hands and begged the water from the lake to heed her call. Fast and agile, the element rushed forward to pool at her feet.

"Good," the Gouram purred. "Now, let it fully engulf you."

Maya's heart began to race, thinking of the last time she had summoned the temperamental element. "I did that once, and it tried to kill me."

"I'm sure it did. You must convince my element that you

are worthy of its power," Batshari crooned, enjoying every morsal of her fear.

How the fuck am I supposed to do that? she wondered.

Concentrate, little halfling, Batshari growled back telepathically.

Maya flinched at the unexpected response but did as she was told. She allowed the water to encompass her entire body.

Now, you will likely die, the Gouram chuckled in her head, the sound a cavernous boom.

Maya's panic climbed with the burning sensation in her lungs. She was going to drown. *No, I'm not.* Within the aquatic bubble, she unclenched her fists and opened her mouth, letting the water in. *You WILL find me worthy.* With the bold invitation, the water jumped down her throat. Maya choked, her instincts telling her to cough it up. Instead, she began to absorb it, she could breathe. Maya had offered her body to the element, and they became one.

～

"BREATHE, MAYA, FOR FUCK'S SAKE!" Thelic began to pound on her chest the moment water had spouted from her mouth. "Breathe!"

Blue light sprang across the ground beneath them. A castor circle, unbroken, and pure.

Maya bolted upright, coughing, and grabbed her aching chest. She dragged the air into her lungs and looked at the worried faces. Even Keela was beside her now, a line of sweat dampening the worried frown. It was entirely possible Keela was perspiring from the heat, but the look on her face suggested she truly had been worried for her sister.

Only moments later, Maya's chest began to burn. She cried out with the pain, thrashing against Thelic's hold.

"What is it!?" Elkin's question was answered when a blue seal appeared below her neck, spanning across her shoulders and down the line between her breasts. As quickly as the burning had begun, a soothing sensation ran across her body and the pain vanished.

"Damn, tricky, confusing, unhelpful, *pain in my ass* water God! Now he's gone and done this?"

"Correct me if I'm wrong, but isn't that a Gouram's mark?" Elkin asked, his throat suddenly dry and face matching his pale-white shirt.

Maya clutched her chest in protest. A low, echoing growl from the departing Batshari caused her to wince and issue a mental apology for her outburst. The cool sensation seeped down from her breasts to pool in her lap. Maya glanced down and blinked as a Finkel covered in sapphire-like scales sat between her crossed legs.

Minus Thelic, who continued to hold Maya, everyone else swept back quickly at the shock of the creature's arrival. It was the same shape and size as Loki. Though, with a straight and regal pose, this one seemed more arrogant than mischievous, like a mini Batshari. Maya chortled at the thought.

"Spirits, not another one!" Keela and Elkin groaned. The shimmering Finkel snapped in their direction before evaporating out of sight.

"You made it." Kadhim had woken with Maya's return and walked over to welcome her back.

"You set this up?" Maya asked the sleepy outlander.

"You almost got her killed," Thelic all but snarled.

"It had to be done," Kadhim said matter-of-factly. He looked at the open flap of the shirt against her chest and the mark that stood stark against it, and smiled. "You did well."

"I'm going to need some goddamn answers pretty soon. Every time I come close to getting information, I'm just left with more questions."

"It would be better coming from Fatari," Kadhim said with a yawn and a shrug.

"That's what Batshari said."

Zarina's eyes lit up at the mention of the Gouram's name and demanded Maya tell her everything. Maya promised she would, in time. By this point the sun had relinquished the day and she was keen to bathe and wash away the blood of Batshari's trial in the lagoon.

As she waded into the pool, the swell of its water around her legs was different. The element, even in its most basic form, now felt like an extension of her body. She rubbed at the dry blood covering her healed torso, the remaining pink scars a reminder of the Gouram's power, and his temper. Thelic joined her, conscious that Maya had been a beacon for trouble since the moment they met, and therefore too wary to take his eyes off her.

It wasn't long before the food had been cooked and the party was called to gather. As they ate, Maya told them everything about her meeting with Batshari, from her mother's promise to her true heritage. Now they could only hope that Fatari would be able to fill in the remaining blanks, tomorrow.

19

FRESH FACES TEACH A DARK HISTORY

SLITTER RIDGE

Leaving the relative calm of the oasis was hard, but a day of travel had already been lost for Batshari's trial. The Water Finkel hadn't been seen since that evening, though Maya could feel his weight on her chest where the seal remained, waiting to be called forward. The verdant of the lagoon faded away into the background, replaced once again with the scraggly rocks of the mountains. The travellers' shoes had all but disintegrated. Only the outlanders, gifted with the ability to fly were left unscathed.

Surprisingly, the group had made good time, and at mid-day they passed the final crevice of the mountain pass. At most the group had expected a few tents; instead, what lay before was a small community of crudely built houses, their backdrop, a beautiful lake.

"This can't just be Fatari's camp," Maya said, echoing the thoughts of the others. Nevertheless, they moved on, down the mountain's back and towards the first of the small dwellings. The community was quiet, and it wasn't until the travellers had passed the first mud and straw-built outhouse that their presence was recognised. A woman gasped and clutched her child close to her chest as she ran from the sight of them. She yelled a warning and others looked up, each in turn dropping their tasks and scrambling to get inside, the loud *thunk* of barriers on doors following thereafter.

"I have a bad feeling–" Maya was cut off by a growl that rumbled to their left. Their right. She spun to the sound of a rumble at her back.

"Fuck. Backs together, face all sides," Keela commanded, bringing up her blades to whatever hid behind them. Following her lead, the others did the same, each facing a side.

Four djincai emerged from the various homes to face each member of the group. In unison they stalked forward slowly, snapping their jaws. The paced quickened and the slow walk turned to a sprint until jaws met steel as the opposing sides collided. Panicked, Maya clutched her chest and summoned Batshari's element. A single, powerful wave, rose from the lake to sweep between the houses. The djincai jumped back at the sound of rushing water, just as Maya's element swept beneath them.

Kadhim and Zarina dropped from the sky and placed themselves protectively between the humans and the other-worldly beasts. Kadhim, bristling at the rude welcome, addressed the djincai currently trying to regain their footing. "Enough of this!" he roared. The creatures stopped and looked each other. "We are here to see Fatari, where is your Elder?" Again, the djincai hesitated. Then, one by one, they transformed into their humanoid form.

The group's concern regarding the beasts quickly changed to panic as they realised, Kadhim and Zarina had led them to an outlander village, a village of enemies.

"Hey, I know you!" A young woman with a thin scar down her face – one of the shapeshifters – pointed in Thelic's direction. "And you!" she shouted, dragging her finger to

Maya. "Both of you were at the Forgotten Forest in Danika!" She gritted her teeth, ready to transform again and tear them apart.

Maya thought back to Danika. To the gateway. To its forest. To the creatures that dwelled there. It clicked. The djinca that attacked her had been struck across the face by Thelic's spear. The woman's scar was now a permanent reminder of that day.

"You tried to kill me!" Maya screeched, ready to summon whatever elements it took to show this shapeshifter she was no longer the same, helpless woman from the glen.

"You would have made a tasty meal then. Not so much now though... too smelly." The outlander wrinkled her nose as the breeze carried the odour of unwashed clothes and bodies across the encampment.

Ignoring the spat, Kadhim once again regarded the naked, transformed man in front of him. "Where is she? Where is Lifaya?"

"Gone, three days ago," the man grunted, stepping away. He glanced back and forth from the humans to Kadhim, uncomfortable speaking with a tribesman willing to protect their enemy.

"And your Elder?"

"Yes, yes, here I am." An old man in a simply woven, priest-like cassock, walked forward to receive their expected guests. One glance at Kadhim and his flame-coloured hands, then to the band of wary warriors behind, gave cause for the old man to smile. "You're late!"

The old man introduced himself as Horticus, Elder of this Ragashian Tribe, a community that worshipped the Gouram of earth – Ragashi. He ushered the travellers into one of the larger, crudely built structures. Inside had a pleasant chill, the clay walls acting as an impenetrable barrier against the sun's rays, instead absorbing the heat of the day to be released in the coolness of night.

Horticus insisted the travellers stay the night to rest and replenish their supplies before resuming their journey. They couldn't help but feel disheartened, Fatari should have been here, should have waited for their arrival. Instead, their expedition would have to continue onwards, if they were to find the flaky Seer. Maya was hesitant to remain with the new and strange tribe, but after five days of harsh travel, everyone was exhausted.

Without room for discussion, they were stripped of clothes with the promise their garments would be returned clean and repaired for daybreak. In the meantime, each was provided with the same, simple attire as the people of the tribe – a thin, green robe tied tight at the waist. As the others left to bathe, Maya wandered the small and muddy community in search of the Elder.

"Where do you think you're going?" Thelic said, crossing his arms at the sheepish grin on Maya's face.

"I wanted to speak with Horticus." She scratched at the thin robe, pulling at the string to loosen the fabric's hold against her body. The dowdy material was a far cry from Wilix's sleek and soft creations they had been wearing, but at least the temporary outfit was clean.

"I'll come with you," he insisted.

Maya had been hoping to catch the Elder alone, believing he might be more open to sharing information without additional prying eyes. She said nothing, though, allowing his company. Her trial with Batshari had put Thelic on high alert, more so than usual. She couldn't blame him for being worried.

Horticus was at the edge of the community's vegetable patch, staring at the mountains to the east. Thelic remained at the far end with a watchful eye on Maya, giving her space as she walked up to the old man.

At the sound of her approach, the Tribal Elder turned and greeted Maya with a kind smile. The earnest gesture touched eyes marred with crow's feet, one of many indicators of a time hard spent in the mountain region. Against skin darkened by days spent under the sun, those blue eyes appeared to glow.

"Your companion is light of trust," Horticus chuckled.

"Does that surprise you?" Maya asked.

"Quite the contrary." He turned to face the eastern mountains once again. "It is a reminder of the dark days behind us...and the darker ones ahead." Grief swept over his face. The thought of one day facing Thelic and other young, human warriors like him, was not a day he would be quick to welcome.

"Who *are* the outla...I mean, the Tribesmen?"

Again, the Elder chuckled but appreciated the diplomatic attempt to correct herself. "We are the original inhabitants of this world, Mayara," he said, his eyes quietly gauging her reaction. "*Avalon*, is a term concocted by the humans for this small slice of our world. In fact, this Realm is known, by our people, as Sythintall. What is now the five territories was once a sacred place, dedicated to the Gouram and elemental sprites." His expression morphed from sadness to anger as he said, "Until the humans came."

She took a minute to consider Batshari's revelation; that she was born of both outlander and human blood; then she thought back to the festival of the Five Majors in Esterbell and Thelic's attempt at a history lesson when she had been brought back to his cabin.

"Humans..." she mused. "So, what are you then? You obviously don't refer to yourselves as outlanders. I'm sorry your people are subjected to such a cruddy label."

He waved away her concern, grateful but accustomed to human ignorance. "We are – to Sythintall – what humans are to the Earth Realm. We are this world's civilisation, the gypsul."

"How have I never heard of that? And why are the two species at war?" Maya sighed, frustrated by her own endless questions but determined to get some answers. "Why can't you all just live together, in peace?"

Horticus empathised with Maya, born of this world but still a stranger. Her questions were not unfounded and many amongst the humans and his own people felt the same way. He himself wished desperately for a solution other than the war of two worlds. But one thing remained true, humans could no longer traverse the two realms. Not without risking Sythintall.

Not wanting to deny her answers, Horticus placed a warm hand on Maya's shoulder. "Let us go and regroup with the others. It is tradition on a night such as this, when guests grace our camp, that I retell the history of our worlds' first meeting."

A BONFIRE BLAZED in the centre of the small community. Gypsul of all ages mustered around the dancing flames, most gossiping about the new arrivals. Children slept on the laps of their mothers or fathers as the older teens danced to music being played on a flute-like instrument, all jovial despite the brewing war. Horticus took a seat at the head of the gathering. All members of the crowd inched closer, excited for the story they'd heard so many times before, most inciting groans of annoyance from their sleeping offspring.

"As you are all aware, we have some unusual callers to our community this night. I tell you now, they are friends."

Keela scoffed at the Elder's assumption before quickly adjusting her position as several sets of eyes cast glances her way.

Horticus continued, "You all know of our history, and that of the humans. But allow me to regale our guests, with the tale of the two civilisations and how Sythintall was changed forever."

Maya wasn't sure if Horticus was considered a good leader. But, considering the easy and infectious display of devotion from the crowd, she suspected he was doing something right. What she did know, was that the Elder had a damn good air about him for storytelling. She settled in, leaning against Thelic's chest as they stretched their legs across the blanket, both listening intently.

"Around 3000 years ago, four of the most powerful human castors journeyed through the gateway to our lands. At the command of their king, Arthur, and his advisor, Maelin, chaos descended upon our world.

King Arthur...and *Merlin*. Maya sat stunned in disbelief as it clicked into place. She knew she had heard of Avalon before, and Yali had hinted of its mythology. It made sense, she supposed, with this world's castors and the gateways hidden at the bottom of lakes. King Arthur was real. Though, she had to wonder whether it was human history or the gypsul, that had incorrectly named the great wizard advisor. She listened as Horticus continued.

"Such an otherworldly appearance of the humans in our realm was unprecedented and shook the very fabric of space and time. Tribal seers believed that, if the humans could escape their visions, their power could rival the great Gouram."

A young girl gasped as others shook their heads. It had been a single miss-step on the part of their ancestors, that had spiralled to what they faced to this day.

Horticus chuckled at the little girl's outrage, placing his own hands on his hips and tutting in agreement. The crowd rumbled with laughter. "This was seen as a challenge to our great Gods, who felt compelled to greet their visitors." He looked up at Maya then, and everyone followed suit, staring at the four visiting travellers. "The Gouram were benevolent and treated the Four Mages with respect as they indeed harboured contracts with their own great sprites."

Maya whispered to Thelic, "I thought there were *five* Majors?"

He shrugged; assuming the old man had simply made a mistake.

Horticus continued. "The Mages, known now as the Majors, possessed a connection to one of the gods of their own realm; an old god that, to this day, dwells deep within the core of their planet. Her name is Gaia."

Maya had heard of this, too. A myth of their world concerning the mother of all life.

"Gaia bound herself with only the most elite of humans, blessing them with wonderous abilities. But there were other, less benevolent spirits and sprites of their world. These would grant power to any with the ability to summon, and willing to pay the price. Chaos ensued. Castors tried and failed to control the power and its host. Great waves wiped out the lands; rumbling earth toppled mountains; and angry winds swept the lands, strong enough to lift an entire herd of shropsin!"

Again, the little girl gave her most dramatic response yet. She leapt up and danced like the wind, lifting the leaves, and throwing them about to signify the great gales. The crowds laughed as the young girl's mother clasped her daughter's arm, dragging the little performer back to their blanket with an apologetic smile to their leader.

Maya realised that Horticus was speaking of tsunamis,

earthquakes and tornadoes, all consequences of natural phenomena or human technological evolution. But, with everything they had seen, she couldn't help but wonder if Gaia really did exist. If these beings her mother had referred to as demons, had truly caused some of the disasters that wiped out entire communities. It would make sense. If people back home, on Earth, found out that the disasters were in part due to black magic contracts with demons... those people would undoubtedly be hunted down.

"The Four Majors turned to our great Gouram for help, to quell the chaos of the Earth Realm and reign in the malevolent sprites. The Gouram, unassuming, granted the humans' wishes and blessed the Majors with a small amount of their essence. In return, a fifth Major would stand among them. One of our own, a gypsul, known as Esterbell. A willing tribute, she was then blessed by Gaia *and* the Gouram. With this aide bestowed, the humans promised to return to their realm, never to return."

A low chorus of murmurs spread throughout the gathering. Horticus allowed the whispers to settle, his pause fuelling the tense crowd. "Yes. One of our own. A gypsul stood as one with the most powerful castors between the two realms. Together, they received the Gods' collective essence and returned to Earth."

"But they broke their promise!" a young boy shouted from the throng of onlookers. Two of his closer friends swatted his head, shushing him.

Keela's hands began to shake with the effort to conceal her annoyance. The Elder was bastardising her history. He was lying. He had to be lying. Esterbell was one of the greatest *Avalonians*, one of the greatest *humans* to grace their history books. A stream of profanities rose to her lips, but she forced them down. Instead, she stood from the blanket, the movement drawing the eyes of the tribe.

Elkin sat at Keela's feet, tugging at the sleeve of her shirt in a bid to get her to sit back down; though, he too found the new version of their cherished history hard to swallow.

Turning on her heel, Keela stormed from the bonfire.

Horticus wasn't offended and drew the crowd's attention by answering the young boy's claim. "You're right. Despite their promise to return and *remain* on Earth, only a single year passed before the Five Majors came back to Sythintall. With them, a mass of human followers."

"But why? Why come here, to our world when they have their own!?" Another young gypsul demanded.

"Because, youngling, the humans began to hunt those born with the ability to bind with elemental beings. A witch-hunt spread across their lands."

Is he talking about the *witch-hunts?* Maya thought about the ones she had read about in books. It seemed that finally she was able to make a connection with what Thelic and Horticus were saying, and her own world's documented history.

Horticus stood to walk between the blankets. A young girl raised her hands to the wandering Elder, and he lifted her into his arms, carrying her as he continued. "The Four Majors lied to our Gods. They never intended to remain on Earth. Instead, they spent their time using the gifted essence to create five gateways. Each stood as a doorway to their realm, bonded to the human summoners, a beacon encouraging them to pass through."

Thelic and Elkin shared a look. This couldn't be true. According to the Elder's story, the humans had purposely invaded. Their history that looked kindly on the Five Majors being invited, offered sanctuary, it had all been a lie.

Horticus continued. "Their gifts allowed the Majors to tap into the elements of this realm, uncharged and unrestrained. After a time, machines and technology began to spring up in places it did not belong. The gypsul rebelled and a war ignited. The humans and their powerful weapons defeated the small might of the tribal warriors, pushing our people back."

The little girl in Horticus' arms leaned away, beckoning for her mother. The Elder walked back to return the child, sadness creeping in. "We realised too late that the humans maintained their bonds with the Earth's sprites, bringing them forth to our world. Sythintall fell ill as the foreign creatures disrupted the balance. Our realm became victim to a new chaos; the veil."

"What happened next? What about Esterbell? Surely she wasn't with them?" A small voice uttered. The boy who spoke already knew, having been told the story numerous times as his parents had laid him to bed. But, like everyone else, he was engrossed, utterly wrapped up in the Elder's words.

"No. Esterbell, too, was tricked. When she discovered what had happened, she convinced Fortus to help her banish the Earths' sprites from this world. Together they used their elemental powers, the essence bestowed upon them by the Gouram and Gaia, to suppress it. Our dear Esterbell lived for ten years after that and bore only a single child. She passed long before her time, a result of her battle against the chaos. With no two castors of both worlds powerful enough to subdue the poisonous veil, it has continued to spread and grow."

"We'll get those humans in the next war," an old lady raised her walk-stick in the air like a battle-axe, shaking it defiantly.

"I remain hopeful that, with the Gouram and Mayara's help, it will not come to that."

All turned to look at Maya. A halfling. Half of her, kin to the gypsul; the other half, an enemy.

"She is Esterbell's heir, and has been blessed by Batshari, the great Gouram of water," Horticus bellowed proudly.

Maya clutched her chest and shrank back as the faces that once damned her, now looked at her in awe, mingled with confusion.

"But…she's human. Esterbell was one of *our* people, she was gypsul," the old, stick-brandishing lady crowed.

The gathering muttered in agreement, their heads bobbing. They were confused, and they weren't the only ones. Since Batshari's claim that Maya was half gypsul, she had often looked at her hands, waiting for them to grow that extra inch or sprout sharp claws.

"Mayara was born from a human *and* a gypsul. She is the first child of two worlds and possesses the essence of both."

Maya felt naked. Horticus was laying all of her newly possessed knowledge, her secrets, bare to these people she didn't know or trust.

That same, confident little girl who had wooed the crowd, approached Maya now. Her mother tried and failed to grab the hem of her dress as she left the safety of the group. As the Elder had spoken of Maya's heritage, she'd stood up. In defiance? Out of fear?

Now, as the little girl drew closer, Maya took a knee to match the child's height. A small hand reached forward and pulled the material of Maya's robe aside. The small smile grew at the crest now laid bare, and she placed her small, taloned hand over the great mark of Batshari.

Warmth passed through them both and the sapphire Finkel appeared on Maya's shoulder. The girl's mother dashed from the crowd, wrapping her arms protectively around her daughter to drag her back from the spiritual being and its master.

"It's okay, he won't hurt you," Maya stuttered quickly in

her effort to reassure them. "I think he's here to help." She patted the Finkel who purred like a cat at her touch.

The little girl, seemingly the bravest of her people and their warriors, clawed from her mother's embrace and raced back to Maya's side.

The Finkel, shy and temperamental, growled at the stranger. Maya stopped stroking to give it a swat on the head. "Be nice," she warned.

With a snort of frustration, the Finkel evaporated, reappearing on the smaller perch of the child's shoulder. She giggled; the sound a cannon amidst the silence as the tribe held its breath.

"What's his name?" the girl asked, reaching up to stroke the creature's head.

Maya hadn't thought of that. "I haven't chosen one yet." She called upon Loki who appeared as usual, a gust of wind rustling her hair before nuzzling into her neck. "This one is Loki. He's a bit mischievous."

Startled yelps and gasps reverberated through the crowd, but the little girl remained in awe at the petite and beautiful Finkel sprites.

"Perhaps you could name it? He appeared to me after I met with the Gouram, Batshari. He's equally as bad-tempered," Maya said, rolling her eyes dramatically.

The girl giggled again. "Did Batshari look like this one?" she asked, her eyes never leaving the Water Finkel.

"No, he appeared to me as a ginormous, cranky shropsin."

"In that case, I think we should call him Baby Batshari!"

Maya cringed at the little girl's suggestion. "How about BB, for short?" The girl loved it and grabbed the newly named Finkel in a tight squeeze before it evaporated.

"Are you and BB and Loki going to help us fight the humans?"

Maya was staggered at the question, unsure how to answer. By all accounts she had one foot on either side of this war, and she had lived her life as a human. Horticus had shown them a darker side of history the humans either didn't know or had long since buried. The war they were fighting, were willing to die for, was based on a lie told by zealots harbouring a god complex. The crowd, too, silently demanded an answer. All Maya could do, was say, "I'll do what I can to stop this war." And for the first time, facing the desperate looks of the young and old tribesmen before her, she meant it.

∾

AS THE CROWD DISPERSED, Horticus was the last to leave. Maya had waited for the stragglers to depart and approached the old man when he was finally alone. She had prepared a verbal beating, unreservedly angry at the Elder for putting that kind of pressure on her without any prior warning.

He beamed as she stormed up, his arms outstretched.

She wanted to thump him. "How could you blind-side me like that? Now your entire tribe thinks I'm God's gift!"

"Well, you *are* a gift, Mayara. Your power is the tipping point on the scales of this war. The side you choose, will win."

"I don't want to choose a side."

Horticus chuckled at that and felt pity for the young woman. "I should hope not! History seems to be repeating itself somewhat, you have a hard road ahead of you, my friend."

Maya scoffed, she'd become so accustomed to hard roads, she felt her feet may as well be made of granite. "I don't doubt it. I wouldn't believe it if you said the hard part was over."

"Truly, you walk the path of Esterbell. You are destined, not to rule, but to destroy the chaos. Only *you* can do what the Gods cannot."

"Didn't Esterbell die in your story?" Maya asked, and the Elder bowed his head in a forlorn admission. That was two, now. Two stories that suggested Maya's inevitable death. Thelic had tried to reveal to Maya the ending to his father's fable. She had stopped him, but his eyes had said it all. Now, according to Horticus, she was destined to fulfil Esterbell's role in the war – stop the chaos and save Sythintall. Possibly at the cost of her life.

"You should stay a few more nights, tell us of your world and your travels through this realm," Horticus offered, trying to lighten the mood.

"We should really get to Fatari. Who knows how much longer she has left to live? I'm surprised she was able to travel at all."

The Elder's eyes widened, alarmed at this news. "What do you mean? We saw her but three days ago. She had been ill, but Lifaya was altogether well by the time she left."

"We were told…Prisia…and Mikosh," Maya stuttered. Did they not know of her condition?

Horticus roared a deep, bellyful laugh, before catching his breath. "That little rasicus, she must have foreseen this." At Maya's confused look he explained. "Fatari must have sent word to Prisia and Mikosh of her *supposed* illness. You hurried here, yes?"

Maya bobbed her head in agreement.

"I'm afraid the Seer can be a little impatient…and over-dramatic." The Elder shook his head, offering a look of apology.

"She lied about dying, to get us to hurry our journey?"

"I'm afraid so," he grinned.

Maya wasn't sure whether to be pissed off or impressed by the sneaky, manipulative Seer. But one thing was certain, they would be staying another night to recuperate, and she was suddenly looking forward to meeting her grandmother.

SHADED HEARTS

SLITTER'S RIDGE

The community was bustling. Hunters had mustered in the early hours and left to restock the village's food supply, but their absence did nothing to dim the looming festivities.

Maya walked the paths between the houses, dodging children and the small, unfamiliar creatures that ran beside them. She wondered at what they were commemorating. The territory of Esterbell had celebrated the festival of the Five Majors weeks ago – not that these people would be rejoicing the exploits of the human colonisers.

"Excuse me," Maya said, approaching one of the women currently lacing several pieces of colourful fabric together. The tribal woman looked up, just as she was threading her long needle.

"Ach! Spirits curse these damned instruments," she swore, sucking at the fresh bead of blood on her thumb. Long, black hair fell forward to frame her freckled cheeks, the thin scar a river of white against sun-bronzed skin.

Maya realised she had approached the djinca from Danika. "Ah, it's you. Never mind, I'll ask someone else." She turned on her heel, eager to make a swift exit and save them both another argument.

"Whoa! Come back. I won't bite," the shapeshifter promised, catching Maya's arm to stop her. "Listen, what happened in the Forgotten Forest, in the glen...I didn't mean to attack you."

"I'm not sure how you can accidentally try to kill someone, but I'd like to hear you try and explain." Maya turned to face the woman completely, resisting the urge to cross her arms and tap her foot.

"It's the fog. It plays with your mind if you stay in it too long, tricks you. When I saw you walking through the trees... well, it wasn't *you*. I mean, you weren't human," she muttered, trying and failing to put her words across the way she meant. "I was sent by Horticus and Fatari to escort you to Slitter Ridge."

"I see, but instead you saw a tasty, human sized rasicus, and decided to stop for a mid-day snack?"

"Yes! Well, no. You looked like a shader. I wanted to kill you, not eat you," she laughed. At Maya's scrunched up expression, she said, "Shaders? Nasty gypsul? The ones that have been wreaking havoc on the human settlements?"

"The humans consider you all to be outlanders, all one people," Maya said, unapologetically. She had yet to understand the difference between the two.

"Of course. I forget that you've lived amongst the humans. I suppose you don't consider yourself one of us."

"I don't know what I am anymore," Maya groaned, truthfully. "But I forgive you, you know, for trying to kill me," she grinned.

"Well, I suppose since I tried to kill you and all, that I should probably tell you my name. I'm Traccia." She offered two hands in truce.

Unsure what to do, Maya attempted to accept the gesture.

She placed her own on top of Traccia's clawed palms and remained still as the gypsul leaned forward to connect their foreheads.

Traccia laughed as she stepped back. "First tribal greeting?"

"Is it that obvious?"

"I wouldn't say that. Here, place your hands on top of mine again," Traccia said, holding her arms out as she had done before.

Maya did as she asked.

"Good, now, when we connect our foreheads, what shape do we make?"

"A triangle, I suppose," Maya answered with a shrug.

Once again pulling away, Traccia touched the pendant hanging loosely around Maya's neck that Thelic had given her. "The triangle is a symbol of the elements. Your pendant shows all four, with the circular symbol for 'spirit' joining them."

Maya glanced down at the pendent and smiled with the newfound knowledge. It wasn't much, but it was finally something she understood.

THEY SPENT the rest of that morning together, and Maya learned of the upcoming Lunar festival. In six days, all three moons would align, as they did every year. During this time, the shroud between realms would blur, and the elemental sprites and the Gods were rumoured to traverse between planes to replenish the lands.

"Why don't the Gods eradicate the elemental chaos, the veils?" Maya asked, it was one of the things she couldn't understand, these sprites were supposed to be all powerful, the chaos simply an open wound. Why couldn't they control it?

"The way I understand it, they can't," Traccia said with a shrug, swearing as the small movement once again redirected the needle into the skin of her thumb. "Here, hold this side."

Maya accepted the outstretched material, keeping it steady as Traccia continued her weave. "It's too strong for them to control?"

"It's not that the chaos is too *strong*. More, it's too *diluted*. The poison that seeps from the gateways is a result of elemental power leaking from two worlds. They can control that which derives from their own essence, but they are powerless against any force born from the human realm."

"That's why they need someone born from both worlds, like a medium?"

"That's what we're told." She regarded Maya. "No pressure."

Maya laughed nervously. The more she learnt, the more she found herself disbelieving. She was a policewoman. A single, London dweller, with a penchant for bad tv-shows and a decent bottle of red wine. Now, she was here; expected to stop a force that threatened to annihilate the realm and its people. *No pressure, sure.* "What about the veil that surrounds the territories?"

Traccia tied a knot at the final loop and held the material up for inspection. "That's a bit trickier. Those Five Major pains in our asses created it to stop more gypsul from rushing in to support the war effort. It's completely man-made, human-made, and kills those who try to eradicate it."

"Kills them how?"

Traccia went still, her eyes glazing over. "Your soul is ripped from your body. At least that's what they say." She thought back to a time she wouldn't likely forget and finally looked at Maya. "My brother was killed by the veil. I saw his body sucked into the void and spat back out again, all colour gone from his skin...lifeless."

"I'm so sorry," Maya said. It was the first she'd heard of the surrounding veil's terrible power, and she could only hope they wouldn't have a need to venture close anytime soon.

Traccia sighed and begrudgingly selected the next piece of fabric to add to her tapestry. "It was a long time ago, when we were kids. I haven't gone near the veiled boundary since."

IT WASN'T long before Traccia was called away to attend to village tasks. Despite her offers to help, Maya was left, once again, to wander aimlessly around the community. Upon enquiry, she discovered that Elkin and Keela had joined the hunting party to replenish the group's supplies for their next journey. Thelic and Horticus, too, were nowhere to be found. So, she continued to stroll.

The sun's rays beat relentlessly against her exposed skin. The dry, musty air parching her throat. As Maya swiped at the constant trickle of sweat meandering slowly from the back of her hairline, she caught a flicker of reflected light in her periphery. The lake. Without a second thought, she made her way to the clear and coolly glistening waters and strode across the dock. With a quick glance around, she undressed to the crude, stretchy underwear and dove in.

Hesitant to rise from the cold depths, she waited for her lungs to burn with the need for air before swimming to the surface. It was quiet, here. The only sound a soft lap of waves breaking against wooden stilts. She lay back to float, enjoying the private moment to cool and collect her thoughts.

"You're not at all reserved, are you?" a deep voice drifted from beneath the pier.

Maya flapped at the sudden break in silence. It didn't take

long to spot the source as her gaze was drawn to Thelic. Succumbing to the heat, he too had opted for a swim and sat on a platform under the shade of the dock, grinning at the half-exposed Maya.

"You scared the shit out of me," she grumbled. "I thought you were a talking, hungry, water creature."

"I may not be a water creature, but I am hungry," he said, sliding into the water to swim over and join her.

Large hands snaked around her waist, tugging at the thin, cotton material there to pull her against his chest. Maya tried, half-heartedly, to resist.

"No way, big man. It's a public place in the middle of the day, someone might see us, and I need to talk to–" she groaned as Thelic traced small kisses along her neck, lingering only for a moment before moving on towards her mouth.

"Everyone is busy," he breathed, his fingers diving below, pushing aside the obstructive material to rub between her legs. "Still want to talk?" he asked, his lip curling up in a smile at her informative moans. She wrapped her arms around his neck, her legs claiming his waist.

Talking could wait.

～

BOTH PANTING AND COMFORTABLY SATISFIED, Thelic and Maya lay on the shaded platform under the dock, hidden from view. Maya told him about her morning with Traccia; about the shaders and the festival, and why they believed Maya might be able to calm the elemental chaos.

He rolled over to face her, leaning up to support his head on his hand. "That's not surprising. We humans also believe the chaos is born from whatever power leaks from the gateways. Though, your mother's claim, backed by Horticus – that the Earth Realm's sprites are the true cause – came as a bit of a shock. Your part to play in all of this is becoming clearer with every outlander–"

"Gypsul," Maya corrected.

"Right. With every *gypsul* we meet. Being born of two worlds, in a way it makes sense that your power is what's needed to end it all."

Maya raked her eyes down the length of his body, bare of the modesty he'd been so quick to highlight she herself lacked. There was no complaint, no hurry to cover him. On the contrary, this was much better. "Why didn't you tell me about the boundary veil?"

Traccia's experience with the barrier was akin to Thelic's. He had lost friends to that wall and dared not go anywhere near it. "I didn't see the need." A fierce look darkened his face, warning Maya not to push.

She didn't. Whatever it was, he could tell her if or when he was ready. So, she changed the subject altogether. "This festival, the alignment of the three moons, do you think it has anything to do with why Lifaya has been so desperate for us to reach her?" she asked.

Thelic wasn't sure, but it was likely. Fatari's ceremony required Maya's essence, bestowed upon her by the four Gouram, and her link to Gaia's power. Perhaps this event, the diminished line between realms, was required to tap into both powers. Only the Seer could give them the answers they needed.

"We should leave at first light, tomorrow," he suggested.

Shouts erupted from the bank of the lake as the hunting party returned. Two men ran at the back of the group; a third, motionless body held between the two.

"Something's happened," Maya realised as the shouts

turned to wails and worried cries. They quickly grabbed their clothes, dressed, and made their way back to the shore.

"It was shaders!" one of the huntsmen barked. "They killed him!"

"Yeah, we were ambushed and fought them off, but they're coming here!" a woman, gingerly cradling a broken arm shouted before being led away to the small village infirmary.

"What happened?" Maya and Thelic had arrived just as the townsfolk were rushing to their houses, dragging their unknowing children behind.

"Maya, it's the ones I was telling you about, the shaders," Traccia said. She was busy attending to a nasty gash on one of the huntsmen's leg, her firm grip on the wound slowing the steady flow of blood.

"What do they want? Why attack their own people?" Maya asked. The shaders were gypsul. It made no sense.

"Because they know we're harbouring *humans,*" the man with the gashed leg hissed. The third hunter whom they'd seen dragged from the woodline, was dead. The man currently glaring at Maya, blaming her for this bloodshed, had been the dead hunter's friend since birth.

"Thelic!" Elkin shouted as he and Keela rushed from the glen, the last of the hunters to arrive back. A quick once over showed no injuries to the two human warriors and Thelic breathed with relief. "There's a pack of those evil outlanders on their way here, now."

"We need to leave," Keela insisted.

Thelic nodded in agreement, turning to head back to their tent and gather their belongings. A quick laugh stopped him.

Maya was outraged. They wanted to run and leave these people to suffer, possibly die because they were kind enough to shelter them? "You've got to be joking, right?"

Pushing past Thelic, Keela descended on Maya. "We get it – you're an idiot with a soft spot for outlanders, but we're going," she said through gritted teeth, her hand clutching Maya's arm.

Everyone had left to attend the wounded, leaving Maya and the others alone in the square. With nobody around to witness their swift exit, the tribe could buy them some time.

Maya shook herself free and stepped back. "I'm not going anywhere. You can go, Keela, really. You've only ever been interested in yourself. Why stop now?"

Keela laughed at that. At the naivety. Maya knew nothing; her years sheltered from true conflict. Nothing Keela did was ever for herself. *She* was nothing, a nobody. Her dark hair had loosened from its plait to flow across stiff shoulders, she brushed it aside with Maya's comment and looked to Elkin for backup.

For once the attention of both, hot-tempered females was unwelcome and made Elkin more than a little uncomfortable. He inched back, both hands raised in surrender. "I'm not getting in the middle of this, but if the little fulsin stays, so shall we," he said, with only a look of apology to offer Keela. "I recognised the leader. It's the same outlander from the bordello at Aqarin Port, the same one you fought, Maya."

She remembered, and so did Thelic. He'd wanted nothing more than to rip Maya's attacker apart, and it seemed he was being gifted with a second chance to do just that.

Horticus was gathering the tribe's fighters at the dock, issuing an order for the shapeshifters to transform and take their positions as the community's first line of defence. Traccia along with three gypsul warriors left with the Elder to take their positions. Maya and the others followed.

In a glen, halfway between the treeline and the last of the village huts, they gathered to wait for the shaders to appear.

It wasn't long before men and women stepped from the shadows of the wood to stand in the open. Unlike the residents of Slitter Ridge, these beings seemed almost feral – desperate to race from their line and annihilate anything and everything. Bloodthirsty. They danced on the spot, sighting their prey. A central figure raised a firm hand, his hounds steadied but chomping at the bit. The man from Aqarin Port. He smiled now, that look of hunger undiminished from their last encounter, as he stared directly at Maya.

Horticus walked forward, Traccia in her djinca form close at his side. The shaders' leader followed suit, a man of his own trailing behind. The remaining warriors watched intently as their leaders met in the middle, waiting for someone to make the first move.

"Where's bird-boy?" Keela asked, moving up to stand with Maya.

After their disagreement, Maya had watched her sister storm from the town centre and head to her hut. But Keela had left only to arm herself and returned to stand beside them for the likely battle to come. Maya nudged her now, a silent apology for their last words and grateful for her presence.

The Ragashian warriors and djincai shuddered with anticipation, their growls rumbling the earth below. Kadhim and Zarina were not among them, absent since the night before.

"Why have you come here, Vakeeb?" Horticus demanded.

"We want *them*," the shader pointed to Maya. "I have business with that one, and you should know better than to help those who caused our people's suffering," he spat.

"They are no threat to our kind."

"Their very existence in this realm is an insult to the Gouram!" Vakeeb bellowed. Traccia snapped her jaws in warning. He chuckled, saying, "You think you're a match for our etiyan warriors?" He raised his hand again and snapped his taloned fingers. Three, lizard-like beasts slithered from the forest to stand amongst the shader's front line. Whoops and hollers erupted from the fighters at the creatures' backs, celebrating the omen of impending battle. The etiyan, though smaller in height, rivalled the strength of the djincai with equally long and powerful tails. Every breath saw cracks in their bellies that glowed red, a fire smouldering beneath the skin, waiting to be unleashed. Traccia snarled, lifting to stomp her two front paws, insulted by the insolence of lesser beings.

Maya summoned Loki and BB to her side the moment the lizards entered the glen, confident they would help her and the Ragashian Tribe should they need it.

Vakeeb witnessed her unspoken challenge and narrowed his eyes, facing the Elder once again. "If you hand us the humans, we will leave your village in peace. We have no desire to spill more gypsul blood today."

Horticus shook his head at the shader's deal, his eyes defiant. "These humans are going nowhere with you. They are the key to our future."

"The only future they face is a slow death at the tip of my blade, or the teeth of the etiyan." With that, he turned to walk away.

Horticus stepped forward, blocked by Traccia's scaled mass from advancing further. "You don't understand. They can end the chaos and lift the veils!" he shouted.

"So they can bring more of their kind through the gateways!? You are *blind,* old man. No better than the God's when this all began!"

"Wait!" Maya shouted across the glen. "Hang on a second."

Keela stared open-mouthed at their supposed saviour as she broke from the defensive line, moving like a violent storm towards the leaders. A curse brimmed as Thelic moved to walk beside her with no word of dispute. Ready to charge forward, Keela stopped as Elkin grabbed her arm, a warning to stay back should her short temper spark the battle.

Maya stopped at Horticus' side, once again facing the man who had once tried to kill her. "My friends and I aren't here to end the gypsul civilisation. I'm new to this, but from the sounds of it, I think we can help," she said to Vakeeb.

"What an inflated ego you have. You think a mere human can stop a chaos the God's themselves have been powerless to vanquish!?" the shader roared.

"She is Esterbell's heir, born both human *and* gypsul," Horticus declared at Maya's defence.

"She's a halfling?" Vakeeb stepped back; a look of utter disgust plain across his face. "Then she is less than worthy, she's an abomination!" He dashed forward again, his face inches from hers as he said, "Surrender to us, and I will spare these traitors." Every word dripped with the threat of the forces at his back. Should she refuse, he was prepared to kill them all or die trying.

Thelic bared his teeth, ready to rip the cocky bastard's smile from his face. "She's not going anywhere with you," he said, echoing Horticus as he pulled Maya back to his side.

"So be it." Vakeeb spun, his long coat billowing behind dramatically as he walked away. Maya moved to object, but the shader's hand was raised into the air, silencing her and signalling his legion to advance.

The gates were open, hounds released, and the ground thundered with the sound of twenty voracious shaders rushing to close the gap between the two forces.

Maya called for the Finkels, readying them. She looked to Thelic who nodded in understanding, retreating with a warning to Horticus and Traccia to do the same. Alone with the dagger at her waist, Maya drew the sharp blade over the palm of her hand. She flinched as the still raw and healing wound reopened, her blood pooling in the centre.

The shaders grew close, the glowing bellies of the etiyan searing across the ground at the head of the pack.

Maya stood tall and turned her palm to the ground. Blood dribbled from the open wound to touch the grass and the ground burst to life. There was no panic from her as the yellow glow of the circle sprung wide, accompanied by the cerulean hue of Batshari's ring. BB was with her, his essence mingled with hers. This time it was different. This time, they were one.

A shockwave shot across the glen, catching the approaching shaders and etiyan and tossing them back. Maya's hands had cast Loki's wind and remained outstretched towards the approaching threat. Turning her palms down, she flung her arms to the ground. The Finkel's force, an extension of Maya, mimicked the movement. The shader army flipped forward onto their fronts in a sprawling mess, like puppets on strings.

Vakeeb screamed for the etiyan to advance, to kill the woman. But she had only just begun, and she wasn't alone. Her wind, complimented by Elkin's own water summoning, locked the shader fighters in an oxygen diminished cyclone.

The etiyan broke through, slithering forward, ready to unleash the fiery torrent at their core. Fire met earth as they collided with Thelic's wall of hard rock and stone, strengthened by Keela's flame. The creatures clawed and pounded at the barrier, their blistering breath disturbing the delicate balance of elements required to keep it standing.

Again, they broke through.

The djincai dashed forward to breach the fresh gap and meet their shape-shifting equals. Claws and teeth snapped in a blur as the powerful beasts tore each other apart.

The leader, where is he? Maya panicked. Flames raced along the grass, its path shrinking the green blades to a scorched mark. A ring of fire burst at Maya's feet, its tendrils lacing around her body in a blistering maelstrom. She dropped to the ground, clutching her throat as the castor circle flickered. Through the blaze, Thelic's frame was distorted.

He was running towards her.

An etiyan burst from the battle mass, knocking him to the ground. Rounding on the warrior, Thelic was too slow getting to his feet and the beast stomped a scaled foot on his chest, its claws cutting the skin below.

"*BB,*" Maya croaked, summoning the Finkel. With its master's command finally uttered, the water sprite disappeared and a stampede of aquatic karkili charged from the nearby lake. Crashing across the glen, the summoned wave washed through Maya to extinguish the fiery trap. She collapsed to the ground, sucking in the cool air.

A scream rang through the glen. The creature had sliced Thelic's chest, and he in turn had swung his spear, cutting the etiyan's webbed hand at the wrist. A second wail ripped from the lizard as the dead appendage dropped to the side, curling in, and transforming back into a gypsul hand. Its head snapped back to the man still trapped below. With a snarl, the etiyan opened its jaws, charging the flame at its core.

Unwavering and not a moment too soon, Maya directed the summoned water creatures towards Thelic. With a sweeping curve, the wave of karkili redirected its path of smothering devastation and blasted the etiyan, drowning its fire-laden guts.

Thelic jumped to his feet, adrenaline masking the pain across his stomach. With a small, and almost imperceptible smile, he brought his spear down to pierce through the etiyan's throat, killing the creature, the shader, instantly.

Maya stumbled to her feet, the effort of wielding two Finkels quickly draining her energy. She couldn't keep this up for much longer. Despite being outmatched easily three to one, the Ragashian Tribe was prevailing over the shader force. Bloods mixed on the battleground. The viscous tack of etiyan gore blending with that of the djincai's colourless ichor. Maya dragged her eyes from a dead creature. The scales morphing back into skin, its form slowly shrinking; returning to its gypsul origin. Traccia's face popped into Maya's head, and she couldn't watch, couldn't bear the thought of those dead eyes possibly belonging to such a vibrant woman. It wasn't her. It was the little girl's mother, the one who had named BB. Anger erupted in Maya.

Across the glen, Vakeeb wove his way through tangled bodies towards Maya. For the first time, he was unsure. This halfling was too powerful. Bound to not one, but two Finkel sprites, and conjuring a castor circle. He had never seen anything like it.

Maya spotted the shader and noted the flicker of uncertainty, his calm confidence shattered by the changing odds. Death permeated the air between them as screeching battle cries sang together with the clang of blades.

Vakeeb shook with rage. His people were being driven back, slaughtered by the foul humans and their puppet djincai; the blasted earth-worshippers.

Maya knelt to the ground, as much to support her shaking frame as to conjure what she hoped would be her final attack. Her hands, slick with blood, spread along the grass at either side of her knees. BB remerged, his shape transforming to the enormous bulk of the shropsin. Loki, too, matched its size; the once petite Finkel sprite towering over the battlefield. Both creatures stood at Maya's side, staring down the simmering shader, awaiting her command to strike.

All became quiet. Blades, frozen mid-swing, sank to the floor as all attention focused on the summoner.

"You have been defeated, relinquish your weapons!"

Horticus commanded, his once white robes now flush with the sticky remnants of his enemies. The remaining shaders scrambled to their feet and made for the safety of the woods. Only their leader was left to stand at the mercy of Maya and the Finkels.

"Why do the sprites heed your command?" he whispered, sinking to his knees at the sight of such a supreme power.

"We have an understanding," Maya replied. "You believe yourself to be cleverer than the Gods of this realm, but they are always watching." She rose to her feet, slowly, her shaking legs certain to betray the projected confidence. "Batshari has plans for those that oppose his will. I should know." She unbuttoned the top of her blouse and pulled the material apart, exposing Batshari's seal on her chest.

Vakeeb, still kneeling before her, scurried back. A hard bump halted his retreat, warm liquid coating his hands. He glanced back and panic gripped him. A man, one of his own, had been drowned and trampled by BB's conjured stampede. The Water Finkel, still brandishing the body of a shropsin, felt the shader's fear and bared its teeth in a malevolent grin.

"What do you want?" he asked resignedly.

"For your people to join us, peacefully, and learn our ways," Horticus declared. At the shader's disgruntled expression and lack of response, Maya wordlessly prompted Loki. She had intended to send a gust of air, just a little one, to hasten the shader's decision.

The dark hearted Vakeeb was rocketed back, landing painfully on his side. He gasped in pain; one hand holding his ribs, the other held up in surrender. Maya made a note to chastise the mischievous sprite, whose wind seemed to chortle.

"Okay, okay! I...I mean, we accept. We will join this Ragashi Tribe," he yielded.

Maya wrapped her bleeding hand in the folds of her robe

and the castor circle began to fade, its absence revealing the tell-tale flora, a result of Maya's gods-given power.

~

BACK AT THE CAMP, Horticus called to the frightened villagers, encouraging them to emerge from their homes. Locks sprung free and doors creaked open, scared faces once again retreating at the sight of the wild shaders. The Ragashian Elder demanded the wounded, all of them, be treated at the infirmary. At sundown he would address the community with what was to come.

Maya had managed to make it to hers and Thelic's shared hut without assistance, feigning an air of ease on the trek back. Finally alone, behind the windowless walls of their assigned dwelling, she collapsed towards the thick futon of their bed.

Thelic rushed forward, his arm wrapping around her waist to cushion the descent, her head barely missing the hardened clay wall. He rolled her over and she grinned weakly up at him.

"Are you okay?" he asked, scanning her smouldered clothes for any burns underneath.

"I feel...sleepy, but otherwise surprisingly ok." She winced, pulling her torn hand back from his chest. The wound had barely stopped bleeding. "This is probably one of the biggest downers to my abilities – having to hurt myself every time." She sighed, surrendering her hand to Thelic for treatment. She felt stronger. The seal on her chest sat like a weight, a reminder of the power that backed her. Usually with a summoning like that she would have been weak for days. Instead, Maya could already feel her strength returning, albeit slowly.

Thelic winced slightly as he bent to return the bandages

to the small wooden box of medicinal tools. Maya caught the small movement and grabbed his wrist, switching their positions to place him on the bed as she lifted his shirt.

"If you wanted me to undress, all you had to do was ask," he said, smiling as he lifted his arms for the shirt to come free.

"You're hurt," Maya said, concern creasing her forehead as she assessed the gash across the hardened muscles of his mid-section.

"It's nothing."

"Not nothing." Reaching down, she removed the same tonics and cleansers she had seen the others use in their treatments. Concentrating, she placed them beside her in order of use before ripping part of the clean bandage to use as a cloth.

Thelic watched as she worked. Maya's once almost golden hair had been streaked with red and darker patches of djinca and etiyan gore. Nevertheless, he was enchanted, and reached up to stroke two fingers down her cheek.

"You were incredible back there, against the shaders and the etiyan," he said, thinking back to her powerful summoning of the karkili wave and the Finkels' transformations.

"I should have been quicker when that etiyan was on you. I wanted to kill it, but you got there first."

Pushing loose strands behind her ear, he cupped her chin, forcing her to look up at his face. Her eyes burned with quietly controlled rage.

"Don't let it consume you, Maya. Or it will kill you, and I can't let that happen."

~

AT THE FIRE-LIT GATHERING, the shaders stood to one side, their clothes bloody and glares shifting through the frightened faces of the Ragshians. Vakeeb sat at the centre of his people, waiting. A clear channel separated the two sides. Seeing the divide upon their arrival, Maya and Thelic sat in the middle. At the opposite side, across the fire, Horticus took his place.

"I know you all have questions. Why do we harbour humans?" Horticus asked on the shaders' behalf. "Why would we accept the shaders, those who threaten a possible peace?" he asked on behalf of his tribe. "I have but one reason. We *must* unite at the face of a single and powerful enemy!" he bellowed.

"The humans!" yelled an overzealous shader. A small number of Ragashians couldn't help but bob their heads in agreement, hearts turning to shadow.

"No. Gypsul and Avalonians alike, we all face a common threat. The chaos."

"You claim this…*halfling* can stop the chaos that chokes our world. You cannot expect us to believe that!" yelled another of the shaders.

Horticus proceeded to explain everything, just as Traccia had educated Maya on the need for a being with power from both worlds.

Maya glanced around and her chest tightened. Traccia was missing from the gathering. Several members of both sides had died this day; and she hoped the shape-shifting woman wasn't one of them.

Breaking his silence, Vakeeb stood from his perch on the wooden bench beside his kin. "Why take the risk? We know what you want old man. We know you want peace with the humans and for one of the gateways to remain open to their realm!" he thundered, the shaders around him shouting their agreement.

This was news to Maya. She had assumed all the gates had to be closed in order to seal the leak.

"One gateway, the original, *must* remain open. This is true for all worlds; it maintains the balance," Horticus countered, disturbed by the shaders' ignorance and lack of reasoning.

"The humans will use it; they will bring reinforcements!" Panicked whispers spread amongst both sides at the shader's outburst. Maya and the others looked on as the two sides battled once again, this time for superiority of opinion. One wanted to kill her, the other to crown her. She sank forward, cradling her head in freshly bandaged hands, weary and craving the quiet confines of their hut.

"Maya, please explain." Horticus held out his hand to her.

Blind-sided, again. She growled, trying to tamp down the annoyance. "What do you want me to say? You shaders have already made up your minds regarding the humans, regarding me. What can I possibly say to make you change your minds?" She finally raised her head to look at the quietened crowd and exhaled. "You've seen what I can do. Now it's down to you to decide what that means."

"You said Batshari has plans. *And* you have that seal." Vakeeb considered Maya, her heritage, and her undeniable power. "You were blessed by the Gouram. What does he intend to do?" he asked sincerely, hushing his people.

Maya told them of her meeting with the great Gouram of water. She told them what he'd told her, what Horticus had told her and what she expected Fatari would tell her. In short, she was to fulfil her mother's promise to the Gods, by using her body as a conduit to stop the elemental chaos from devouring this realm.

A long silence dragged between them, Vakeeb weighing up this new information against the teachings of his people. He stood and stepped towards Maya, the tip of Thelic's spear stopping the shaders' leader only a few paces back. He knelt and offered his stone dagger, a humbled sign of allegiance. His followers and tribesmen gawked at such a sight, before quickly following their commander's lead.

A wave of heads descended before her, shader and Ragashian alike. And Maya sat, feeling more awkward, and more pressure than ever. She was going to kill Horticus.

21
SHADOWS REVEALED

ZAMKORA DROP

"We should've killed Vakeeb, *at least*. To make a point," Thelic grumbled.

Maya stretched, rolling from the futon to the cool floor. Still aching and tired from the battle the day before, she dreaded the impending journey and willed her body to sink beneath the clay tiles. At least the shaders had deigned to stay with the earth-worshipping tribe and promised to keep away from the human settlements. If war descended, they would battle humans together.

A soft plimsole thumped against her head and she sat up. Thelic grinned from the other side of the bed. He'd packed both bags and wanted some fun while they still had time. She held the shoe in one hand, smacking it against the open palm of her other, ready to exact revenge.

A soft knock at the door broke the stand-off. Elkin had come to get them for a final meeting with Horticus before their departure. With a heavy sigh, Maya chucked the shoe at Thelic, grabbed her clothes, and dashed from the hut past the bewildered redhead.

. . .

THE GROUP HAD PLANNED to meet Horticus at the dock. Zarina and Kadhim were already there, having heated words with the Elder.

"You two missed all the fun, yesterday," Maya teased on approach, offering an easy smile to reassure them everyone was well.

"We heard," Kadhim said, grimacing at the thought of what had transpired in their absence. "I'm sorry we weren't here to help. Though, I'm more concerned about the outcome." Kadhim turned back to the Elder. "Keeping the shaders here, trying to bring them back around to our way of thinking is a fool's errand, Horticus."

"I'm inclined to disagree. Our young halfling here seems to have swayed their hearts and steadied their minds," Horticus replied, beaming with pride.

Kadhim sighed, raising his hands in defeat as the stubborn Elder turned to beckon Thelic forward. Pulling the map free, everyone crowded in close and watched carefully as Horticus indicated their best route to Fatari. She had moved on to a Pavinicum encampment. The path looked long and dangerous, the crude sketchings of terrible beasts along the chosen route a bad sign of things to come.

Keela grinned. She had enjoyed their journey thus far. It had been much more exciting than she'd expected, and certainly beat training Bandaar's soldiers at Esterbell Keep. The thought of Bandaar darkened her mood. If she returned having failed him, she didn't know what he would do. Kill her? Banish her? He was a difficult and unpredictable man, especially when it came to his family.

During the hunt the day before, Elkin and Keela had managed to catch an impressive haul of the rabbit-like rasicus. The creature had been a staple in the travellers' diet since day one, and Maya couldn't help but groan at the notion of the days to come eating the same thing.

What she hadn't been aware of, is that later that same evening, Elkin had gone to the dock, armed with a spear and considerable fishing skills. Fashigi, the fish of this world, lived in abundance in the depths of Slitter Ridge's lake. He knew this, having seen the multi-coloured fluorescent beings on his swims. Over-night, both catches had been stripped, dried and salted, ensuring the meat was suitable for travel. He presented the pack to Maya now, noting the additional source of protein. He would do this for her, these little things, to make her life more comfortable. It was the least he could do.

Maya had consistently been impressed by the warrior's preparedness and experience. With everything they'd been through, she had come to care deeply for Elkin, their lecherous and wonderfully kind cook. Maya looked at the others talking amongst themselves of the journey to come and wondered where she would be if Thelic hadn't picked her up that day in the glen. Every member was so important to her in their own way. She chuckled at Keela's stiff posture. Zarina was flirtatiously brushing a lock of hair from the Esterbellian woman's face. They'd all come so far and grown close. She was torn, desperate for their journey's conclusion but miserable at the thought of one day leaving them behind.

Upon the group's departure, the villagers waved from their stoops and children followed to the treeline. Somehow, they had won the hearts of the gypsul here at Slitter Ridge and could only hope it would go as smoothly at the Pavinicum settlement.

According to Horticus, the journey was split into three parts. First, they would take the low mountain trail to Zamkora Drop, the only path in the sheer cliff down to the water's edge. There they could expect to find the lonely Batsharian water-raker. He supposedly charged an extortionate fare but was their only choice for safe passage to

Kavakin Shores. From there it would be a straight line across the desert to Fatari.

∽

THE PICTURESQUE BEAUTY of the glen surrounding the lake was left behind, replaced once again by the dead, ash trees and dust covered stony mountains. Weaving their way through the pass, the familiar, dark, and looming clouds lumbered above. Rain fell in great torrents to soak through the Transumian silk cloth and drenched the filth at their feet. The air grew musty and thick with the humidity but cooled them somewhat. They trundled on, deciding it pointless to take cover and wait for the persistent rain cloud to move along.

"So, where did you go?" Maya shouted over the pattering shower to Zarina. Their Svingoran companions had opted to travel on foot with the group as far as the Zamkora cliffs. Wary of the creatures that lurked within the mountain pass, they figured a larger group might act as a deterrent to any curious predators.

"We flew to Etiyan Vale, to see Fatari," Zarina replied. "She is well by the way, no sign of impending death. Though I imagine she will outlive us all anyway," the shape-shifter giggled.

"Yeah, we heard," Maya said. "The Pavinicums she's staying with…"

"The Fire Gouram worshipers? They're nice…so long as you aren't human," she grimaced awkwardly looking from Maya to the others. "Fatari will keep them in line, I wouldn't worry."

Maya wasn't worried. Perhaps it was cocky, but after what they had survived, a little confidence was deserved. "Why does the Seer travel so much across the Outlands? Is it to hide from the Keepers hunting her?"

"That, and she's trying to unite the separated tribes, in case this war comes to pass. Though, she hopes that won't be the case." Zarina had once told them of two prophecies conveyed by the Seer, Lifaya. One resulting in the death of all humans and gypsul, another in which they all unite under one ruler. Maya wondered if that had been what Fatari was trying to achieve all this time.

A bird flapped overhead, ducking quickly behind the cragged edge of a rock higher up the mountain. Kadhim quickly transformed and flew away in pursuit. The group stopped to wait, confused at his sudden burst of action. Maya leaned in to ask Zarina what was happening, but the gypsul held a finger to her lips.

In the eerie quiet of the cavernous valley, several squawks echoed along its walls, accompanied by the rapid beat of wings. Moments later, Kadhim returned with a small bird hanging dead between the sharp curves of his beak.

"A picorin," Elkin wondered aloud upon seeing the brightly toned creature.

"What's going on?" Thelic demanded. Kadhim had returned to his humanoid shape and passed Thelic the lifeless bird. "Shit," he muttered, his eyes darting around the cliffs.

"What's wrong, what is that creature?" Maya asked. When she first saw the bird in Kadhim's beak, it had been a beautiful shade of violet. Now, the creature was as black as a starless night sky.

"It's called a picorin, they're very intelligent creatures," Elkin explained, taking the fowl from Thelic's hands. "Every territory uses them."

"Uses them for what?" Whatever it was, it wasn't likely to be good.

"Individuals are selected to train these creatures as hatchlings. They change colours, you see?" He lifted the bird's wings to show Maya the colour that was still fading to its baseline black. "These changes in colour are used to indicate things like distance, direction, numbers…whatever the bird had been trained to detect and report."

"I don't understand, you think it's being used to keep an eye on us?"

"And pass our location or heading to whoever might be trailing us," Elkin said. "You see this colour? It may be a signal to its master that we're heading east, then change to a different shade and relay our distance."

Kadhim and Zarina took to the skies to do a sweep on the road behind them. Meanwhile, Elkin explained to Maya that the picorin is not an uncommon sight in these parts. Many are caught close to the Zamkora Cliffs, and it could just be a coincidence.

It was long since dark by the time they broke through the mountain pass. The wind whipped across the plains, its salty taste a clue to what lay beyond the nearby cliff edges, easily seen from where they stood. Thelic looked at his map and determined the valley road had taken them too far north in relation to Zamkora Drop. Dusk had descended quicker than expected, only a silver edge of moonlight visible through a crack in the clouds. Too late in the evening to journey south, they decided to retreat into the sheltered pass and rest up for the night. Their trek to the Batsharian ferryman could wait until morning.

With the final tent erected to ward off the drizzle, Kadhim and Zarina returned from their search with nothing to report. A full sweep of the valley, from the Ragashian Tribe's settlement to the cliffs, gave no indication of anyone following. Just to be safe, they took their usual shifts to keep watch for any predators or unwelcome guests.

The following morning, thundering rain had seen the travellers through a restless night, and they looked forward to leaving the mountains and its dark sky behind them. With no end to the torrent and little cover, only cured meat was offered to nibble on as they headed south.

A single wanderer traversed the north road towards them; the first they'd seen outside of Slitter Ridge since arriving on the barren shores. Whoever it was, wore a long cloak that concealed their face and clothes beneath. Maya rested her hand on the hilt of her short sword, instinctively readying herself for a fight. Luck throughout their travels seemed to wane the closer they got to Fatari, and none were taking any chances. A glint of metal peeked out from beneath the cloak. Kadhim and Zarina dropped from the sky in front of the hunched over stranger.

The cape was ripped from his body, a tall, lean man revealed beneath. He swung his sword towards Kadhim, but Zarina moved to block the sharp blade that sliced across her chest. She howled in pain and fell back, her body shimmering with the desire to transform and flee but ultimately unable. Kadhim quickly summoned a blistering wind to surround the man and the others raced forward. Maya and Thelic stopped, surprised to find they in fact knew the stranger. Dixol, Alaara's bodyguard. He had tracked them using the picorin from the docks at Fortus.

"What the hell are you doing here?" Maya yelled over Kadhim's whirlwind as she stooped to assess Zarina's wound with Elkin. Luckily, the slice was shallow and would heal quickly for the Svingoran shapeshifter. But blood had been spilled and Fatari's location possibly jeopardised. If Kadhim had his way, the human would be put to death.

Released from Kadhim's elemental prison, Dixol hunched over breathing heavily. Keela took possession of the Fortusian's sword, and she looked at him quizzically. She searched the full archives of her memory trying to find his face and came up empty. He was not Bandaar's man, though she was sure one would follow, prepared to finish the task on her behalf.

"I'm here under Alaara's orders," he wheezed. "I was to follow you and report your locations to her."

"Damn that woman," Thelic seethed. If that was true, then Jaxum knew of the encampment at Slitter Ridge. The location would be marked as a future target when the inevitable war ignited. "She intends to use this information to win the war. She always was a desperate attention seeker."

Thelic's unkind words sparked a fury in Dixol, his loyalty unwavering. "She isn't reporting to Jaxum! She wants to help, truly. She believes there's more to this war than the Keepers are telling their people."

Thelic shook his head and looked to Maya, a knowing glance passed between them.

"She's right, isn't she?" Dixol asked, already sure of the answer from their expressions. He had seen them with the outlanders at Slitter Ridge and witnessed Maya's incredible power. "Please, let me come with you. I'm sure I can help, and I can't return to her empty handed." He dropped his head, begging them.

Thelic realised something then, recognising the desperation. "You're in love with her," he said.

Dixol looked up, his face the picture of utter despair at the possibility of failing his task. He truly was here at Alaara's bidding.

"You can't come with us," Thelic decided.

"We have to kill him," Kadhim said. He stepped towards

Dixol, flipping a small knife over and over in his hands, a look of pure hatred in his eyes.

"Wait, please don't! You say I can't come with you, and I'll accept that, I won't breathe a word to anyone. I don't even know where you're going!" Dixol pleaded. The Svingoran's cool expression didn't flicker as he took another step forward.

Maya moved to stand between the two, blocking Kadhim from his kill. "You're not murdering him," she warned, her own eyes mirroring his cold ones.

"Look at what he did to Zarina! Get out of my way, Maya. This realm could do with one less human," he said darkly, pushing her to the side.

Thelic reached forward and grabbed the front of Kadhim's shirt, pulling him down before grabbing the knife wielding hand and pinning it back. He leaned down, his breath a stroke on Kadhim's ear as he said, "You touch her like that again, ally or not, I will rip your arms off." With his free hand, Thelic reached down to help Maya stand. Brushing herself off, she offered the same to a quivering Dixol.

"He's coming with us to Kavakin Shores," Maya announced to the group. She turned to Dixol. "Once we reach the shores, you can ask the water-raker to take you to Fortus docks. It'll be much safer than travelling by land without your bird thing."

"My picorin? You've seen it?" Dixol asked, hope renewed for his small friend.

"I killed it," Kadhim spat. Shaking free of Thelic's loosened grip, he stormed over to Zarina to check on her.

Dixol dipped his head, silently mourning the loss of the picorin he'd spent years training to perfection. He could only hope the creature had died swiftly at the hands of the shapeshifter.

∾

WITH DIXOL IN TOW, they continued south before cutting across the open plain, heading east to Zamkora Drop. Maya realised as they reached the cliff's edge, just how appropriate the name was. The drop itself was enough to kill. Those lucky enough to miss the ragged rocks below were just as likely to perish from the height of the fall into the choppy waves. A small and jaggedly carved stairway was set into the rock; the only way to reach the water without walking to the southern tip of the island.

Kadhim and Zarina transformed and took flight, assuring the others they would meet again at Kavakin shores. While the two shapeshifters had managed to fly them a short distance at Yatiken Point, the journey overwater was both too windy and too long to carry passengers. At least with two less people, the ferryman wouldn't be able to charge as much.

Waves crashed violently against the face of the cliff, soaking the treacherous stone stairs already coated in a natural, slippery algae. Elkin went first, followed by Maya, Keela and Dixol, with Thelic to hold up the rear should the Fortusian make any sudden moves. The spray of salt water lashed at their faces and stung their eyes. Progress down to the lonely water-raker's boat was slow and arduous, no one daring to hurry the pace.

The final steps led to a small cave, naturally eroded into the rock over millennia. With shaky legs and frazzled nerves, the open floor and break from the spray was a welcome relief. Through the dark and narrow passage, a second tunnel opened into a cathedral cavern. Light flooded the open space from gaps in the roof, long vines hanging from its crevice ripe with flora. The crash of waves against the outer walls echoed within, its effect a constant hum as the sound bounced amongst the walls. At the far end, a small, stone-built house sat lopsided at the edge of an inlet. Moored there, was a boat.

Maya couldn't help but wonder many things about what she saw; how the Batsharian had managed to build his house in such a perilous place, and how the hell he ever managed to get any business somewhere so out of the way.

Channels filled with a gaseous liquid lined the walls. As Elkin made a move towards the house, a line went taught at his ankle. A tripwire. Movement bobbed around the windows of the dwelling and an old, haggard looking man stepped from his door with a burning torch. He placed it in the channel and stood back. Flames shot along the wall, setting the shadows of the cave alight to reveal his visitors.

"Who's there? Wadd'ya want? Go away, I'll not be ferrying anyone!" he bellowed, the sound easily carried across the empty space. They moved forward, with no choice but to convince the old man of their need for his service.

"We require passage for five to Kavakin Shores and then passage for one to any of the docks in Fortus," Thelic said, moving to the front of the group.

"It's not cheap. Bad time of year to be travelling these waters. Creatures be mating," the man tutted, waving his torch at the group in a warning to stay back. He stopped then, his cataract-ridden eyes struggling to adjust themselves. He spotted Keela and grinned. It wasn't a pleasant or comfortable thing. At best the ferryman's smile was disturbing, with most teeth missing and the remainder a dull yellow stain. "That's a woman," he whispered.

"Well spotted," Keela muttered, her skin crawling as the man's gaze dipped south to her legs.

"I'll take you across the water, *and* to Fortus."

"Dare I ask what the price may be for that?" Elkin asked.

"Her." The ferryman pointed at Keela, who threw her head back and laughed.

"Me!? Punching a little above your weight don't you think, tiny man?" she crowed.

"I *want* sex with that one," he said, pacing back and forth. "One night, all to myself and then I'll take you wherever you want."

Keela stopped laughing as she realised this shell of a man was offering a serious proposition – a ride for a ride. Bile rose in the back of her throat. Elkin choked back a laugh as he watched Keela's face turn from amused to infuriated in record time. Maya, Dixol, and Thelic were all too gobsmacked to say anything.

"Alright, sugar. You want me? You've got me. Why don't we go inside and get comfortable?" Keela crooned, putting a little extra sway in her hips as she walked up. Everyone stared, wide-eyed. The Batsharian especially, he couldn't believe his luck.

"The rest of you stay there, don't come in. I want privacy with the woman, ya hear!?" He drooled as Keela stepped up to his porch and stroked the unkempt, bearded face before opening the door to his ramshackle of a home. "I'm gunna make you scream," he whispered.

"Oh, I won't be the one screaming," Keela purred with a wicked, perfect smile of her own. The others hadn't moved, didn't move, barely *breathed* as Keela disappeared into the perverted old man's house.

"You don't think…" Elkin began, but he couldn't finish the sentence.

"We can't let her do this, with that…thing!" Maya ran to the front door of the house. It was locked. She banged on the frosted glass panel, demanding she be let in, demanding Keela's release. A small squeak and a thump could be heard from inside. Moments later, the front door opened. Keela stepped out, clothing intact and hair slightly mussed.

"That was quick," Thelic laughed.

"I didn't *actually* do it, you little insect."

Maya let out a breath of relief and hugged Keela, who froze at the sudden and unwelcome contact. Sensing the discomfort, Maya jumped back. "So, what *did* you do with the old man then? Where is he?" she peeked around Keela to see the man face down on the floor. "Did you kill him?" she squawked, rushing through the door. The man was breathing, but a large welt was slowly rising on his forehead where Keela had struck him with the hilt of her blade. Maya chuckled. He deserved a lot worse.

Tying up the old man, they lashed him to the backseat of the boat and gathered some oars from a shack at the side of the inlet. Being the only members of the group still conscious that had any experience manipulating the water element, Maya and Elkin stood at the bow and BB was summoned to her side. Without the use of the castor circle, she guided the Water Finkel to manipulate the currents and push the boat. It worked and the ferry rocked forward to drift into the open water.

The paddleboat was exactly that; a small, wooden vessel just big enough to cram all six people. The voracious water below proved a difficult beast to tame as waves three times the size of their ferry loomed overhead. With every wave too big to circumnavigate or threatening to capsize them, Elkin was forced to focus on intercepting and creating a path through.

They had only made it halfway across the channel when Elkin succumbed to exhaustion and could no longer wield his lowly Warkoon's power. Darkness fell and the unaligned moons had once again shrouded their light between far-reaching clouds. Only Maya was left to guide the boat, and she was blind. Their only hope, now, was that BB understood to go straight east to the shoreline. If not, they would likely travel in circles.

Moonshine finally broke through, and dark, mountainous shapes appeared in the distance. For a moment, Maya was worried they had somehow been turned around and gone back the way they came. She sank to her knees, her forehead slick with sweat. Thelic's arm remained a steady anchor wrapped around her waist, the only thing stopping her from toppling forward into the churning water. With murmurs of encouragement, he kept her steady as she guided the boat to the sandy shore.

The ferryman woke to the scrape of wood along the sand. Feeling the tight, leather binds around his wrist and realising what they'd done, he flapped about like a captured fish, demanding to be released and demanding his woman. Keela smiled down at him, before lifting to slam the heel of her foot on his genitals. A high-pitched squeal erupted from clenched lips, and he dipped his head, willing away the black spots around his already ruptured vision. Thelic, Elkin, and Dixol muttered a prayer and cupped their own privates self-consciously, steering clear of the Esterbellian warrioress.

Everyone disembarked, Dixol and the old man included. They would spend the night on the shoreline together where it was safest, before travelling their separate ways. Elkin started the fire and the others laid out blankets. From the shore, a vast expanse of desert dunes stretched to mountains far in the distance, with no trees or shade in sight. Maya wondered if they would be better travelling in the comparative coolness of the night. As she settled on the blankets her eyes grew heavy and hands shook with fatigue as Elkin's fresh meal wafted from the fire.

Maya had once offered to cook in his stead, but he refused. Cooking was a passion. The chance to woo and charm a lady with an expertly cooked meal was one of the few things he believed he truly excelled at. Maya begged to differ. He had been immensely useful on their travels; a capable fighter; an excellent healer and damn good company. Though, his cooking was something spectacular, especially considering the conditions he was expected to work in. Together, they enjoyed the fashigi with a healthy dose of mead, a reluctant peace offering from the old man's stash in return for his release.

As the others slept, Keela and Elkin took first watch. The desert wind lifted the sand from its dry perch to whip around in delicate spirals along the dunes. Howls and crows of far-off beasts stalked the night and yet the group slept peacefully having grown accustomed to unfamiliar landscapes. None of them had travelled this far east. Even Elkin, who seemed well acquainted with all the nooks and crannies of their small slice of Avalon or, as the gypsul claimed, Sythintall.

Keela poked at the fire and added another dry log, the remnants of small trees that sprung forth at the beginning of every year, only to wither and die with the heat of the scorching desert. The silence between the two warriors and old friends had become comfortable again. Their history left behind in the wake of everything they had faced in the recent weeks. Elkin watched her now, trying to determine where he stood in her eyes. Friend? Foe? Former lover? She was unreadable.

"Stop staring, you're creeping me out," she muttered, poking the embers.

"What do you think would have become of us if I hadn't left?" he asked, the shadows cast from the flames emphasising his serious expression; unusual for the light-hearted man.

"Honestly? I think we would have killed or left each other," she said truthfully. "I mean, with us, it was all sex when it was good, and arguments when it was bad."

"Isn't that the fundamentals of a relationship?" A smile cracked the hard line of his jaw. He chugged another mouthful of the old man's delectable mead, commending both his taste in drink and his taste in women as he passed the mug to Keela.

She accepted with a shake of her head in response to his question. "That isn't the kind of life either of us wants or needs, Elkin. Not in our line of work." She avoided his stare, eyes focused on the fire. "We...I, need someone who is there for me. Someone who understands my..."

"Hard-headedness?"

She chuckled but nodded in agreement. "We were good when it lasted, but we had no real future. We were too different, our souls never married up."

He accepted the mug she handed back and dropped his gaze, disappointed but understanding her reasoning. Deep down it still hurt. He believed they'd had a chance back then, a chance to be happy. It was Fatari's prophecy that had changed everything, changed him.

ELKIN WOKE to Keela violently shaking him. They had fallen asleep during their watch. He stood, too suddenly, and a wave of nausea racked his body. He looked at Keela, then to her twin. Two Keelas. Grabbing the mug abandoned at his side, he wiped a finger around the inside of the rim, and a slight but slimy residue was noticeable.

"It's sikospin," he said. The old man had drugged them. A quick glance at the shore confirmed it; the boat and its owner were gone.

"How the hell did he get it into the bottle without one of us noticing?" Keela asked, taking the mug to see for herself.

"I'm not sure. Perhaps it was already laced?"

With little choice, Dixol was forced to join the group as they packed up and began their journey, trundling across the undulating dunes. Ruins of old towns littered the terrain. Abandoned and utterly desolate, they stood half buried beneath the sands. These were their only navigational markers, their only means of finding Lifaya. A half-destroyed statue of a creature, an etiyan, lay on its side.

Thelic regarded the crude map and Horticus' added drawings. The statue was clearly marked. They were on the right track but not even halfway to the Pavinicum Tribe's encampment. Despite the clear skies Kadhim and Zarina were nowhere to be seen. The group pushed on nonetheless, confident the gypsul would use their flight to find them.

As the sun loomed dangerously above, their skin turned red and sore to the touch. Another small, stone and mud-built town loomed on the shimmering horizon and the travellers took shelter in one of the dilapidated buildings. There they slept until nightfall, determining the sun a far more lethal adversary than any predator that roamed the dunes at night.

Thelic thanked whoever was watching over them for the clear sky and starlight as they woke, crucial for night-time navigation. Like the evening before, beasts hollered from behind the dunes, some far and others chillingly close. A lurid hiss seemed to follow their tracks. A creature stalking them, hidden beneath the sands.

Thelic recognised the sound instantly. It was the same sound he'd imitated at Yatiken Point, the hiss of a grokus. A long and thick bodied creature, the grokus bore no arms or legs, just pure muscle slipping beneath the dunes. These beasts were known to favour two types of terrain – water, and heated sands. An odd mix that no human or gypsul could explain, but a fact proven by the countless victims in both environments.

The sand dipped and bowed; its surface disturbed by what stirred beneath. Thelic whistled to the others in front and unwrapped his spear. Signal conveyed, Maya and the others followed suit and slipped their own weapons from their sheaths. The grokus was here, and it was big. Maya was at least ten feet ahead of Thelic, and yet, the line of shifting sand stretched between them.

They stood still and held their breaths. Thelic took one step, two steps towards the pulsing grit. He raised his spear.

Four eyes blinked beneath the sand, their lids sliding horizontally. Gills puffed and the grokus broke from its hide, teeth snapping, mere inches from Thelic's face.

He swung his spear and the grokus clamped down on the recently sharpened blade. It shrieked. Every member dropped to their knees, weapons falling to the ground as they cupped their hands over rupturing eardrums.

Maya summoned Loki and commanded him to whip around the grokus. The snake-like creature dove to ground, hiding once again beneath the sands.

"Where is it?" Dixol screamed, shifting his body left and right to survey the sand.

Maya shushed him, listening for the hiss. Sand shifted to her left. Without hesitation, she swung her small sword and plunged it into the ground. Another shriek sounded. The creature's tail shot from below and ploughed into Maya's stomach. She flew, five, six, seven feet into the air before plummeting back down. With a thud barely softened by the sand and sharp rocks, she landed painfully on her side.

"Maya!" Thelic roared, racing towards her unmoving figure.

The creature tried to block him, but Keela had jumped on the writhing centre of its back, her blade barely breaking the hard scales. Shaking her off, it dove once again to the protection of the sands, swimming rapidly through the lightly compacted silica.

Dixol spotted the slithery mass and leapt into the air,

coming down hard on the grokus' muscled body. It doubled back, head breaking from the sand, and clamped down on the Fortusian's head.

Blood sprayed the white dunes. He died instantly.

The distraction allowed Keela and Elkin the opportunity to attack simultaneously, both swords split through the beast's skull. One final cry and the grokus was killed, Dixol's body rolling from its razor-edged mouth.

"Maya? Hey, wake up." Thelic cradled her bleeding head. She had landed on a small cluster of geodes, her body bruised and battered. "Maya?"

She blinked, roused from unconsciousness by his voice. A sharp reminder of the beast they were facing sprang to memory and she shot up. "Where the fuck is it?" she screeched. Thelic steadied her, telling her it was dead. But she saw that now. She saw Dixol, his head crushed like a watermelon, unrecognisable in the open jaws of the lifeless creature.

22
FATARI

KAVAKIN

Maya shivered as the desert temperature plummeted with its sun. After tangling with the grokus, they stopped at the first abandoned village they could find on their path ever east. Nobody had slept that day, the silence eerie when all preferred to hear what creatures hunted them. The bays and hollers began as the last of the sun's rays dipped out of sight. Maya shivered again and longed for the coat Brijid had given her in Danika.

Thelic wrapped one of their blankets around her shoulders, offering the same to the others. She warmed but continued to tremble. Dixol's face, half eaten and disfigured, burned into her mind.

They stopped at a lonely building, preparing to rest as predawn lit the sky. A familiar squawk overhead accompanied the flap of wings and Maya stepped from the crumbled home just as Kadhim dropped to the ground in gypsul form. Relief washed over him at the sight of her. He registered the graze above her brow and strands of golden hair brittle with dry blood. Once again, he hadn't been there when she'd needed him. He brushed her face with the back of his hand.

"I'm fine," she laughed awkwardly, stepping away.

He pulled back and asked what happened, a blush creeping up his neck to paint pale cheeks. Maya told him of the creature and Dixol's death, joking darkly that Kadhim had gotten what he wanted in the end.

"I'm not against humans, Maya. I just consider this quest a priority over any and all life here...all except yours."

Again, his serious expression and proximity caused her to step back. She wasn't sure how the gypsul felt, but life was complicated enough without a love triangle being added into the mix.

"Listen, Kadhim–"

"The Pavinicum encampment is close. If we leave now, you should be there by late morning," he said, cutting Maya off.

Grateful for the change in topic, she ducked back inside the stone house to relay the news to the others.

A SHIMMERING SANCTUARY appeared in the distance. Maya was sure her mind played tricks. Just another abandoned village in the never-ending trek across the sands. As they got closer the haze dipped to reveal tall fruit trees and stone buildings, intact, with cloth-covered verandas and shaded courtyards.

"Welcome to Etiyan Vale, the last great town of Kavakin," Kadhim said, leading the way.

Zarina stood, leaning against the first of the taller, mud-bricked houses and waved to the approaching band of travellers.

"You found them! I was beginning to think they'd been eaten," she chuckled before registering the grim faces. Maya told her of Dixol's unfortunate fate, and she apologised.

"You all must be starving, let's get you out of the sun and fed."

A short woman with long, white hair and a single rune on a face crinkled with time, stormed from the central courtyard. Thelic and Keela braced for a fight, but Elkin and somehow Maya, knew the old gypsul. She raced forward, pushing the warriors from her path, and embraced Maya.

Fatari.

Lifaya had spent their years apart clinging to her visions of Maya's face. She'd watched her granddaughter grow into a beautiful woman and could hardly believe she finally stood here, in her arms. As the chaos grew, Fatari's power had waned over time and as Maya travelled the territories, she had been fraught with worry, unable to track her progress.

"Grandma?"

The Seer wept at the title, the only title she truly cared about, and squeezed Maya once more. Stepping back, she gazed upon her granddaughter, taking in everything her visions as of late could not provide. Maya was strong with a firm grip. Her eyes, burning emeralds, full of passion and strength. Though Bandaar had left his mark in those eyes, she looked just like Jaseen.

"You have grown so beautiful, Maya. Like your mother." Fatari had seen the vision of her daughter's death, the last she'd had of Maya. Prisia, the Elder, had told her of Maya's progress to Cantor and her assembled guardians. "I'm so sorry about your mother, but she died the only way she would have wanted; protecting her children."

Maya felt the back of her throat go dry at the mention, unable to speak momentarily as the wave of grief passed. Lifaya embraced her once again. "I'm also sorry about how Traccia greeted you, the djinca you met in Danika. I told her to stay beyond the portal's bleed. By the time my vision came through, it was too late."

"It's fine," Maya assured her. "Traccia explained everything at Slitter Ridge. It wouldn't have mattered anyway. I had to save Jacob before coming to you, I don't see how it would have gone any differently had she greeted me as intended."

"Yes! I almost forgot to say, your brother is well."

"You've seen him? In your visions?"

"I have. The gateway spat him out in a place named Teg-sas. He was able to contact his father and should be home now."

Maya chuckled with relief. Teg-sas. Translation – Texas. Her brother was safe.

THE SEER FERRIED them through the small town. Each of the houses, bound by mud and clay, stood two bricks thick and two-stories high with domed roofs. Small windows circled the tip like a crown, the design a method to cool the interior with a through-wind, permitting only minimal bugs and dust in its wake.

Lifaya led them on, through the town, to a rounded tower. Grand in size while simple in design, there were no flared eaves here, or any such majesty. The wooden door, its only entrance, sat peculiarly several feet high. With the frame's base at knee hight, the tower's visitors were forced to step up and over the threshold. A warm wind rushed towards the door as it opened, the sand at their feet denied access to the hall by its clever design.

Inside was surprisingly chilled. Large pots bursting with long, dampened reeds ran along the wall of the circular room. As the temperature rose throughout the day, the water would evaporate from the tall plants, moistening the air with a cooling effect. The method was ancient, but effective. A long, stone slab sat plainly in the middle of the room, with blanketed pillows upon which to perch. Lifaya asked them all to remove their belongings and to have a seat and rest. Food and drink would be brought in momentarily.

Children, the oldest barely fifteen, entered the hall with steaming pots of meat filled buns and large jugs of water. The travellers ate and drank voraciously; their rationed diet leaving them half starved. In such a desolate place, a shortage of food and suitable drinking water would not come as a surprise. But as they finished the first serving, a second was brought in almost instantaneously.

A young girl dashed through the door, her amber hair bobbing across small shoulders. Running to Lifaya, she leaned up on tiptoes to whisper in the older woman's ear.

The Seer chuckled, shooing the girl away before addressing the group. "Your quarters are ready."

There were so many questions. Weeks spent waiting for the moment Maya could finally get the answers she craved. Keela yawned next to her, thereby prompting a similar effect across the group as Thelic and Elkin stretched. Everyone was exhausted, her questions could wait.

Lifaya guided them under the colourless verandas to several smaller domes. These were to be their sleeping quarters. More importantly, each member was pleased to learn their living space for the foreseeable future came with a shower. Such a luxury was afforded by an advanced system of channels buried beneath the town, which led to an underground water system. Clothes, too, were arranged for each member of the group, long sleeved and appropriate for the unforgiving environment. Despite the early hours of the day, Fatari left them to bathe, change and get some rest.

≈

UNABLE TO REST, Keela wandered the shaded courtyards of the vale, making her way to the outskirts. From there she gazed out at the horizon; only sand and dust glaring back.

"You should not be here," Lifaya announced, sliding down the dune to stand beside her.

Keela snorted. "And here I thought the Seer was a kind woman." She looked at Fatari, at the rune on her forehead and elongated fingers. "Though, I suppose even *that* was untrue. I thought you were human."

"I warned your friend to leave you in Esterbell."

"He did leave, though I think he's beginning to wonder about the validity of your prophecies."

The Seer gripped Keela's arm, forcing her to turn so they stood face to face. "You have a choice, Keela. There are many sides to this war, and you must choose."

"You act like I have a choice!" She ripped her arm from Lifaya's taloned grip. "Some all-knowing seer *you* are."

"Your father, or your sister, Keela. One of those choices will kill you, and I think you know which it will be." Lifaya let that sink in before putting hands on her hips. "I know you've been leaving hints, breadcrumbs for his soldiers."

Keela stepped back, affronted by the accusation. "I've done no such thing!" She didn't want her father's soldiers anywhere near this mission.

"I saw! The vision was clouded but I saw the messages exchanged on the dock. The recipient, a water-raker, secretly bore Esterbell's emblem. You're the only one with any sort of connection to the foul man." Lifaya dropped her arms and her shoulders sagged. Maya would be devastated should Keela choose to abandon them. Keela needed a wakeup call. "You crave his approval, and it will destroy you. Bandaar can never provide the love you need!" Keela recoiled at the verbal slap, dropping her head in embarrassment. "There is still time, Keela. Your fate is not set in stone. Make your decision."

Keela was left alone on the dune with her thoughts. One question stood glaring above the others. If not her, who had been liaising with Esterbellians on their travels? Who was betraying them?

∾

MAYA COULDN'T SLEEP. Tossing and turning, the questions burned and beckoned her to find Lifaya. Slowly, she got up from the bed and yelped as a hand shot out to wrap around her wrist, dragging her back beneath the covers. Thelic's warm, hard chest dwarfed her. Wrapped in the iron embrace, his heat seeped in, relaxing the stiff joints suffered from their journey.

Feeling her squirm, he let out a warning growl of complaint, wrapping his arms tighter across her back. "Go. To. Sleep," he rumbled.

"I can't wait any longer, Thelic. You stay here and rest, I'm not going far."

He cracked open one eye and groaned in defeat, releasing her, and swinging his legs over the lip of the cushioned bed. Both dressed in loose, cotton trousers and a tight, long-sleeved tunic, Thelic attached the spear and its sheath to the belt at his waist, before following Maya out the door.

Together, they took their time, enjoying the sun as they explored the sheltered walkways and admired the domed structures. With every territory and every town, children were seen playing in the streets while the older generations worked the stalls or tilled the land. Here, children and teenagers worked the town pump, swept the household entrances, and tended to creatures in the paddocks. The presence of grownups was sparse. Other than her grandmother, Maya had seen two, maybe three adults since their arrival.

Maya spotted Lifaya storming into town, her long, frost-coloured hair billowing behind her. Elkin stepped from behind one of the buildings and grabbed the Seer, whispering something in her ear before dragging the old woman into the tower hall.

Maya and Thelic followed.

"Why did you tell me that prophecy?"

From behind the door, Maya recognised Elkin's voice, tense and upset.

"To save your life, Elkin. If you had stayed, Bandaar's darkness would have consumed you," Lifaya said.

Ignoring Thelic's amused expression, Maya pressed her ear closer to the door, barely able to hear the muffled voices.

Elkin paced the length of the great, stone table, "Why didn't you tell me? Why not tell me that Keela would come?"

"Because you would have waited for her." Fatari sighed and sat on one of the long cushions. "You shouldn't have allowed her to join you, she was supposed to stay behind."

"What do you mean? She's still in danger?" Elkin stopped pacing his eyes burning into Lifaya.

"She has a choice to make. She knows this, and she knows the consequences of choosing poorly..." Her eyes drifted, seeing something beyond the scope of any mortal or gypsul. "Though I fear it may be too late." She lifted her eyes to meet Elkin's. "She will betray you, boy. Best to do as I warned and cut ties."

Elkin laughed and Maya recoiled from the doorway. The sound wasn't humorous or joyful, the laugh was cruel. She leaned in again to listen as he said, "*Her*? Betray *me*? Your powers are waning old woman."

The mounting anger of the towering man wasn't what gave the Seer pause. "You–"

"I love Maya as if she were my own sister. Know that I would never do anything to harm her." Elkin's anger evaporated and he backed away from the speechless Seer. Turning on his heel, he ran from the hall.

Thelic and Maya pressed against the wall as the door flew open and their friend raced past into the town. Inside, Lifaya still sat at the stone table, head cradled in her hands.

"Are you ok?"

Lifaya jumped up, banging her knees on the underside of stone, "Spirits, Maya!"

"Sorry, I didn't think seers could get spooked," she laughed.

"Ha, it doesn't work that way, sweetheart. I don't know everything that's going to happen, at all times."

"How *does* it work?" Maya asked, settling onto the cushion beside her grandmother.

"Your guess is as good as mine. There's only one other seer written in our history, Esterbell. Those before her have been lost to time. The power comes from contracting with a Gouram. Some receive the gift, others do not." She shrugged, the questions regarding her power no longer troubling.

Thelic settled onto one of the pillows that lined the walls. Setting the spear to his side, he leaned against the hardened mud, his eyes drifting heavily. Since Maya's arrival in Danika, he'd been unable to sleep peacefully. Everywhere they went, someone or something seemed intent on killing them. It was a surprise they'd made it this far. With the Seer close by, he could close his eyes just for a moment, and allow that exhaustion to swallow him.

Both Maya and Lifaya watched the hardened warrior drift into a dreamless sleep. Revilo's son. Lifaya had recognised the brown crop of hair, chiselled jaw, and grey eyes the moment he'd brandished that spear at her in Maya's defence.

Despite the odds of fate branching a new course since the prophecy, they'd found each other.

"He's done well getting you this far."

"You met his father, didn't you? That old fable, it was one of your prophecies."

Lifaya nodded. "Fables and prophecies, all forged in the growing chaos," she said, remembering the Fortusian guard. He, too, had been quite ruggedly handsome.

Maya removed the recently repaired chain from around her neck and handed it to Fatari. "I promised Thelic he could have that, to restore his family name and return to his home territory. That's why he came."

Lifaya eyed Maya dubiously. "I think we both know why that young man has come this far, and it has nothing to do with an old stone." She waggled her eyebrows knowingly. "Anyway, it was not yours to promise. This is a crucial part of the original gateway. Have you ever seen the Gouram Stone's glow?"

Maya remembered the thin line of radiant light which led her through the fog in Danika. "Yes, once. But it hasn't glowed since."

"I'm not surprised, its energy is depleted." She tucked the necklace into the folds of her clothes. "Before you leave, I will show you how to restore it. Don't worry."

"Leave!? We just got here!" Maya blurted. Thelic woke abruptly and grabbed his spear. He sat up, one eye struggling to remain open. Maya whispered an apology and told him to go back to sleep.

"Maya, what do you think your purpose is here, in Sythintall?"

She raised her fingers counting off the items on her to do list. "Find and rescue my mother and Jacob; find Mikosh, your ex-husband; and find you. Batshari and Horticus hinted at a larger purpose, but I'm hoping you'll tell me otherwise."

Fatari chuckled. "And how is that errant former husband of mine?"

"Drowning in vice."

"Pah! He never changes. That's why I left the foolish old man," she bellowed, banging a fist on the table. Calming herself, she regarded her granddaughter once again. "Tell me of your life, Maya. Of Earth and your family there. Tell me all I've missed."

Maya told her of Jaseen's disappearance, her work in the London Police, Jacob's grand achievements, her adoring stepfather, and of Yali.

At her granddaughter's sudden despair, Lifaya told her not to worry, that Yali was doing fine and recovering nicely.

"Who was Yali to you?" Maya asked. "She can't be your sister; she doesn't have the gypsul…features."

"She was my friend, and my guard," Lifaya said. "That is a story for another time, but yes, you're right. She is human."

Encouraged to continue with her story, Maya spoke of their journey through the territories and made the introduction to BB and Loki. Her grandmother was thrilled and commended her ability to work with the temperamental sprites. But there was only so long she could put off telling Maya the truth. That her journey had only begun, and how it all stemmed from a moment in time when two beings from two different worlds, fell in love.

A moment of silence drifted between them as Lifaya considered where she might begin.

"Tell me everything, Grandma. I need to know."

"Horticus told you the history of the Five Majors, so instead we will start with *your* history, how you came to be who and what you are. It starts with your parents, Jaseen and Bandaar."

Maya settled in and listened as her parents' story was laid out for the first time. Bandaar wasn't always so obsessed with the gypsul and the chaos. A catalyst precipitated this when their firstborn, a son they named Qaylan, was absorbed by the boundary void."

"I had a brother?" Maya couldn't believe it, not one but two siblings, and she'd had no clue.

"He was killed when Jaseen was pregnant with you. It happened just after a wave of new humans came through the gateway in Esterbell. The power of their collective bindings to earthly sprites shook the foundations of Sythintall. The portal bleed, only of mild concern at that point, spread like an errant woodfire from the gateways."

"But I thought the veil was a problem since the first war?"

"It was. Esterbell and Fortus' combined sacrifice meant that any humans who crossed over were stripped of their contracted sprites. However, the more the humans crossed, the more that power to seal the sprites waned. Since the death of the great Majors, we have failed to control it."

Unable to sit still, Maya stood to walk the circular confines of the large hall. "Horticus told me why my power is so important." She stopped, a disturbing thought only just occurring to her. "Is Jacob a halfling too? Like me?" If Maya died, would he be expected to take on whatever quest she had been promised to?

"Technically, yes. But he's not like you. He holds slight traces of your ancestor's contracted essence, though not enough to enable the gift, as is the case with most children of castors. Whereas you not only hold *Esterbell's* remnants, but that which the Gouram gifted to you themselves." Her eyebrows furrowed as she pondered. "Your father, too, passed something of his own to you. What that contract is, I have no idea. But whatever it is, it must be strong, just like the combined power of Esterbell and Fortus all those years ago."

"And you know how to tap into that power so I can use it to stop the chaos?"

The Seer became somewhat frustrated. She should have brought the scrolls with her, but she couldn't afford for them to fall into the wrong hands, or risk them being destroyed. Bandaar still possessed the dark one, the most dangerous. "I have three of the four scrolls required to enact the old rite… but they aren't here."

"Well? Where the hell are they?"

Fatari had left them with a woman she could trust at the far western boundary. Nobody would find them there. The place, known as Daqarmi, was a maze of trees that secreted a naturally occurring gas. Those who entered would suffer intense hallucinations. Most either died or got so turned around and paranoid, they never returned.

"Those scrolls are only part of the battle, Maya. You see that seal on your chest?" Maya pulled the folds of thin material apart, revealing Batshari's mark. "That is only the first of four, should you hope to survive the ceremony."

"Bloody hell. Don't suppose you know where I'm supposed to find the other three?"

"Possibly. There are old temples scattered around the five territories, at least one dedicated to each of the Gods."

Maya slumped back onto the pillows beside her grandmother and buried her head between her knees, warding off the pounding headache. "Bugger it all to hell," came the mumbled whine.

Lifaya draped an arm over Maya's shoulder, pulling her in tightly. Without looking up, Maya asked for the story of her parents and how they met. Lifaya leaned in, keeping a good hold as she spoke of two young warriors, one the Keeper of Esterbell and the other a wonderfully gifted castor, a gypsul.

"Bandaar was a young ruler when he met Jaseen. He had not long passed through the gateway before taking control of the territory in an unprecedented coup. Keen to bolster his position, he travelled the territories and the unclaimed lands often. The void that surrounded the land fascinated and terrified him, but he wanted to know more. He wanted to know who or what, if anything, dwelled beyond that border."

According to Lifaya, it was during his exploration of Kavakin shores that Bandaar met Jaseen, a beautiful warrioress of the gypsul, and incredibly powerful. His men had been frightened at her appearance; always taught to shun and avoid the original inhabitants of *their* Avalon. But Jaseen entranced him. Bandaar found himself visiting those lands more and more, just to get a glimpse of the woman. On one such visit, he found Jaseen, injured. Her town on the shores of Kavakin had been savagely attacked by humans who wished to rid the lands of gypsul and claim it for themselves.

Bandaar saved her, bringing Jaseen back to Esterbell for advanced treatment. At first, he kept her hidden. But eventually, they fell in love, and he convinced her to change. With power never before seen, he transformed her hands and runes to conceal her true heritage.

In turn, she taught him the true history of the Four Majors and he believed her, damning the human mages but allowing his people to live on in ignorance.

"Why wouldn't he tell the other humans? Surely his influence would have gotten the message across?" Maya asked.

"At this time, a political war was brewing amongst Avalon's leaders. Many wished to snatch more power for themselves." Lifaya continued with her story, moving on to Qaylan's birth.

Bandaar and Jaseen were thrilled, the boy was born a young and already powerful being as was evident by the castor circle that shone upon his entry to the world. Fatari chuckled at the rekindled memory. Jaseen had been frightened to death, unsure where to begin with such a powerful child, a halfling. Bandaar, too, doted upon his son relentlessly.

On Qaylan's fifth birthday, Jaseen had discovered she was pregnant with Maya. It was on this day, that the first of two prophecies would be foretold. Fatari had seen a bright future, where the gypsul and humans lived together in harmony. She tried to convince Bandaar to change the tides, educate his people of the true history of the Five Majors but he refused. Almost a single year passed after that, during which time more and more humans had flooded through the gateways.

Bandaar grew distant from his family, a darkness beginning to swell inside with every new arrival. All potential threats to his position as Keeper. Jaseen sensed this and blamed the stress of keeping a territory and a family. She convinced him to travel with her to the Outlands, to get away for a while. There, on the southern shore of Kavakin, Qaylan's powers led the young boy astray. He walked into the void, never to be seen again. With the loss of his son, Bandaar slowly began to drive himself mad with a new mission – to eradicate the chaos by whatever means necessary.

"This is all because he was grieving?" Maya interrupted. Thelic, woken by the hum of voices, sat awake and listened to Lifaya's re-telling of Maya's history.

"Be quiet and listen to the damn story," Lifaya barked. Thelic chuckled at the Seer's outburst and rose a finger to his lips at Maya's affronted expression.

Jaseen had grown frightened of Bandaar's obsession and left Esterbell to visit her mother during the later stages of pregnancy. Three days later, Maya was born in Bodhisia's valley. Like her brother, the child's birth was bathed in light from a spectacular amount of power. Unfortunately, Maya emerged half dead, the remaining life rapidly leaving her tiny body. Frightened, Jaseen called to the great Gouram. They had been watching the event as a result of their own self-interest. The Sythintall Gods had made great plans for

Qaylan, but his death had come, unforeseen, to shatter their hopes of saving the realm. Maya was their last chance, and a deal was struck.

"Ok, this is the part I'm wary about." Maya slapped both hands on the table, ignoring her grandmother's exasperated look. "Other than the obvious, what is this life of servitude I've been told about?"

"Who told you that?"

"The God of grumpiness, Batshari."

"Spirits, Maya. You can't say that!" Lifaya placed the tips of her fingers and thumbs together, both hands creating a rough circle in the gypsul gesture of prayer as she muttered an oath of obedience to the Gouram. Swatting Maya for her ignorance, she continued. "Jaseen begged the Gods to breathe life back into your body and they accepted."

"Yeah I know, a life for a life."

"Exactly! You help return life to Sythintall and your debt is paid!"

"That's not what Batshari suggested."

"I was there, this is the deal that was struck!" Lifaya shook her finger at the air, as if in warning to the Gods that she bore witness and refused to suffer any treachery. "Maya your...rebirth, I suppose, was one of the most spectacular things I've witnessed in my long life."

When the Gouram combined their essence and revived baby Maya, the entire valley was lit in the most beautiful colours. Flowers, trees, and fountains of water, sprung from the earth. Blazing fires erupted from deep lava channels and wind sang through the valley.

Maya rubbed her temples. This was a serious amount of information to digest, and she was still recovering from Horticus' historical revelations. "What about my original power, before the Gods blessed me? What was that about?"

"Part of that was from Esterbell, but the rest...I have no

idea. I can only assume it has something to do with your father as both you and Qaylan displayed the same at birth."

Before Maya could question her grandmother further, Keela burst into the room.

"ESTERBELLIAN SOLDIERS!" Keela hollered.

Maya, Lifaya and Thelic stood at once and rushed from the hall. Children of the tribe remained frozen in the streets, sensing the mounting chaos but unsure what to do. Seeing Lifaya, they rushed towards her, and she told them to head for the caves, that the humans were coming. Quick to follow orders, the young gypsul dropped whatever it was they were doing and dashed from the scene.

"Where's Elkin?" Maya scanned the streets as they ran, with no sign of their friend.

"He's with them!" Keela yelled behind her.

Maya stopped and the others slammed to a halt with her. "What is *that* supposed to mean?"

"I was wrong, Maya." Lifaya said. "I didn't see…I thought it was Keela, but Elkin has been with Bandaar all along."

"Bullshit!" Maya yelled. There was no way.

"It's true, Maya. I saw him. Elkin left to meet the soldiers and led them here." Keela had remained on the dune where the Seer had left her. She knew by then, who their traitor was. Thelic would never betray Maya, they were matched. Elkin had confirmed as much when he had found Keela, and she watched him walk into the desert, his only explanation that Bandaar was right.

"Fucking idiot," Thelic rasped, rage and betrayal clear in his voice. "Keela, how many soldiers did you see? How much time before they get here?" he asked. Something had been different with Elkin, something lost or longing. It was so subtle that he'd brushed it aside. A resounding scream through the vale answered Thelic's question.

They were already here.

At least twenty soldiers, all displaying the Esterbellian crest, charged across the dunes, their swords ploughing through the chests of fleeing children.

Lifaya screamed as the young child that had served the travellers their first meal at the village, was bowled over by the soldiers' karkili; blood and brain matter scoring the sand as the small body was trampled.

Kadhim and Zarina charged from their rooms, ushering the remaining villagers behind the line of defence, where Maya stood with Fatari and the two human warriors.

"Maya!" Elkin beckoned from the centre of the riders. They stopped at his command, a large, empty courtyard standing between the two sides. "Come with me! Your father can stop this chaos!" he begged. "I am sure, now, that the Seer lies. Give me the scrolls, and we will go to him together."

"You're a bloody idiot, Elkin." Thelic roared. "You left his service, why band together with him now? Why betray us?"

"Elkin, remember my warning?" Fatari cried. "This may well be the moment. This choice possibly determines your fate!"

Elkin laughed; a maniacal rage inherent from too many years under Bandaar's thumb. "I bow to no fate. I will not be intimidated by an old woman!" He raised his hands, ready to summon the water from the depths of the town.

"Then you will die." Fatari dropped to the ground and summoned a blue castor circle, three times the size of Maya's.

Water from underground channels sprung from the ground and coalesced into a single, powerful wave. Elkin's summoning was outgunned by the dominant Seer, the water bowing to a higher power. Bandaar's men met the challenge, and water met fire. Thelic, too, conjured the earth accompanied by Kadhim and Zarina's powerful wind, and sand whipped from the ground to blind their enemies. Maya and Keela continued to call to Elkin, begging him to reconsider.

One of the Esterbellian soldiers summoned a boulder from the sand, its target the Seer. Thelic jumped forward and launched his own. The stones collided in mid-air with a crack, one bounced and plummeted towards Elkin. Keela screamed and rushed towards him. Soft, dark hair brushed his face as he fell from the karkili, just as the boulder collided with flesh.

A soft whimper passed Keela's lips, and she collapsed to the ground at his feet. Elkin dropped beside her; the elements of water, earth, wind and fire raging above. He gingerly placed his hands beneath her body, rolling the limp form into his arms. Blood and sand stained her beautiful face, her chest and heartbeat still. She was dead. The Seer's prophecy had come true.

Maya felt the tears race down her cheeks, and darkness once again welled inside. Their father's darkness. A shader's retreat. She unleashed it.

A bloodied sword dropped to the floor and light flooded the vale. Maya hovered just above the ground, where all four of the castor circles shone, dull and broken, but powerful, nonetheless.

BB and Loki whipped ferociously at her enemies. Drowning them. Suffocating them. Fatari and her friends, too, were battered by the elements as they tried to calm Maya. Her body climbed higher into the air, her hands outstretched, commanding the elements to destroy the humans that threatened her new-found family.

Etiyan Vale shook and hummed with the summons, but it was short lived. Too much power and too few of the spiritual seals exhausted her small reserves of energy quickly. She screamed, willing herself to summon more, more, more of the elemental rage.

A child's cry broke the trance. He was trapped beneath a pillar destroyed by Maya's wind. She choked, elemental essence consuming her. The earth opened beneath her feet, ready to swallow its un-anointed master, and she plummeted toward the void.

Thelic raced for the pit and summoned Loki. With the Finkel's help, Thelic was lifted from the ground and caught Maya, landing roughly on the other side. Placing her down, he manipulated the earth to return to its tempered, sandy state.

"Get the child!" she croaked.

He looked from her to the young boy. He was still crying, trapped under the rubble. Thelic raced towards the toppled veranda, this time summoning his own contracted power to remove the debris from atop the child. Relatively unharmed, the boy raced from the battlefield, towards the caves.

Maya stood, sheer willpower and adrenaline the only thing keeping her upright. Only five of the soldiers remained, her power had all but obliterated the rest. Thelic slammed his hand to the ground and a large wall of sand erupted from beneath like an ever-shifting wave.

"Maya, go with the others and get to the caves!" Thelic yelled.

"Like hell. I'm not going anywhere," she growled. Kadhim and Zarina also scoffed at the suggestion; instead transforming to fly over the battlefield unseen, and tackle the soldiers from behind.

Fatari faced Elkin. He remained, crouched over Keela, her bloody head soaking the Esterbellian crest. "Let me see her," she said.

"Get away. This is all your fault," Elkin spat, not bothering to look at the Seer as he stroked damp strands of hair from Keela's face.

With a low mutter, Fatari summoned the water once again. Its powerful current dragged him from Keela's side, and he roared with pent up rage, clawing to keep hold of her body. As before, he was powerless against the element as it wrapped all but his head into a tight ball. "Right. Now, stay there and be quiet." Kneeling on the blood-soaked sand, Lifaya pushed her hands to hover over Keela's broken form and summoned Batshari's power.

A pattering of small feet echoed in the distance. The soldiers, whose arms had raised in preparation for their next onslaught, stumbled back. An army of children bolted over the dunes from the cave entrance. Balls of flame burst from the tiny force and small etiyan jumped between Maya and the others, crashing into the remaining Esterbellian soldiers. With all of them working together, the battle was quickly won, and the children cried with victory.

Flames died out and water retreated. Amidst the death and despair, the vale bloomed with life. Grass, unnatural against the landscape, blanketed the dunes with desert flowers peppered amongst the sand's ripples.

Lifaya held Keela to her chest in a bed of yellow petaled blossoms. Maya turned to go to them, but her body froze as the last of her energy drained away. Clutching her chest, she fell to the ground.

THREE DAYS LATER, Maya woke to the soft sound of the minor and diminished chords of a stringed instrument. She lay and listened to the notes, sad and lonely. She sobbed as the reality of the battle hit her. Thelic had been asleep on a bed of pillows next to her. At the sound he bit back his own tears of relief and shifted, moving to her side.

"Spirits, you two are a sad pair."

Maya bolted up at the familiar voice, and Keela grinned from the end of her bed. She was alive.

"Well, it's about time you woke up," Zarina teased as she and Kadhim entered the small room to join them.

"I'm glad you're all okay. What did I miss?" Maya croaked, settling back against the pillows.

"Your crazy grandmother summoned Batshari's power," Keela explained. "She manipulated the water in my blood and restarted my heart. She saved my life." Keela was still reeling from the events that transpired that day; her temporary death...and Elkin's betrayal.

"Elkin?" Maya whispered.

Keela and Thelic shook their heads in response. One of the Esterbellian soldiers had survived the children's attack. In all the commotion, he had managed to free Elkin, and they'd fled together.

Lifaya burst into the room at the sound of voices. There was no coddling from the old woman. Instead, Maya was chastised for chasing shadows and allowing dark thoughts to consume her. She cursed Yali for not better preparing their kin before the crossing and that she herself would not be able to train and follow Maya on her next journey.

"You're not coming?" Thelic asked.

"I'm afraid not, these children have no one left to protect them."

Maya sat up, a difficult manoeuvre after several days of lying down. "I've been meaning to ask, where are their parents?"

"Most left, their hearts blackened. They became the shaders I'm sure you've heard of."

"Surely not all of them. They left their children?"

"They believe they're fighting to *protect* their children, Maya. But no, not all of them. Many died after venturing too close to the void." That reminded her, and she uttered a warning. "The void will call to you, Maya. Your power is too great to ignore. Do not go near it!"

Maya promised to stay clear, her yawn breaking the tension, and Lifaya shooed everyone from the room to allow her granddaughter to rest, giving the broad-shouldered Thelic a raised eyebrow when he refused to budge.

THE NEXT MORNING, Maya was up and about, stretching her legs and trying to regain some movement. Thelic and Keela were with Fatari, planning the routes for their next voyage.

Maya liked this place. It was peaceful, something she had felt was lacking since she stepped into the lake at Yali's house. She looked up. Last night, the three moons had aligned. Lifaya explained that Maya's display of power against the soldiers had been intensified by the moons' orientation. The only thing to explain how she had been able to summon all four circles to that extent without being ripped apart.

One year. That was all the time they had to find the scrolls and track down the remaining Gouram before the next alignment. She could only hope that the war between humans and the gypsul didn't break out before then, before she had a chance to stop it. Loki nuzzled against her legs, and she chuckled, bending to pick him up. Well, at least she'd have company. Her little spirit guide.

A soft breeze swept across the dune beside her, and with it, a whisper. Maya froze at the sound. She was alone. Though, the unfamiliar voice begged to differ, as a cold hand wrapped around her throat.

ABOUT THE AUTHOR

Kate Craft is an emerging writer of fantasy romance. With CHAOS FORGED A FABLE, she debuts into the world of published authors with nothing but excitement and an arsenal of future projects waiting to be brought to life.

Kate Craft studied at the University of Roehampton, graduating in 2014 with a BSc in Psychology and Criminology. She continues to live in less than sunny England, dreaming of fantastical worlds.

Website: www.katecraft.com

instagram.com/book.cove

ACKNOWLEDGMENTS

There are a number of people I would like to take the time to thank…mostly for putting up with my incessant need to talk about this new world!

Dad, despite being outside of my intended demographic, the time and effort you put into editing the first drafts was out of this world. If I had any doubt (which I never have) of your love for me, this certainly would have put those fears to bed.

My Fiancé, and the Bodster, bringing the world of Avalon to life has been a journey to say the least, and has come with sacrifices found in the very real world of our home life. Your endless support has enabled me to chase a dream I thought to be well out of reach!

Mum, thank you for your wonderful and completely baseless belief in me - I know it's always on hand exactly when I need it.

Finally, to my wonderful editors, Alexandra Slingsby and Katherine Bent. Thank you for being the first people to read and love my book as much as I enjoyed writing it. Without your help and encouragement, this book may have struggled to see the light of day.

STREET-TEAM

Thank you to all of the absolutely incredible bookstagrammers who took a chance on my book AND helped me launch it!

Find them on Instagram:

@thebookcollectionuk
@a_reads_alot
@readit.with.red
@books.of.amber
@bookishcharli
@life_tell.me.a.story
@the_bookish_palss
@fantasy_fiction_fanatic

Printed in Great Britain
by Amazon